FALLS THE SHADOW

MIKE NICOL

FALLS THE SHADOW

CATALYST
PRESS

El Paso, Texas

Published by Catalyst Press.
www.catalystpress.org

© 2026 Mike Nicol

In North America, this book is distributed by Consortium Book Sales & Distribution, a division of Ingram. Phone: 612/746-2600 cbsdinfo@ingramcontent.com
www.cbsd.com

First edition, first printing
1 3 5 7 9 8 6 4 2

ISBN 978-1-960803-31-3
Library of Congress Control Number 2025936337
Cover design by Georgia Demertzis

Something wicked this way comes
—*Macbeth*

Acknowledgments

Writers are always in search of names. I have to thank Bruce MacDonald for giving me the names of Joey Curtains (*Agents of the State*), Hardlife Macdonald (*Power Play*), and Exit Kutoka in this novel.

Characters

Captain Zara Dewane (Internal Crime Unit)
   Kyle (son)
   Ashton (ex-husband)
   Elsi (mother)
   John (father)
Warrant Officer Wynston Adams in the ICU
Josephine "Jo-Jo" Lanski (attorney for the ICU)
Brigadier Wiseman Sithole (head of the ICU)
Colonel General Kaiser Vula, promoted to general
   Lady Vula (wife)
Captain Alicia Hendricks (police officer)
   Duifie (lover)
Sergeant Langa Mpho
Sergeant Kikiha "Exit" Kutoka
General Duncan Maale (head of Police Intelligence)
   Sipho Mpungose (Maale's attack dog)
Minister of Police Lebo Majoro
Luna Maplewood (clairvoyant, sangoma)
Jaco Cilliers (kayaker, prosecutor at the National Prosecuting
   Authority)
Big D (diamond diver)
Straight Abe Margulies (diamond dealer)
Janet of the Cape

PART ONE

PART
ONE

The Livelong Day

1

They drive to the killing in Wynston's green Mercedes-Benz.

Which is: a 1974 model with bread-loaf headlights, left-hand drive, vinyl seats, enough room inside to fly a drone.

Nice.

It's been resprayed that snazzy green, even the hubcaps.

Under the hood, a reconned four-cylinder with a manual gear shift, a high whine from the diff in the upper gears.

Alarming when you first hear it but music to Wynston.

That's Wynston Adams, Warrant Officer. Twenty-seven years old. Close-cropped hair. Sleeves of his linen jacket hoicked back from his wrists. Number two in the Internal Crime Unit, Western Cape.

In the passenger seat, Zara Dewane, Captain. Thirty-nine years old. Hair caught in a short pony. Wearing a red (as in ox-blood red) leather bunny jacket. You could call it her uniform. She's head of the Internal Crime Unit, Western Cape.

At 10 a.m. they left Cape Town city center on the N1, branched off at Canal Walk onto the West Coast road. That's twenty minutes ago.

All of that time, Captain Zara Dewane's said not a word to Wynston. She's sunk in her thoughts. Can be like that sometimes. Some think she's being aloof. She's not. It's just her way.

Wynston knows this. He's the one who breaks the mood.

Bravely says, "I'm running her in so we won't be going fast."

No fokking kidding. Zara distracted. Hearing him but lost in her thoughts. Thinking they could do with more speed but what the hell, half an hour's hardly going to change the world. Gives her more time with the four photos on her smartphone. The ones sent yesterday of the two children, a boy and a girl; the woman; the man.

Gives her slow-hooded eyes more time to look from the pictures to the passing scenery: scrub, salt bush, the sea a dancing blue beyond. To wonder how it happened. Well, not how, the how's obvious. So's probably the why.

Says to Wynston by way of response, "It's a nice car. If you don't mind that whine. Or the left-hand drive."

Zara knows the man in the photograph. Knows in the sense of having seen him around the Saldanha police station. Never to talk to. Just a smile and a passing greeting. He was one of the locals when she was stationed there. Stationed there for two years to get her out of the way. Quarantined, while the brass figured out what to do with her. Now there's this.

The killing.

Hears Wynston say, "The reason it's left-hand drive is my motormac friend Baz, he got this Benz for me."

Knows Wynston's talking out of nervousness. Can't handle her silences.

"Belonged to a German lady who went back to Berlin. Not surprising because it was insane what happened to her. Though nothing actually happened to her actually, but the engine was shot. I mean that, hey, literally. Shot with 9mm APs, you know, armor piercing. Two bullets through the radiator caused hectic damage, went on to whizz-bang around the engine. What I can say, if it wasn't an old Benz she'd of been history, the German lady. Posted one-time to the celestial choirs. Praise the lord this is a tank. A Panzer. So the APs died inside the engine compartment. Car comes to a dead stop, the German lady hops out with a Glock, lets off a few rounds at the tsotsis. Which gives the boys second thoughts. They're not into a shootout so they're gone. But the German lady's freaked. Forty years living here, she's never been robbed, mugged, raped, nothing. Like she thinks this is paradise. Except now it's paradise lost, I'm telling you. There on Main Road, Claremont, eleven o'clock at night, paradise was almost closing down for her. You got to ask what's a sixty-something woman doing driving around alone at that time of night? Yarrah, man, this's Cape Town. Anyhow. The German lady sells her one 'n' only car ever. Brought out with her when she came here. Baz phones me to say, 'Wynston, this one's for you. Come 'n' check it out.' Which I do. Post-haste. Because when Baz's got something, he's got something. Like pristine inside you can see. Three hundred thou miles on the clock but you wouldn't say so. Now it's a new engine besides. And you got this big steering wheel, a manual gearbox. What's not to like?"

Gets no response from Zara.

A tentative throat-clearing from Wynston. "Captain, can you tell me why we're going to Saldanha?"

"Sure," she says, coming back from the pictures of the children. "Why'd the tsotsis shoot the car?"

"Because, the way I heard it, the German lady, she tried to ride them down."

"That's different."

"Wilde deutsche Frau. Wasn't gonna take nonsense from the tsots. They had to shoot the car to stop her."

Zara back to looking out the window at the scrub flats. Shooting cars is one thing, shooting people another.

Wynston says, "Can you tell me?"

"Sorry," she says. "Sorry. I was going to tell you, of course. Am going to." Looks at her smartphone, a photo of the boy filling the screen. Says, "Something I don't get is why dads shoot their kids."

Thinking: What's that feel like? You stand there over your kids, they're sleeping. How do you decide which one to shoot first? The boy or the girl? You make a decision, you aim down at the kid's head. Are you calm? Are you crying? Are you hyper-ventilating? Sweating? Then you squeeze the trigger. What are you thinking? Are you thinking? Are you in shock, such despair you have no thoughts, no feelings? Even when you're looking at your child lying there, dead? Do you want to rewind, after you've fired, like it's a movie you can pull the bullet back into the gun. Is that what you want to do? Or are you so far gone, you're committed to taking out your whole family? Move on to the next one.

She glances at Wynston. The guy's staring straight ahead, must have felt her eyes on him but doesn't make contact. In ten months has learned to tread softly with her.

"So what do you think?"

"I dunno," says Wynston. "I dunno why a dad would do that."

"You must have an opinion."

Wynston says nothing. Hands locked tight on the white steer-ing wheel. Then before she can speak: "This's why we're going to Saldanha?"

"Sort of.

"What's it got to do with us?"

"Ummm! Not sure totally. It's what we've gotta find out."

Zara's thinking how the shooting must've happened one night back in the small cottage. An isolated cottage in the middle of nowhere. So isolated you even wondered why it was there. He shoots the kids: two shots make a helluva noise. His wife wakes up. It's a small cottage, one room, the kids sleep behind a hang-ing blanket separating them from their ma and pa. His wife's sleep-fogged, she doesn't know what's going on. Pietie, she says, Pietman, what's happening? Then she sees the gun in his hand, cause he's lit the kerosene lamp so he can shoot straight. Pietie, what's it you're doing? Or maybe, Pietie, what's it you done? Either way she's coming into the scene, realizing what's going on. And by now she's staring at the big naught of Pietman's pistol. No, Pietie, no, man, please, Pietman, I'm your queen.

To which he comes back, maybe, like this: You whore, Lizbet, you been putting your poes out for Manfred. Then, brings up the pistol. Opens a hole in Lizbet's forehead. Because Pietman Malgas is a crack shot.

Zara now imagining Pietman standing in the room. Children dead behind the blanket. Lizbet dead, collapsed back on the bed. Pietie with the gun in his hand brings it up underneath his chin, shoots his own brains out.

She sits with this image for one, two miles: the man's knees buckling, Pietman Malgas going down backward. Splayed out on the floor, the pistol fallen from his hand.

Inside the green Benz with the bread-loaf headlights, there's the whine of the diff; outside, the industrial yards of Saldanha coming up over on the left.

That's where they'd found the plumber, Manfred, dead in his van outside his workshop. Someone at the police station knew about Manfred and Lizbet and when Constable Pietman Malgas didn't come to work, they went to Manfred's place. Found the horrorshow.

Wynston says again, "What's it got to do with us?"

Zara scrolls through screens on her phone to a map. Says, "This cottage we're going to is other side of Saldanha."

"I don't get it," says Wynston. "This's a family murder. What's it got to do with us when a cop shoots his family?"

"Guns," says Zara. "They found boxes full of them."

2

"Right inside this place," says Captain Alicia Hendricks, station commander at Saldanha, opening the door to a shed. The shed attached to the cottage where the Malgas family had lived. No more than a lean-to arrangement of bricks and tin without foundations. "Just lying under a plastic. My people couldn't believe it. Me neither. Brought me back from my leave."

The captain is in uniform, Brassoed stars on her shoulders.

A compact, quiet-spoken woman, six months into her posting. Zara and Wynston standing with her at the door of the shed, staring down at the emptiness where once were crates of guns.

She closes the door. "If you'd have asked me, I'd have said Constable Malgas was straight, honest. Okay, I didn't know him for long but he was a polite man, very quiet."

"That was my impression, back when I was here. Always a greeting with a smile." Zara steps aside, shades her eyes to look over the downlands to the distant sea. Great place to live if you liked solitude. But: "Heckuva long way from anywhere out here. Back of the moon."

"I suppose. You are thinking it's a good place to store guns?"

"Not sure what I'm thinking. Maybe." A glance at the captain. Her sunglasses in her hair, cigarette elegant between her fingers. Young for her rank, for her appointment. Station commander was a position Zara could've had if she'd kept her mouth shut.

"Going on what I understand, he was born here," the captain says, tapping off ash onto the sand. "When his people died, he moved back. The farmer didn't mind having a policeman on his lands. Then the member goes and does this. The last person I would've said." She takes a long drag.

"You're reckoning because his wife was having an affair?"

"Open and closed for sure certainty. The problem with these bhutis, they don't talk. They shoot first." The captain exhales, flicks away the butt of her cigarette. "Look, I got some stuff for you so you don't have to come into the station. I don't want any bad vibes."

"From us? We're not making trouble."

"From my members. Some of them don't like you guys."

"I know most of them from when I worked here as acting commander. That wasn't so long ago. A year and a half back."

"Precisely what I'm getting at. For them you've gone over. They can't get that right in their heads."

"Shit, man. Hardly what I'd call going over."

"You know what I mean."

"Uh-uh. No, not really. We're after the people jacking the system."

"I know that. Except some of them don't see it the same way."

Wynston clears his throat, says, "We get this a lot."

At which the captain turns, inspects him. Zara watching the smile on her lips, wondering what the station commander's thinking. Wynston a good-looking man. Snappy, sharp, has a lot of muted phone conversations. Women, she assumes.

"I suppose, Warrant. So you got to get used to it. Members think it's bad enough being shot by gangsters, don't want to have their own sort coming after them."

"We don't go after them. Unless they're corrupt. Or torturers. Or killers."

The captain knocks another cigarette from her packet. "You live in a strange world, Warrant." Flicks a lighter, draws hard on the cigarette, blows smoke from the corner of her mouth. Gestures at their cars. "Come, let me get the file."

They walk without speaking round the cottage over the sand and scrub to the cars. The cottage is standard farm-abode: middle door, window either side. Chimney structure at the one end. The sort of place water colorists find attractive.

Speaks to Zara of a hard life. You lived here, you'd sell guns. You'd put out in some way.

There is crime tape over the door, hanging limp. The place looking bloody desolate.

The captain bends into her car, a snazzy maroon Mazda CX-5, comes out with a file, places it on the bonnet of Wynston's Benz. Says, "You don't see many of these cars anymore. Why'd you want to drive one like this when you can drive something modern?"

Wynston shrugs, does a turn-up to his lips.

"Ja, okay. What I've got in here for you is his cell phone contacts, list of the weaponry found in the shed, his bank statements. I can tell you, there's nothing big gone in or out of his account in a year." Hands the file to Zara.

"Doesn't mean he didn't have one you don't know about."

"I don't think so, Captain. Not Constable Malgas."

"We'll see," says Zara. "You'd be surprised about some people. Meantime we need to check the guns."

Impasse.

The captain contemplates the farmlands, smokes her cigarette. Zara waits her out.

Checks the file, runs her eye down the list of gun types. Mostly the usual: Rugers, Glocks, Siggies, S&Ws, HKs, Berettas, cop guns; also Russian military-issue pistols, two SR-1 Vektors, the pistol favored by the Russian special forces. Interesting.

Is about to speak when Captain Hendricks says, "They told me about you, you know, when I reported the guns. One of them called you a jackal."

Gets a laugh from Zara. "I can guess who."

Any one of half a dozen men. Including her brigadier boss, the useless bastard kicked sideways by the top brass to babysit the Internal Crime Unit. ICU, which got quips tweeting across the service. "A cop arrested a gangster. The gangster died. The cop landed in ICU." Or: "In ICU for a colonoscopy today. Crap story."

"Fine. I can show them to you if you want but that's all. They're evidence."

"We need them for our evidence."

"Sure. You know the scene: subpoena them."

The two women doing the eyeball, Zara holding it until the captain looks away. Thinking sometimes women act just like men: all aggro. Like, my lewe fok, Eloise, what's your problem?

Says, "These guns, you got any idea of their origins?"

A headshake from the station commander. "No. Nothing. Except they're not from my station. We've got everything accounted for."

Of course. Wouldn't expect anything else. A woman this tight would have an inventory for every ballpoint pen. You had to wonder where they went to school, her type. Some leafy-suburbs girls-only convent. Not a public local on the windy Cape Flats. Step into my world, Captain Hendricks.

"Any chance of checking out the actual cell phone?"

Not worth the question but worth asking anyhow for the annoyance factor.

"The contact list's in there. The cell phone number. It's pay-as-you-go but you can check with the service provider." The captain stubs a length of her cigarette into the sand. "I must go, Captain. You want to look inside the cottage, be my guest. The door's on a padlock. It's open. Lock it when you're through. Good luck."

End of story.

Zara and Wynston watch the captain do a fast reverse to the right, straighten out, wheel-spin in the soft sand as she accelerates the SUV.

"Don't know about why that captain's so worked up," says Wynston.

Zara laughs. Admonishes him with a brief "Enough." Turns away toward the cottage. "I'm going inside."

Wynston follows her in. A smell of August cold and damp, of wood char: the remains black on the chimney hearth. Blood stain on the flagstone floor beside the double bed, beside the table. Blood stains on the children's beds.

"What're we looking for anyway?" from Wynston. "We're here about the guns."

"Come on, Wynston. We're here about Pietman Malgas, you know that. Why'd he have the guns? Where'd they come from? Where'd he plan to send them? Saldanha probably haven't done a search, except for the basics. To them it's a family murder. Open and closed. You heard her."

"So what's it we're looking for?"

"You know the answer to that."

"You'll know it when you find it. Bit of a pissy cop-show answer."

"Works every time."

3

What doesn't work for Captain Alicia Hendricks is having Captain Zara Dewane on the case. She's heard the stories about her predecessor. How in her time at ICU she'd had a bunch of cops disciplined. Two ranking officers demoted. Of a cop cousin put away for fifteen years. An actual family cousin. Caught with a bag of poached abalone. Her own cousin! A man with a family. A hero of drug busts. What'd that say about loyalty? The woman was a jackal, feeding on corpses. A traitor to the police service.

Captain Hendricks pulls into the car park outside a convenience store. Switches off. Sits staring at the dribble of people hanging about the supermarket. Smokes a cigarette. Decides Captain Zara Dewane can be an issue. Keys through her contacts to the name of Colonel Kaiser Vula. Gets him on the third ring.

Imagines the man in the State Security Agency—the Aviary, to those in the know. His office down a long corridor. View of Table Mountain from the big window. Imagines him in his wheelchair pulled up against the wide teak desk. The neat in-tray. The laptop with its tropical-island screensaver. The man's large hands on the desk. The notepad and the fountain pen. The colonel's stiff upper body in uniform. The bitter face. The dark angry eyes. Because Kaiser Vula never got over taking a hit for the president. Ended up a paraplegic. And now that robber president disgraced in Dubai living the high life.

The voice at her ear saying, "Do we have a problem with this woman?"

A question Captain Alicia Hendricks contemplated on the sand road. Says to the colonel, "She's a jackal."

Which gets a snort. "I am listening."

"She will subpoena the guns."

"Of course. What about the Russian pistols? Did she notice them?"

"She said nothing."

"Good. But she will wonder about them soon. And the contacts in the cell phone?"

"A short list."

"Not all of the names?"

"No."

"Better. Destroy the SIM card. Get rid of it. Today. Cut it."

A possibility Alicia Hendricks has foreseen. A possibility that makes her hands sweat. "It is in evidence."

"Pah! What does that matter? In our chaos, evidence is missing all the time. Lose the phone, Captain. Not a problem. I will sort the service-provider records. The jackal captain will find no trace. Is this all we are to worry about?"

"Yes, Colonel."

"Then it is nothing. You can sleep easy, Captain."

"Yes, Colonel." If that were only true. She sticks a cigarette between her lips, pushes in the car's lighter. That idiot Malgas. What a cockup! About to disconnect the colonel when he says, "Wait."

She waits.

"You need to find a new warehouse, Captain. Very soon. There will be a shipment tomorrow or the next day. I will confirm. Somewhere safe, Captain, where the jackal can't find them. We cannot have these problems. No one likes it." A pause. She can hear the sound of traffic. Then: "Stay together, sisi. You can do this."

With that, he's gone. Leaving Alicia Hendricks in her car outside the store, blowing smoke at the windscreen. It was supposed to be a quiet posting. A starter position to launch her career. A place to make her mark. Now this. So quickly into this nightmare. As if she'd never had a choice once Vula had championed her. As if the problems were waiting for her to fix. She crushes the cigarette into the car's ashtray. Lights another. What a frigging balls-up!

4

Exactly what Colonel Kaiser Vula wants to avoid. Digs through his briefcase for the tin of muti—some powder his wife had acquired. Your actual gray powder from a witchdoctor, a white sangoma, but it works. Takes away the discomfort. The irritation of his whole life. Kaiser Vula stirs a teaspoonful into a glass of water. Slugs it down. Waits for the relief. One, two minutes, the ease goes through him. Not only the physical ache, also the rage. Helps him think past the anger.

Here he is, fifty-five years old.

A para with a colostomy bag.

But he is still a soldier, still has his job.

On return to duty after the shooting had refused to be boarded. And they'd humored him with a big office, a mountain view, two couches, a minibar fridge. Even stocked it with a bottle of Johnnie Walker Black. Hung on the walls three colorful township scenes to remind him of his beginnings. A framed signed photograph of the current president, his smiling moon-face bestowing beneficence. Few in the Aviary came down the corridor to his section. Left to his own devices, Colonel Kaiser Vula devised his own payback.

Now he pulls from his briefcase an old-style cell phone: what they call a burner in TV shows—a cheap pay-as-you-go special. He likes the term "burner." The burner going to set fire to the coming days. A total scorched earth. Torched monopolies. Torched capitalists. The land taken back. Wheels himself away from his desk across the room to the window. Looks up at the mountain, the ridge-line cut hard against a clear sky. Gray against blue. The ice blue of winter. His preferred season.

He thinks of Captain Hendricks, of her nervousness. She is new. She will be good if she can hold her nerve. Already she has proved useful. But she needs reassurance. Signs that the new warriors are in control.

With quick fingers, Kaiser Vula Telegrams a call. Thinks, Maybe the time is coming. Maybe there should be another example to show who holds the power.

There have been others: a top cop shot dead as he arrived home.

A politician assassinated.

Whistle-blowers disappeared.

But it is never enough.

To the answering voice, the colonel says, "Sergeant Mpho, you remember what we talked about?"

A silence. Colonel Kaiser Vula waits it out.

"About the ICU captain?"

"Yes. That exactly."

Another silence. Then: "I have the hearing tomorrow."

"I know. It will be alright, you will see. But even in this case, perhaps you need to give the jackal woman a fright." He liked the word "jackal." Captain Hendricks had found a good word. Dewane was like those animals: howling on the veld, skulking under bushes.

"Tjow!" A whistle of exclamation. "That is dangerous. She will know me."

True. To the top cop, the politician, Mpho has been a man in the street. Could be a gardener going home, hurrying to catch a taxi. No one has a reason to think differently. With Dewane it is different. She could recognize Mpho. Will recognize him. That is a risk, should something go wrong.

Colonel Kaiser Vula gazes up at the mountain. Holds back an exclamation. Says quietly, "Use Exit. He can do it. Tell him, Go to her house. Warn her to watch out for her son. You with me, Sergeant?"

That will make her stop. The trouble with a woman like Captain Dewane, she is clever. She gets ideas. Sees blood on the walls, the slip of money from hand to hand. Thinks she is superior. That you can't touch her in ICU. That she knows about policing. Security. Protecting the state. She knows nothing.

"Get Exit to persuade her, Sergeant. That way she will not be at your hearing."

With that, disconnects. Hears his smartphone chirp: his wife's ringtone. Lady, she who must be obeyed. Who has been his major support: nursed him; changed the shitbag before he could manage it himself, fueled his anger when he wavered. Who gave him unimagined sex when no other woman would look at him. He who had once had them begging him to their beds.

"I have made an appointment for you," she says.

Lady will do this, arrange his life, which irritates him. But there is no other way.

"Impossible today." It isn't.

"It is for tomorrow morning. You can stop at her on your drive to the Agency, she is not far off your route in Rondebosch. We have agreed for half past nine. You will go, Kaiser?"

Yes, yes. He says he will.

"Her name is Ms. Maplewood. It is her powder you use. You will see, Kaiser, she has important things to say to you. Without even knowing you, she has told me about your life. And her muti has helped you more than all the Western medicine. She is highly recommended by all the sangomas. They know her as a wise woman."

Perfectly true. On all counts.

"What things does she want to say to me?"

"She will tell you. She has not told me."

"I do not believe in these people."

"This one is different. Trust me, Kaiser. My life is for you."

Also true. Lady Vula is a good woman. Loyal. Ambitious for him. He knows this. He knows that without her he would be useless. A para in a wheelchair. Instead he is a colonel.

"With Ms. Maplewood, you will realize, she has the power to see beyond."

Which would be useful. Especially in a career move from the Secret Service Agency to the South African Police Service. Then he would be in control of Police Intelligence. And, with Ms. Maplewood's foretelling, would know all.

Kaiser Vula says goodbye to his wife, glances down into the

empty parliamentary precinct. He had saved a bad man from death. Only to become a crippled hero. No one is interested in a wheelchair veteran. Except they should be. He knows where the shallow graves have been dug. He has the dirt. A store of intelligence. Useful intelligence. Better still, he has networks. Agents. Spies. Reporters. Wherever there is a pie, he has a finger in it. If anyone should be head of Police Intelligence, he is that person. Not like the yes-man General Duncan Maale or his attack dog Sipho Mpungose.

He phones General Maale. Drops a teaser: ICU are pulling a cover-up. Guns, ammunition involved.

"Leave it with me," says General Maale. "I'll put Mpungose onto it."

Then after chit-chat: "You are a wasted man at the Aviary, Colonel. You should come across to work for me."

Colonel Vula smiles to himself. "I am at your service anytime, General."

"Let me make a plan. I have been thinking of changes."

Colonel Kaiser Vula lets the smile fade, become a scowl. He needs power. He needs recompense for his condition.

5

Which is not too dissimilar to the question Captain Zara Dewane asks.

Puts it to Warrant Officer Wynston Adams. "Why's a guy do this? For the money?"

The two of them forty-five minutes into searching Pietman Malgas's cottage.

"Suppose," says Wynston.

"Doesn't look like it though, does it?"

Zara Dewane standing at a clothing cupboard. Not much inside: in the hanging section some dresses, some jeans, new puffer jackets, two uniforms. Sundry trainers, a pair of police boots beneath them. In the drawers: underwear, T-shirts, a couple of folded jerseys. Nothing new. Even in the kids' area, no place to hide: a chest of drawers with clothing, a box of toys. The whole interior a wysiwyg, what you see is what you get. Nowhere to stash bundles of cash.

"So what d'you think of the captain?" Zara getting to the topic they've both been circling.

"We're not her favorites."

"When're we ever their favorites. It bothers you?"

"Sometimes. It's getting less 'n' less."

"And the captain?" Zara walks over to a heap of magazines, old newspapers stacked in a corner. Above them a shelf, a photograph of Pietman and a woman propped on a Bible. Attractive people. Young, full of life, laughing.

"She's alright. Doing her job. Even helped us out a bit."

"Or she's given us only what she wants to."

"Could be."

"Maybe also too protective. Makes me wonder."

"Nah, Cap," says Wynston. "Now you're overthinking it. Too cynical."

"Happens in this job. All the stuff we've got to look at."

Zara moves the photograph aside, picks up the Bible. Holds it upside down, flips the pages.

Wynston laughs. "A believer's not gonna put money in a Bible."

"I would. Who'd look there?"

When nothing falls out, Zara tosses the book onto the bed. Then bends down, opens it, thumbs through the front pages. An old copy inscribed with a name that is Malgas but not Pietman: Steveboy Malgas. The date back in the 1970s.

"Your family have old Bibles?"

"And Qurans. We're mixed up: some Catholics, some Muslims."

"Us too. Evangelicals also after I married one. Though nobody bothers much anymore with the god-stuff. Once my gran wanted me to wear a headscarf. When I was a teenager. I even did for about a week, but it didn't last." She pauses at the contents page. "Check this out?" Holds the book toward Wynston.

"What'm I looking at?"

"You're the detective, you tell me."

"I dunno."

"The dot, bozo, the dot."

"What dot?"

"Right next to Steveboy's name. Steveboy-dot-Malgas."

Wynston squints at it. "In this light, it looks like a smudge. Maybe even mold on the paper."

"You need to get your eyes checked." Zara pulls back the book, lets the pages flap beneath her thumb. There, at the back, written in the margin, a Gmail address and password. "My lewe fok."

On her phone, Zara opens Gmail. Puts in the address, the password. Only two emails in the inbox. Both opened, both with attachments. One the current month, the other the month before. Zara downloads the current attachment: a bank statement. Password protected. Turns to Wynston.

"Look in the file, read me out Malgas's ID."

He does. Zara inserts the digits, opens the file. A current statement with a balance of R25,000.00. Bank charges. No interest. One deposit the previous month.

"What's his balance in that account, the one she gave us?"

"Eight hundred."

"What've we got here then, you think?"

"Dirty money, no question."

"Absolutely right. Quick money for the guns. He was their storeman, I'll bet." She glances around the dim interior. "I'll bet somewhere here's a SIM card or another phone. Whoever deposited the money's not going to be named on the captain's list. That person got hold of Pietman off the books. We got to look again, Wynston."

They do.

Behind drains, sinks, in the loo cistern, under ledges, beds, cupboards, at the back of drawers. For another half an hour, they go into the nooks and crannies.

Until Zara says it's a waste of time. He could've wrapped it in plastic, stuck it under the third rock to the right. She points out the door at the wide world.

"Could be anywhere in the veld. Better we call it a day, go back to start the paperwork."

Thinking what she really wants is an hour or so on the ocean in her kayak. If they went now, she could be in the water by four. Enough light to paddle by until well gone six. Says, "I'm in court all day tomorrow, so you're on your own. No heroics. Just the paperwork."

"Yes, Cap." Wynston mock saluting.

Zara raises her eyebrows. "Watchit." Has them both laugh.

When they hear a car. Go outside to see Captain Hendricks stopping next to Wynston's green Mercedes-Benz.

"Oh yeah, wondered if she'd come back," says Zara. The two of them standing outside the cottage watching the policewoman walk toward them. A clip in her pace, her focus on lighting a ciga-rette. Zara shifts her stance, wishes the woman hadn't returned.

"Thought you'd be gone by now," says the captain, exhaling smoke. "Find anything?"

"Nah." Zara shakes her head. "Your guys did a thorough job." She pauses, looks full into the captain's face, seeing what could be complete indifference. A bland nonchalance. "Something we can help you with?"

"No."

Which leaves the question: why've you come back?

"So is there a problem?"

"No problem."

Zara considering how to take this one on, telling herself, Keep it cool. No need to get riled. Says, "There's one thing we're won-dering about, there could be another cell phone or SIM card."

"You think. Why's that?"

"It's the way these guys work. At least the careful ones. Usually we find other phones."

Captain Alicia Hendricks takes a long pull on the cigarette, holds the inhale, letting some drift out her nostrils. Slowly exhales, says, "We looked. You looked. There's nothing." An upward tilt to her chin. That cigarette going back to her lips.

"Cool character" are the words circling Zara's mind. You meet us out here. You hand over information. You allow free access to the place. You ride away. Then you return. Maybe not so cool, after all. What happened in between going and returning? A rethink? A worry about something? A need for surety? She's bumped into this type before, these women with concerns, always checking up. It's good meeting policewomen who strut the rank. But there was something off with this one. Something too anxious. Like she knows there's a jackal drifting in. Which brings a twitch to Zara's lips, the nickname she's garnered. No hassle if they wanted to call her a jackal. Jackals clean up. Leave the bones to bleach in the sun.

She smiles at the captain. "We're just going. Nice meeting you. I'm sure I'll be in touch."

The captain nods, squashes the butt of her cigarette into the sand. "Drive safe."

In the car, Wynston says, "Seems to me we're causing her some concern."

"Got that feeling too." Zara giving him a smile. "But maybe she just doesn't like the idea of the ICU. Not many do."

Thoughts shifting to the next day's hearing. The dagger-looks she'll get. The hissed insults. The anger that she's the enemy. She hates hearings. The sleeplessness of the night before, the anxiety twisting her stomach throughout the day. Tomorrow will be no different, probably even worse. Right now she needs to paddle on the ocean: cut over a glassy sea, the flash of sun in the water, the sharp slap of the prow bouncing on a low swell.

6

Zara launches at Three Anchor Bay. A cherished spot: small beach, a lapping sea, wind protection when the southeaster pumps. What's not to like?

Today is windless. Still a chill in the air. Perfect for a hard paddle to Camps Bay and back.

She greets others at the storage sheds, keeping to herself. Lugs the kayak to the water's edge, straps on a life jacket over her wetsuit.

A guy says to her, "You want to buddy up? Five of us're going hard to the Sentinel." He waves at four kayakers drifting in the bay.

She squints at him. Has seen him around to nod to, say hi. "Some other time."

He pushes out of the shallows. "No sweat, have fun. We're here most afternoons. You should join us."

"One day. Maybe."

Not looking at her, flutters a hand: "See you, Captain. Keep up the good fight." With that, the guy paddles fast toward his friends.

Leaving Zara wondering how he knows her, who he is. Considers shouting after him to find out. Then thinks, No, don't do that. You have a profile in newspapers, on social media.

Also she's acquired storage at the Bay against the odds.

Long story short: a whistle-blower cop she got reinstated knew a guy who knew a guy who magicked her the slot. Like brilliant. Aside from Granger Bay, no other place on the Sea Point coastline you could launch. But here you can slip into the water no problem. Which she does now.

What Zara paddles is a Dagger Stratos sit-inside. Fast on the open sea, stable for quieter moments. For those contemplative times when you want to float between the sea and sky. Think impossible thoughts. Her ideal kayak. Also there is a spray skirt round her waist buttoned to the cockpit. Makes life drier, warmer.

She's about to begin paddling when her cell phone chirps. Not an easy task, getting it from the waterproof pouch round her neck. By the time she does, the caller's rung off.

Kyle. Her son.

She calls him back. "What's up, spaceman?"

"I wanna come home," he says.

"Two more days, then I'll fetch you. That's what we agreed."

They've got this arrangement, she and her ex, Ashton: one weekend Kyle's with her, one weekend with him. And a sleepover midweek. Except this week Kyle's with him for three days. As a trial run at Ashton's request. But Kyle's not buying into this anymore. There was a trial run last month that had Kyle in tears. Ashton raging, saying he isn't to blame. It wasn't his fault. The boy was aggro. That Kyle had backchatted. Called him a lousy dad. When he was giving the boy so much: Nikes, surfboard, skateboard, laptop, smartphone, tablet. What other thirteen-year-old got that? Then walking out of his own house, leaving Zara and Kyle sitting there for an hour until he'd got over himself. What Zara couldn't figure was why she'd ever had a child with this guy. Not that she didn't want Kyle. She treasured him. She just didn't want Ashton. Only upside was Kyle getting older. They could both outgrow Ashton.

Now Zara says to Kyle, "What's going on? You can tell me."

"Dad's shouting at me."

The words cutting into her. Her son sounding on the edge of tears. "Over what?"

"Nothing."

"Has to be something." Of all the moments to have this conversation. When she needs to reach out, pull him to her.

Silence. Which she lets go on until she can't any longer. The ache in her needing resolution.

"Come on, tell me?"

"Mom, he just goes ballistic."

"Why's that?" Knowing it doesn't have to be much to get Ashton shouting. She'd gone through plenty of that herself. Before realizing Ashton was a mistake.

"Yesterday he promised me we'd go surfing this afternoon. When I said I was ready to go, he said he'd never said anything about going surfing. He lies, Mom. He lies to me. I told him he's lying."

Wrong move, boykie, thinks Zara. Don't call him out. Says, "Kyle, listen to me. You're listening?" Hears an intake of breath. "Go and say you're sorry. You must have misheard him. Tell him you don't want to upset him but if he's got the time, you'd really like a surf. Leave it there, don't push it."

"Mom, he told me I'm a waste of space."

The hurt in his voice, opening an ache in Zara. The desire to hit Ashton. Punch him in the fokking face. A nose crusher.

"I wanna come home. I want to live with you all the time."

There you go. On the line. Which makes her raise her eyes to the horizon. The empty horizon. But that's all it takes to collect her thoughts.

"I can't do anything now, Kyle. Just stick it out. Two more days then we'll talk about it. Okay?"

Eventually gets a quiet "Okay" that breaks her heart. Again looks out at the horizon for a moment, wondering if she should cut the kayaking for the afternoon, confront Ashton instead. Knowing this isn't the right time. Would lead to lawyers, more money wasted getting nowhere.

So she pacifies her son. Tells him he can surf all weekend. Then, when he's accepted the status quo, says hang in there. Strikes out with fast vicious strokes, as if the blades are slicing across the bastard Ashton's face.

You should've gone to Kyle. Rescued him. Taken him home. Told Ashton to fuck off. Run to his lawyers if he wants. And where would that have gotten you? Nowhere. Right back in the war zone. My fok, when's this gonna end?

She keeps up the pace: left pull, right pull. Her thoughts self-critical: why had she let him possess her those years ago? Why had she been seduced by his love-bombing? His manipulations? His lies? Why hadn't she seen the man was empty? An alien. My lewe fok, Eloise, an alien sucking the life from her. Until she'd gotten out.

And still he has power over her, because he has power over their son. And through Kyle can wreck her moments of solitude.

Knife a deep pain into her heart. It isn't the boy's fault. It is Ashton wielding the blade. Or is it? Is she maybe the problem?

Once Zara had asked a psychologist this exactly. Was it her attitude? Was it her job? What could she do to do things differently? How could she change?

Never thought she'd find herself sitting in a shrink's rooms. Never thought she'd be asking these questions. Yet those questions had her awake in the dark hours, doubting every move she made. Did her cop training make her too strict? Too tough? Was she pushing emotions aside? Not going there. Not allowing her instinct to win out? Was she lacking somewhere? Maybe Ashton couldn't do anything differently? Maybe that was just the way he was? Maybe she had to work around it? In the dark hours, here was calm, assured Zara, way out to sea without a paddle.

Which brought her to the shrink's sunny room one midmorning. A home practice on the side of the mountain. View of the sea she kayaked in out the front; view of the mountain's Twelve Apostles out the back.

After she'd told the therapist about being a single mom, being there always for her son, being a daughter with no parent issues, the therapist said, "You're a cop."

Statement.

She replied, "Not in the normal sense."

"Meaning?"

"I cop cops. You've heard of the Internal Crime Unit?"

The therapist shook her head. "Not as such."

Zara gave her chapter and verse. Added how she was shunned by normal cops. How they called her the jackal.

"And you're okay with that?"

"Yes. No. It's difficult. But I manage. I handle it."

"You believe in what you're doing?"

"Absolutely."

The therapist made notes. Looked up, said, "Tell me about your ex."

Zara did. How he'd caught her on the rebound. How she'd

fallen for his charm. How she'd wanted to be loved. Then, after they'd married, how she found herself covering for him. Realized there was something odd about him. A kind of chaos. Temper outbursts. Affairs. The trinkets when she'd said she would leave him. The way he'd talk through the night about how he needed her, how painful his life was, how she gave him purpose. And every time she stayed. Until she didn't. Until she took Kyle, walked out. Moved in with her parents for some months. Then bought the Woodstock house with the view of the bay.

"My ma always said she was wary of Ashton. Right from the start. And maybe I was too. When I think about it. But I was also mad for him."

The therapist laughed. "That's what happens. Love, lust, it's a madness that comes over us. What about his family? You haven't talked about them."

"Ja, well. For starters his mother hated that he'd married other side of the tracks."

"Sorry. You mean he's white?"

"As a sheet."

"Okay, but you could still visit her. Do birthdays, Christmases, that sort of thing?"

"Sure. There was family stuff, but there was always an undercurrent."

"What about his dad?"

"Dead. He died when Ashton was a teenager, thirteen, fourteen."

"Difficult. But listen …" She straightened in her seat, leaned forward on her desk. "From what you've described, Ashton could be a narcissist. I'm hazarding a guess, making an assumption, so don't quote me. He'd need to be diagnosed professionally."

"That's never going to happen."

"That's the thing. Unfortunately, most narcissists won't go anywhere near therapy. Or if they do, they manipulate the therapist. I've heard of that happening more than you'd believe. Normally, in this sort of situation, I advise my clients to run for their lives. But you can't. You've got Kyle. You're trapped. Be careful. This man could cause you great pain."

Not that Ashton had ever tried physical abuse. Knew better than to start with her. She'd have him locked up one-two-three. Despite his outbursts, Zara believed that Ashton had not hit Kyle either. At least, Kyle had never said so. Physical violence wasn't Ashton's way, his way was to keep changing reality, make it unreliable until you didn't know what was real, what was fiction.

"Look," the therapist had said to her at the end of the session, "there's not much I can do for you. Except to say, 'Keep on questioning yourself.' You're in a stressful job. You're in a stressful situation. Being self-aware is the best thing you can do. Not easy, I know. But you've been doing it, which is why you're here. So if you need to see me again, all you've got to do is call."

A call Zara had not, has not, felt the need to make.

Back to Zara in her kayak somewhat down the coast.

She's slackened the paddle rate, gone into an easier rhythm, more the style she's used to. Opens her eyes to the surroundings: before her, a string of fishing trawlers coming off the horizon. To her left, the cliff face of apartments fronting the sea. About her, other kayakers missioning home; here and there fishermen in small boats. She paddles on, her heart rate dropping, the easy dip and pull of the blades lulling her. Gets her mind back to: the gun-cache, the ICU hearing, Ashton's aggression pushed down beneath the slap and sparkle of the ocean.

Off Camps Bay, she encounters the Sentinel paddlers returning. No ways they could have gone all that distance south. Probably turned back at Llandudno.

"Join us," the mysterious dude calls out, but she waves them on. The last thing she wants is to join a pack of supers doing time-trials. Watches them pass, easy as dolphins.

Sits on the water off Camps Bay, thinking of her life. Not the cop life she'd hoped for, not like her dad's: who'd nailed serial killers; against the odds put a bunch of rapists away; could end a gang war with a loudhailer; had gone up the ranks despite discrimination. A man bemedaled. With citations. The man who'd told her: "Don't back down. What you're doing in ICU's got to be handled. If we'd had it in my day, I'd have done what you're doing. We damn well needed it." "Damn" being as far as her dad went with swear words.

"My lewe fok, Eloise." Being *her* go-to phrase.

7

Here are two men on the promenade, backs to the sea, eyeing the women jogging past. Hordes of joggers on this late winter afternoon.

"You know she's here?"

"Of course, my brother. It's cool."

"How? How d'you know?"

"I was told, okay? I have information about her. Don't worry."

"I don't worry. You must worry. You have the problem."

"No problem, my brother."

This last from Sergeant Langa Mpho, the smaller of the two, really into the passing parade.

"Haaita, man, look at that bum. What can you say? That is a bum." Holds out his cupped hand. "The way I like it. Big."

His gaze on a woman running alone toward the lighthouse: braids bunched up on her head, shiny Lycra leggings, sports top. Running easily, plugged into her music.

"You get me. Not like skinny white girls. What's their problem? Always they're worrying, 'Is my bum too big?' No bum is too big."

"When's she going to be here?"

"Hey! Yoh, my brother! Mamello, mamello, patience. She will come."

The two gents in jeans, winter hoodies, leaning against the railings.

The other one is Sergeant Kikiha "Exit" Kutoka. He's a tall

thin man. Turns now to the sea. Watches the kayakers coming into Three Anchor Bay.

Says to Mpho, "You know she goes out on the sea?"

"I know." Mpho laughs. "Do not worry. It is a thing she does. That is what I have been told."

"But you have not seen her doing it?"

"No, my brother. I myself have not seen her doing it. I said, 'I have information about her.' Her cell phone came here. Now it is coming back. We must wait."

"You know her? What she looks like?"

"Of course. I have seen her. She has questioned me. Many times."

"What is she like?"

"She is the jackal. I will show you when she comes. Relax, my brother. For now enjoy the shiny bums."

But the tall sergeant can't, he's antsy. Until the small sergeant says, "That is her." Points at the woman coming up from the beach onto the promenade, carrying a paddle.

The two sergeants further down the promenade watch her. Watch her cross the street toward the petrol station. Stop beside a Polo hatchback parked at the curb. Glance around before tossing the paddle on the back seat, getting in.

Sexy-looking babe to Sergeant Exit Kutoka. More his type. Lighter skinned. He likes these Cape women, they are sassy, full of backchat. And they can drink: wine for wine. Great pity she is on the other side.

"Let's go," says Langa Mpho, "we must follow."

Not something Exit is keen to do. "What for? We have her address. I can go there anytime." Actually not a job he is keen to do. Full stop. No point. The disciplinary hearing won't find against Sergeant Mpho. He will walk anyhow. They always do. Says, "Why must we do this?"

"You know," says Langa Mpho. "My brother, she is the jackal. Come, we must hurry, she is going."

They trot toward their car. Mpho rabbiting about how this

isn't about him. "There is more going on, my brother. I can't tell you. But you can become rich. Believe me. I know. I have the information."

Their car is Exit's old Honda Ballade with false plates. Still enough push under the hood to surprise any rev-rev boys who take him on. They buckle up. Exit waits for a gap, does a fast U-turn, to position five cars behind the captain's Polo. Langa Mpho sitting next to him wearing a beanie, dark glasses.

Exit says, "I will do this by myself. She will recognize you."

"No, no. Not possible. I am just another black man. But forget that, my brother, we are a team. You and me, that is how it works, my sergeant." Mpho takes a pistol from the bag at his feet. A Ruger with a long-nose silencer. Ejects the clip, checks it, slides it back in.

Exit glances down at the weapon. "Where is that coming from?"

"Yoh, man, relax. This gun is safe. No jammings, no misfires. I have tried it myself."

8

Zara hears a screech of tires. Is in her car waiting for the green at the Three Anchor Bay traffic lights, on a WhatsApp chat to Wynston. The topic: Pietman Malgas's secret. Zara saying to Wynston to focus on that, find out all about it. Adds, "Look, I've been thinking about things, and best to keep matters between us. Understand? No more phone calls."

Then comes the tire squeal, she glances in her rearview, sees a car U-turn. A blue Honda Ballade. Guys behaving badly. Says to Wynston, "You know what I'm saying?"

He says he does.

She disconnects, turns left on the green toward town, notices the Ballade, now two cars back.

Opposite Giovanni's Deliworld Zara pulls into the parking lot, the Ballade behind her finding a space further down. Zara registers two guys, nothing out of the ordinary. Heads across the street to the deli. At this time of the afternoon the place buzzing. The coffee corner chock-a-block. A clutch of people at the food counter. From a cheerful woman, orders a takeout of chicken schnitzel with sautéed potatoes, creamed spinach, roasted peppers. At the sweets counter, selects a small baklava. Although she has wine at home, takes down a shiraz from the wine racks. What more could a girl want? Good food, good wine, peace and quiet.

Back in her car, about to ignition, her cell phone rings.

Josephine Lanski, attorney for the ICU.

"At last. Where've you been, Captain Zara? Five times in the last hour I've been told to leave a message."

"But you didn't."

"No."

"So what's it?"

"Just checking in that you're still good for tomorrow."

Zara smiles. The woman is hyper. Doesn't expect anyone to do their job.

"Why wouldn't I be, Jo-Jo?"

"A hundred reasons. Could be the red curse is on you."

"Bit anti-fem."

"You know me, Captain Zara, nothing's too bloody weird to say in our diverse complexity."

"Whatever that means."

The lawyer ignoring her, saying, "This time we're going through without postponements."

"Let's hope."

"It's not a bloody hope, it's a certainty. Our girl is all fired up. She'll be good. She's got us behind her."

Zara watching the blue Honda Ballade come slowly across the parking lot to the exit. By the looks of the two in the front seats, no-good boyos: both behind dark glasses, the driver with his hoodie up, the other wearing a beanie pulled low over his ears. Probably hadn't even got out of their car. Maybe been there for a drug drop or pick-up. She shakes her head. What is the city coming to? The local cops need to keep an eye out.

"So, are you?"

"Am I what, Jo-Jo?"

"Up to bloody speed."

"Would I not be?"

"I don't know, Zara. This case is more than two years old. They've dumped you into frauds and murders and syndicates and organized crime from the chiefs to the constables, every reason why you'd have overlooked a lowly rape from before your time."

"I haven't."

"Right. Your scene. Do your thing."

"No probs. She's still on to testify?"

"As of yesterday. All go, like I said. We've got your investigation. We've got signed affidavits. We've got enough to nail him. Get Mpho disciplined at least."

"Don't hold your breath."

A cluck-cluck-cluck of the tongue: "I'm the eternal bloody optimist, Captain Zara. It's why I do this job. In the hopes of justice."

Zara presses on the sound system, winds up the volume. 4 Non Blondes kick in with "What's Up."

"You remember her, the singer?"

"Vaguely."

"Vaguely. That voice. I could wake up to that voice. She's enough to make you fancy women."

"I do. Fancy women."

"Ja, of course. Sorry, hey."

"Who's she anyhow?"

"Linda Perry when she was a babe. When we were all babes. I came across her again the other day, now she's the soundtrack to my life. Once more." Zara singing with Perry about going out in the morning, filling her lungs, shouting the lyrics of "What's going on?"

"Okay, okay. You and me both, sister."

"These days, the eternal question." Zara ignitions the car. "Sight yous, Jo-Jo, as they say in the classics."

Keeps Linda Perry in full voice over whatever goodbye Jo-Jo said. And stays such, belting out "Spaceman," "Dear Mr. President," "In My Dreams," "Superfly" along the elevated freeway, up Nelson Mandela Boulevard, Zara tapping the music against the steering wheel, on the rise takes a left into Woodstock upper. A few streets down Roodebloem left again into Chamberlain, drives slowly to the end, finds a parking space outside her Victorian.

The gods were smiling when she'd bought this home.

Except.

There's the next-door neighbor on his stoep. Beer to hand. Chair tilted back, his feet on the porch railings. Admiring the view.

Which is, admittedly, a great view over the lower city, the harbor.

The neighbor a reporter with no fixed partner. Zara has seen a merry troop of sisters going in and out of his place. Day and night. Never the same ones. Studs Karsten, the neighbor, not averse to putting the moves on her. Like now. She's hardly out of the car, he asks if she wants a beer.

"Chilled, the very best for you," he says, getting up, coming halfway down his front steps. "Devil's Peak IPA."

Of course, what else when you live on the mountain's slopes?

"Things to do, Studs," she says. "But thanks, nice idea."

Bends into her car for the Giovanni's packet on the back seat. Comes out with it, shrugs the strap of her briefcase over her shoulder.

"You want any help with that?"

"I'm good." Zara closes the car door with her foot. Presses the remote lock in her hand.

"I've got stuff for a salad would go with your Giovanni's. A pretty good red I could bring over.

"Another time, hey. Tonight's about work catch-up."

"You got a story for me, perhaps?"

"Not really."

"What's that mean?"

"It means maybe but only tomorrow. Maybe I'll be in touch."

"You always say that."

"Live in hopes, Studs. Someday it has to kick in."

"What?"

"The good times.'

"Forget it, my sister. This is as good as it gets."

"You journos have a bad attitude."

Studs snorts. "Like you guys don't. Come on, Zara, you got to be sitting on a good story. A whole heap of good stories. Let me do a profile of you."

"That'd go down well with my brass." She leans forward to unlatch the gate, goes in, pushes it closed with a backward reach of her foot.

"Neat maneuver," says Studs. "You should play soccer."

Zara starts up the steps to her front door, hasn't gone halfway when she catches sight of a blue car out the corner of her eye. Stops to look: a blue Honda Ballade. The car coming on slowly. Closing. Sees the hand with a gun at the passenger window. Hears Studs say, "What the hell!"

Then the shots. One. Two. Three and four fast.

A zing of a ricochet, a smash of glass behind her.

The car accelerating away with rubber burn.

Sees Studs pitch forward down the steps.

Now she's crouching, the Giovanni's packet with the wine beside her, Z88 in one hand, phone in the other. Watches as the car slides round the corner at the end of street.

My lewe fok, Eloise!

Gives thanks Kyle isn't with her.

9

"You mad," shouts Exit Kutoka. "You really mad." Putting foot, gearing down to take the corner, the car slipping, rocking as he fights the steering wheel.

Langa Mpho laughs. "Tsho, man, tsho-tsho. You see that? You see that, man?"

Boys on skateboards jump out of the road, give the finger as they pass. One holding up his phone.

Exit thinking, Not good. Saying, "They videoed us."

Mpho corkscrews in the seat, waves the gun. "No sweat, my brother. What're they gonna get, a blue car with fake registration." Resettles himself, slips the pistol into a pocket in the footwell.

"It's my car," says Exit. Takes the next right into Kitchener.

"And so what's the thing? You're not even licensed. You have no problem." Mpho thumps the dashboard with a drumroll. "Slowly, wena, slowly."

No possibility of slowly for Exit. Instead he guns toward Roodebloem, takes a sharp left into a bumper to bumper. The traffic backed up at the lights. Sits there antsy, checking the rearview mirrors. Riding the car on the clutch.

"Relax, my brother," says Mpho. "Where's the problem?"

"The problem? Number one is Instagram. You want to be trending?"

Sergeant Langa Mpho smacks his knee. "Cool. I have no problem. We can be hashtag-blue-lightning."

Exit pulls off his mask, his beanie. Tells Mpho to do the same. The traffic lights change, Exit goes right into Main Road. Plans his exit through Salt River, onto the highway, figuring he can get to Gugulethu. Get lost in the township.

Says to him, "You could've killed them."

"No ways, my brother, no ways. That's not how you do it to kill someone. Aikona, no. When you want to kill someone, you do it standing on the sidewalk. Steady, aim, fire. That's the story."

"You were shooting wild."

"Of course. When I shoot true, there is no escape. Now the madam has a little fright. Something to keep her waking up tonight. Keep her heart jumping. Tomorrow, she's not going to be so full of shit. She's gonna think about her words."

Langa Mpho turns to his phone, taps out some WhatsApps. Exit drives on in silence.

Where they end up is Mzoli's, facing a dish of mixed meat

(sausages, chops, ribs), a side order of pap and salsa. Black Label beers.

Mpho welcomed by sundry and all: the braai masters doing the elbow-knock, "Haaita, my bra"; patrons back-slapping, "Molo, my bru"; even Mzoli himself comes out to bump fists. Langa Mpho no longer Langa, now Bra Langa. "Howzit, bhuti, nice to see you."

This effusiveness eases Exit's anxieties, as does the Blackies going down. Exit absorbed by the clients, leaning back on the plastic chair, watching Bra Langa work the scene. Like he is some celeb. Chatting to even the whiteys. Packets changing hands. Always odd to see whiteys there. Exit sucks at the beer bottle, considers this: some tourists with their guides getting into the township vibe. But also local whiteys hanging out as if Mzoli's is in one of the leafy suburbs.

Mpho plops into his seat. Pushes a bag at Exit.

"Advance payment." Keeps his face serious, then flashes teeth. "Smile, my brother, we're talking serious money. Count it." Slaps his shoulder. "We gotta go. Get the man his order." Downs the dregs of his beer.

As he's getting up, this white guy pushes him back into his seat. A big flesh man type. Bodybuilder arms. Thick-necked. Shiny dome. Says, "Nyet, Bra Langa, we need to have face time." The flesh man swinging a chair between them, sitting. "Who is my friend?" Giving Exit the eye.

Mpho does the introduction. No names for the flesh man, only "my Russian friend."

Who wants to know of Exit, "You are a police too?"

"Of course," says Mpho. "Special Services."

"Good." The Russian looks from Mpho to Exit, back to Mpho. "You can get me a special? This is possible?"

"Of course."

The man leaning in closer. "Twenty-two. With a nose."

Bra Langa nods. "Of course. Hollows?"

Exit watching the Ruskie grin. "You are, how you say, on the ball, Sergeant Mpho." The man rising. "Tonight, yes?"

Mpho confirms. Right here at Mzoli's, about an hour. Writes the price on a paper napkin, gives it to the Russian. The Russian shrugs. Says something in his language, holding up a finger at both of them. "No shit, my friends. We do not want that."

Walks off to a table at the far end.

"Let's go," says Mpho. "Business is business."

They don't drive far. Out of the township to a suburb. Exit unhappy about the locale. Keeps at Mpho: Where we going? Who we going to?

Gets from Mpho a "Wena, my brother, wait. I know. It is all fine."

Arrive at a house in a wide street. Lights on behind curtained windows. Long grass on the sidewalks, low walls round the house. No security fence. No electric wiring. Open driveway gates. Only thing: they pull into the driveway, spotlights come on, light them up brightly. A dog starts barking in the house.

"Where's this?" says Exit. "Who's here?"

Gets no answer from Mpho because Mpho is out of the car, trotting to the front door. Exit waits, sees the door open, a woman standing there. The woman in camo trousers; a chunky jersey. Stands aside to let Mpho in. Exit wondering, Who's this? In three months they've never been here to drop or collect. The worry coming back to him. The worry about being with Sergeant Langa Mpho. The man playing hero-guy, no one to touch him. Makes Exit think of snails. The old proverb about the track of slime so easy to follow.

Then five minutes later, Langa Mpho's leaving through the front door with a carry bag. The woman not appearing this time. The door quickly closed as Mpho sashays toward the car. Hamming his walk like he's some comedian. Grinning wider than a crocodile.

He stashes the bag in the boot, slides into the passenger seat. "There we go, my brother. All good."

"Who was that?" says Exit.

"A somebody."

"A somebody who?"

"Doesn't matter. Let's go. Hamba, hey. Back where we belong."

On the way, Colonel Kaiser Vula comes through on Mpho's phone. Says, "Sergeant, are you with Sergeant Kutoka?"

Mpho says he is.

"Put me on speakerphone."

Mpho does.

A silence. Exit pictures the colonel in his wheelchair. His face set: the downturn of the lips, the black eyes, the short hair shot with gray. Sees him in his uniform, always in his uniform, the shirt never creased, the sleeves buttoned at the wrists, his hands gripping the hand rims. Then hears him say, "What happened, Sergeant?"

Exit thinks, The voice is like the man. Tight.

"We did it," says Mpho.

"You did it," repeats the tight voice. "You know what you did, Sergeant? You got a trending hashtag drive-by. That's what you did, my sergeants. A nice clip for everyone to see on Instagram. This is a top prize, Sergeant. This is a new way to advertise. Sergeant Langa Mpho going viral. High five, my bhutis."

Exit can see the man swivel the wheelchair in the middle of his large office. The thick vein standing in his neck. The knuckles tight on the hand rims. Then the yell: "You fucking moerheads." Flecks of spittle catching in the downlights. The rest Exit feels as a cramp in his stomach. Keeps his eyes on the road. Does not look at Langa. Hears the anger until Colonel Kaiser Vula goes quiet.

Then: "Moerheads, do you know what you have done?"

Neither of them answers.

"Talk. Do you know what you have done?"

"No, my colonel," says Mpho.

"What you have done, my moerhead sergeants, is you have put a man in hospital. Maybe he is going to die. Maybe he is not. He is in ICU, my moerhead sergeants. He is what they call 'critical.' He is a reporter, this man. Other reporters want to know why he is shot. They will be asking questions. They can see the movie on Instagram. When they look on their phones, they see a blue Honda come round a corner from where the reporter was shot. They can see skidding. They can see skateboarders jumping left and right like Bart Simpsons. Everyone's laughing. But in the back of the car there is a man waving a gun. They can see this Sergeant Mpho. They are going to ask questions. Why was this reporter man shot? What did he know? Or they will ask, 'Maybe he was not the target? Maybe it was the police captain from Internal Crime who was the target?' They will ask questions. These are questions we do not need."

Exit stops outside Mzoli's.

"Do you understand me, Sergeant Mpho?"

Sergeant Mpho says he does.

"Then you, moerhead sergeants, go home and cause no more kak tonight. Except that car. That car must burn."

In the quiet outside Mzoli's, Exit says, "This is my car."

"We can make a plan," says Mpho. "A spray job. Tomorrow the car will be white. Will cost money but there is money. Come, my brother, we have business here. The legless one mustn't scare you. Afterwards, I got one more quick 'n' easy to sort."

10

In the late hours Wynston Adams puts a hand over his wine glass, says to Zara Dewane, "Enough. I need to sleep."

She pours what's left in the bottle into her glass. "You can go in Kyle's room. The bed's got clean sheets."

The two of them in pulled-up chairs before a wood-burning stove.

"You gotta go to bed," says Wynston. "There's the hearing tomorrow." Looks at his watch. "Today."

Zara opens the stove door, slides in another log. "I'll go now-now." Watches him heave out of the chair, walk unsteadily down the passage to the bedroom. Calls out, "Thanks, hey, Wynston. You're a good gabba."

Gabba?

My lewe fok, Eloise, second time in one night. Where'd that come from? Like something dredged out of her family's lingo from back in the day.

But she means it.

Because he had been a true colleague. More than that, a true friend.

Had got to her in twenty minutes. Same time as the local SAPS, same time as the ambulance. By then she had her hands well bloodied trying to stop journo-neighbor Studs from bleeding out. Most of his stomach looking pretty eviscerated. After the medics had gotten him away, there'd been a bunch of cops milling around. No crime-scene technicians available so the local detective became the investigating officer, collected what rounds he could find. Had a constable take down Zara's statement.

And then her mother pitched up. Out of the proverbial blue. Burst from her car, pushed her way through the cops, onlookers, private security officers. A smart woman with iron-gray hair in a pixie cut.

"What's going on, Zara-sweet?"

"Ma! You shouldn't be here."

"Looks to me like I should. What's happened?"

Zara took her inside, to the kitchen at the back. Explained the situation.

Her mother's reaction: "Where's Kylie? You've got to come home. You're not safe here."

More explanations from Zara. Plus: "My colleague Warrant Officer Wynston Adams is with me. I'm fine. I'm alright here, honestly. Those guys're not gonna come back."

Getting the dubious eye.

"We worry about you, you know. Your pa and me."

"I know, Ma, I know." Introducing her to Wynston to get her off the subject.

"This is my mom, Elsi."

And Wynston was charming, reassuring. Ten minutes later

was escorting Elsi to her car. Elsi saying to Zara, "You better phone your pa."

Which Zara did. As a retired cop, he knew the hazards. Expressed his anxiety, said he'd calm her mother. Added: "It was bad in my day. But you've got it worse, bokkie. Be careful."

She disconnected as Wynston returned.

"That's a force of nature, your mother. Hectic. Can see where you get it from."

Zara smiled. "I'm a kitten in comparison." Went indoors to change, then phoned Brigadier Sithole. Before he heard it through the grapevine.

"You're alright?" the brigadier wanted to know.

Zara, now wearing a chunky hoodie, sweatpants, thick socks, no shoes, flicked hair off her face. Was feeling hyper, charged. Riding an upper. Was about to draw the cork on the Giovanni's bottle of wine.

"What's happening, Captain? You are okay?"

Said she was. Put the call on speakerphone, left the corkscrew standing in the cork. Told the brigadier about the blue Honda. The two guys.

Got a long pause from her brigadier. Imagined Brigadier Wiseman Sithole at home, other side of the country. At home in Menlo Park, Tshwane. She'd been there twice for briefings. Nice place. Swimming pool. Braai zone. Fake lawn. Big house. High walls. Electrified fencing. Security cameras. His veggie patch: spinach, cauliflower, broccoli, onions, cabbage, all sorts of herbs: arugula, basil, rosemary, thyme. The brigadier's pride and joy. One day, every day, it would be his office, he'd told her. Until then, the brigadier ticked off the weeks to retirement. His children out of the house. His wife in the lounge, watching television. Zara knowing the last thing he wanted was trouble from the Cape. Heard him say, "From what your warrant says, low caliber."

"Point-two-two. Silenced. You could make more noise clapping your hands."

"The car didn't stop?"

"Not for a moment."

"You can't say they were professional."

"They seriously wounded my neighbor."

"Yes, I am briefed by the warrant about your neighbor."

Zara kept silent. Drew the cork.

"He's a journalist, the shot man, the warrant says. Does investigations. You are sure they weren't after him?"

Zara thinking, My lewe fok, Eloise, I told you they were following me. Said she didn't think so, not at all.

"Fine, alright, fine, I suppose. That's the car I see on Instagram? The same one you saw before?"

She said it was. Poured two glasses.

"You couldn't identify them?"

She told him not a chance. They wore masks. Beanies. Were too far away. At the time she first saw them, had no reason to think anything suspicious. A pause again. Zara pictured him taking in a sip of Johnnie Black.

"You think it's to do with tomorrow? The hearing?"

"Maybe. Maybe not. There're other things going on down here. Today we got a cache of guns at Saldanha, it's in my report tomorrow. We have leads to bank accounts. Warrant Adams is on it, doing traces." Corrected herself: "Will be doing traces tomorrow. Maybe someone's spooked that the case has come to us."

"Could be." The click of a fingernail against glass. A change in tone: "Listen, Captain …"

Zara clenched her teeth, anticipated *the talk*. Gripped the back of a chair.

"Listen to me, Captain, for tomorrow at the hearing, you stay with what you know, alright? You don't go to deviations like I've heard you. You stay on the point. You give straight evidence. Facts. Forensics. Eyewitness. You tell what you know, you do not say what you think. You keep to the path of facts. I do not want wanderings of speculations. I do not want you turning a spoon in this pot. I do not want to get more messages from the higher floors for me to keep you in line. I do not want this sort of trouble, Captain. You hear me? I do not want whisperings, jokings behind me when I walk down the corridors. This job is not my choice. I have told you this before. This job is my duty. So enough. Do not cause problems for me tomorrow. I know you and that Lanski lawyer. You have no boundaries. You want women's rights. I want women's rights. But tomorrow you give your evidence then leave it. No funny stuff. You exit the hearing." He said something in his mother tongue she didn't understand. Then went quiet.

Zara waited. Always the same lecture. As if she was that person. He'd never understood her, her way of operating. She took it. Rolled her eyes but said nothing to contradict him.

Eventually he said, "You with me, Captain?"

"Brigadier," she said. Wanted to scream but didn't.

"One more thing. Today Brigadier Mpungose from Police Intelligence came to see me. He told me there is talk about shutting down the ICU. There are people at the Aviary who want us to stop our investigations. We cannot let them, Captain. We must be one hundred percent within the law. We are OMO-washing-powder clean. Nothing must be with a stain. We cannot lose credibility." He stopped. "Are you with me?"

"Yes, Brigadier," said Zara.

His voice softened. "Good. Now, where are you? At home? You have protection tonight?"

Zara told him, Yes, Warrant Officer Adams was staying over. Her home-security people would do regular checks.

She released her grip on the chair, reached for her wine, took a long pull. Pushed the other glass toward Wynston. Drank a second mouthful, refilled her glass. Feeling the wine's warmth in her stomach, an easing of the tension in her neck. Heard the brigadier wishing her well. That they would talk tomorrow after the hearing. That he would see if he could arrange police protection for her.

Zara said, "Cheers, Brigadier." Could picture the crystal tumbler in his hand, the man wanting to take another hit. Knew how he resented ending his career at ICU. Some desk job pushing papers would've been more his style. She said goodbye again, tapped off the connection.

"You can't say that to him," Wynston said.

"What?" Zara taking her glass down by another half. "What? Toast him with a cheers?" Expecting the tremors any second. "What're you saying?" Grinning at Wynston. The wine kicking in nicely. She'd been shot at before. Four or five times. After the first shootout, the shakes had set in pronto. So badly she was useless. Had to walk around to quiet her heart rate, let alone steady the trembles. Second time there was a delay of hours. Same delay the times after. She couldn't escape them, but a drink helped. Definitely. She finished the glass.

"Yarrah," said Wynston. "Slow down, Cap."

Zara refilled her glass. "I can drink. I was the target. You heard him, the brigadier. What'd he say? Was I the target? After I'd told him, he still says, 'Was I the target?' He still thinks maybe they were after my journo-neighbor. He knows. He damn well knows this's about the hearing." This time Zara sipped her wine. Glanced at Wynston. No ways she had enough Giovanni's morsels for two. He would finish the schnitzel in a mouthful. Said, "You want a pizza? I've got Woolies margheritas." Opened the fridge. "I've got chorizo, peppers, chilies, olives, sun-dried tomatoes I can chop up for toppings. Or anchovies. You want anchovies rather?"

Wynston said the chorizo would be good. And the rest. Just not the anchovies.

From the freezer, she took two pizzas. From the fridge, the rest. Began slicing the peppers.

Said, "You think this guy, Langa Mpho, was trying to scare me? Got a gabba to drive him?" She paused, knife raised. "I reckon they were watching me from Three Anchors. They were at Giovanni's, in the parking opposite. They followed me there. Thing is, how'd they know I was at Three Anchors? Huh? How'd they know I was there? They musta seen us get back to the office from Saldanha."

Wynston shook his head, finished his wine. Refilled. "All they gotta do is ping your phone."

Zara went back to dicing peppers. "I suppose. Like how they traced and killed that other cop."

"Exactly."

She pointed the knife at the wood stove. "You want to get that fire going?" Told him where to find the firelighters, the matches.

Said, "So how'd I know if they're doing that to me?" Still no trembles. This was okay. Maybe going to be okay. Zara put the chorizo on the chopping board, sliced off ovals. "There some way we can find out?"

"I'll sort it," said Wynston. "Not that difficult."

"Like now."

"Like tomorrow."

Zara's phone rang: Jo-Jo Lanski.

"Zar, I heard. You okay? You want company?"

"No problemo. I'm fine. Wynston's here." Zara tapped to speakerphone. "I'm making pizzas. Drinking wine. We're all merry."

"Good. You think it's Mpho hunting you?"

"Could be. I dunno. There were guys following me. Probably pinging me, Wynston says."

"Bloody Christ, nasty one. That's how they nail you. As you get home. Keep the Z loaded."

"It's on the table. Hey, Jo-Jo, tomorrow, Sithole says we got to be cool. Not cause any crap."

"Sithole se gat."

Zara smiled. "Very rude. But, yes, he can be an asshole."

They disconnected. Zara glanced over at Wynston struggling to light the fire. Smiled. Maybe he could catch a crooked cop, maybe he could even machine a piston head to hear him tell that story, but light a fire! No ways. She let him battle. Stuck the margheritas in the microwave to defrost. Wound up the oven to a high heat. Wondered, looking at him, a pretty boy, why he'd never tried it on with her. Not that she was game. But he was what? Twenty-eight, twenty-nine, had women on speed dial. A flirter. A sharp dresser. The custom-fit shirts under a natty waistcoat. The pressed chinos; Italian lace-ups, never trainers. The duster coat, for heaven's sake, an occasional flamboyance. Zara expecting him to come in one bright morning with a Stetson. Sign up for the Wild Bunch. Wynston's hip tastes unlike her what-you-see fashion sense: tight jeans, slip-on sneakers, flat soles. Out and about she wore that leather bomber jacket, red (ox-blood red), that just covered the pistol. Her hair pulled back in a short ponytail, like now. Brown hair, green, skeptical eyes, usually no lipstick, like now. Sometimes red lipstick on special occasions.

She took the pizzas out of the microwave, forked on the topping, spread it around, stuck them in the oven. Went over to help Wynston with the fire.

"I don't do fires," he said, standing up.

She jostled him aside, knelt down to feed in more kindling. "Let Mommy help." Had it blazing right off. Looked up at him, "How'd you manage to machine a piston head?"

"I didn't. Baz, my motormac friend, did it."

"I thought you said …"

"Ja, well, I was there to help."

Zara laughed. "You're such a bullshitter sometimes, Wynston. Is this what you tell your girlfriends? That you're Mr. Handyman?"

"I never said that."

"Not in so many words." Zara emptied the bottle into their glasses. Flopped into a chair, pulled it up to the wood stove. Said, "This is not how I expected this evening to go." Gestured for Wynston to sit. Could feel the trembles starting. She set the wineglass on the floor, gripped her hands in her lap. Clamped her teeth. Didn't want Wynston to see this tension in her. Said, "What's this thing you've got with old Mercs anyhow?" Anything for distraction. Fought against the shaking that wanted to jiggle her knee, get her feet skittering.

She heard but didn't hear Wynston going on about his car and its diff whine, and the badge he had to buy for a thousand bucks, how he could steer by that star. She kept the shakes in check, drank wine, ate her pizza. Got Wynston to talk more about himself. Drank wine. Kept her muscles taut. Couldn't stop the shakes in her thighs. Got up to search for chocolate. In the bathroom, knocked back three paracetamols. In the kitchen, opened another bottle. Drank off a glass. Gave Wynston more wine, a third of the chocolate slab. Ate the rest herself. Heard Wynston's stories of clubbing at the Black Hole, doob raves on Dassen Island, stories, too, from the other side of the blue line: drag racing in the small hours, abalone diving along the reserve coast. Hours hiding in kelp beds to escape the conservation officers. Stories she couldn't believe. That Wynston could be so left field. Told him, laughing, "Wynston. Enough. I didn't hear that stuff." Drank wine. Realized the shakes had subsided. She could relax.

"More wine?"

Which was when Wynston put a hand over his wine glass, slurred, "Enough. I need to sleep." Said, "You gotta go to bed. Don't drink anymore." Staggered off to her son's bedroom. Zara calling after him that he was a good gabba.

Saying "gabba" for the second time that night.

My lewe fok, Eloise.

Now she sits before the dying fire, her thoughts zeroing in on her life: her son; days mired in work; colleagues who've spurned her; no lover; the difficulty of dealing with Ashton. Gets maudlin. Wonders, as always, what she'd ever seen in her ex. Why she hadn't listened to her mother's cautionary; her own gut telling her there was something off. Placid, quiet, hesitant Ashton. Ruthless, angry, heartless Ashton. To see him standing at a braai, beer in hand, you wouldn't guess the anger, the rage beneath the skin. But she'd seen it. Heard it. Felt it. At least you got out, she tells herself. Except. Except until Kyle was his own man, she was tied to his father. And all the upset he caused. The old story.

Only way to handle a sociopath, the therapist had said, is to praise them. "Give him fuel. That's what he's looking for. Something to still his inner rage. Something to make him feel better."

Remembers Kyle's heartfelt plea to come home. Because Ashton has blown up for some reason.

She opens another bottle of wine, fills her glass. Reaches for her cell phone. Keys Ashton. Gets a croaky "What do you want?"

"We need to talk."

"It's too late. Go to sleep." Then the kicker: "Have you been drinking?"

How'd he know that? How could he hear it in her voice?

She grips the phone tighter. Comes on the rational pacifier.

"Look, Ashton, listen, I know you're worried about Kyle. I know he can be a handful sometimes. Exasperating even."

"You're not joking."

"You just got to give him space. He likes to do his own thing."

"He needs to listen to me."

Which she doesn't rise to. Keeps her voice level.

"Sure. I've got to repeat myself with him too. But he's a kid. Not even a teenager yet. I think you're doing pretty well with him. I know you're worried that I'm not managing but I am. We are, Kyle and me. This is working for all of us, the three of us. It's a good arrangement: you get him for a once-a-week sleepover, every second weekend he's with you. We're co-parenting. You're good for him."

Zara thinking, Where're you getting this stuff from? All cool, calm 'n' collected. Completely deceitful.

"That's not what he says."

"He doesn't mean it."

Completely rational!

"He does. You're telling him. I can hear you in his voice."

"I'm not. I absolutely am not."

A silence. That silence that is always the workup to his rage. She goes in, hoping to forestall him. Why not? You're on a roll, Zar, lather on the soft-soap.

"Look, please, no more visits to the school principal. It's embarrassing. For me and for Kyle. Also please, no more lawyers letters. You know I have custody, that's our divorce agreement. I've given you more than was legally set out. Can't we just keep it the way things are? We're both his parents. Like I said, we're co-parenting."

Will you listen to yourself. You're being creepy.

Predictably, it gets Ashton coming back at her with a "Listen to you. I don't need your words of wisdom. I don't need the calm rational Zara. I know what you're like. Really like. Why d'you think the cops all hate you? Because you're the bully, Zara. Always telling people what to do. Always ordering them about. High and mighty Captain Zara Dewane, the moral voice. The nation's conscience. Don't come lecturing me. Especially not when you're drunk. I don't have to listen to your crap. I can get you anytime. I'll break your kneecaps. This is not over by a long shot. You disgusting vernon."

Zara holds the phone away as if that will quieten him. Thinks, Here we go.

"Don't kid yourself, you disgusting vernon. You're pathetic."

Vermin. He means vermin. He never can get the word right.

She hears him splutter. Then it comes: "You're lowlife, the great Captain Dewane is a nobody." Followed by a string of insults ending with the whore of Babylon. Which Zara has heard many times. Reckons the reference is some allusion to his evangelical pretensions. No other way Ashton would've gleaned such knowledge.

Realizes then that he isn't shouting. His voice is hard as if he can't breathe, but he isn't shouting. Isn't talking softly either.

You did your best. You didn't shout and scream. You were reason personified. Enough now.

She disconnects. Drinks the last of the wine in her glass, stares at the dying embers. One day there will be no more Ashton.

The Dawn Chorus

11

Zara hears Wynston get up. The flush of the loo. Drifts in and out of sleep to the sounds of his leaving. His soft tread creaking the floorboards. The gush of water into a glass in the kitchen. The opening of the front door, the latch clicking fast as he closes it. On her cell phone, sees the time: 6:30. Her mouth dry, foul tasting. Her head sore. Yet she hadn't drunk that much, surely. She groans, tries to get back to sleep. Another half an hour. Another forty-five minutes.

But no, five minutes later the phone: Wynston.

Grouches: "What?"

"Mpungose's been killed."

"What? Say again?"

"Last night. In an operation. They shot him. It's on the news."

She blinks, rubs her eyes, tries to focus.

Brigadier Sipho Mpungose dead! The number two at Police Intelligence dead. Unbelievable.

"You're sure it's him?"

"OTS News. Tune in. Really, he was shot. I can't believe it."

The implications worming through her hangover. His death will open a big hole in the hierarchy of Police Intelligence. Minus the brigadier's authority in the upper echelons, Sithole will be lost. A weak man, easily brushed aside. Without Mpungose,

ICU will be ignored, laughed at, derided. It doesn't bear thinking about.

Zara swings out of bed, grimaces at a flash of headache behind her eyes. Wonders why she's slept in her bra. Wonders at the tracksuit pants.

"I'll get back to you, okay. I need to phone Sithole." Needs to pee too. Staggers through to the bathroom. The damn seat up as Wynston had left it. Jesus! Men!

Wynston still on at her: "It's gonna mean problems for us."

"I dunno, Wynston. Let me get sorted. Find out what's going on. Give me half an hour, okay?" She disconnects. Gets sorted.

After a glass of water, two Tylenols, stares at her image in the mirror. The mussed hair. The wine stain on her teeth. The puffiness around her hooded eyes. Her eyes? Don't look like her eyes. More like the eyes of a zombie. Runs a shower. Under the deluge, her thoughts not hopeful. Without Mpungose, Sithole won't fight for the ICU. He'll cave at any resistance to their investigations. Why bother to fight. He's retiring soon. Even likely that on his retirement, ICU might be closed down, as he's intimated. What then of her position? Her job? Back into uniform? Or worse, exiled to a back office to shuffle papers?

She stands a long time under the hot water, these thoughts going round and round. Then realizes her period has started. Today of all goddamn days. Maybe another reason for the headache. Comes round every month yet so often takes her by surprise. Like she can't get used to it. She dresses: no jeans today, no leather jacket. A black suit, her court attire. Even red lipstick. At that point starts fantasizing about Coke and a chip gatsby. Could pick one up on the way to the hearing. That'd settle the day.

But first Brigadier Wiseman Sithole. The call goes to voicemail. She gives it five minutes, phones again. He answers.

"We can't talk now, Captain. I'll be in touch after the hearing."

"But. Mpungose?"

"Not now, Captain. Not now."

Dead air.

Zara clenches her phone. Inhales to the count of three. Lets her breath out in a huff.

12

Comes the morning, comes a fiery sky.

Driving this red dawn is none other than Captain Alicia Hendricks behind the wheel of her maroon Mazda CX-5.

To be honest, she hates the daily commute up the West Coast, sixty miles from Cape Town. Hates the Saldanha posting. The pettiness of the harbor town. The stink of the fisheries, the ugly homes, the cramped lives. The sense that she is at play in an endgame she can't foresee. Is buoyed only by the colonel's promise of a posting soon in the city.

"How soon?"

"Give it another three months, Captain. Surely not too much to ask." That way he has of spinning his chair to face you. The glare in his eyes. The accusation that he can no longer walk. That you are among those to blame. Merely because you are part of the walking world. Your only option to look away, let his temper subside. "Come, Captain. Relax. Your patience will be rewarded."

Two months to go.

And then what? Police Intelligence? The division the colonel is angling for. That would suit. That would get her onto a career path. Major. Lieutenant Colonel. Colonel. Brigadier. The targets Alicia Hendricks has set herself. A stratosphere above the likes of oily Sergeant Langa Mpho. Above the violent jealousies of a Constable Pietman Malgas. Or the sniffling twitches of a Captain Zara Dewane.

Her thoughts are interrupted by OTS News on the radio.

"In breaking news, On The Spot has learned that Brigadier Sipho Mpungose has been killed in a major police operation last night. The operation was focused on a house in the upmarket

Tshwane suburb of Waterkloof. OTS has learned that the house was owned by a brother of a senior figure in the African National Congress. Details are unclear but a police spokesperson said, 'At 01:00 hours this morning, a special task team entered the premises of a house in Waterkloof. Shots were fired by security guards on the premises. During the exchange, Brigadier Mpungose was wounded in the head. He was rushed to hospital but died at 05:00 hours this morning. The South African Police Service expresses its sincere condolences to his wife and family.'"

Alicia breaks out her first cigarette of the day, fires up. Thinks, Hoozah, hoozah. Sometimes the world turns to your advantage.

Now what about Kaiser Vula with his ambitions to leave the secret service? Surely he'll angle to join the cops? With Mpungose gone, he could aim for the position. Be the ideal candidate. Who else comes with his intelligence background? Who else has such Struggle credentials? The man is a veteran. A national hero. Surely the chief of Police Intelligence will look to Vula? She leaves the cigarette between her lips. Presses through to other channels. Gets everything from music to chats about god's presence in the world. Catches a snippet about warring factions in the ANC. Wonders if the snippet is linked to the cop raid. The invisible game being played. With Mpungose off the board, Vula can make his move. Her cigarette down to the stub, Alicia Hendricks crushes it out, lights another. Decides to phone the colonel. Two miles on, pulls off at a farm gate, digs an old Nokia from her bag, gets through to Vula.

"I know why you're calling," he says. "I have heard the news report too. It is very sad but also very interesting. Mpungose was an important man. He will leave a gap that should be filled quickly."

"What will happen, Colonel?"

"I am sure there will be a temporary appointment. This has become the ruling party's modus."

"Will that be you?"

"It is possible. But it is not automatic. We will have to see what powers will pull the strings."

"It should be you."

"I am not the only one they will consider, Captain. There are others from the Struggle. New dogs barking in the backyard. Now, I must talk to the chief of Police Intelligence and give him my condolences. Ah, one more thing: that shipment, I have postponed it."

They disconnect.

Captain Alicia Hendricks accelerates back onto the N7: the sun risen, hope rising eternal in her breast. Maybe the colonel will be promoted and transferred to the police. Maybe he will get her out of Saldanha sooner. Maybe, maybe, maybe. A host of possibilities. Without Mpungose and his support of the ICU, there will be less oversight of the police. More room to maneuver. Almost suppresses a desire for another cigarette. She should stop. She will if the world changes. Presses in the lighter. Fidgets a stick from the packet. Sets it between her lips. As the car gathers speed, takes her hands off the wheel, raising her fists in triumph.

When her smartphone in the holder rings: Tamora Gool.

No coincidence.

The top bitch of the Mongols not wasting a moment.

13

Colonel Kaiser Vula rolls up to the breakfast table. Still in his pajamas, under a thick robe. His wife, Lady, sitting there in her fluffy fur coat over silky black pajamas. No toweling gowns for Lady. Only the faux fur she's taken to wearing on winter mornings. Suits Kaiser if that's how she wants to play it.

"I suppose little miss is all excited this morning," says Lady. Raises a finger of toast smeared with marmalade to her mouth, crunches down. "What has miss got to say?"

"That I should become Maale's right-hand man."

Kaiser Vula helps himself to putu porridge and sausages. Pours a mug of coffee. "This is a dreadful thing that has happened, this shooting."

"Of course. This is painful for the Mpungoses." Lady wipes crumbs from her lips. "It is a tragedy. To lose a father and a husband and a valued policeman is an awful thing. Truly cruel. Violence is one of the burdens we suffer in this country. Look at you. You have to endure the consequences of doing your duty. You could have been killed. I could have been a widow. But we have gone on. We have ourselves. We have our life. This is what happens. This is what matters. The world goes on through Sturm und Drang, as the good Germans would say."

Sturm und Drang!

Kaiser Vula glances at his wife: takes in her lively face, her unblemished skin. These days, her hair in short braids with beads. Takes years off. Smiles. Gets a smile in return, a tilt of the head. Fingers adorned in black nail varnish reaching across to stroke his face.

"Later," he says, swallows a mouthful of sausage and pap, laughs at the glint in her eyes. Knows what will happen when she helps him in the shower.

How she has changed since his wounding. Now takes Virgin Active sessions four times a week. But she's kept her bums, round, firm. And he has come to love her again. Appreciate her. That she has not turned away from his … his maiming, his shitbag. Has brought new vooma to their sex life with leather apparel.

"I will phone General Maale after breakfast."

"Phone him now. He will need you, Kaisey. The little miss is right, you should be the general's new right-hand man. For the moment. We all know this. Maale knows this. You are the man with the strings. The smiling puppet master. Maale should be your right-hand man."

The smiling puppet master! It must be all the books she reads, Kaiser Vula has decided. These days she comes out with strange words, unusual phrases. His literary wife.

So even as they sit at breakfast, he phones General Maale. Goes through the condolence protocols, edges the conversation to what happened.

"Ah, my friend, that is the badness," says the general. "That is the worm that eats at our hearts. It is what the prophet says, we have turned everyone to his own way. We fight against ourselves. You can see it, we are comrades no longer."

Kaiser Vula makes eye contact with his wife. Presses the general to speakerphone.

"These are our people killing us. Our very own people. Let us look at you, Kaiser, you were shot by a veteran, a man of the Struggle. This is unacceptable. We have forgotten our ways. We are living in our own evil."

Lady Vula holds up her hand like a beak, her fingers imitating a mouth chattering. The problem with Duncan Maale, Kaiser Vula knows, is his sermonizing. As a lay priest, he loses no opportunity.

"And now Brigadier Mpungose has been slain. And why? Because a man wanted to enrich himself. Colonel, we are in a bad space, our hearts are deceitful and desperately wicked."

The moment to interject. Kaiser Vula helps himself to toast and butter, says, "What happened?"

"It is not completely what you hear on the radio or the television."

"No. There are not many times when it is."

"This is the truth exactly. These reporters all write fiction. Sipho Mpungose, the lord have mercy on his soul, was working with Brigadier Sithole, you know the brigadier from ICU?"

"I have heard of him."

"They were investigating certain matters. I cannot tell you more at this point; the investigation is now most critical. But what I can say…" He pauses. "Perhaps you know already, Kaiser. Because you are a man with more fingers than ten."

"I know only what the news reported."

"But all intelligence finds its way to Colonel Vula, is that not so?"

"I cannot say, General."

Lady Vula silently claps her hands. Mouths, "Oh yes. Oh yes."

"Last night Sipho led a special team to arrest a man who was once a policeman. One of our brothers. One of us, Kaiser. It is a true sadness that we are now this way. It is a disgrace. It is our disgrace. I cannot tell you who this is because there has been no arrest. Now the lawyers are talking. What happened is still unclear. Inside the house, there was a shooting. There, shots were fired. One man was wounded. Sipho Mpungose was killed. All this happened where there were no witnesses, I am told. The task force was outside. Sipho's gun was not fired. The only people who know what happened in that room are the wounded man and the suspect. What can you do with people like this? Now our brigadier is dead. For no reason. He is dead because some men were too easy with the triggers. Ah, Kaiser, what more can I say?"

Kaiser Vula lets the question hang over his breakfast table. Looks across at his wife looking at him over the edge of her coffee cup. A connivance in her eyes. He can imagine her thoughts: Be *the* man.

Hears General Maale saying: "Today is a day of grief, Colonel. We must mourn our dead comrade. He was a comrade before all others. Tomorrow we can think of other matters."

They disconnect.

"A mess," says Kaiser Vula.

"An opportunity," says Lady Vula. "Come. You must dress, you have an appointment with Luna Maplewood."

14

"I've got money for you," says Tamora Gool to Captain Alicia Hendricks. "I'm sure you want it."

Alicia Hendricks hears the snicker in Gool's voice. The sarcasm. Feels her body stiffen with tension. The woman never lets it go: always the reminder that, cop or gang leader, they are both the same. From the same place. Playing the same game. But they aren't. For starters, she doesn't dish out poison to kids.

Or smuggle abalone.

Or use a hammerman to get her way.

Alicia Hendricks fastens both hands on the steering wheel, says, "The usual place." Keeps her voice hard.

The usual place being a small shopping center parking lot in the suburbs. No cameras. Surprisingly, no car guards.

"I don't think so. Not this time. We should change it." This from Gool. Putting it out there.

"Why?"

"Because."

"Because isn't a reason."

"It's enough."

"It's stupid."

"Stupid! You think it's stupid. You want me to teach you, my friend? You're a cop. You know how these things work. You don't use the same place too often."

"In our case, that's nonsense. Three times is not too often." Alicia knowing she is arguing to be difficult. The shopping center is out of her way. Across the northern suburbs. An hour's drive there, an hour's drive back. They could find somewhere closer. More convenient to them both.

"Also I want ammunition. Not that much: a hundred rounds, 9mm."

Alicia Hendricks explodes. "Jissis. You think I can conjure it up just like that?"

A pause, a silence. Then: "Ja. I do, liefie. It's your reputation. So when, hey? This afternoon, maybe?"

"You think you can just call this anytime you want?"

"Why not? I'm the buyer. I'm the client. Where's your customer service?"

Alicia Hendricks clamps her teeth. Keeps her eyes focused on the car ahead. The thing about gangsters: the men want you to play mommy; the women want a servant. That is the way with Gool. More larney than the larnies.

"Listen, there's something else."

Here we go. Alicia Hendricks puts her foot down to overtake. The guy ahead's driving like an asshole. Says, "Like what?"

"Stones."

"Stones?"

"Ja, man, stones. Diamonds. You know, rough ones."

The woman has no fears. Is getting above herself, in Alicia Hendricks's scheme of things. Needs taking down a peg or four.

"Are you mad?"

Tamora Gool barks a loud laugh. "I'm adding to your product range. Making you more marketable. Let me tell you, there's lots more in the pipeline. This could be a profitable side hustle for you. Have a look at them at least. Yes? What do you say?"

Alicia Hendricks says nothing. Lets a silence tick by.

"You still there, Cappie?"

"I can't do this afternoon," she says. "Tonight."

Before Gool can say anything, Alicia Hendricks names a street in a railway suburb. The street where her sister lives. The sort of street where everybody is indoors by dark, watching Netflix. Says 9 p.m. Between numbers thirty-three and thirty-five.

"No ways. Not at night."

Alicia's turn for a derisive snicker. "You scared of the dark?"

"I'm scared of what you cops hide in the dark. I like to see what's going on."

"Nothing'll be going on. Just you and me."

"And the transaction."

"Whatever."

"Good. Cos we don't want shit, Captain. You and me, we're both living in the material world. We got our debts. So, this afternoon, usual time. At your new location. Tell them at Saldanha you're going to meetings in the city. You're the commander, you got the authority. You can tell them anything."

The last thing Alicia Hendricks wants is time arrangements made by Tamora Gool. But what other options? She presses her off. Thinks half a chance she'll have that woman sorted out. Give her what for with a sjambok. Except devil you know. Devil you want to keep onside.

15

Zara Dewane finds parking in a city side street. Sits for a moment to still her pounding head. To check out she hasn't been followed. Nada. If there was a tail, they were good. No cars turned in, no one peering round corners. At this end the street is empty. Further down there is movement outside New York Bagels. A courier guy sitting on his bike, waiting for an order. Someone putting chairs and tables on the sidewalk. She could do with one of their espressos: the dark brown foam, the solid taste. Instead washes down another Tylenol with a guzzle from her bottle of water. Her thoughts clearing, focusing now on a gatsby and Coke. Salvation being one street down at an Indian takeaway. As she locks her car, a car guard appears. Makes her start. Makes her reflex grab at the Z88 which isn't there. So much for anti-surveillance training. So much for being alert when people are out to get you.

"No, my sister, no, man, I's not trouble." The car guard backing off a pace, holding up her hands like Zara has a gun pointed at her. "I's a guard to keep the troubles away."

"You better," Zara says. Then laughs. "Where the hell were you?"

The guard laughs with her, points at a wheelie bin lying on its side.

"In it?"

"Welcome to my home."

My lewe fok, Eloise. How had she missed her? Zara shakes her head. "You want a gatsby?"

The woman looks at her.

"Yes or no?"

"This is breakfast time, my sister."

"Yes or no?"

Now the car guard's turn to shake her head. Like this is one sad craziness eating a gatsby for breakfast—meat, fries, salad stuffed into a long roll. For breakfast?

"Yes. Thank you, my sister. Calamari with extra chili sauce, asseblief, my sister. An' a cream soda." The woman fishing in her pocket for change.

"Ja, ja keep the two rands. Just look after my car, hey?" Zara heads off. Not a chance in hell the woman could look after the car. She's lucky to have a patch on the street before the Congolese moved in. Lower down, they are the guys controlling the curb parking, the car parks.

Zara buys the takeaways: one a calamari with extra sauce; the other a Vienna sausage; a straight-up Coke; a green cream soda. Two paper straws. Goes back to eat, leaning against the bonnet of her car; the guard sitting on the wheelie bin.

"Is sister with a babbelas hangover?" the woman wants to know.

"You could say," Zara replies. Wonders if she smells of booze.

"It's good for that," the woman says, holding up her gatsby. Then: "Is sister a gatte?"

"It's that obvious?"

The woman gives her a grin. Good teeth. "I sees your cowboy move. Gunfight style."

"Ja, I'm gatte," Zara confesses. "But the good police."

"There's no good police," the woman says, staring hard at Zara over the top of her roll. "Cape Coloureds shouldn't be police."

Zara goes mock offended. "Hey, I've just bought you breakfast."

"Maybe yous an exceptional."

They eat in silence for a while. Zara feeling the greasy food settle her stomach. The Coke bringing back some pep to the day. Getting to the stage where the gatsby is getting to be too much gatsby. She pats the corners of her mouth with a paper napkin.

"What's your name?"

"Janet."

Sips at the Coke. "Janet who?"

"Janet of the Cape. Who's yourself?"

Zara tells her. Asks why she sleeps on the streets, doesn't use the shelter.

Janet chomps gatsby. Says through a mouthful: "I's got my many reasons. I's a free soul. There's all rules in the shelter. I's got a nice person I know. She's got my room."

"You've got a room but you sleep in a wheelie bin?"

"I told you I's a free soul."

Zara's phone rings: attorney Jo-Jo. She stabs a greasy finger at the green button. "What's up?"

"You heard from the witness?"

"We last spoke a couple of days ago. Why? What's the problem?"

"She's not answering my calls. Yesterday she was all fired up."

"Could be in a taxi."

"Maybe."

"Don't panic."

"Says she who got shot at last night. How're you? Where're you anyhow?"

"To the first question: fine. To the second: not far, having breakfast."

"Wynston's with you?"

"No. Why, should he be?"

"Cos you're a bloody target."

"Ja, ja. I can take care of myself. I'm a big girl."

"Meet me in twenty," says Jo-Jo. "Let's hope this time it happens."

Zara disconnects. Sees there's been another call: Ashton. He's left a voice message. She plays it on speakerphone.

"Listen, you ... you! I don't know what your case is but refrain from phoning me. At all. Ever. I'm going to a lawyer. It's better that Kyle lives with me. Has some stability in his life."

"Oo, there's a angry man," says Janet. "I's had experience with a angry man. Sometimes theys get psychopathic."

"You think?" Zara more amused at the woman's earnestness than her opinion.

"I's telling you. Even for a cop, you gotta be careful."

"Yeah, well." Zara wipes her hands on what's left of the

napkin. Offers the remains of her gatsby to Janet. Says, "I'm not diseased."

Janet takes the roll. Eyes her up and down. "You got a backyard room for me?"

My lewe.

"We's sisters. Same color, mos."

Zara amused, giving this some thought. The there but for the grace of thought ... Being on the street a wild dangerous place. Besides. She has a room. That's been locked up since she moved in two years back. Did she want someone in the backyard? Not really.

"How're you gonna earn it?"

"You's got me then," said Janet. "Good company. Also I's protection. There's a lady at my beach house will be a reference."

Which collapses Zara.

A beach house?

"There by Muizenberg. Miss Vicki's a lawyer, mos."

"Seriously?"

"Serious."

Zara gives Janet a business card, scrawls her street address on the back. In exchange, gets the name Vicki Kahn, the name of a legal firm she recognizes, and a cell phone number.

"Phone her for a voucher," says Janet.

"I will," says Zara, heads for the hearing, thinking some days start weird.

Witch Hunts

16

All the way to the appointment with Luna Maplewood, Colonel Kaiser Vula stays engrossed in his iPad. Flicking through news reports of the death of Brigadier Sipho Mpungose. Plenty of commentary: the rot in the ruling party; corruption in government; the president's culpability. Glowing testimony of a good cop, father, husband, friend. Of course, Twitter on fire: everything from bring back hanging to just deserts for cops. All predictable. Mostly vitriolic. Gladdens Vula to see the state of disquiet. Chaos means opportunities.

Only when the driver does a slow trawl down a suburban street does he look up. Either side, gabled houses set back behind front gardens. No one around. The driver stops the black Merc at a driveway gate, says, "It's this one, Colonel."

Colonel Kaiser Vula gazes on a stone path between rose beds. A Victorian house. Two bay windows either side the front door. Before he can move, the door opens, a woman stands there, raises a hand in greeting. She must have been waiting at the window. Colonel Vula doesn't know if he should be flattered or wary. In his experience, those who wait, wait with bad intent.

The driver pushes him up the garden path. The woman standing, smiling at the steps of her stoep. She wears bright blue Skechers, gray jeggings, a chunky jersey, her hair top-knotted, the ends strung with beads. Looks to be no more than early thirties. He'd imagined an older woman. Some rich colonial type gone native in African print dresses, leather sandals. He raises a hand in greeting.

"At last I get to meet you, Colonel," says Luna Maplewood, all smiles and happiness. "I've heard so much from Lady." Then her hand goes to her mouth, her eyes suddenly bright: "Oh! Oh! Wow. Awesome things going to happen to you. That's hectic. How exciting. Come in, come in."

"I'm sorry. What are you saying? What awesome things?"

"Come in, come in. I will tell you all."

Once they've negotiated the steps, Colonel Vula waves his driver back to the car. Looks up at the attractive Luna Maplewood. Imagines her breasts free behind the soft wool. Small breasts, he pictures. Like Lady's. Easy to cup. To tweak a swollen nipple. He shifts in the wheelchair. Shakes the image from his mind, shakes her hand. Soft skin, yet a firm grip. Says, "What has surprised you?"

"I'll tell you," she says. Smiling a lovely smile with a hint of white teeth. "But first tea, my special brew. This way." Goes ahead of him into a lounge.

"This tea is from some muti man?" he asks.

She glances back at him, coquettish. "Why not? They know what's needed. We know it works." Indicates a chair. "Can I help you get comfortable?"

"No, no." He stops her with a raised hand. "I spend my day in this wheelchair. I'm used to it. I have gotten used to it."

Again the lovely smile.

She pours tea. Places a side table next to him, the teacup on it. Offers a shortbread biscuit.

"Could you tell me about that incident, the shooting, that caused you this terrible condition?"

The woman wasting no time with preliminaries. He bites into a biscuit, washes down the sweetness with a mouthful of tea. Surprisingly pleasant. More chamomile than the acidic tree bark, he expects. Flashes back to Nandipha of his virile days. She'd used a gray powder on him to excite their sex. But he is not about to tell Luna about Nandi or her parties. Tells instead about his loyalty as an officer to the president.

"The disgraced president Zama," she adds.

The blot on his career.

"In my day, we did not know he was corrupt. We thought he was a strong man."

He tells her about the attempted assassination in the palace grounds. How the crowds were ululating, singing, reaching out to touch their president. How he, a major then, saw the assassin moving through the people. How he leapt forward to save his president, took two body shots. But brought the hitman down.

"I did what any officer to the president should do."

At the end of his story, Kaiser Vula smiles at Luna Maplewood looking at him with steady eyes. In earlier years he would have had this woman. Instead he eats the rest of the biscuit, finishes his tea. Sees empathy there in her face. Perhaps even admiration.

"That was brave."

"As I have said, it was my duty."

"Are you angry now?"

"Because I am left like this?"

"Yes." She sits opposite him, other side of a coffee table. Sits upright on a straight-backed chair, her legs crossed. The jeggings emphasizing her thighs. Firm thighs. The thighs of a Virgin Active. He brings his eyes back to her face. "Also because you did it for a bad man."

He considers this. Yes, he resents being a paraplegic. Yes, he resents that he's taken a bullet for a thief. Yes, he resents how it has affected his career. Yes, he is angry.

"I suppose you could say that."

"Do you? Is this what burns in your heart?"

"No. I have my rank. I have an essential job."

"You have your wife too."

"I have Lady."

"She is a special woman."

He watches her pick up a leather bag from the coffee table. Hears the knock of bones.

"There is something of the future I can tell you straight away," she says. "It's exciting. Time for celebrations." Such enthusiasm in her voice. The song of the young.

"What is that?" Kaiser Vula keeps his voice muted. What is happening that now a white woman should throw the bones? A pretty white woman. What does she know of ancient lore? Yet here he is. Here Lady has sent him.

Luna Maplewood puts down the bag, swipes at her phone screen. "One minute." Holds the screen toward him. "Look at this."

He looks: a display of police ranking insignia.

"When you arrived, I saw your colonel rank change," she says. "You now have this one." She points at the insignia for a general: crossed swords, four shields.

"What do you mean, you could see them change?"

"I did. They were replaced before my eyes as you arrived. How exciting is this. Congrats, General, congrats. Whoohoo. You should be pleased. You have leapt three rankings."

Her attention goes back to the bag. She opens the drawstrings, is about to spill the contents on the coffee table. But doesn't. She frowns. Glances at him.

"What is it?" Vula struck by the change in her face: how it has darkened. How her eyes are now sunken.

She jumps up. "I'm sorry," she says. "I don't feel well." She has her hand over her mouth, brushes past him. "I can't ... Not now." And runs from the room.

Kaiser Vula calls after her but gets no answer. He listens to the quiet of the house. He can't hear the woman Luna Maplewood. The house is so silent, he imagines he is alone. As if the woman has vanished. For the first time he takes in the furnishings. Two sofas covered in a flower-patterned material, arranged to form an L. A deep easy chair near the window. Next to it her straight-backed chair, now pushed away at an angle. On the coffee table, a bowl of semi-precious stones on a white beaded cloth. Hardly the furnishings of a sangoma. The pictures on the walls too are strange. Too modern for his taste. Splashes of color, a chaos of paint. He wonders if he should go in search of the woman? Or wait. He waits. Another five minutes tick by; then he hears the creak of floorboards.

"Hullo, Mr. Officer," says a woman's voice. "Miss Luna is too sick to see you anymore. She says she will phone to make another appointment for you."

Colonel Kaiser Vula swings his wheelchair to see a tall woman in a nurse's uniform. "Who are you?"

"I am Sister September. I help Miss Luna. She is very sorry she can't see you now."

"Is she alright? What's wrong with her?"

The woman shakes her head. "Miss Luna has turns. Sometimes the turns are bad. Like today. Please, you must go."

17

The sidewalk opposite Caledon Square police station.

Here Zara Dewane finds Jo-Jo Lanski. The lawyer with her bag under one arm, phone and cigarette in her other hand. Standing up against the wall of a building, trying to write in a notebook. Saying, "I want you to find her. Ping her bloody phone. Go to her place. Just bloody find her. She's got to be here."

Turns at the fall of Zara's shadow.

"Thank bloody Christ you're here."

"Where else was I going to be?"

"Dead last night. If whoever'd been more on the ball."

"But they weren't. So here I am."

Jo-Jo giving her the once-over. "Very natty, all in black. Where'd you breakfast?"

"In a back street." Zara waves over her shoulder. "With a very nice bergie. We ate gatsbys."

"You did what? Gross, man. That's disgusting."

"Wasn't too bad. Did the job."

"Oh shit!" Jo-Jo stubs her cigarette against the wall, flicks it into the gutter. "You're bloody hungover."

"Earlier. Not so much now."

A heavy sigh from Jo-Jo. "Come on. Come on." Taking Zara by the arm, heading across the road to the police station. "You bloody cops. You're always bloody drunk."

"And lawyers aren't?"

Which gets no response, except Jo-Jo's hold falls away as they enter the building.

The disciplinary hearing is in a second-floor room. The two women going up the stairs at a clip, then down a long corridor.

Jo-Jo complaining how they always hold their disciplinaries at the back, out of the way. "Out of sight, out of bloody mind," as she puts it.

The men waiting for them. At least, Zara thinks, no bonhomie, everyone subdued. Two captains behind the table; the defendant on a chair to the side whispering to his union man. All full of himself.

"You could've had a woman cop to hear this," says Jo-Jo to the captains, dumping her bag on the table. "When're you boys gonna get with the program? Bloody hell, man."

One of them looks up at her. "There's a major coming. She's late. Like you."

Jo-Jo on the point of responding when Zara pulls her aside. "Leave it. Don't start with them."

Guides her to chairs facing Sergeant Langa Mpho.

"Bloody bozos," says Jo-Jo under her breath, sorting through her papers.

Which leaves Zara to stare at the sergeant. She's not liked him from the get-go. Right there, at the first interrogation, he'd been far too arrogant. Far too big man. Lying to her. Accusing the eyewitness woman of making it up. Of being racist. Getting at him because he was black. Even when she came back with the eyewitness report, he'd held out. Said it was a conspiracy. He was a good policeman. With a good record. But she'd heard differently from some of his colleagues. Colleagues who said he touched them on their breasts, made lewd remarks. But these colleagues wouldn't go on the record. Sergeant Langa was protected, they said. Protected from high up. Which might've been why it had taken so many months to get this hearing. Postponement after postponement. Had to make her wonder then if he'd been in the blue Honda, if he'd shot at her. The man was too relaxed. Like he knew something they didn't. Even for a disciplinary hearing, he should be more wound up.

Sits there staring back at her: hard, aggressive. Face tight as a snarl. Zara astounded by the audacity, keeps the eye-lock until he looks away. Moments later he flicks his gaze across the room, seems to be smiling. Yeah, she thinks, you might reckon this is a joke, Sergeant, but wait. We'll get you.

The major comes in, gets the proceedings started. Zara doesn't recognize her but likes that she pays her co-arbiters scant heed. Barely nods a greeting. Is businesslike. Has her papers ready. Speaks with a pencil in her hand, her eyes steady on the errant sergeant. Tells him he is accused of two counts of rape at the Manenberg police station. The first two years back, when he had assaulted a woman after arresting her for soliciting. The second nine months previously, again having arrested the same woman on the same charge. A week after that assault, the woman had reported the incident through the offices of Women Together. She had supplied an affidavit. Her accusation was supported by a witness who had been in an adjacent cell at the time of the second assault. An affidavit from said witness included in the matter. Said witness to give testimony. The matter investigated by Captain Zara Dewane of the Internal Crime Unit. A finding that he was culpable.

"It is lies, my Major," says Sergeant Mpho. "All lies."

The major remonstrates with him. Tells him he will have a time to speak. Looks over at Jo-Jo. "I believe the alleged victim is dead. We extend our condolences. But we can still proceed. May I ask how she died?"

"Cancer," says Jo-Jo. "A month ago. She would have been here if there hadn't been so many postponements. But you have her sworn statement."

"And the eyewitness?"

"You have her sworn statement as well."

"Will she be here?"

"Yes."

"Today? This week? This month?"

Smiles from her co-arbiters. Sniggers from Mpho and his police union rep.

"Directly," says Jo-Jo.

"I want to get this over with, Advocate. We haven't all day." She points her pencil at Zara. "Captain Dewane, apart from the testimony of the deceased and the eyewitness, why have you recommended disciplining the member?"

Zara stands up. Takes a folder from her briefcase. It contains notes but is more a prop than a prompt. Never stand with empty hands, she had learned. Give them something to hold. "I interviewed many of his colleagues," she says, "and his superiors. The impression I got was that the sergeant was a law to himself. He does not respect the role of the police as the guardians of society. Also I found him evasive, arrogant, dismissive of the internal process. A woman has charged him with rape. With being raped twice. You know what happens in the police cells: assault, torture, rape, sometimes murder."

"We all read the *Daily Maverick*, Captain Dewane. What we need is the evidence. Not gutter journalism. With this rape, there is no evidence."

"There are the sworn statements."

"I would prefer to hear the eyewitness. Where is she? Advocate?"

"I'll find out," says Jo-Jo, leaving the room, smartphone in hand.

"You, Sergeant," says the major. "Don't lie to me, did you attack this woman?"

"No, my Major," says Sergeant Mpho.

"Did you rape her?"

"No, my Major."

"Did you have sex with her?"

"I cannot lie, my Major. She was my girlfriend. Sometimes she was staying in my house."

The union man laughs, says, "This is true. I can swear to it."

"Captain Dewane, did you know?"

"No. It's news to me."

"Maybe you needed some more investigation. Some more facts."

Zara feels the hammer in her head. Wants to yell, My lewe fok, woman, what's wrong with you? They're lying.

But says, "The victim said she was raped. Twice. By this man. A witness said she heard the victim screaming. It is there in the eyewitness statement." Zara searches for it, reads: "She was screaming. She was telling him to stop. She was crying. I could hear him punching her. Then she was quiet and I heard him making sex gruntings. Afterwards, she was sobbing. And I think praying. Suddenly she shouted, 'That man, Sergeant Mpho, he raped me.' She knew we were others in the cells. She wanted us to know what had happened." Zara puts aside the statement. "There it is. Sworn to. Attested. Everything the law requires."

"For this hearing, it would be an advantage to hear the witness testify." The major looks away across the room. "Advocate Lanski, what is your news?"

"Her phone tells us she is somewhere in the city. But she is not answering my calls." Jo-Jo sits down beside Zara. Says quietly, "We're bloody screwed."

Not that Zara needs to hear it. She watches the major confer with one captain then the other. The captains nodding in turn.

The major speaks: "You see my problem, Captain and Advocate. We have the word of a dead woman. We have a statement from a witness who refuses to appear. How can I discipline a member when there are just words on paper? It is not enough. What signals do I send our other officers if I take action? This is what I have to consider. I have to consider the morale of the Service. If I take action because of these statements, I tell our members we are doing witch hunts. Every day these members face violence. They don't know in the morning if they will be alive that night. We are a brutal society. I cannot tell them we do not support them. Like you, I know there are the bad apples. But they are few. You can find them. You can throw them out. That is your task. But we cannot make discriminations on flimsy grounds. We cannot live by allegations. You do good work in ICU. I know that. But this one is not good enough. I find problems in this matter." She turns to her co-arbiters. They nod again. "So. We are in agreement. I cannot make a ruling against you, Sergeant Mpho. You can go. Captain Dewane, please do not waste police time without proper evidence."

"You are wrong," says Zara.

The major pauses in collecting her papers. "I'm sorry, Captain, what?"

"I said you are wrong."

She frowns. "Respect, Captain, respect." Touches her epaulettes.

"Don't," hisses Jo-Jo. "Let it go. There are channels."

Zara speaks through the hammer blows behind her eyes. "This finding is wrong." Hears her words as an echo. Sees the major go rigid.

"Captain!"

Is now in freefall. "You have legal documents before you. You have all the evidence you need. Your finding is unreasonable."

"Stop it!" From Jo-Jo.

"Enough." From the major. "I know you were shot at last night, Captain Dewane. I am considering that. But you must keep your place. You must watch what you say. You are showing insubordination. This is something I cannot allow. You have gone beyond my tolerance. And for this I must take action."

"Apologize," says Jo-Jo. "Just bloody apologize."

"You want to discipline me? For questioning the procedure?"

"I will."

A last glare from the major as she leaves the room. The two captains grinning, giving mock salutes.

"Bloody hell, Zara," says Jo-Jo. "You have bigger battles. What the hell d'you want to get under her skin for?"

"Because I've had enough. Enough of these sham hearings."

"Time you went back to boxing. A couple of rounds would sort your aggro."

Not a bad idea anyhow, Zara thinks.

True Heroes

18

"We don't have to do this," Exit Kutoka says to Langa Mpho.

"We do, my brother."

"You are off the complaint. No evidence. Case dismissed. You told me."

"She is a jackal bitch, my brother. She is a problem. We must give her another lesson. This we must do for all our comrades."

"No, we must stay away. We have our business. We do not want this woman chasing us."

"When we are finished, she will not chase us. We will make her frightened, my brother. The captain then will even resign. It has happened before."

The two cops a block away from the police station. Straight line of sight to the entrance. Where Captain Zara Dewane stands with Advocate Josephine Lanski. They watch the two women part, the captain stepping into the traffic.

"There we go, my brother. You follow her."

"And you?"

"I will be in the car, watching where her phone goes. Maybe she is going to her office, who knows? That is what we need to find out. Yes, yes, hurry, my brother. Go."

Exit Kutoka crosses the street. Very bad feelings about this in his stomach. Very bad feelings about his friend's plans. The woman is dangerous. He's heard stories about her. She pulled a gun, she'd shot an attacker. Stories were she fought back. She was not afraid. Yet here was Mpho wanting to give her a beating. Yoh, stupid. But what can he do? They are one.

He follows the woman up Albertus Street into Harrington. Loiters until he sees her get into a car. Come past him heading for the Castle. He phones Mpho, rushing back the way he'd come. Jay-walking the traffic to get to Mpho waiting in the car, the still-blue Honda Ballade.

"Down, down," he says, pointing toward the traffic lights.

They pick up Zara Dewane in her Polo going round the Parade. Sit three cars back all the way across town. Exit certain she's noticed them. The woman isn't one of the stupids from the upper corridors. This is the jackal. Why'd he even let Mpho take the Honda?

"Where's she going?" says Sergeant Langa Mpho, as they turn into Portswood Road. "This is dead-end city."

19

"You better just bloody calm down," Jo-Jo Lanski had said to her outside Caledon Square. The two of them on the sidewalk, Jo-Jo about to light up. "I don't want to be arguing the toss against them. I don't want you in the stocks, okay?"

Zara had muttered again about pretend hearings. Then, with a raised hand to say goodbye, stepped into the traffic. Drivers hooted, yelled. She gave the finger in return, dodged between the cars.

Heard Jo-Jo shout, "You're a bloody mad bitch."

Nothing wrong with that. Turned to blow a kiss, give her a thrill.

On the way through the back streets, Zara stops for a double espresso at New York Bagels. The headache now a sharp pain behind her left eye.

"And please, like chop-chop," she says to the man taking her order. These guys have the Cape Town slo mo big time. Even a coffee can take ten minutes. For her, they do it in five. She takes the paper cup with a nod, the first sip going into her veins like a drug.

"That hit it?" says the barista.

She gives him a quick smile. Why not? The guy makes good coffee. Goes off up the street to her car.

From a distance, can see no sign of Janet. The only car guard a Congolese in a yellow reflective vest, peering at his smartphone. She flashes her ID. The man backs off.

"Where's the woman who was here?" she says. The wheelie bin now upright against a building entrance.

The man gives her a dazzle of whites. Says he doesn't know any woman. Says this is his street every day. There is no woman. Says he looks after the cars to keep away the tsotsis. Look, Madam Policewoman, no problem with your car.

"Better not be," Zara says, balls the paper cup, lobs it into the wheelie bin. Which gets an appreciative whistle from the car guard. Then she sees, there under the windscreen wiper, a note: Janet was here. Neat handwriting. She holds it up at the car guard. "See this? You chased this woman away."

The man glances at the note, shakes his head. "No. There was no woman here. Every day I am here. There is no woman."

Zara opens the door of her car, dumps her bag on the passenger seat. Turns back to the man. "Watch out, okay? You cause trouble, you'll go back to the DRC. Understand?"

The man shrugs. As she pulls away, can see him in the rearview mirror, tapping at his phone. How'd it happen that everywhere you parked, there was a car guard? Beaches, forests, shopping centers, streets, everywhere. Always someone comes hissing out of the shadows, saying they'll look after your car. No end to it. Not that they'll do anything to stop a tsotsi bent on stealing it.

She drives toward the Castle, skirts the Grand Parade, goes up Strand Street into the city across Buitengracht, takes Dixon to Somerset along to Main Road. At the Giovanni's traffic circle, remembers the meal she hasn't eaten. Comes out at three o'clock heading for Portswood. Whoever had located office space for the unit had looked for the cheapest, most out-of-the-way, most rundown part of town. Rented two adjoining rooms on the second floor of a two-story building. From the windows views down into a dank courtyard, across at a blank wall. At least blue sky above. At least windows that can be opened in the stifling summer heat. At least off-street parking under trees. At least no car guard. Plenty of Janets in the area, some she knows by name. None with the audacity of Janet of the Cape. She wonders if she'll see her again.

In the office …

Ah, the office.

When she'd moved in, she'd sent Brigadier Sithole photographs of the office.

Photo 1: the two desks, two round-backed office chairs circa 1960s.

Photo 2: a bank of two metal filing cabinets.

Photo 3: a small table in a corner: on it a kettle, tea bags, a Bialetti coffee maker (bought at her own expense), a two-ring gas hob, three mugs. Beside the table, a bar fridge with (usually) a bottle of sour milk.

Photo 4: tatty sun blinds at the windows. Again bought from her purse at the Milnerton street market.

Photo 5: the wooden floors without rugs or mats, also showing a credenza with a wireless printer.

WhatsApped: This is what they think of me.

Got the reply: So what.

Hadn't bothered to send a photograph of the security: an outer grille door, a metal door, an inner grille door. Three keys to get in. Big deal. Still not exactly Fort Knox. The only slight advantage, anyone intent on breaking in needed to find the offices first.

A couple of months later, Zara sent Brigadier Sithole a photo update.

Photo 6: stacks of files on the floor.

His WhatsApp response: There is no budget for admin. But I can consign a warrant officer in a few more months.

What Zara didn't send him was a photograph of her desk chair. Cost her a couple of grand but at least it was comfortable. Then Wynston came. Took one look at his round-back, changed it for some sort of ball chair. Something to do with strengthening his core muscles.

She liked Wynston from the get-go. The guy wasn't full of bullshit. If he wanted to perch on a ball that was his lookout.

It is on her comfortable desk chair that Zara now sits, facing the window. A thin line of sun on the floor that will be gone in half an hour. At her temples, the dull throb of the hangover, when she remembers to think about it. Arrayed on the desk, four cell phones. Her workaday smartphone; three burners. One marked Intel; another Brig; the third, Misc. Intel is a mole she's cultivated in Police Intelligence. Brig is her unit head; Misc a useful number when she wants a private phone conversation. Zara operates on the basis that her calls are monitored: undoubtedly by the secret service; probably by SAPS internal.

Her neighbor Studs is on her mind. She puts a call through to the hospital, goes through the hoops until a superintendent tells her that "Sorry, Captain, I have to inform you that sadly Mr Karsten died a few hours ago. Very sorry, for your loss."

Which socks her.

That could've been you.

For long moments she stares at the strip of sunlight. Watches it slowly fade. Her thoughts eliding; a heaviness settling in her chest. Studs gone. Just like that. When you were the target.

Then she has to get up. Drink a glass of water. Pace the small office. Until a calm returns. And she can force herself back to her day.

She sits. Checks the phones to find messages on two of them.

On her smartphone, a catch-up from Wynston: he is at the bank, will probably need a warrant. Be at the office soon. A query from the brigadier about the hearing. Then three messages from Ashton:

1. I am his FATHER. That's me. I am not some Villain.
2. Be the mother he values to Kyle.
3. Newsflash, this is NOT going to happen again.

Whatever this means. The trouble is, Zara realizes, his WhatsApp messages make him sound ridiculous. More than ridiculous: a coward and a bully. It is difficult to take him seriously. Yet she has to. He is Kyle's father; he has rights. If the therapist is correct, he's also a narcissist, more particularly, a sociopath. And as the therapist has said, sociopaths, like scorpions, can do nothing other than hurt and destroy.

She saves the messages. You never know what might come in useful one day.

Sends a message to Wynston to push as far as he can with the bank.

To the brigadier, a cryptic: They let Mpho off.

On the Intel phone, the message reads: Call me.

She does.

The woman who answers says, "I've heard an intercept, Captain, this afternoon the Mongols' woman, that Tamora Gool, she's meeting some female cop she calls Cappie. We're gonna do surveillance. You wanna be there, you better stay hidden." Gives the time and place.

Brightens Zara instantly. She's up and away, out of the office, heading for her car.

They come at her as she leaves the building.

20

What she hears is her car alarm going off. So. Goes down the flight of stairs at a clip. Her tote bag over her shoulder, car keys in one hand, phone held against her ear with the other. The brigadier again. This time wanting to know why she'd questioned the disciplinary officer. Telling her the major was going to write up a complaint for insubordination.

"What is going on with you, Captain? The unit doesn't need this sort of bad reputation."

"I'll explain."

"You will. In writing. Today. You hear me, Captain, today, not next week, not tomorrow, today. A full explanation. We lose another case, what do you think we look like? A joke. They think we are a joke. I can hear them laughing at me."

Zara about to say she has to ring off, her car alarm is sounding. Doesn't need to. The brigadier has disconnected.

She slides her phone into the bag, realizes, again, no gun.

The building's entrance is a wide door, glass panes either side. The one pane cracked and taped. Both fronted by a lattice work of metal protection. Fifty feet of paving between the building and her car. Three cars in the parking area. Two at the far end belong to a couple from an IT start-up. Guys she's only seen once or twice. Her car opposite the building entrance, its hazards flashing, the hooter unrelenting. No one visible.

She aims her remote at the car, shuts down the alarm. Pauses. Opens the door. Steps out.

The first blow comes from her left. A straight punch to the head that explodes the world. Has her staggering, her arms up in defense. Her vision black. The second blow takes her across the shoulders, the hard strike of a club. Her knees buckle, she goes down. Loses a shoe. The damn pumps she'd worn for the hearing.

Even as she sprawls, she realizes there are two of them. The one has no weapon but his fists, the other is the dangerous one. She can hear them panting, the scrape of their boots on the paving as they dance about her.

For long moments, they let her lie. And she does, not moving. Listening. Her head clearing, her vision returned. In her mouth, the taste of iron, grit on her palms. Then from her right, a kick below the ribs that makes her grunt with its force. Yet gets her to her feet. Unsteady. Getting rid of the remaining shoe. The bunch of keys still in her fist, the keys now protruding.

In vague form, she sees two men, watching her. Taking their time, playing with her. The one with the club, feinting, forcing her backward. The whistle of the club with each wild swing. The club a golf iron. He thumps the ground with it. Smacks it against his hand. She can imagine him grinning.

She sees their blue cop boots, their cop trousers; the one wearing a black T-shirt, the other a zipped jacket. Their faces hidden in balaclavas. The men: one short, the other tall. The one stocky, the other slim. The one with the club, in the black T-shirt, could be Langa Mpho. As per height and build.

They shift about her. The one in the zipped jacket keeping his distance.

"You're cops," she says. "You're Sergeant Mpho." Her voice sounding strange. Thinner than she means.

No response.

"You won. What's your case?" she says. Winds the tote bag around her left forearm. Lunges toward the one in the zipped jacket, slashing with the keys in her fist. He pulls back, avoids her.

Giving the Mpho one a clear target to hit her in the lower back, the club head striking near her kidney. A pain that makes her groan, stagger into the man in the zipped jacket. He pushes her away. Zara reels, sucks air. The ache in her side forcing out another groan. As she is shoved between them, takes another blow on her shoulder.

She turns to the Mpho one. The keys in her fist held low. Steps at him. Her vision blurred, bisected. He raises the club above his head. Swings down, the force of it glancing off her protected arm. The car keys snagging in the man's T-shirt, wrenched from her grasp as he whirls away.

Her arm on fire from the hurt. She glances over her shoulder at the man in the zipped jacket, at how he keeps a distance. Returns to face the one she believes is Mpho. Sees him kick her keys across the paving, out of reach. Decides then they will not kill her. Their aim to hurt, to break her bones. To warn: don't mess with us. Just as the shooting had been a threat. And thinks, Run at him, knock him down.

Is about to when the man in the zipped jacket grabs her clothing.

Holds her. For the other to take a swing. The Mpho one coming at her; white teeth gleaming in the mouth hole. Hard dark eyes.

Zara Dewane leans back, lets zipped-jacket man take her weight, swings her legs out at the Mpho man. Catches the club strike on her bare feet. The club clattering away.

Hears the man swear.

Hears someone shout, "Hey! Hey, julle-you! What the fuck, man!"

Hears a car pulling in. The hooter blasting.

21

Through the morning, Colonel Kaiser Vula ponders the witch's prophecy: General. Nice. General Kaiser Vula. That sounds like him. A deserved rank. But where will he be as this general? Here at the Secret Service Agency? Or elsewhere, Police Intelligence, preferably? Is he being pushed aside? Or raised up?

Ah man, the questions, the questions. How can a young woman in a suburb know about his life? And what is wrong with her? Bright one moment, sick the next. These women with their connections to the ancestors. Always a problem. Never can you tell where their heads are.

Then Lady phones, wants to know what happened.

He is at the mountain window of his office, looking down on the square. Two men on the cobbles smoking: MPs, probably, who should be in the House. But what good are they anyhow? Zombies. Of no use to anyone. Sleeping on the benches and being paid huge salaries for their laziness. While beyond them, the good citizens in their patience keep the lights on. Although the lights are out as much as on these days. Ah man, electricity blackouts. The incompetence of the government. Truly the people deserve proper leaders. Not the useless comrade cadres. His eyes go upward to Hoerikwaggo—the god of Table Mountain. Is he to be a general? Is he on the edge of ascendancy?

"She said a strange thing," says Kaiser Vula to his wife.

"Tell me."

"That I am to be a general. Not a colonel anymore. A four-shield general."

"You see, Kaisey, she knows. That Luna knows. She can tell where these things are coming from in the future. She has that connection. Didn't I tell you how it would be? You are a worthy man. You are a man of importance."

"She is also a strange person," says Kaiser. "Suddenly she was ill and disappeared. What is that business all about?"

"I will find out. Come home, Kaisey. This is a good day for us."

Not long after they've disconnected, while he sits there communing with Hoerikwaggo, his phone pings. A selfie of Lady in her gear: the leather chaps, the nipple tassels. Her hooked finger, beckoning him. She is a remarkable woman. To have nursed him. To have stayed with him when she could have had her choice of men. To have supported him. To have encouraged him. To have invented a new life for them. This was Lady. She who should not be disobeyed.

Colonel Kaiser Vula raises a salute to Hoerikwaggo, summons his driver.

22

She sits on the ground where the zipped-jacket man dropped her. Wynston with his gun out, shouting at the men to stop. They don't. They run. Jump a fence, disappear into the bush on a vacant lot.

"Pity you didn't shoot them," says Zara, trying to get her breath back. Pains lancing through her body.

Wynston ignores this. Holsters his pistol. "They're cops," he says.

"No reason not to shoot them."

"You don't mean that."

"Don't I?"

The tech woman comes up. "You alright? Man, that was hectic."

"Who're you?" says Wynston. His hand back on his gun.

"Hey, hey, hey, hokaai," says the techie. "I just work here. There at the end. I saw them beating her. Who're you guys, anyhow?"

Wynston flashes an ID.

"Oh shit, I didn't know. I've seen you here before, nè?"

"We work here," says Wynston.

"Tsho, man. Whyn't you based at a police station?"

"Good question," says Zara, rubbing her feet, thinking, Probably wouldn't be any safer. Gets up unsteadily. Nothing broken in her feet. She brushes off Wynston's helping hand. The pain in her side more intense than the pain in her feet, making her wince as she straightens, trying to massage away the ache.

"You better go to a doctor," says the techie. "That skollie was mad-woes. Lucky, he didn't hit your head."

"Would've eventually," says Zara, "when he'd finished playing games." She turns to Wynston. "His prints'll be on the golf club." Bends to pick up her shoes, her car keys, groans at the movement. My lewe fok, Eloise. Her body going to be a mess of bruises, swollen black 'n' blue. Going to hurt like hell for days.

Kyle would take it badly. He always did when she got hurt. This not being the first time she's attracted trouble.

A "shit-magnet," Jo-Jo Lanski calls her.

Counted off on the fingers of one hand—although you could go both hands—in random order there'd been: a hammer attacker (she'd shot in the leg); a knife wielder (who'd stabbed her in the shoulder before her colleagues jumped him); a car jacker (immobilized with a Taser); a loony who'd tried to bite off her ear (calmed down by an uppercut); an irate gambler (subdued with pepper spray) in a casino. Wasn't even her pepper spray, was one snatched from the dealer at the card game. It pleased her that she'd only had to shoot once. An experience she didn't want to repeat. Though she'd had to pull the Z on a couple of others. Afterwards joked she could have squeezed the trigger on most of them. But, what the hell, you couldn't shoot all the scum dogs, could you? Much as you'd like to.

Zara unlocks her car. Every movement an electric sizzle. One positive: it'd stopped her hangover. One negative: also period pains clutching at her stomach. Says to Wynston, "Thanks, you're a good man to have around." To the techie: "Thanks for the concern."

The woman at her car door, responding, "Should you be driving? Can't you go with your colleague?"

"I'm fine," says Zara. "Really."

Really not, but hardly likely to admit it. She watches Wynston wrap a plastic carrier bag round the golf-club handle. Bit of luck there'll be a print. Bit more luck, they'll know in six or seven days if there is a match. Luck supreme, the results wouldn't go missing.

"Follow me," she says to him. "I've got to go home and get changed." Her black suit trousers with a tear at the knee. The jacket smeared with dust. Her blouse missing buttons. "And take a shower." Rub arnica on the bruises. Where she can get to them. Wynston will have to do where she can't reach. What else are warrant officers for?

23

They get out of the area fast. Drive into the Waterfront, take Dock Road to the elevated freeway. Tension in the car. Exit Kutoka driving in silence, keeping to the speed limit, not wanting to attract attention. Thinking: Today, today the car must change color. With Mpho, it is crazy. There is the man he shot, now he attacks a policewoman. Insane. Wazimu. This Langa Mpho is mad in the head.

Mpho talking non-stop. About how they'd fixed her. The bitch would be in pain for weeks. The jackal would be hiding away to lick at her wounds. For this, there would be grateful people. People who would thank them.

Exit's thoughts also on Captain Zara Dewane. She'd recognized Mpho. She said his name. She'd come to the station. Want to question him. Want to know who the tall guy was with him. The one who'd punched her in the head. Had held her fast for Mpho to strike. She'd work it out. She had the golf stick. She would have fingerprints. She would say, You, Sergeant, you are in trouble. She would point her finger at him. That finger straight as the barrel of a gun. Maybe then, even Mpho's big man couldn't help him.

Exit takes the N1, M5, N2, M10, M18 to Gugulethu, drives down NY144 to where they have the woman eyewitness captive. Outside the house, they sit in the car. Speak for the first time.

Exit says, "She recognized you."

To laughter from Langa Mpho. "No way. She was too frightened. She was being beaten."

"She said your name."

"No, man, she was taking a chance. No ways she knew it was me. How is she going to do that? Tell me, how? My face is hidden. There is nothing to say it is me, Langa Mpho. She is clever that one, but not that clever."

"She's a cop. She knew it was you come straight after the hearing. She knows your shape. Look how we're dressed, man? Half in police clothes. She saw us. She knows us. She knows you. Believe me, she will be here to look for us."

"Tsho, no man, Exit. You spook for nothing. We have given her a lesson. There is no more to this business. Come, we must sort out the woman."

"What do you mean, 'sort out'? We must let her go."

"Yes, my brother. My case is finished. She cannot give witness anymore. So we do not need her. She is free to go."

"Go to the police."

"No, she will not do that."

"She knows us."

"What is she going to say? There is her word; there is our word. We give her some blue notes and she is our friend, believe me."

They enter the house. No woman. There is the chair where they'd tied her. Cut cable ties on the floor. A back window open.

"Impossible," says Mpho. "She is the Houdini woman."

"What about her phone?" Which he'd carried with him all morning.

"We can sell it. There is always someone wanting a phone."

Exit sees shadows in the backyard. The shades of his ancestors, gathering. This is not good.

24

On the car's clock: 1:59 p.m.

Captain Zara Dewane and Warrant Officer Wynston Adams heading for Lavender Street, Bellville. To check out the meeting. Wynston driving Zara's car.

Zara biting back the pain. The ache at her kidney, the burn across her shoulders, the stinging on the soles of her feet. Has to keep shifting in the seat. The shower and arnica not much help.

To distract herself, says to Wynston: "So what you're saying is the bank statements show the payment was from a commercial entity."

"Uh ha. Umuzi Trading."

"That's all you got?"

"A Cape Town street address, in the city. Bree Street. Google puts it back between Bloem and Buiten."

"We'll check it out later. How many payments?"

"Three. Two for five thousand. One for ten."

"Dates?"

"The 10K this month. The others last week of last month, consecutive days."

"That's it? No withdrawals? Bank charges?"

"Month-end bank charges, that's all. For one month. The account was new."

"In Malgas's name."

"His name. The Saldanha police station's address. I didn't know you could do that."

"You can't in the city. In small dorpies, the banks don't mind."

Zara groans.

"You okay, Cap?"

"Okay enough." Leans forward to massage her kidney. Lewe fok, it's sore. She needs stronger painkillers but there's been no time for pharmacy stops. Endure it, Eloise. She sits back, gazes out at the strip hustle of Voortrekker Road. Urban ugliness. The garish colors. The bright brand names writ large. Realizes she hates this side of the modern world. Especially with the hurt in her body.

Eventually they turn down into the suburb. Find Lavender Street.

On the car's clock: 2:15 p.m.

Either side of the street, 1950s houses, some needing paint, others spruced: frontage of two bedroom windows, wooden door with security grille, lounge window. Driveway to a single garage. Flowerbeds, mostly canna lilies. Low precast concrete walls edging the pavement. The sidewalks of unmown grass, mostly. Here and there, the house-proud tended their strip as they did at thirty-three and thirty-five.

Zara and Wynston cruise the street in Zara's hatchback. His big green Merc not exactly ideal for surveillance work.

Zara wearing dark glasses, a throbbing like hell along her forearm, across her lower back, her kidney. With each breath, gets reminded of the kick under her ribs. Swears she's going to get that Langa Mpho.

Says to Wynston: "I'm gonna nail Sergeant Mpho. I'm not taking that kind of crap from the likes of him."

"You don't know it's him."

"I do. It was him, the squat little fucker. No ways it wasn't. I sat looking at him for an hour, I know his pudgy shape. The other guy I don't know. Lanky type. I'll get to him too."

Some ten houses after number thirty-five, Wynston pulls in, keeps the engine running.

"What's the plan?"

"You see anyone else doing surveillance?"

"Uh uh."

"Supposed to be Anti-Gang on this one."

"Maybe they're still coming."

Zara checks her watch: 2:23 p.m. "They got seven minutes. Maybe position a bit further back, turn the car round so we're facing number thirty-five." Takes binoculars from the cubbyhole. "You know that Tamora Gool, jumpy as a spider. Fulla shit every time we confront her. She sees anything weird, she's gonna light out. And if the other one's a cop, she'll be freaked all the time." Zara winces. Rubs the spot over her kidney. My lewe fok, he is in for it, that Mpho. Big time. "But we're not doing anything, okay? Just checking out the scene. File work only."

"Ja, ja," Wynston nods. Drives to the first intersection, makes a U-turn. Comes back slowly on the opposite side from numbers thirty-three and thirty-five. Goes on down the street. At the next intersection, does a U-turn, pulls to the curb.

"This'll do," says Zara. "We've got a line of sight. And far enough away, they won't notice us."

On the car's clock: 2:26 p.m.

"Still no Anti-Drug?"

"Not that I noticed," says Wynston.

"Lazy buggers."

"They might be here."

"What d'you mean? Like hiding behind the rhododendrons in someone's garden? Like they're gardeners? I don't think so."

A maroon Mazda CX-5 glides past in low gear.

"Seen that car before," says Wynston, pointing. "You don't see many that color."

Zara looks up from her phone. Thinks, My lewe fok, Eloise! Her? Says, "It's Hendricks. You gotta be kidding me? Captain Alicia Hendricks? What's she doing here? She's not Anti-Gang."

On the car's clock: 2:29 p.m.

"That's her," says Wynston. "Definitely. No mistaking. You drive that sort of car, that color, you'll be noticed. Long way out of her ecosystem." Wynston attaches a 400mm lens to his camera, resting it on the steering wheel.

"Ecosystem. Hell's sake, Wynston, what's this ecosystem business?"

"A term. It's what they mean by 'your place.' You know, the lingo."

"Yeah, the lingo." Despite the agony in her arm, Zara has the binocs up, watching the Mazda slowing down opposite number thirty-three, thirty-five. "Hell's she doing?"

"Upcoming," says Wynston. "Other side. Right into frame."

Zara stops a moan, shifts her focus to the approaching vehicle: a BM, what else? M5 black. Hunched there on the street like a beetle. Shiny. Reflecting. Poised.

The two cars stopping opposite one another: the Mazda's red taillights glowing. If Hendricks reaches out, she can touch the other driver.

It isn't Hendricks who reaches out, it's the other driver. To hand over a plastic carrier bag.

"You on that, Wynston?" says Zara. "You think the good captain's getting a takeaway from her favorite auntie? Like samosas or something? Maybe shucked perlemoen? Crayfish. Special biltong." Zara liking the click-click-click of Wynston's digital camera. All the evidence mounting up. The two of them watching the plastic bag disappear into the Mazda. "Auntie Gool paying for services, you think? Jirre, who'd have thought the Saldanha woman would be doing this?" Zara wondering if this is legit or not. Doesn't voice her thoughts.

"Maybe it is samosas," says Wynston.

Zara sucks in her breath. "Don't make me laugh. It hurts." Sighs. "Ja, of course it is. In Lavender Street, back of nowhere's exactly where you'd meet to hand over food goodies."

"It's where her sister stays," says Wynston. "Number thirty-five. Hendricks's sister."

"You know that?"

"S'trues."

"How come?"

"I'm a detective." Wynston giving her a grin. "I found out."

"So not only a man with smooth hands." Zara shifts to glance at him. Holds in check the ache of the movement. "You know, you give a nice rub. You want to change professions, you could become a masseur." Teasing him. Knowing it unsettled Wynston. Anyone else might have her up for sexual harassment. But Wynston is cool. Sees it for what it is: taking the mickey. Wynston certainly not her type. Even if she knew what her type was.

Zara pushes the pain aside, focuses back on the women.

"And now?"

There is Tamora Gool, arm extended into the space between the cars, dangling a small Ziploc bag from her fingers. Captain Alicia Hendricks seemingly reluctant to take it. Tamora Gool jiggling the bag. Enticing her.

"What's she got there now? Not more samosas, that's for sure. Probably not sweeties either."

"Only one possibility that it's maybe," says Wynston. "That being Tamora Gool."

"My thoughts, precisely. You got pictures of that exchange."

"Plenty."

"What I'd like to know is what they're saying."

25

Which is.

Tamora Gool: "Look, take it. Do me a favor, get them checked out by a dealer. This's high value, honest to god. Good quality. You think I'm spinning you, I'm not spinning you, cross my heart."

Captain Alicia Hendricks thinking, Watch it. This is Mongol Gool. Slippery as butter. Quick as a mongoose. Is probably recording what they say. As she is on her phone's recorder. All the same, decides to play along. "How much?"

A laugh from the ever-cool Tamora Gool. "I'm not gonna tell you that. Go to your own guy, get your own pricing, you're not gonna believe me anyhow. Once you've got a figure, we can negotiate."

Alicia Hendricks looks at the plastic Ziploc, looks along the street. Hesitant. Wondering, What's the catch? Says, "We've got no channels for diamonds."

"You mean you've got no channels for diamonds at the moment. Don't play helpless with me. All you've gotta do is ask around. You're the police. You can do anything."

"You think it's that easy? It's not."

"Really? You want me to believe that? C'mon, I'm not born yesterday."

Alicia goes back to scanning the street. Some cars parked against the curb. Nobody visible. Nothing out of the ordinary. Says, "Who cares what you believe? I don't. I'm telling you how it is."

Tamora Gool shakes the stones. "Yeah. Okay. Whatever. Moving on. Take the sakkie. It's a lucky packet, a lottery, can't you see? You don't even need a ticket. You just take the baggie, see what it's worth. What've you got to lose? Nada. Nothing."

"Except I'm giving you leverage."

"No more than I'm giving you. Anyhow, we're not talking leverage, we're talking mutual benefit. You don't drop me; I don't drop you. Sweet and simple." She shrugs. "In any case we're just talking, Captain H. Finding our common ground. What the Americans call 'reaching out.'"

"You're fulla shit, Gool. I know you, there's always some angle you're working, yes? Why're you bringing these to me?"

"Why not? You'd do it too, if you were me."

"I'm not you."

"Next best thing."

"So why?"

Alicia Hendricks hears Tamora Gool sigh. "Because. Because I've got a source and I'm spreading the love. This is an opportunity, Cappie. A whole new line of business. Much higher profit margins, nobody getting hooked on drugs, no broken homes, no rape, no kiddie abuse. No assault. Clean business. Clean conscience. The big oukies, your De Beers, Anglo, Debswana, your Rockwell, don't even feel it. Doesn't touch their bottom line. Believe me. This is white monopoly capital, FTU. Free to use. Take it, join the club, make your own decisions. I'm telling you, this is better than cash. No paper trail, money deposited anywhere in the world." She jiggles the bag. "Take it. Feel the weight."

Captain Alicia Hendricks does. Finds it surprisingly light, not what she's expecting. Opens the Ziploc: six or seven stones inside. Unattractive chunks that could've come off any gravel patch. "What d'you want for this?"

Tamora Gool smiles. "Now we're talking. By my count, for that little baggie, I can get ten AKs, fifteen pistols, 9mms would be good, one hundred rounds per, and, maybe, how about five machine pistols? Uzis, Berettas, I don't mind. Fifteen-round clips would make my day."

"Jesus. Are you mad?" Alicia thinking, Okay, time to end this. This was dangerous with Gool taking things to another level. A level that needed the colonel's blessing. No chance she'd venture into trading that amount of weaponry without backing. Says, "Where'm I going to get that lot?"

"Ah, come on, Cap H. From your treasure chest. Your personal cache, wherever you've got it. I'm reckoning you're sitting on enough guns to start a small war."

"What you're wanting's enough for a big war."

"For peace, my sista. Not war. Peace. Quiet on the streets. Everybody safe 'n' sound. Because after war comes peace time. What'd the man say in that book, 'War is peace?' What I can do with that firepower is bring peace to the streets."

Alicia Hendricks doesn't laugh. Lights a cigarette. Through the exhale says, "The Mongols're the Anti-Gang squad now?"

"Better than them," comes back Tamora Gool. "The streets're where we live. We know what's happening. We know about all the shit coming in. You think you do, you cops? You think you know about the drug trafficking? You know nothing. Not a single clue. I've seen its heartache up close, in my family, my friends. You sell me those guns, I can do a clean-up, then we're all winners. No more little kiddies caught in the crossfire. No more teenagers smacked on tik. What you say, Cap H? This is win-win. You take the diamonds; I get the guns. You've got fat stored in that little packet. Fat profit. You'll be smiling. Smiling. All. The. Way. To. The. Bank. Check it out for yourself. What we're talking about is once in a lifetime. You 'n' me, we can make a score for the community. Be true working-class heroes."

"I'm not like you."

"We're the same, Captain. You 'n' me. Same story. Same streets. Same bullshit. Except I don't smoke; I've got respect for my body. You should quit."

The black X5 rolls forward. Tamora Gool's parting words: "Enjoy the crayfish in the plastic bag. Maybe coffee next time, ha ha? Get back to me, alright? Any hour. Anywhere."

26

Afterwards. In the warm glow.

After he has showered, changed into a tracksuit, the one with the white cord running down the legs, the one with the red-mouthed Lacoste crocodile on the left breast. After he's poured a Johnnie Black over two ice cubes, wheeled himself into his study, he lets the images return.

Of Lady in her chaps. The white tanga. Her jacket open, her breasts visible with each rise of the whip. The knife he'd used to cut the tanga strap. Of Lady lowering on to him.

He tastes the smoky whisky.

Thinks, General. Ah man, that would be a worthy rank. With that rank, he would achieve his ambitions. Ambitions of wealth. Of power.

And sits there in the warm glow. Basking. When the name General Duncan Maale lights up his smartphone screen. The theme: *Star Wars*.

He connects: "General."

"Yes, Colonel Vula, yes, we cannot pause even on this sad day. Your name has been mentioned by my colleagues. You have been present in my mind. So now we must talk. Can you talk now?"

"Certainly, General." Colonel Kaiser Vula wheels himself to his desk, switches on a voice recorder. Takes a notepad from a drawer.

"Yes, Colonel, I want to offer you an appointment, yes. An appointment to join Police Intelligence. It is important work we do. You could say the most important in the Service. That is how serious is the loss of Brigadier Mpungose. I ask you if you could consider taking his position. With the rank of general."

General.

Ah man, the woman Luna Maplewood was right! She saw the future. Vula, both amazed at her insight, glowing with the general's request. No question he won't take such an appointment. But he stays quiet.

"I understand this is much to ask of a man in your position at the Secret Service Agency. But everything can be arranged, Colonel. It would be no problem to transfer from the Agency to Police Intelligence in SAPS. We already have a close working relationship with the Aviary. So this can be done without disruptions. Of course you would have to come to Tshwane, away from the mountains and the sea." A chuckle. "But there are other things, other compensations, Colonel. So, yes, I ask you to consider this appointment."

"I will," says Colonel Kaiser Vula. Who has considered it already. He will take the position. It is what he wants. What is his due. Closer to the center of power. He will know more. Get to know more.

"There is one other matter," says General Duncan Maale. "Yes, a request from me personally. I would like to invite you and Mrs. Lady Vula to a special game lodge for the weekend. We can discuss everything in detail there. Perhaps after the welcome dinner. It does not give you much time, yes, I apologize. But in this world, we have unexpected things happen and we must act with what occurs."

A pause. While Kaiser Vula sips at his whisky. Keeps the smile from his lips.

"Thank you, General," he says. "We are honored." Ah man, how was that?

"Very good. My staff will make the flight bookings for you and Lady Vula. At Tambo International there will be a driver to meet you. He will take you straight to the safari lodge."

After they have disconnected, Colonel Kaiser Vula stops the recording, calls his wife. Has her listen to it.

"You see, Kaisey," she says, "Miss Luna knows everything."

27

"You're going to live," the doctor had said. After prodding, poking, raising a fire in her body. Not her normal doctor. This one a male with his golf bag ready and waiting in the corner of his consulting rooms.

Every time she'd said ouch, he had come back with an "Umm, I wouldn't say it's that bad. Your kidney's going to be sore for a while. Your arm too. That's a nasty bruise. The thump to your head's not worth an MRI. Your shoulder's taken a hammering but it's just muscle bruising. What'd he hit you with?"

"A golf club."

"Explains it." Without telling her what it explains.

Had written her a script for painkillers. Warned her to stick to the dosage.

"You don't think I will?"

"With you cops, there's no telling."

Her pharmacist had said much the same. Added, "Don't take these till you're home. They'll make you woozy."

Woozy sounded good.

At home she doses up, then lowers herself carefully onto the couch. Stretches out along its length under a blanket, her back against the armrest. Groans at the ache and pain in her side. Hasn't stopped her drawing the cork from a bottle of wine, pouring herself a glass. A malbec she's been saving for a special meal, a special night. Whatever that meant these days. Hasn't been anyone special for a special meal in what, months? Not quite a year, probably nine months, but she doesn't want to think back that long. To hell with it. You don't need someone else to open a bottle of malbec. Not after such a day.

She closes her eyes, lets the wine lie in her mouth. Succulent. Almost chewy. Behind that, the painkillers taking the edge off her hurt.

Goes over her day: hearing Studs had died when it should probably have been her; that bastard Mpho getting off the disciplinary; attacking her, then Captain Hendricks meeting with gangster Tamora Gool. Not to even bring her own bruised body into the line-up. The constant pain in her side. She swallows the wine, takes another mouthful.

At least there is the uneaten meal from Giovanni's. At least there is the malbec. She swallows. Takes the rest of the glass in one hit, pours another.

You stripped out being a hammerman's target, you got over the rough and tumble, there was stuff to work with. Trouble was how to play it. Confront Hendricks? Much as she'd love to shove the photographs down her throat, ask her what the hell she was doing with a gangster in the middle of the street, for heaven's sake, despite that ... waiting would be best. And what was in the plastic bag? What was in the Ziploc?

That was one side of the story; the other was Umuzi Trading. You take the positives, Zara always took the positives, there is stuff to do.

About then, about halfway through the second glass, her phone rings: Sithole.

"Captain Dewane, I've heard what happened."

Damn Wynston.

"Are you okay?"

Not really, but managing, thank you, courtesy of malbec and pain drugs. "A bit sore but otherwise functioning, Brigadier."

"You need to recuperate. Stay home tomorrow. Take a long weekend, even Monday if you want to. I will see if I can arrange some security."

Zara thanks him. Thinks like hell she'll be taking any time off. Thinks like hell he'll be able to arrange some protection. Everyone is under-resourced. Nice consideration though.

"It is a pity about the Mpho disciplinary, I had hoped they would be stronger in their ruling. Perhaps if there had been a witness to testify. You must work harder on the witnesses, Captain. This is always our weakness. I think maybe we should change from Advocate Lanski, there should be more authority in our cases, in how we produce our evidence."

Zara wanting to argue, tell him there is nothing wrong with Advocate Lanski. That people are scared of cops, even witnesses, see them as another kind of gangster. The kind that has the law on their side. Until he puts muscle into the ICU, nothing will change. Which brings her to Police Intelligence. With Mpungose dead, what now? She phrases it circumspectly.

"It was a dreadful thing that happened to Brigadier Mpungose."

Silence.

Then: "Yes."

She waits.

"Have you heard of this man Colonel Kaiser Vula?"

Zara says she hasn't.

"Some years ago he saved the robber president from a bullet."

Which is more fact than you get from the brigadier most days. The man polite, concerned, but not really a fount of knowledge.

"What a pity." An unfiltered response from Zara because she can't help herself. The robber president being on a list of those she'd gladly see in orange overalls.

Predictably no comment from Sithole. Except: "The colonel is a man from the Aviary."

"You mean Maale's taking someone from outside SAPS?"

That is weird, unusual. Or perhaps Maale is being told by the police commissioner to take this Vula. Which is more like it to Zara.

"That is what it would seem to be."

"Of his own choice?"

"Perhaps. Perhaps not." Sithole sitting on the fence, as ever, doesn't surprise her. For a career cop, he'd long ago learned the wisdom of the three monkeys. Understandable. But sometimes you do need to speak your mind.

"I will meet him this weekend. We have been invited to General Maale's bush lodge."

Interesting, thinks Zara. Brigadier Sithole building his defenses. Or capitulating to higher powers more likely. Says, "Is it going to help us in ICU?" Doubting that it will.

No response from the brigadier.

To Zara, taking a spook into Police Intelligence might make sense at one level. The man would bring with him a network, probably international contacts, background dealings, secret negotiations between the security departments, potentially compromising information on politicos, government officials, party high-ups. On another level, it suggested infiltration. Manipulation. The nefarious tentacles of the governing party. Where was this going? Times were, she wondered if the job was worth it. The odds so stacked against them, the corruption so pervasive, what were the chances of ever getting things right? The good cops would keep on being killed or frightened into retirement; the bad ones forever gathering in the shadows.

She pushes the thoughts aside, hears Sithole telling her again to take time off. The Saldanha cache can wait a couple of days.

Zara not convinced about that. Reassures him she will relax with a TV series.

After she disconnects, thinks of phoning Wynston, find out why he's been onto Sithole about her. But she doesn't. Downs another glass. Before she can phone her son, there is her mother. Taps her to speakerphone.

"My god, Zara-sweet, I couldn't believe this. First the shooting, now you're assaulted. You've got to come home to recuperate."

"I'm fine, Ma." Zara reaches for her glass, sucks in air at the movement. Thinking, the only way her mother could know was from Jo-Jo.

"You've seen a doctor?"

"Yes. He says I'm fine. Badly bruised. Hurting. But he's given me painkillers."

"Jo-Jo says you were bloody lucky. To use her words. That your lovely colleague Wynston saved you."

Which makes Zara smile. "You could say that."

Can hear her father in the background saying something.

"Your pa wants to know if this was random?"

Her pa would realize damn well it wasn't random. Was giving her an out, something to pacify her mother.

Zara takes it. "Most likely," she says. "Two skollies trying their luck."

They talk some more about where she's been struck, how black and blue the bruises are. Then Zara says she has to phone Kyle.

His first words are: "Are you going to pick me up tomorrow?"

Sticks a dagger in her heart.

"I can't, love, I'm on duty."

"You're always on duty."

Partly true, admittedly. She needs to give him more of her time.

"We've got all weekend, okay? How about we hire a two-up kayak, go for a long paddle?"

Which gets a favorable response. Although she isn't sure if her battered body will take it, but what other options? Maybe promise him a surf down the peninsula. Long Beach. He loves the Long Beach break.

"Is Gran and G-pa picking me up?"

"They'll be there." An arrangement she still needs to make. "I'll be round soon as I can."

"And I'm with you next week?"

"Every single day."

What was it about his father that got to him? Was getting to him more and more? At one level a silly question, the boy was picking up a vibe. Because Ashton had never hit him. Certainly, Kyle had never said so. Raged at him, of course. Yelled and performed, called him a waste of space, a mommy's boy, a disgusting vernon. Confiscated his tablet and cell phone for days on end. Said he was withholding a privilege because Kyle hadn't done his homework. That was typical Ashton. Irrational. Vindictive. But then he was on the narcissist spectrum. If the therapist's assumptions were anything to go by. Not that this excused anything. Not that this absolved him of responsibility. It didn't. Okay, unlike normal people, he couldn't change his behavior. He had no moral basis. But that didn't mean he couldn't be condemned, criticized, sanctioned. He was trouble. Because, as she'd read, with sociopaths there was only one way: destruction. Wasn't there some quote about boys killing flies for sport? That was true of sociopaths, they were willful, destroyed people for the sport of it. Why she hadn't twigged to that long before Kyle was born would be a mark against her forever. But, for now, something she had to live with. Something she had to find ways of dealing with. Like not challenging him. Like praising him—hard as that was. But, for Kyle's sake, that had to be the way.

With the blanket wrapped round her shoulders, Zara picks at the Giovanni's meal. Has microwaved everything first but what would have been a treat last night is fuel now. Even so, good-tasting fuel. Is about to start on the baklava when she hears knocking at the front door.

No. The last thing she needs. Still wrapped in the blanket, goes to the door, squints through the peephole. A bergie on the stoep. Absolutely the last thing she wants.

"It's only me, Mrs. Police," says the bergie. Janet of the Cape. "You remember, nè? From this morning."

My lewe.

Zara opens the door. The woman standing there, showing the business card where Zara had scribbled her address. Not expecting to hear from the woman anytime soon. The woman wet, wearing a black bin liner as a raincoat. Her hand on the extended handle of a battered airplane cabin bag with wheels.

"I's come about the room you said about."

"My lewe fok, Eloise, why didn't you go to the shelter when the rain started?"

"I's Janet, not Eloise," says Janet. "Please, Mrs. Police, maybe even for one night in your room. I's not a bothersome." She unzips her bag, brings out a bottle of Old Brown sherry. "For nightcapping after the livelong day."

Oh lord, preserve me, thinks Zara. Says, "Come, I'll show you." Limps through the house with Janet following.

In the outside room, Janet says. "This's a nice place you got, hey." Sits on the bed to get a feel of the mattress. Looks at Zara: "You been fighting?"

"Something like that."

"Ag no, shame. It's mos a hard life for a Mrs. Police when you also got the curse. Yous need a sweet doppie. Sherry for the cherry."

And Nothing Is But What Is Not

28

It's the early hours of Friday morning. To be precise: 4:14 a.m.

What do we have?

We have two policemen in a white, unmarked VW Caddy van on the N1 highway leaving Cape Town. A flask of coffee on the seat between them. In a plastic box, a selection of samosas, sandwiches, biltong, dried sausage, fruit. The men in jeans and puffer jackets, standard-issue boots.

Weather conditions: 50°F, rain.

At this hour, the traffic light; the city still asleep.

They are beyond the city limits, nine miles to the Huguenot Tunnel. Their destination: Cape Gate Wire and Steel Manufacturers, Vanderbijlpark, Gauteng. Estimated travel time ten hours. The men are hoping to effect delivery, be home by Sunday.

Their load: six crates of pistols, revolvers, rifles, shotguns, ammunition, gun components. A cache of AKs, machine pistols, ammunition from the long past days of the Struggle. The entire haul a result of a firearm amnesty on illegal or unlicensed firearms, the weaponry destined for crushing and smelting.

The two men have done this run with a similar haul once before. No hassles, although they were tense then. Not convinced of the major's decision to use an unmarked van. But it had worked. "Ja, my boys, you've got to hide in plain sight, really," he'd said to them afterwards. "That's the trick."

The trick absolutely.

Also two days out of the station, off the streets. No having to deal with people's kak. Plus extra overtime bucks. Plus two days driving in the wide country. Jirre, man, it was beautiful out there. So much space. And nobody there. Maybe it was time to transfer to a dorp.

This trip, the two men more relaxed, less uptight at headlights staying too long in the rearview mirror. Still have ready firepower in the footwell: a handgun each, a pump-action.

They talk constantly, these two men: about fishing, sport (their soccer club, major matches, players, referees), their superiors, their wives, their families, friends, colleagues, court cases, the samosas.

At this point, they have been on the road forty minutes, have almost finished the coffee. The driver is talking about going fishing with their major on his boat. There in the deep waters beyond Cape Point when yellowtail are running. They should organize it when they're back. The major is a good oke. Not one of the high and mighty. The driver's eyes flicking from the rearview to the side mirror, his concern with the headlights behind them. Till he says, "What you think?"

"Dunno. Slow down a bit, let him overtake."

The driver eases off on the pedal from 70 to 60 mph.

That does it. The vehicle behind, swinging into the fast lane to overtake. Comes alongside. A cop van. Its blue lights going on. A loud voice telling them to pull over.

"Ag no, man," says the driver. "What's their case?" He shifts onto the hard shoulder, slows to a stop. "Go 'n' see what's their problem, I'm not switching off."

"Heita, look at our brothers," says Sergeant Langa Mpho to Sergeant Exit Kutoka. "Here are good members behaving."

"No shit with them," says Exit. "We are all police."

"Of course, my brother. Never, my brother. All we want's the van."

Exit pulls in behind the Caddy van, keeps the engine running, the lights on bright. Watches Langa Mpho, carrying a 12-gauge, walk over to the cop. The cop holding up his papers, saying something. Langa Mpho doesn't hesitate. Swings the pump-action at the cop's head, knocks him down. Steps over his body, slides into the van from the passenger side.

Exit wondering why he is with this man. He assaults people. He kills. He is dangerous. Knowing he is with him for the money. With the money he can leave the police. Find another job, escape from the mad world of Langa Mpho. Never see the lunatic again.

Then comes the white lightning: a flash in the front of the VW van. He knows what that is. That is Mpho firing the pump-action. Shit, shit, no man, no. He isn't supposed to do that. The driver's door opens, a body falls out. The door closes slowly, the van moves off. "Oh lord, my savior," mutters Exit. Now there is a dead man. He swerves the police vehicle round the body, follows the Caddy van down the highway, accelerating. This isn't how it is supposed to happen. They've agreed: a no-violence hijack. Because no one is going to argue with a pump-action shot gun. Isn't as if there is money in the van. No one would want to die for a haul of old guns. The cop driver and his sidekick would surrender. Walk away. Except now there is a man unconscious, another one shot. Two of their own. This time there will be comeback.

At the R304 interchange, they come off the highway, head west. Ten minutes later, the cargo van pulls onto the gravel shoulder. Exit stops alongside. Shouts at Mpho, "Why did you shoot him? You did not have to shoot him."

Langa Mpho holds open the van's door. "Do you see blood? There is no blood. The man is not dead."

"How? How is he not dead?"

"A blank. It was a blank." Mpho walks to the back of the van, opens the doors. "Come. You are too worried, my brother. There is no problem. Those men will be a little hurt for some days, that is all. Come now. We must move the load."

They do until there is a crate left, no more room in the pickup truck.

And now? Exit to Mpho.

His response to break open the remaining crate.

"We can put the guns in loose. Come on. Hurry. We must go." Mpho carrying an armful of weapons from the Caddy van to the police vehicle.

"If someone stops."

"No one will stop."

No one does. Three cars pass, none of them slowing down. Each one pumps Exit's anxiety.

They leave the van. Throw the keys into the veld.

"You see," says Langa Mpho. "We are a team. We are the superstars."

29

Now it's 5:50 a.m.

Zara wakes to her workaday phone. The tolling bell of a WhatsApp message. An ominous clang that she's been meaning to change. First thing in the morning, it stops her heart. She gropes for the phone on the bedside table. Sees the time. Groans. Partly because of the pain in her body, partly because she has to meet Wynston in forty-five minutes. Taps at the phone's screen, brings up the message: Stop. Or we'll kill you.

My lewe.

She closes her eyes, feels the drag on her heart, counts to ten. Knows nothing will change, the message will still be there when she opens her eyes.

Stop. Or we'll kill you.

Not the first death threat she's received. But that doesn't take the edge away. The instinctive feeling that this is Mpho. The short-ass worried that she'll come for him.

She forwards the message to Wynston. The techies he knows can triangulate its location. Which is about all they will learn from it. By now the phone would have been SIM-swapped or thrown away.

Still, who needs this kind of awakening to the day? Especially to a gray dawn.

Sometimes enough to make you think, Enough of this shit. I'm outta here. Going to become a lawyer. Earn big bucks. Get out of the firing line.

The firing line that gunned down Studs Karsten. And just because he was her neighbor. A thought that escapes as a groan.

With a sigh, Zara gets out of bed, stands at the window watching sheets of rain curtaining the city, hearing the gurgle of runoff in the gutters. Moans again at the pain in her side. When Wynston phones.

"That's from Mpho."

"Probably. If he's that stupid." She turns her back on the dismal day.

"Or that full of himself."

"Which he is."

"What're you gonna do?"

"Nothing. Nothing to be done." Zara heading for the bathroom. "Wait 'n' see what your guys come up with."

"You won't …"

"What?"

A pause. She grimaces at herself in the mirror over the basin. There is light in her eyes. A twitch on her lips. Knowing what Wynston is about to say.

"Take him on."

She likes that. Says, "Like I'd do that? How can you even think I would?"

"I know it. You would too."

"Yeah, Wynston. In your dreams."

But of course he's right. She'd take on Mpho the first chance she gets. An ache in her kidney or not. Until then she agrees to meet Wynston in an hour at the offices of Umuzi Trading.

Twenty minutes later.

Here's Zara in jeans, T-shirt, her sloppy house jersey, sitting at her kitchen table scanning the news on a laptop. The usual international crap (Houthi pirates, migrant drownings, Boko Haram shootings); the usual national crap (the dithering president, the robber ex-president laughing in his Dubai hangout) plus a developing story: two cops hijacked on the N1. A photo of the guys looking bedraggled. Stunned. The caption: Cops hijacked by cops. That's interesting. Especially if the hijackers are your actual cops, not just fake cops. Question is: what'd they get, the hijackers? A cop van, the cops' handguns, or was there something in the van? Not her concern. Yet. Zara flips through screens to a story of a local young swimmer's triumph at the Olympics. Something upbeat to go with toast and a Bialetti of coffee. When the knocking starts. A soft knock at the back door, more like the scratching of a cat. Then the husky voice, "Mrs. Police, ag, man, Mrs. Police, how's about a mornings coffee perhaps?"

Janet of the Cape.

My lewe, Eloise.

Zara opens the back door.

"Mornings, mornings, Mrs. Police, you mos remember you got a overnight visitation."

Zara says she has. Hard to forget. Indicates the bread, the toaster, the coffee. Says she has to leave in five minutes. If Janet wants to spend the day, she can take toast and coffee to her room.

"That's what I's thinking, Mrs. Police," says Janet, slipping bread into the toaster. "But I can do payback time also. If you want it, I can vacuum attack. Be a dust buster. How's that for a thing?"

"Impressive," Zara says. "But where are your references?"

The toaster pops. Janet spears the slices with a knife. Drops in two more. While she smears on butter and marmalade says, "I's my own best reference. S'trues you can't have a better C of V. But also you can phone Miss Vicki. I mos gave you the number."

Zara does.

Gets this Vicki saying, "I wondered where she'd gone."

Gets a reference: "Janet's an A. Completely trustworthy. You'll like her. Tell her it's time she came back to her Muizenberg beach house."

Zara has the call on speakerphone.

Janet chirps, "I's coming, Miss Vicki, just got to help Mrs. Police out quick sticks."

"Okay," says Zara, "you've got a deal. The room as payment."

"Brilliantine," says Janet.

"Only thing," Zara with a raised finger, "no more 'Mrs. Police.' Call me Zara." Strips off the house jersey, straps on her Z88, with a painful grimace shrugs into her red leather lummie. Janet standing there crunching toast, admiring.

"Yous look very zootie tootie, Mrs. Z."

"I'm not married," says Zara.

"Yous mos married to the job, Mrs. Z. I can see it."

I like "Mrs. Z," thinks Mrs. Z.

Another twenty minutes later.

Here's Captain Zara Dewane—aka Mrs. Z—with Warrant Officer Wynston Adams, mounting the stairs of a musty building. On the first floor going down a passage to stand outside the closed door of Umuzi Trading. The door made of stippled glass: on it a simple logo of a black zigzag arrow separating the word "Umuzi" from the word "Trading."

Wynston knocks. No reply.

"As I expected," says Zara, her hands shading her eyes as she strains for shapes behind the glass. A light on inside. She knocks harder. No movement. No sound. She takes out her lock picks, has the door open before Wynston can protest.

"Your standard one-cylinder Yale. You'd have thought they'd have done better than that."

They enter a cold room that stinks of cigarette smoke. Stale cigarette smoke. Opposite the door, a window with closed venetian blinds. In the center of the room a wooden desk, two wooden chairs either side on wall-to-wall carpeting. Two armchairs beneath a framed poster of Table Mountain in a corner. Three peninsula beach posters tacked on a facing wall above a bank of metal filing cabinets. Opposite the desk, a whiteboard with the words "The people that walked in darkness have seen a great light" pinned alongside a current calendar. Behind the desk, a table with a printer/scanner/photostat machine, a ream of A4 paper, beneath it a wastepaper basket. Empty. As are, Zara finds, most of the drawers in the filing cabinets.

"What do you think the people walking in darkness is all about?"

Wynston shrugs.

"Maybe it's about nothing," says Zara. "Or a quote or something. Sounds like it's from the Bible."

The desk drawers are locked but might as well not have been. Coming open with a sharp yank from Zara. In the top drawer, a writing pad, date stamp, stapler, a collection of ballpoints and whiteboard pens. Some plastic folders (empty); a stack of bank statements going back four years.

"Handy," says Zara. "No need for a subpoena then. All yours, boykie."

"You want me to photograph the lot?"

"C'mon, Wynston, use your head. Do the last six months. We can come back for the rest if we have to."

While Wynston takes photographs, Zara goes knocking on doors along the corridor.

Three down, at the offices of Eastern Enterprises, finds a short dumpy man in a dark suit standing behind a desk. Smiles at her.

"I am Mr. Yan. How can I be of assistance?"

Zara waves her cop ID, asks if he knows who works at Umuzi Trading. Says there is a light on.

"Yes," says Mr. Yan, "there is always a light shining. Sometimes there is a woman who comes to the office on a Saturday at the midday. I know this time exactly because of the noon gun. Maybe she comes once every month. A very nice person."

"You've met her? You've talked with this woman?"

"We have said good day greetings."

"That's it? Nothing more?"

Mr. Yan shakes his head.

"Have you been into the office?"

Again Mr. Yan shakes his head.

"Are you here every day?"

"There is either me or my partner Mr. Lijan," says Mr. Yan.

Zara hears Wynston close the office door, join her.

"Where is your partner?"

"In this precise time, Mr. Lijan is in China for the export arrangement of many products for our business."

"I see," says Zara, thinking, More Chinese crap to fill up the cheap stores. "And this woman, the one you've said hello to, can you describe her?"

"Most certainly," says Mr. Yan. "We are of the same height, she wears short brown hair. Maybe I would say she is thirty-and-something years old. She is dressed in those tight pants and with the Nike shoes. But her face is always in a covering scarf."

"White? Black?"

"Like you," he says, pointing at her.

Which describes a vast sector of the population.

"And does she stay for long, when she's here?"

"Maybe for an hour. Never for very long at one time. She is like a ghost person, we know she is here when we smell her cigarette smoke."

"Not a bad start," says Zara to Wynston as they leave the building. Zara with her fingers pressing into her side to ease the pain.

There is rain in the air with cloud over Lion's Head. It will come down hard soon.

"You go to the office, check the statements. I'll be in later."

"Why's that?" Wynston moving quickly toward his Merc.

"Routine. The guy working my neighbor's case wants another chat. Now that he's dealing with a murder, I'm being helpful. I wanna stay on the inside of that one."

As she presses her remote, hears Wynston calling, "Hey, wait, wait." Turns to see him jogging toward her, holding up his phone.

"You won't believe this."

"Try me."

"Saldanha. The Saldanha area. That's where they say the phone was. Mpho's phone."

My lewe fok, Eloise. She opens her car door. "I'm more than curious. That's helluva interesting. Saldanha's big. They able to be more specific?"

Wynston hunches into his jacket, his thumbs dancing on the phone keyboard. Has to turn his back as a gust sweeps down the street bringing spatters of rain. Zara ducks into her car, hears his phone chime.

"Looks like they're saying somewhere to the north of the bay," says Wynston.

"More curious," says Zara. "Get in. We're gonna take a drive."

"To where?"

"Pietman Malgas's cottage."

"What about my car? Someone'll steal it. Or I'll get a parking ticket."

"Hardly," says Zara. "Nobody'll be out in this weather doing parking tickets, let alone stealing vintage cars. The brothers are all at home smoking zol. Get in. Let's go."

30

Colonel Kaiser Vula sits at breakfast. Consumes an egg on toast, two rashers of bacon, fried tomato, fried banana. Behind him, rain patters on the window. Opposite him, Lady Vula reads from the screen of her phone.

A message from Luna Maplewood: I can tell you more. The insignia I saw on your husband's shoulder is the insignia of a general. It was as clear as reality. This I wanted to let him know before the turn came on me. These turns happen from time to time when the energy in the room becomes too intense. You see sometimes I am overwhelmed by these energies. Please tell the colonel not to be worried. His ancestors support him whatever he does. I am truly sorry about the interruption to our session. I would be happy to see him again whenever he feels like it. I shall come to your house. We must be so careful these days.

Kaiser Vula frowns. What does she mean "we must be so careful these days?" She is one weird sister.

"She is a very strange woman," he says. "Very disturbed." Wipes toast crumbs from his shirt. "I am not sure if I should see her."

"It would be a good thing. But first we have this safari weekend in the bush. We have matters to arrange."

"What matters?"

"You will become second-in-command to Maale but that is not enough, Kaiser."

"We don't know that."

"It is what Luna predicted."

True.

"She is always right. But now: you know Maale is a weak man. He cannot make decisions. He cannot act. He is a cadre deployment propped up before by Comrade Mpungose—may he rest in peace—now he will be propped up by you. This is not right. Maale must be assigned somewhere else. He is not good for Police Intelligence."

"Impossible. He has years ahead in this job."

"He can be moved sideways."

He sees the glint in her eyes. The glint of the plans she rolls out in her scheming. Who would ever have guessed the once-shy Lady Vula would have come this far?

"Minister Majoro is your friend, she will listen to what you say. Perhaps you could suggest she redeploys him to the Internal Crime Unit when that useless Brigadier Sithole retires. It is a better place for him. And for you. In ICU, he will be completely useless." She snickers. Holds up the coffee pot, her eyes quizzical.

When does she think of this stuff? As she potters about the

vegetable garden among the spinach and the broccoli? As she pulls on her leather boots? She is worth double her lobola. No wonder men look at her. He's seen them, their secret glances. They sense her allure. As if she gives off a scent.

"Yes, yes," he says to her offer.

She pours. A steady hand, a steady pour.

"There is another way. An accident."

Colonel Kaiser Vula takes a mouthful of coffee, holds it to savor the bitterness. There is always the other way. A car accident, for example. He swallows. Says, "No. It is not possible to think like that."

"We have heard of it before."

This is true. In the Aviary, car accidents raised eyebrows. Brought forth titters. Heita, there goes another one. Especially when the deceased was high profile. And he knew men who could do it. One man in particular. Which is a thought worth entertaining. An arrangement that will require planning. But it is not impossible.

"No," he says again. "We shouldn't think these thoughts."

"We can think anything, Kaiser," she says. "There is no harm in thoughts."

31

Captain Alicia Hendricks drives the sand road to the cottage of Constable Pietman Malgas. The cottage where Pietman had killed his family. Stuck the barrel of a Z88 into his mouth, blown a hole in his skull. Drives slowly in her Mazda SUV, thinking murderous thoughts. Like WTF did Mpho think he was doing? Going out on the razor's edge. Going freelance. Putting everyone in jeopardy. The whole network. Stabs at the car lighter, lights a cigarette. Blows smoke at the windscreen. Can see two men standing beside a police van at the cottage. She stops beside them. Adjusts her cap, gets out.

Her first words to Mpho: "Are you mad?"

The man salutes her, shifts from foot to foot. "No, Kapitan."

She sucks at the cigarette, exhales. Sucks again, exhales. Her gaze on Mpho. His eyes on the ground.

"Why did you bring them here, Sergeant? There is no one here. Anyone can help themselves."

"This is where Captain said to bring them."

"Last time, Sergeant. Weeks ago. When the constable lived here. Malgas is dead. There is no one here. Do you see anyone here?" Gestures at the crime-scene tape still stuck to the cottage door. Grabs at the door handle, rattles the door. "Do you hear anyone? Do you see anyone?"

"No, Captain."

"No, Captain." She looks away from the two men at the long silent scrub veld. "You didn't tell me about these." Brings her gaze back to stare at them. "I didn't know about these. Where do they come from?"

"They are amnesty weapons, Captain."

Captain Hendricks crushes her cigarette butt into the sand. Would like to grind the head of Sergeant Langa Mpho similarly. "How did you get them?"

Mpho clears his throat. "From an interception, Captain."

An interception. A frigging hijacking. Jesus Christus. "You hijacked them."

No response.

"Tell me, Sergeant. You hijacked them. Yes?"

"Yes, Captain."

"Is someone dead?

"There is no one dead, Captain."

"Where? Where did you do this?"

"There on the N1."

Jesus Christus. "And no one saw you?"

"There were some cars that passed. No one stopped. When people see police lights they don't stop. You know."

"You had the blue lights on?" There was some sense in that.

"Yes, Captain."

"You and him? Who is he?"

"Sergeant Exit Kutoka, Captain."

Captain Alicia Hendricks lights another cigarette. Wonders if Colonel Vula knows about Sergeant Exit Kutoka. If he doesn't, he will not be pleased. As she isn't pleased.

"And this police van?" Thumps the bonnet. "Where does that come from?"

"We got it."

"I can see you've got it. Where did you get it from? Who checked it out? Who is going to check it in? How can you take a police van, Sergeant?"

"It is no problem, Captain. It will be all finished this morning. No one will know."

She can believe that. No one with a handle on logistics, rosters, schedules. Everything a chaos, made you wonder if the police existed.

But says differently. "Someone knows, Sergeant. Someone knows that Sergeant Langa Mpho took this van. Someone knows how long you took it for. Why did you do this? You cannot make schemes on your own, Sergeant."

"No, Captain."

"This makes problems for everyone when you do this. Now we have to leave the weapons here where anyone can find them." She looks from one man to the other. There is something about Kutoka. About the shape of his face. He doesn't look local. But how did a foreigner get into the SAPS? That isn't possible. She exhales smoke from the corner of her mouth. "You put the boxes in the outhouse? Let me see." Leads them round the cottage to the makeshift hut. Inside five crates, a stack of handguns piled on them.

"Why are these loose?"

"To fit them in."

And they think this is okay? To leave them lying visible for any passing veld walker to help himself?

Then Mpho comes in with: "Is Captain going to pay us?"

For fuck's sake!

"With what? Pay you with what? Do you see FNB on my cap? ABSA? Capitec? Standard Bank? Do you see these badges?"

Sergeant Mpho shakes his head.

"No, you don't see these badges. Because I am not an ATM bank for you to get cash. I am not social services. You want a grant, you go to them. You don't come to me."

She watches Mpho keep the subservient posture, head bowed, shoulders slumped. Knows this is for her sake. How he'll deride her to Kutoka once she's gone. Such are men. Such is their babbling.

Hardly hears his mumbled "We can take it somewhere else."

"What? What'd you say?"

"We can move it."

"Oh yes, where to? Take it where to? Put it all back in your bakkie, take it where to?"

"Wherever Captain wants."

"Uh uh." Captain Hendricks closes the shed door. There isn't even a lock on it. Time to bring this to an end. "No, Sergeant. What is going to happen is, you and the sergeant will go back to Cape Town. You report for duty when it's your shift. You hear me? You hear what I'm saying? I will sort this."

"But we need money."

"I will phone you." The man finally looking at her. A raw hatred in the redness of his eyes. But she can live with that. Men like Mpho don't scare her. It is women like Tamora Gool who worry her. "Now go." Watches the two men slope off to their van, drive away.

She finds a padlock for the shed door in Pietman's cottage. The place cold, quiet, unnerving. As if the bodies still lie where he had shot them. The children who had never woken up.

Outside she sits in her car with the door open, fires up another cigarette. Thinks about guns, diamonds, Tamora Gool, Big D. It is time to see Big D.

32

On speakerphone, Colonel Kaiser Vula to Sergeant Langa Mpho. Lady Vula listening.

"I might have a job for you, Sergeant."

"Yes, my Colonel."

"Are you with me?"

"Yes, my Colonel."

"What is your roster? Are you on duty today?"

"This afternoon, my Colonel."

"I will talk to your station commander. And over the weekend?"

"It is my weekend off, my Colonel."

"Good. Be ready to travel this afternoon. We are away for the weekend."

"Yes, my Colonel."

"You must be at Cape Town International at 1:00 p.m. We will meet there at the departure terminals, you understand?"

"Yes, my Colonel. For how long, my Colonel?"

"For two days in civvies. No uniform. We will be in the north. Any questions?"

"To where in the north, my Colonel?"

"That doesn't matter, Sergeant. As long as you are ready."

"I am, my Colonel. My Colonel …"

"Yes."

"My Colonel, is there some payment that is possible?"

"There will be payment. Major payment. After the job."

"Thank you, my Colonel. If I can ask please, my Colonel, please for some front payment, my Colonel."

"After this weekend, Sergeant, there will be payment. You must learn to control your spending of money. I am not your wealth manager."

"No, my Colonel. It is just, my Colonel, that it is for extra expenses, my Colonel. To make the ends meet up. There are many things for a young baby, my Colonel."

"You have a child?"

"Three children, my Colonel. Two are in Eastern Cape with the mother. This one is here with me in Beirut, in Khayelitsha, with the mother."

"I know where Beirut is, Sergeant. I thought you were in Gugulethu."

"Sometimes, my Colonel. When it is most necessary."

"Good, Sergeant. Now I repeat: check-in at the airport at 1:00 p.m. You cannot be late. That is clear?"

Colonel Vula disconnects, ensures the call has ended.

"You are sure of this man, Kaiser?"

"Can we be sure of any man?"

Lady Vula lays a hand on his shoulder. "I am sure of you."

Of course you are, he thinks. Since the bullet put me in this chair, I have been your world. Uncharitable thoughts, he knows. For without her, he would not have managed to continue in the Agency. He would have been nothing. At pasture in some evergreen frail-care facility. She has kept him angry. He raises his arm, puts a hand over hers.

"Mpho will do what he is ordered to do. Money is his god."

She tinkles a bell, goes to sit on the sofa. "As good a god as any other."

They sit waiting for the colonel's driver. At the front door two suitcases. In the colonel's bag a snubby Taurus .38 centerfire revolver to pack the necessary punch. A constant companion. Plus an off-the-street .22 Ruger with a silencer. Will do the job he has in mind. The pop so soft, snapping your fingers is louder.

Earlier, while he dressed, he had considered taking his rifle. But traveling with a rifle, even for a colonel in the Aviary, is difficult. Papers. Forms. Permissions. A bureaucratic nightmare. Undoubtedly there would be hunting during the weekend. Difficult for him but not to be missed. Maale would have a selection of rifles available. Others would need rifles too. There would be the camaraderie of old comrades selecting their weapons. As they had once done as guerrilla fighters.

Now the prospect of a hunt stirs Colonel Kaiser Vula. The anticipation among the men. The tension. The quiet on the Jeep when prey are sighted: the unconcerned kudu browsing. Then the shot. The fall. The startle as those still living bolt. Out on a hunt in the bush there are possibilities. Somehow they will have to accommodate him.

He hears the car arrive. The slam of the driver's door. The footsteps on the path. The knock. In such details, he thinks, is a fate decided.

"Ready," says Lady Vula. "We have plenty of time to catch the plane. Perhaps we can have a sandwich at the airport before the flight."

33

Sergeant Langa Mpho ends his call to Colonel Kaiser Vula. Glances at Exit Kutoka.

"The colonel, he has a job for me. For the weekend."

"Not me?"

"Me only."

"Where is this job?"

"Away."

"You mustn't go."

"That is not a possibility."

"What about the money?"

"There is no problem with the money. He has told me he will pay."

"When is he going to pay?"

"Man, my brother, there's no problem. The captain has always paid. The colonel has always paid. Sometimes in cash money. Sometimes to my savings. It is alright. He has said payment is after the job. After the weekend."

"When is after the job? After the weekend? Next month is after this weekend. When people do not pay, there is a problem. First the captain wouldn't pay, now the colonel says after the weekend. It is always this problem with money. You mustn't go on this job."

"Ah, of course I must go."

"I do not like it."

"You frown too much, my brother. You must relax. I am sunny like my name. They will pay, the colonel and the captain. And so I have no worries. Also we know where the captain has a flat. We have seen where the colonel lives. We can go there any time. They know this. They know if they do not make the payments, then there will be a visit. A knock on the door in the nighttime. This is something they know about."

"We cannot do that."

"In what is a worst case, it is a possibility." Langa Mpho sits forward, points up the road. "There. Look there. She is leaving."

From where they wait, almost half a mile away beside a windmill, they watch Captain Alicia Hendricks turn her Mazda onto the dirt road to Saldanha. "We can go back."

"Back? For what is this we are going back?"

"One box, my brother. One box for our insurance."

Which makes sense but will cause problems later. "You said they always pay."

"Insurance, my brother. Insurance. Everybody has insurance."

There is no arguing with Mpho. Exit says nothing, starts the van, heads back to the cottage.

"I know what you think," says Mpho. "But it will be safe, my brother. I have a secret place to keep it. Then we can make our own sales. You know, for me this is already a business."

Fine, thinks Exit. But what about the job for the colonel? "You must not go."

Langa Mpho laughs. "Leave it. You are like a woman with your fuss. Why not go? Now he has told me about the away job, it shows he has demand for us."

"It is not good."

At the cottage, they break the padlock on the shed, extract a crate.

"She will know it is us," says Exit.

"Never, my brother. There are always ghost robbers on the veld. Even now probably someone is watching us."

34

This time it is no cruise at fifty in a green tank. This time it is Zara Dewane driving on the far side of the speed limit at 80 mph. Trying to ignore the ache at her kidney. Beside her in the passenger seat, Warrant Officer Wynston Adams scans through the photographs he's taken in the offices of Umuzi Trading. Occasionally glances up when Zara complains about a slow driver or pulls out to overtake.

"So what've we got?" she wants to know.

"Not much," says Wynston. "Bits 'n' pieces coming in: R3,000, R5,000, R10,000 in January. Nothing in February. But then R140,000 in March. In April R300,000. Only R12,000 in May. In June R1,000. July sweet-bugger-all. The soon as anything's in, most of it goes out to leave a low balance. Right now that's at R2,000. Whatever trading Umuzi does, it's erratic. Only consistent thing is R5,000 paid each month from March into the same account. That's five payments. That's R25,000."

"Which is how much was in the Pietman Malgas account."

"Exactly."

Zara thinking, So okay this is the account whoever (probably Hendricks) uses to pay Pietman but why leave bank statements in the desk drawer? So okay Captain Hendricks is probably running an operation trading in stolen firearms but why then a fake office? You don't need an office just to keep bank statements. Who prints out bank statements these days anyhow? Unless Captain Alicia Hendricks has this little hideaway to keep her records. Has scrubbed her digital copies. Because Captain Alicia Hendricks is paranoid of the internet or expecting bigger things? And Captain Alicia Hendricks has set up something that looks real should the revenue service come knocking. Which they do so often these days, the bastards.

Zara's thoughts stop as the car in front brakes. She hoots. Swears: "My lewe fok, Eloise, what are you doing? Who brakes suddenly like that?" Frowns at the pain of the sudden movement to her body. Glances at Wynston, his eyes on the road ahead, his knuckles white. "So this's maybe the start of the laundry business. Money comes in, money flies off somewhere else."

With that swings the car out to overtake. Wynston making guppy noises, pointing ahead. Okay, there is a car in the distance, nothing to get worked up about. She has her foot flat, the Polo in third, the engine revs, pushing 4,000 rpm.

"Trouble is we're no further down the track. All we know for certain is about Malgas. The rest's going to need subpoenas. Which can take time."

The oncoming car now flashing its lights. Zara checks in the rearview, sees she is beyond the slow moron, eases back into the left lane. Waves a "calm down" to the oncoming as it goes hooting past.

Wynston gulps. "Yes, maybe."

"Yes maybe what? Don't whisper."

"Tshoo, man, that was scary."

Zara laughs. "Ah, c'mon, Wynston, there was miles of space. Don't exaggerate." She pauses, thinking no wonder he drives an old Merc, he doesn't want the needle pushing more than sixty. Says, "What do you think's going on in that account?"

"What you said. But it's small-time. I'd thought we'd be seeing bigger figures."

"Me too. Maybe this is just a side hustle."

They drive on in silence until Zara punches in a CD of Linda Perry's "In Flight."

Something defiant.

As they turn onto the sand road to the Malgas cottage, Wynston says, "You really think there's something happening here?"

"Short answer, yes."

Zara stops well back from the cottage. Switches off. They sit, the wind rocking the car, stare at the cottage forlorn on the scrub flats beneath a rushing sky.

"You see that?" Zara points at tire tracks in the wet sand.

"Yup. Two cars probably."

"I'd say. Let's go have a look."

They step into the bitter gusts, hardly a wonder there are no trees. You had to live close to the ground to survive this howling. She rubs at her side to ease the stiffness. Flexes her arm. Then zips up her jacket, puts her shoulder to the wind. Thinks, Why'd anyone choose to stay out here? Sort of place could strip your bones. Limps off against the pain toward the cottage.

Where the cars had stopped earlier, Zara spots a cigarette butt. Stained with red lipstick. Round the back of the cottage, at the shed, finds another.

"Captain Hendricks," says Wynston.

"We could get DNA to check."

"Hey?"

"Joking, Wynston. Joking." On the ground next to the shed door, a broken padlock. "There've been visitors." Zara opens the door.

And there, inside the shed, the treasure trove: a stack of four crates, on top of them a plastic bag of handguns.

Jackpot.

"Wow, Cap," said Wynston, taking a pistol from the bag. "Have to be guns in those crates, don't you reckon?"

"Nice," says Zara. "Wonder where they come from? Out of our stores? Amnesty hand-ins? A heist at some military base?" She peers into the plastic bag, thinking, What if these were the guns from the cop-van heist? Not impossible. Bit of a drive to get here but not impossible. She'll have to follow up.

Wynston opens a crate, reveals an armory of different makes.

"If I had to guess," says Zara, "I'd say unlicensed firearms handed in by the public before the might of our law came down on them. Though given the might of our law, they needn't have bothered. But good citizens are good citizens."

Wynston jots down some serial numbers. "We might get lucky."

Yeah, thinks Zara, miracles do happen. Pops a painkiller to ease the ache in her back, kidneys, the cramps of her period pains. The more important consideration: being here when the collection is made? Because one thing is for sure, they won't be stored here long. Nobody's that stupid.

35

The diamond dealer is younger than she'd expected. Couldn't have been more than mid-thirties. Big (as in tall and muscular). Blond. Tanned. Wearing a tracksuit, sheepskin UGG boots. Looks like a surfer. Is a surfer. Has a longboard in the lounge of his house in the Port Owen marina.

"Howzit, Captain. Come in, come in."

She enters an open-plan lounge/dining room/kitchen with tiled floors, kilims, furniture that looks like it'd been bought at auctions, a massive oak dining table. To one side a blazing wood-burning stove. A young woman had wafted out of the kitchen, waved at her, disappeared into the house.

Always amazes Captain Alicia Hendricks how close the marina is to Saldanha in miles but how far away in lifestyle. In summer, you entered the marina, you entered the chardonnay world of board shorts and bikinis. In winter, you entered the marina, you entered the pinotage world of Swedish sweaters matching for him, her, they.

She'd got there by asking her team at the station for the name of a local diamond expert. Without hesitation, they'd named this blond dude. Big D. Because he'd been diving for diamonds in the concessions since he was sixteen. He knew stones.

"Big D'll check out a stone, feel it, tell you its value," one of her sergeants had said. "You get three other valuations, they'll be in the same ballpark, plus/minus a coupla rands. What d'you want this for?"

Which she hadn't answered except by way of a faint smile.

Now here she is in Big D's home spilling stones onto his oak dining table. Watching him pick them up, look at them individually, close them in the palm of a large hand, set them in a row on the table.

"Lekker," he says to her. "You just wanna know how much?"

She just wants to know how much.

"Okay, these are ocean diamonds, okay. They're brought down to the sea by rivers over millions of years. That's good. That's why they're the best. Cos only the good ones can survive that long. What happens is you get guys like me go out and pick them up out of the gravel on the ocean floor. You look closely, you can see they're clean, you can see the inner light. You don't even have to have these cut, they're beautiful like they are." He looks at her with ice-blue eyes. "What I'm saying is there's a lotta Gs here."

"How many?"

He gives her a figure.

Sjoe. Enough to make you crave a cigarette. Enough to cover the hijacked crates, which is good. And still keep her in debt to Tamora Gool, which isn't.

Big D scoops up the diamonds, returns them to the Ziploc. Hands it to her.

"Can I ask where they came from? I'd say probably Namibia."

"I don't know yet," says Hendricks. "We're working on it." Part truth, part fiction.

On the way back to Saldanha, she phones Tamora Gool.

"I have what you want."

A laugh. "That was fast, Captain Amazon. So when do I collect?"

Captain Alicia Hendricks ignores this. "I also have a value figure."

"Never doubted you wouldn't have. We can talk about that too at the collect. So when?"

"This afternoon."

"You gonna tell me where?"

"This afternoon."

36

"Coincidence? I think not," says Zara to Wynston on the way back to town. Wynston driving. "Cocky-boy Mpho's right in this thing. Thinks he can send me death threats from way out here, that I'm not going to put three and four together. He's got another think coming."

"It's a stretch," says Wynston.

"You reckon. I don't." The more she thinks about it, the more convinced she becomes.

But first.

"We need eyes on those guns." Knowing there isn't a snow-ball's of that happening. Who'd they get to do it?

"You mean post a cop guard out there? Even a couple of cops? No ways the brigadier would give us budget."

Too true.

Technically the Saldanha station should be responsible, the cache being in their area. But how can she trust Hendricks, especially after her meeting with Tamora Gool? No ways. No chance.

What she wants is to do it herself. But alone would be stupid. With Wynston not much better. Anyhow, not the sort of thing she could ask of Wynston. The only other possibility is a camera.

"Easy enough," says Wynston.

Except that means putting in a requisition form. Something else the brigadier would question. In short, getting a camera up and running in less than three days would be a miracle. And then what, even assuming the guns haven't been moved already? Have a feed from the camera through to her phone so she can watch the crates being taken in real time? No chance of doing anything about it. Wonderful. Best seats in the house.

So back to Mpho.

Says to Wynston, "Find out where the cops who were driving the van are. We need to talk to them."

Turns out one is in hospital with perforated eardrums, the

other—a warrant officer—at home recovering from concussion. He can see them.

They find him in a semi-detached in a neat street. His wife fussing, saying they aren't to be long. Offers them tea, coffee, water? They opt for water. Shows them into the lounge. They wait on a two-seater couch, knees jammed against a coffee table. Can hear the wife cajoling her husband that he isn't to let them stress him. The warrant comes in wearing a shapeless jersey, green tracksuit bottoms, sheepskin slippers. Smiles, says, "Don't stand, sit, sit, it's okay." He is okay. The hospital'd done MRI scans, there were no problems. Just this helluva big lump on his head. The guy had whacked him with a pump-action. Out for the count, hey.

Zara and Wynston introduce themselves. Say they are ICU.

Click, click. Zara's pen against her teeth.

"You think this's cops?" says the warrant, now sitting opposite them on a matching couch. His hand gripping the wooden arm rest. "Actual cops?"

A tense bugger.

"Sure," says Zara.

"I've heard there're syndicates using fake cop stuff doing booze heists."

"Actual cops doing that too," says Zara. "Your incident we think was done by members. Could you tell us what happened?"

He does. In minute detail. From the moment they drove out of the compound to the first sighting of the headlights in the rearview.

"At that time, there's not much traffic so we had them for about five minutes right behind us. We slowed down. They slowed down. That's when they put on the blue lights, told us to pull over. Okay, we were pissed off but we thought it's our guys doing their job, what the heck."

"Is that why you got out of the vehicle?"

"Ja. I had the papers, the permits, in my hand. I was just gonna let him know there's no problem here, we're men in blue."

"Did he say anything?"

"I greeted him, he said nothing. Just comes up and whack!"

Zara nods. "You get a chance to look at him? See his face?"

"No, man, it was dark. But I can tell you he was a short oke. Stompie, you know. What you call stocky."

"White, Coloured, Black?"

"Black. I'd say Black. That's what we'd both agreed cos my co, the driver, he got more of a look at him. Even in the dark, we reckon Black."

Zara clicks her pen, taps her teeth. "One last thing, any cars come past while this was happening?"

"A couple. Nothing much. Like I say, it was quiet. Too early for the traffic."

By now, the guy's wife is back, hesitant in the doorway.

Zara says to her: "We're done. Thanks." Looks like the warrant officer has more than one station commander in his life.

"What you think?" Zara says to Wynston as they drive away. Wynston going slowly down the neat street of sandy sidewalks. Secure suburb where no one much bothers with fencing. "Could be Mpho."

"Could be. It's vague though. Sure, Mpho's been after you but we don't know why."

"You reckon we don't?"

"Not specifically, uh uh. Can't be about the rape. He got off. Why go for revenge? Okay, the shooting in your street happened before the hearing but why'd he mess with you afterward? Doesn't make sense."

"Maybe it's not about him. Maybe he's working for someone else. Maybe he's just the soldier following orders."

Wynston waits a beat before responding. "Could be too. But, yarrah, Cap, that means it could be any one of our cases."

"Not any one. One of the high-profile ones. Or maybe it's not even a case yet. Maybe it's just someone wanting to frighten us. Someone who's worried that we're going to be onto them soon. I dunno. That's an outlier. More likely, most likely, it's a case we're on."

"I would say."

"So we need to talk to Mpho."

At the Gugulethu police station, they hold up ID, say they are ICU. Want to speak to a Sergeant Langa Mpho. The duty cop buzzes the station commander. Tells him there are two ICUs wanting Mpho. The station commander comes through—a big bhuti without a smile—wants to know what's the problem. No problem, says Zara, they'd like a few words with the sergeant. Maybe in an interview room. Doesn't need to be a mind reader to know the station commander is aggro, doesn't want them in his precinct.

"What about?"

"An investigation," Zara says. "Nothing official at this stage. Just like to talk to him."

Is told Sergeant Mpho is being seconded to an operation for the weekend. He has to be at Cape Town International at 1:00 p.m.

Ninety minutes away.

Zara holds the big bhuti's eyes. Until he says, "Come. You have five minutes." Tells the duty cop to summon Mpho. Then leads them down a passage to a small room. The only furnishing a table, four chairs. Thick bars at the window.

Five minutes they have to wait for Sergeant Mpho. All that time the station commander stands there not saying a word. Mpho comes in. Glances at Zara, Wynston. Salutes his boss.

"These people want to ask you questions," says the station commander. "You know Captain Dewane."

Zara thinking Mpho doesn't look happy. Not the defiant Mpho of the previous day's hearing. Now he's unsure, keeping his eyes averted. Decides to open with an accusation.

"You were in Saldanha this morning." More a statement than a question.

"Not me. No, Commander." Mpho's immediate response.

Comes too quickly for Zara.

"Don't tell me, tell the captain," says the station commander.

"You were at the cottage of deceased Constable Pietman Malgas?"

"No, Commander. I wasn't at that place." Mpho's eyes focused on the window.

As if you want to fly away, thinks Zara. "Why were you there, Sergeant?"

"It wasn't me, Commander. I don't know this place."

Zara deciding, What the hell, sometimes the only option is to call it straight out. Says, "Don't lie to me, Sergeant. You were there. I know you were there. You sent me a WhatsApp."

"It wasn't me, Commander."

"You threatened to kill me."

"Hey, hokaai, stop-stop." The station commander coming in, hand up as if he is directing traffic. "Do you have the proof of this, Captain?"

"Yes."

"What proof?"

"For the moment, I cannot disclose it."

"Show me the WhatsApp you got."

"Not at this time." Zara going back to Mpho. "You also attacked me yesterday. You and one of your friends."

"It was not me, Commander. The captain is wrong. Where is the proof?"

"I have camera footage."

The station commander again: "You can identify Sergeant Mpho?"

"That is part of our investigation."

"It was not me, my Commander."

"You had better be sure of your case, Captain. These are serious matters you bring against the sergeant. You must have proof. You cannot have only allegations."

"I have more," says Zara. "This man, your sergeant, is suspected of being involved in other criminal matters. Serious criminal matters. This time it will not be a disciplinary hearing. It will be in court. Our investigation is finalizing."

"Stop." The station commander with his hand in the air again. "You must stop this way, Captain. You are threatening my member. You must come with your questions and your proof and then you can interview my member. But this way is not the right way. What you have are only some complaints."

"I would call them more than that. I would call them accusations. And I would thank you, Station Commander, to let us do our job, our duty. We would like to speak to the sergeant alone." Zara watching the station commander puff out his cheeks, raise his shoulders, bounce on the balls of his feet.

"I cannot do that. Where is the evidence? When you bring the evidence, then the sergeant can account. But you have no evidence that I can see. You have come to threaten my member with fake news."

My lewe fok, Eloise. Zara pointing her pen at the big bhuti. Counts to ten. "Are you going to let us talk to the sergeant alone, Commander?"

A plaintive from Mpho: "This captain is against me, my Commander. She has prejudice."

From the station commander, a shake of the head. "No. It is not the right way. When you have evidence, then it is a different matter. Until that time, this conference is over. You can go, Sergeant."

Mpho heads for the door.

"He should stay," says Zara. "One moment, Sergeant."

Mpho ignores her, opens the door, then hesitates.

"Go, Sergeant," says the station commander. "You do not have time to waste." Mpho goes quickly, smirking. To Zara, the station commander says, "We are finished. You and the warrant must leave."

Zara doesn't move. "You do not want to do this. I will be reporting what happened here. I will be reporting your attitude."

"I am not worried. It doesn't matter, Captain. ICU is nothing. We are the real police. You are only two in this province. Now, please, for peace and quiet. I ask you to go." The station commander shifts his eyes from her to the door. "I do not want trouble."

Then you shouldn't be a cop, thinks Zara. With a nod, indicates to Wynston that they are leaving.

They go back down the passage, the station commander behind them, into the charge office. The buzz stopping as they enter.

"Stay safe," says the station commander.

As Zara and Wynston are about to drive away, knuckles rap at her side window. A face leers: Mpho. He spits, his saliva spraying across the glass.

My fok.

Zara is out of the car fast, ignoring the pain flashing through her body.

"What's your case, Sergeant?"

He grins. "No case."

That does it for her. The audacity, the quick comeback. And the sight of Mpho's smirk, his self-satisfaction, the taunting in his eyes. Despite the pain in her shoulder, she whacks him a solid backhand swipe full in the face. Sends him staggering, his hand going to his jaw. He will come at her, Zara can tell. Well, let him. Holds her fists ready, her stance relaxed. Sees Mpho steady himself. Prepare to rush her. She steps forward, pops a straight right to his cheek.

Mpho grunts, keeps his ground. Shakes his head. Zara ready to unleash a left hook.

Except.

Except for the station commander's bellow. Which stops her.

"Captain! Sergeant!"

Zara keeps focused on Mpho. "You try that again, I'll put you down."

Mpho backpedals. The grin sliding across his face. Says quietly, "You in for big-time shit, my sisi. You cannot hit me."

Zara takes a step forward. "Don't you my sisi me." Watches Mpho back off again, turn, head for the charge office.

Hears Wynston saying, "Come, Cap. Leave it. Let's go."

The last thing she is going to do. Like hell the short fucker will get away with it. "No ways," she says. Walks toward the station commander. "You saw what happened?"

The man one step up looking down at her. "I saw that you hit the sergeant."

"After he spat at me. You saw him spit at me?"

"No. I did not witness that action."

"He did. I want him disciplined."

"I will talk to the sergeant."

Zara shakes her head. "That's it? He spits at me and that's okay? You'll talk to him. I want him disciplined."

"Come," the station commander beckons her into the charge office. "You see what is happening?" He gestures at Sergeant Mpho at the desk saying to the duty officer he wants to lay a charge of assault.

"What can we do?" says the station commander to Zara. "We are police. You, Captain, me, the sergeant, we are police. We know what the law says that he can make a charge."

"He spits at me and then he gets to charge me with assault!"

"He has the law. He has the witnesses. Even your warrant saw how you hit him."

"My warrant saw him spit."

"Perhaps. It is possible. All these matters will be under investigation. Maybe you want to make a charge?"

"I wouldn't waste your time. You have murders. You have rapes. You have serious gang violence to deal with. Those are proper police matters. Not spitting or minor altercations."

Enough, she thinks. There is no dealing with these people. Turns her back on the station commander, indicates to Wynston, time to go.

In the car Wynston says, "Why'd you hit him?"

Zara's turn to grin. "Because he's an irritating little shit with enough crap to his name to get him locked up for a long time. And because I wanted to."

Let Linda Perry take it away with "Bang the Drum."

37

"On this trip you are my security, Sergeant. For me and my wife. We will talk about the other matter when we are in private."

This Colonel Kaiser Vula says to Sergeant Langa Mpho at Cape Town International Airport. The two meeting in the domestic departure lounge before the flight to OR Tambo International that Friday. Says to him in a quiet voice. Sergeant Mpho bent slightly forward to catch the colonel's drift. The two of them positioned at the glass windows facing the runway.

In his muted tone, Colonel Vula says, "The other matter ... the one I mentioned earlier ... You are with me?"

Sergeant Mpho says he is.

"This matter is important," says Colonel Kaiser Vula. "As it was with the other two occasions. It is important for our country, for our democracy, for the rule of law. It is state business. In these matters we cannot be bulldozed. We must be revolutionaries without sentiment. We must be as committed as we were in the Struggle. Are you with me?"

Sergeant Mpho says he is.

"I trust you, Sergeant. You have earned that trust. This is why you have been selected," says Colonel Kaiser Vula. "I know that you, Sergeant, will do the right thing. In the right way. As you have done before. For this you will be well, how shall I say, rewarded. Are you with me?"

Sergeant Mpho says he is.

"Do you trust me, Sergeant? Because this is also important."

Sergeant Mpho says he does.

"Then we will talk about this matter later. At the lodge." Colonel Kaiser Vula clasps the rims of his chair, angles himself away from the window. "I can see that we must board," he says. "My wife is alerting us."

"Can my Colonel not tell me a little more," says Mpho, "about this matter."

"Patience, Sergeant. It is best this way. It is better that you do not know too much. What I can tell you is you will be honored. You are a warrior, Sergeant. A chosen warrior."

38

In the ICU office, for an hour in the afternoon.

Here are Captain Zara Dewane and Warrant Officer Wynston Adams going through bank statements. The stash Wynston has photographed. This time being thorough, line by line.

Outside, it's a dismal gray afternoon. Inside, there's a single heater for warmth. A packet of Romany Creams for sustenance.

At one point, Wynston said, "And what happens now?"

Which stopped Zara clicking the pen against her teeth. "About what?"

"About Mpho charging you."

"Search me. Probably won't go anywhere."

"You're not concerned?"

"Nah. But I'll put money he was on that heist. He's the short oke who clocked the cop, shot the other one with a blank. Stored the weapons in the Malgas cottage. That's our man. Sergeant Langa Mpho."

At another point, Zara said, "Money comes in. Gets transferred to another account. Like a clear paper trail that no one's worried about. No one's expecting to get found out. How stupid's that? And here I've got two amounts going to a Vula Holdings back in Jan and Feb. A couple of hundred thou. Vula come up in your lot?"

"June," says Wynston. "Fifty thousand."

"Nice round figures every time."

"And another in July. Same amount."

"Funny thing, I heard that name before. Just yesterday. Sithole told me there was a Vula from State Security going to be transferred to Police Intelligence. To be Maale's number two. You don't come across a name for years, then pop, you hear it twice."

"It's coincidence. I read this piece once that we see meaning in small things. Like when coincidences happen we think it's important. It's how our brains work. Always looking for a story. For connections."

"I'm just saying. I've never heard of this Vula guy. If he's going to be like Mpungose was, that's okay. But I dunno. The Aviary's a dodgy place. Putting a spy into Police Intelligence is asking for trouble. Where's his allegiance going to be?"

"It might work."

"Can't see the spies wanting to help us out. Can you? They've got sticky fingers in all the money boxes."

Then half an hour later, Brigadier Sithole rings. To give Zara hell.

Shouting on speakerphone: "What's this you have done? What's this story I hear that you hit some sergeant? In the name of the almighty presence, what the hell are you doing, Captain? There's a charge of assault against you. We cannot have this happen in ICU. We are the guardians, we are the moral center." Followed by a run of Zulu which Zara can't follow. Followed by a quieter "I am disappointed, Captain. I feel betrayed. That you have betrayed our duty, you have betrayed what we stand for. You have let me down. You have let down the name of the service."

A pause. While a frowning Zara thinks, What's your problem? Glances across at Wynston, the guy full-on embarrassed.

Says to the brigadier, "There was a reason, Brigadier."

"There was no reason to do what you did, Captain. There is no reason to strike another police member. You leave me no choice. I have no options. You are on suspension leave. From now. From this exact minute. You hear me, Captain? You will clear your desk. You will go home. You will not make contact with Warrant Adams. You are going nowhere near the office until this matter is finished. Do you understand me, Captain? No more investigations. No more inquiries. You stay away from everyone. You are on suspension until this matter is finalized. This is an order. Obey it. Do not go against me."

"Brigadier, we have found new evidence ..." says Zara, realizing she is talking to dead air.

"My lewe fok." More a sigh of resignation than a protest. Wynston looks up; she pulls a face.

"What?" he says.

"What nothing. We carry on. Nothing changes. He's in Pretoria. We're stuck out of the way where no one's gonna check on us."

"What if they do?"

"Ah come on, Wynston. Who's to bother? Like anyone cares if I'm suspended. Like they'll send someone round to check. You can see that happening." She bends down to pick up the spray of bank statements. "We're just getting somewhere with this stuff. We're not gonna quit now. Not for our almighty presence in the north."

Yet she can't help feeling sucker-punched. Stabbed in the back. Thrown under the bus. Whatever. A resolve pumping adrenaline, putting a slight tremble into her hands.

When Jo-Jo Lanski phones. "Bloody hell, doll. What've you gone and done now? Beating up the rank 'n' file. Bad girl, Captain Z, bad girl." Ending with her raucous laugh.

Brings a smile to Zara's lips. "Jesus, how did you know?"

"I know everything. Because I'm ICU's attorney of record. Anyhow, news gets around, Captain, in case you hadn't noticed. You heard from the brigadier yet?"

"Just heard. He put me on suspension."

"Couldn't really bloody do anything else, could he? Punching a member in the face, not once, twice nogal, is going to bring that kind of response. Especially backed with a charge of assault. Got to hand it to our little friend, Mpho, he's not one to ever let an opportunity go to waste, is he?"

"He's also been stealing guns."

"Lovely. Of course he has. But let me guess: this's a hunch? You've not got enough to charge him with."

"Not yet. He'll slip up."

"Except you're forgetting you're suspended."

"So what?"

"Thought you might say that. Look, Zara, listen, just be bloody careful. Smacking a member's one thing; breaking a suspension order's another. Bloody hell, you've got to take it down a step."

"I'm fine."

"I'm not talking about how fine you are. I'm saying be bloody cautious. You know what that word means: avoid potential danger. You got that?"

"I've got it."

"I bloody hope so." With that, conversation over.

And Wynston at her desk showing a WhatsApp on his phone: *Serial numbers are from weapons in the consignment hijacked this morning. How do you have those numbers?*

"Don't answer. No. Rather say they were on the driver's manifest. Say that's how we know."

Wynston taps a response.

"What're we gonna do about those guns now?" He flops back into his chair. "We can't leave them there. We should report it."

Zara looks hard at him. "Why?"

"It's the right thing to do."

"And that makes it the right thing to do?"

Wynston not meeting her eyes. "Ja. I think so."

Tick, tick, tick.

"Okay. Who're we gonna tell?"

Wynston rocks back on his chair. "Police Intelligence. I don't know. Some branch dealing with this stuff. Maybe even Hendricks."

"Pah. Given her friendship with Gool, not likely. Wouldn't surprise me if she's in on this."

"Why d'you say that?"

"Gut feel. I know Tamora Gool from way back. You watch how this goes."

Tick, tick, tick.

Zara thinking, Chances were that whoever had stashed the weapons at the cottage would want to be moving them soonest. Wouldn't want weaponry spending too much time in a shed in the middle of nowhere. Chances were they'd make a move this weekend. Her thoughts focusing. No one knows I know. I could go out there. Spend the weekend in the Malgas place. See who comes to collect. Make the arrest. Or phone it in, let the big boys and girls take the credit. That'd give Sithole something to chew on. That was a plan. And then how to tell Kyle? That hurts her. Would hurt even more when she told him and he got that look on his face, the sadness, the disappointment. "Ah, Mom, do you have to? Can't you just stop being a cop for once?" To which she'd have no ready answer. Except to turn away so he couldn't see her eyes watering. Then would come the hyped alternative. How about a weekend with Granma and G-pa? Endless surf time: real waves plus the internet. Ice creams. Chocolate. Hot chocolate. His favorite supper: mac 'n' cheese. "You wouldn't even miss me."

"I will."

"But you're okay with that?"

He'd say he was. He always did.

To Wynston she says, "I'll sort it."

He looks at her. Shakes his head. "If I can mention that's not a good idea."

"What?"

"What you're thinking."

"You can read my mind now? So what's it I'm thinking?"

"Going out there alone."

She laughs. "You reckon that's what I'm planning. You think I'd do that?"

"Yes. I know you, Cap. You're crazy bedonnerd."

39

Beachfront, Bloubergstrand. Middle of the afternoon.

Captain Alicia Hendricks waits in her car. No music on the

sound system. No talk radio. Who wants sound when you have the sea? A rough sea driven by a dying northwester. Patches of sun lighting up the water: the magic after the cold front. Only rags of clouds without rain littering the sky. She smokes, watches walkers, joggers, lovers, bored surfers despondent that their waves are blown out. Waits.

Her phone rings: Duifie.

Saying in Afrikaans, "Where are you, my darling skattebol?"

Thrills Alicia to hear that sexy voice. The new love in her life. Who'd flown in like a dove. Landed on her table while she'd sat in the sun at Truth café one Saturday afternoon.

"Mind if I join you?" Plonked her latte on the table. Slipped onto a chair with lithe grace.

How could you mind this blue-eyed, black-haired dazzle in the white dress smiling at you? Her long legs, her sandaled feet, her toenails dove gray.

Duifie.

"How about coming to me?" says Alicia. "Close the shoe shop early. You can do that?"

"Sure."

"I'll be home in an hour. With biryani."

"Chicken?"

"Chicken, mutton, fish. Whatever you want."

"Switch on the electric blanket. I'll bring red wine."

They settle on chicken.

A warm thought that there'll be Duifie tonight. Captain Alicia Hendricks crushes out her cigarette. Lights another. Looks at her watch. The woman is late.

Earlier she'd phoned Tamora Gool. Given her the time and place.

To Tamora Gool's "Ah, so romantic. By the sea."

One cigarette later.

There's Gool's large BMW M5 pulling up next to Hendricks' Mazda CX-5.

Frigging statement wagon, is the riled thought that goes

through the captain's mind. Sees Gool hop out of the BM, tap with red nails on the Mazda's window. Hendricks pops the door lock.

"This's cozy," says Tamora Gool, getting in. Then, waving a hand in front of her face. "You don't half smoke, hey. You get flu, you're gonna be straight to ICU."

"My car," says Hendricks. "You want to talk to me, this is where we do it."

"You phoned me, remember."

Alicia Hendricks stubs out the cigarette. Squashes it into the car's ashtray. More butts in there than cigarettes in a packet.

"You gonna have to get a new car soon," says Tamora Gool. "Your ashtray's full."

"Listen. You want this or not?"

"In your interests, ma'am. Your obedient servant listening."

"Ah, cut the bullshit attitude."

Tamora Gool sits staring at the sea. Hendricks watching her profile. The twitch at her lips. A beat. Ten beats. She turns to Alicia Hendricks.

"Climb down, okay. We both want this. We're doing business. We don't need crap. We're not macho men. So tell me where I collect."

Fair enough. Alicia can hear Duifie laughing at the retelling in bed. So what'd you say then? I told her to get stuffed. You didn't.

Dead right she didn't.

She told Tamora Gool where to find the cottage up the West Coast. Added, "I'd go there ASAP if I were you."

"Like tonight?"

"Ja, like tonight. Don't leave it any later."

Tamora Gool had smiled at her. Opened the car door, got out, leaned back in. Said, "You're a cool chickie, Captain Alicia Hendricks."

Which will give Duifie the giggles when she tells the story that night.

Captain Alicia Hendricks drives off, thinking maybe it is time she quit smoking. Especially if it is too hardcore for gangsters.

40

"I's not gonna let yous down, Mrs. Z," says Janet.

"You better not." The two of them in the kitchen, Zara loading a cooler box with fruit, tomatoes, cheese, a packet of beef patties from the fridge. From the freezer, a bag of frozen rolls. Out of the grocery cupboard a couple of packets of pasta, some onions.

"I's here every hour."

"You better be."

Zara thinking, Don't forget coffee, the Bialetti, water. Adds these to a cardboard box of utensils, plates, cups. Also on the check list: ammo, Z88, torch, spare batteries, candles, LED lanterns, the gas cooker. Painkillers.

Then limping to Kyle's room—the pain in her side making her grimace—to check he'd packed his stuff: hoodies, T-shirts, shorts, jeans, Crocs. Surfboard, skateboard, wetsuit. Shouted to Kyle in the bathroom to get a move on. Janet behind her watching.

"Don't forget the wax, Mrs. Z."

How the hell does she know about surfboard wax?

She does because: "My old landlord there by Muizenberg with Miss Vicki, Mr. Fish, he was a surfer."

"Oh yeah." Zara occupied checking the hoodies for food stains, thinking, Fish! Odd name. Fish. Pealed a distant bell. "Was? Why'd he stop surfing?"

"He's dead from being shot."

Which gives her pause, the story coming back vaguely. "Shot! When was this?"

"Back inna old days, before the plague. Out there in the Murderers' Karoo. Mrs. Z mos knows, it happens in your lines of business."

"He was a PI?"

"Exactimonti."

My lewe fok, what a weird coincidence. "Fish Pescado, right? That's his name?"

"Exactimonti."

A story she'd orbited. Had involved old operatives from the Security Branch, left four dead bodies in its wake. Yet hadn't even made the morning news. Hushed up. Put down to another mysterious farm killing.

"So you knew him, hey?"

"Like a hope to grope. Mr. Fish was a mensch true 'n' proper."

Small-town Cape Town. All the same, a weird coincidence bumping into Janet of the Cape. Or was this the universe speaking? Not that it matters to Zara. Some things you just accept: they are what they are. Someone comes into your life, you trust them or you don't. She trusts this bergie. Something about her she bought into. Still worth a cautionary.

"You leave my booze, okay?"

A shock-horror gasp from Janet of the Cape. "Mrs. Z! I's scandalized, totally. I's mos got a small supply. Mind yous if yous wanna leave a token for appreciation, I's not trying to dissuade yous. In the analogies of wisdom we say, clear your frown with a dop of Old Brown. Like I told you, that's my complete standby specialty."

"But it's low now?"

"In a way of saying."

From the cabinet in the living room, Zara takes out her one and only bottle of sherry. There remains: a whisky bottle half full, a bottle of brandy three quarters gone, vodka unopened, gin maybe a tot or two down. Three bottles of malbec. Hands the Old Brown to Janet.

"Don't drink it all at once." Zara checking her out.

"Me! Never on Sunday." The bottle disappearing into the pocket of her coat. "When's Mrs. Z gonna be coming home again?"

Good question. "Depends," says Zara. "Maybe tomorrow. Maybe Sunday. Definitely Monday morning."

Janet nodding with each day. "In that cases, yous needs enough sanitaries."

Stops Zara in her tracks. The second time Janet has referred to her having a period. "You think I've got the monthlies?"

Janet shrugs. "Ja, mos."

"How d'you know that?"

"I got witch senses." Said straight-faced without a cackle. My lewe!

Zara shouts again for her son: "Come on, Kyle, we've got to go."

Driving away from her house, Zara thinks, What're you doing? You leave all your possessions in the possession of a bergie! One you don't even know! Imagine Janet of the Cape sprawled in front of the flatscreen sucking on a bottle of Old Brown. Streaming reruns of *Miami Vice*. Crazy. Yet, also, she isn't that bothered. As house-sitters go, Janet probably no worse than a professional. You just have to listen to Jo-Jo's scary stories in that department to never leave home.

As she crosses the suburbs, Zara's thoughts flick to her suspension: a nuisance, but no regrets at having smacked Mpho. So he'd charged her. So Jo-Jo could handle that one. Might even be a way to get Mpho nailed.

Enough.

She glances at Kyle. "You're being awfully quiet. What's that you're watching?"

Kyle focused on a YouTube clip on his phone. Looks up. "I don't know why you can't stay home for the weekend. You were going to."

She reaches out, puts a hand on his arm, squeezes. "Hey, it doesn't get better than a weekend with Granma and G-pa."

"I wanna stay at home."

"I told you, things have changed. I've got to go away. It's my work."

"Ah, Mom." Her hand shaken off.

She grips the steering wheel. The rejection stinging. "We've been through this, Kyle, please. Don't make it any harder. This is how things are for me."

How things are: the constant tussle. Being a cop. Being a mom.

Being a mom so much more difficult. At times like these when you've got to farm out the kid. Your child. Because otherwise you can't cope. Otherwise you look weak. A girl in a man's world. And all she wants to do is hug him to make it better.

But that's not going to happen. Instead they sit in silence. In her head, the constant loop: Please, Kyle, please, please, please.

Fifteen minutes later, she stops outside her parents' house. Kyle not happy, which pulls at her heart but what alternative has she got? Being the child of a cop isn't easy. At least there were his grandparents. For him, a weekend with them probably better than a weekend with her. Truth be told.

Zara's father opens the door at her knock, reads the look on her face, notes the overnight bag she carries. Raises his eyebrows.

"Don't start," Zara says. "I've been through it already with Ma."

He smiles at Kyle. Comes in with: "We'll take you surfing. Long Beach if you like."

And then her mother appears, saying, "There's macaroni cheese for supper."

Which might have been the two things that clinched it for Kyle.

Or the point Zara then conceded about Ashton. Because Kyle pushed home his advantage.

"I don't want to go to Dad's again."

Zara strokes his arm. "We can't do that. He's got legal rights."

"What about my rights?" He shrugs off her hand again.

"You're too young for those sorts of rights. When you're old enough, you can make those decisions."

"I don't want to be there."

Zara glances from her father to her mother. Gets blank expressions of, Difficult, but your baby. Don't get us involved.

A great help, Zara thinks. Then says to Kyle, "Okay, how about you only go to him one weekend a month? I'll speak to your father, but I can't promise anything."

"Okay."

"He'll give you a hard time when you're there."

"He does already. Takes away my phone. Says it's a privilege. Why've I got a phone if he can take it away? He even switches off the internet."

Father Villain at his best.

What'd she ever seen in the guy?

She gets a goodbye peck from Kyle, watches her father usher him away. Wants to hold him, but he'll squirm free. As he does. "Mom, you're smothering me."

"I know what you're feeling," says her mother. "He'll be fine. Right now, more important, how are you?" Daughter and mother walking down the short path to Zara's car. "Still hurting?"

"Mostly my kidney. My arm if I bump it."

"You should be taking it easy. Not playing cops and robbers like this."

"Ma, I've got no choice, you know. There's just the two of us in the unit."

"Yes, well. Wynston's still a boy despite his rank. You could ask for backup." She reaches for Zara's hand, slips her a small tube of white pills.

"What's this?"

"Homeopathic."

Zara has to laugh. "You never stop."

"You're my daughter."

"I've told you I've got painkillers. Heavy-duty stuff."

"Consider this backup. Much more effective. Three under your tongue three times a day. You'll see. Nature's remedy without the toxic chemicals."

Watchman, What of the Night?

41

A game reserve somewhere northwest of Tshwane. A cluster of lodges around a waterhole. The waterhole floodlit. There are hippo snorting in the reeds; buck, giraffe, zebra drink there in the day. Sometimes lions pass through. Here you might think you were not part of the rushing world. In the silence of the hot bush during the day, this could be another time. A time long past. In the dark hours, you are convinced of how it once was. You know you are secure, yet there is an unease, a fear.

It is a discreet location that has hosted international missions; government conferences (lekgotlas by another name); gatherings of social institutions concerned with civil rights; boards of high-powered companies. It is a place where plans are made, strategies determined, discussions facilitated, where breakaway groups can talk freely before formulating policy. In the paneled meeting rooms, there is the fume of fine cognacs, single malts, Havana cigars. The aromas of living. This is a place of understandings: whispers, nods, handshakes. The quick meeting of eyes, the brief smile of complicity. A place where men and women find their place.

In well-appointed lodges. Each with en-suite bathroom, jacuzzi, sitting room. Picture windows onto the bush. Thick curtains. Loungers on the deck for a beer at the end of the afternoon. Judiciously positioned massage cabins.

Boardwalks connect the lodges to the main house, where a banquet has been arranged for tonight. The guests have arrived. Been welcomed by the lodge manager and his staff, shown to their quarters, told there would be pre-dinner drinks at seven.

On the manager's list, the guests are: General Duncan Maale, head of Police Intelligence, and his wife; Brigadier Wiseman Sithole, head of the Internal Crime Unit, and his wife; Colonel Kaiser Vula, special officer in the State Security Agency, and his wife. Two majors from Special Investigations, both unaccompanied. Both women. The minister and entourage are absent. Apologies received. All protocols observed. Of course, each of those present have their own security officers, accommodated in private suites. Of course there is also on-site guarding. But no obvious surveillance cameras. Because this is a secure venue, a discreet location.

Where newly arrived Kaiser and Lady Vula sit with drinks. Gin and tonic from the minibar, three cubes of ice, a slice of lemon. Sit as you do when on safari in the quiet hour at dusk. The hour of guinea fowl calls. Of francolins. The hour of reflection.

Time to consider the drastic option, its inevitability, its necessity, any flaws in the course of action. Time for Colonel Vula to wonder if he has made the right decision. In all conscience. All things considered. The ideals of the revolution. The authority of the state. The power to change the country for the people. The commitment to governance. The service to the people. The people are paramount: their freedom, their rights, their dignity. The totality of their lives within a just paradigm. No wrong ideals, no corrupt institutions, no power-mad person can jeopardize the democratic project. Nor can the meek, the indecisive, the chicken-hearted. The revolution calls for decisive measures. Yet the man is personable. Harmless. Doesn't deserve such a drastic outcome. And what of his family?

Considering this, Kaiser Vula wonders aloud to his wife, "Is this right?"

Watches as she sips at her drink. Turns to him with a smile.

Lays a hand on his thigh. "A touch of conscience, Colonel. That is not like you. What of the others?"

"The others were different. For the first thing, they were ruthless men. For the second thing, I did not like them. They were flies."

She squeezes his thigh. "Resolve, Kaiser. This is the way. It is not your fault Maale is the wrong man in the wrong job. There is no other way than this. You know he will not step down. And then as his number two, he would thwart you with every obstruction. Where then would be the options? You could even say he is a counterrevolutionary. Resolve, Kaiser."

"I am resolved." Finishes his drink. "Where is Mpho? It is time we talked."

42

They reach the Malgas cottage after dark, Zara driving. All the road, Wynston sitting tense, shut up, hands clenched in his lap. There've been some touchy moments in the dismal dusk. Moments involving oncoming cars. Flashing headlights. Extreme overtaking. Throughout Linda Perry presiding. When they turn onto the sand track, Wynston stretches, yawns, letting go of nervous tension.

Zara says, "Boykie, you'd better stay awake. There's a long night ahead for us. Plus we might have visitors."

Thinks more likely that'd be Saturday or Sunday. Could be day or night. Out here in the isolation, daylight isn't a problem.

Wynston says, "I must be out of my mind."

A laugh from Zara. "Yeah, well, that goes for you and me both, my brother."

At the cottage, she cuts the engine, lets the silence pervade. Switches off the headlights. In the darkness even the walls of the cottage disappear. Until slowly her senses adjust to the black solitude: to the ghosting abode on the pale scrublands, the screech of insects.

Again she wonders, Who'd live out here?

Says, "Come. Things to do."

First, they check the weaponry in the shed. Shine torchlight on crates: all present and correct.

Second: unload. Establish no electricity, no gas, only a dribble of tap water in the cottage.

Third, Wynston drives the car behind the cottage, covers it with a tarpaulin.

Fourth: supper. On the gas cooker, Zara boils pasta. Serves it with chopped tomatoes, shavings of Parmesan.

Fifth: the beginning of the long night by candlelight. The long night in the cottage where Pietman Malgas shot his children, shot his wife, shot himself. She can never stop remembering this.

Before they settle, Zara takes a walk into the veld. Looks back at the cottage. No lights flicker at the windows. No sign of life. No clues of their waiting.

Back inside, she sprawls on a couch. Tries to make herself comfortable among the lumps and bumps. Her own lumps and bumps dulled with her mother's little white pills. Which seem to have helped. Unless it is mind over matter. She has her Z88 within reach. A box of rounds on the floor. Her phone off. Opposite, in a chair, Wynston wrapped in a blanket. The time 7:56 p.m. Slow flickering hours ahead.

Says, "You wanna sleep, you can. I'll wake you at midnight. There're beds."

Beds with blood stains.

"You could turn a mattress."

Wynston shifts in the chair. "I'll sleep here. It's okay."

She looks at him in the dim light. Loyal guy. Dedicated. Says, "Shouldn't you be jolling on a Friday night?"

Gets back a "Ja, I should."

"You don't have to be here."

"It's okay, Cap. *You* don't have to be here either. You're not supposed to even be on the job. Suspension is suspension."

"A technicality." The end of this line of discussion. Zara wishing they'd brought wine. Maybe she should shoot into Saldanha. Convince a hotel barman to slip her a bottle under the counter. A possibility. A distinct possibility. Especially as they'd hopefully recognize her from when she ran the cop shop, be conducive to helping her out. "You fancy a dop?"

"Oh ja. You've got a bottle?" Wynston pulling himself upright.

"Not exactly. I can get one."

"Where?"

"At the hotel."

A doubtful glance from Wynston. "I could go."

Zara shakes her head. "They don't know you. They know me from when I was stationed here. They're cool."

"I dunno. Someone else might recognize you."

"Hardly. Anyhow, so what? No reason I shouldn't be here. So: a bottle and maybe some cards. You think Malgas has cards?"

Zara swings her legs off the couch. Hears Wynston say, "I think being here is fucked up."

"Yeah. How?"

"He killed here. A week ago, there was a live family in this place. Now they're all dead. Except ..."

"Except what?"

"They're here still."

"You mean their ghosts? You're worried about their ghosts?"

"Can't you feel it?"

"What?" My lewe fok, Eloise.

"A presence. It's creeping me out."

Zara laughs. "You mean you don't wanna stay here alone. My tough-guy Wynston's afraid of ghosts."

"It's damn spooky."

"Look. I'm going to be gone, what, half an hour? Ten minutes in. Ten minutes to make the purchase. Ten minutes back. Not the end of the world."

"Maybe I'll wait outside."

"It's cold and wet out there."

"Even so." But he makes no move in that direction.

"Okay, boykie. Your choice." Zara picks up the car keys. "What'd you prefer? Shiraz? Pinotage? Cab sauv?" Doesn't wait for his answer. Adds: "Maybe one of each, hey?"

43

At six o'clock, Lady Vula lies back in the jacuzzi with a glass of bubbly in hand. In the sitting room of their lodge, Colonel Kaiser Vula hands Sergeant Langa Mpho a .22 Ruger pistol, eight rounds in the clip. Gives him the silencer separately.

Tells him, "With this, there is no noise."

Sergeant Langa Mpho buries the gun in the pocket of his coat. Inspects the silencer.

"From an American friend," says Colonel Kaiser Vula. "It is the latest model." He beckons the sergeant to bend closer. "You are with me? You understand why you are here?"

"My Colonel has told me nothing," says Mpho.

"Now listen," says Colonel Kaiser Vula. "After the dinner, when everyone has gone to their lodges, I will stay on to talk with General Maale. You will find us there. I have seen the dining rooms have wide doors onto the viewing deck. These doors will be unlocked. You can come in. Pop, pop. You leave. Get rid of the gun. Maybe throw it into the waterhole. You have a minute before I shout for help. Go back to your room. When the search starts for the attackers, your orders will be to secure my lodge." The colonel studies the sergeant. The man is in deeply already. He will do this. He is also a man who likes money. "Are you with me?"

"The general?"

"Yes. It is the general. Are you with me?"

"I am, my Colonel."

"Quick, quick. No wild shootings like the other day. That was stupid. That was reckless. You must be professional. Focused."

"Yes, my Colonel."

"Now tell me this one last thing: do you want rand cash or Cayman dollars?"

A flash answer: "Cash, my Colonel. Can I ask my Colonel how much?"

"More than last time."

"Thank you, my Colonel. Can I ask my Colonel how much?"

"This will pay R400,000. In dollars, $25,000. You still want cash?"

Mpho nods.

Kaiser Vula smiles. Even though the dollar offer, the Cayman offer, is better, Mpho is not stupid. Knows about paper trails. Can get a bit reckless sometimes, sometimes dangerously freelance but mostly controllable. A useful handyman. An on-call hammerman. "Fine. Go."

Watches Mpho leave. Can hear his footsteps on the boardwalk fading.

Kaiser Vula wheels himself outside. Sits for a few minutes on the deck. At the edge of the floodlit waterhole, a shadow stirs. Then another. A third. Three hyenas come out of the bush, come to drink. He watches them lapping at the water's edge. Then one pauses. Raises its head. In seconds all three are gone, soundlessly. He waits on, expecting whatever has given them fright. But the bush stays silent, nothing stirs at the waterhole.

All that disturbs the quiet is a ping on his smartphone. He scrolls to a WhatsApp message. An unknown number. Opens a meme of a handgun. It floats across the screen. Then is suddenly gone, deleted.

To a man blasé to death threats, this is yet another. He hisses in irritation.

44

"Well, look't who's here? Hey, Cap, surprise, surprise."

Zara turns from the bar at the familiar voice. Sees Big D coming at her, arms wide. A full-on bugger-me-pleased-to-see-ya attitude.

"Whatcha doing here, Caps?"

She goes into the clinch, pain shooting through her body.

Feels his hand slide down her back, grab her bum. Pull her into his crotch.

"Watch it," she says, pushing back.

Big D releases her. "I still dream about your tits, Cappie."

She laughs to cover her aches. "You and lots of others."

Once they'd had a fling. Well, not once. Three times. If you counted it in nights. When she'd been acting station commander at Saldanha. Living there with Kyle in a grim two-bedroomed rental near his primary school. After she and Ashton had separated. Not the best of times in her life. A bit mad that she'd moved on Big D one weekend. Or he'd moved on her. In this self-same bar. Ended up in one of the rooms for the night. Well, that night. Then the next two at Big D's place in the Port Owen marina. In fantasyland. But every moment there'd been Kyle-guilt at the back of her mind. Kyle with Ashton for the weekend. When all she wanted was time out, an escape from her life. For just a few days. When here she was with this blond dude and his liquid tongue. This blond dude feeding her grapes, filling her up. Yet all she could think of was you shouldn't be doing this. You've got a son. You're separated, not divorced. Listening to the Adonis body saying she could bring her boy over. Knew why she'd never taken up the offer of weekends there with Kyle. I'll take him surfing. We'll go diving for crays. You can come here any time. This's paradise for a boy. Yet she never did. Big D was dangerous. Dangerous to fall in love with. She recognized that much. There was talk of battered women. There was talk of diamond deals. She didn't need another fucked-up man. So when he'd phoned, she'd smiled. Said, "We'll do that." Never did.

Now here he was, so close she could feel his body heat.

"Hey, man, what're you doing in this neck? Slumming it? You still catching bad cops in the city?" Smiling at her. His hand on her forearm. "That's gotta be a full-time job."

She doesn't answer him directly. Says she is up the West Coast for a weekend break. Says she'd forgotten to pack wine. Which is why she is there buying bottles from the friendly hotel barman.

"Is it," he says, those blue eyes dancing at her. Not listening. She can see that, scheming something else.

"Your boy's with you?"

Before she can answer, he says, "You should come over for a braai. Afterwards, there's a break I know, I can take him surfing."

"I dunno." Zara wondering how she'll get out of this one. Says, "I'm with friends."

Doesn't faze Big D. "Hey, no worries, man. Bring everyone. We can party." Keeping up that how-good-to-see-you-again smile. A finger now tapping at his lips. "You know, this's funny seeing you. This morning I met the station commander. Not the one took over from you. This one's new. Well, okay, she's been there a while, like six months, she says."

"Hendricks?"

"Ja, that's it. She came to see me. She's cool. It's like all the pretty birds are joining the SAPS." He winks at her. "Listen, man, stay 'n' have a catch-up drink. A quickie."

Zara thinks, You shouldn't. You should go. Get back to Wynston. But there is the nag: why'd Hendricks come to see him? A Big D transgression? Highly likely. Or a Hendricks issue? Could be a case. Could be something more personal. Whatever: worth finding out. And how much would another half an hour matter anyway? Which was more or less how things had started those years back. Which isn't lost on her.

"Okay."

"What're you having?" he says.

She screws up her face at a sudden bite of pain. Clutches her side.

He notices. "What's up?"

"War wound."

"Looks sore."

"It can be if I move wrong. Nothing that a drink won't sort out. Make it a short beer," she says. "Tell me about Hendricks," she says.

"Thought that would catch you. Find a table, I'll bring the beers."

She finds a table, checks her phone. A missed call from Wynston two minutes ago. She hadn't even heard it. Taps out a WhatsApp: *What's it?* Leaves her phone lying on the table. Watches the blond dude approaching. There'd be eyes on him, on her. This is his drinking hole. And many would recognize her. Wonder what is up between them.

"Two frosties," he says, putting her beer before her. Pulls up a chair. "Cheers." They clink glasses.

Zara takes a mouthful, feels the tingle of evanescence on her tongue. Watches him slurp the foamy top off his lager. Wipe the back of his hand across his lips. "That's lekker. So. Why're you so curious about our captain?"

"Ah, it's nothing. Suppose it's because she's got one of my old jobs. I liked working here." Not totally true. She hated being there because it was banishment. But liked being there because it was different. The harbor. The railhead. The surrounding farmers. Always something happening. The lagoon close by for time out in a kayak. She watches Big D take another draft. Can see why she'd gone for him. The man gives off vibes. Very sexy. Very bloody dangerous, as Jo-Jo would warn.

"She wanted advice," he says.

"Oh yeah?" That can only be about one thing. Diamonds. Her phone screen lights up. A WhatsApp from Wynston.

"You want to get that?" says Big D.

"In a moment. Tell me about your advice to her?"

He laughs. "Still the one-track Zara. Won't let go of the bone."

"So tell me."

"Slowly, man. Slowly. You've got to build up the suspense. Like a writer."

"D."

"What?"

"Stop buggering around."

"Alright. It was about some stones. Really nice ones. Either someone lucked in higher up the coast, Port Nolloth, Orange River mouth, more likely Namibia, maybe, or these're …"

"What?"

"You know. Stolen."

"She didn't say?"

"No chance. She's a cop. You cops're cagey."

"But what'd you reckon?"

He drinks beer. Does the back-of-the-hand wipe again. Grins at her. "Naa-mibia. That's where I'd put my money. New stones. Absolute beauts."

"How many? A lot?"

"You could say. The right place you'd get well over a coupla hundred kay."

"Sjoe." Zara muses, pictures a handover in a suburban street involving one Tamora Gool. Says, "If she wanted to get a value on them why'd she come to you, not go to some proper dealer?"

Big D pulls back, mock hurt. "I'm the best there is. How can you say that?"

"Because this is IDB, she's wanting to keep it all under the radar."

More mock horror. "I'm not illegal. I'm not a diamond buyer."

"Course not. Furthest thing from anyone's mind." They both laugh. Time to change course. "So how're you doing, D?"

"Genuine?"

"Genuine."

"Stoking, man. Stoking." His eyes going across the room to a far table. A young woman in tight jeans, fluffy pink scoop-neck stands up, sashays toward them. She comes up, sits down in Big D's lap, full-on possession. "Meet my honey," he says. "Elmari," he says, "this is Zara. She was SAPS here once upon a time."

Elmari sticks out her hand, doesn't smile.

Five minutes later, Zara, two bottles of red clutched to her chest, walks across the hotel parking lot to her car. Thinking that piece of work isn't going to last in the Big D world more than a few months. If that. The man is welcome to her. With Elmari on the scene, a fat chance she'd take up his invite to pop round for a braai. No ways in hell. Actually, no ways in hell Elmari or no Elmari.

She sets the bottles on the passenger seat, sticks the key in the ignition. Before she turns the engine, looks at her phone to see what Wynston had wanted.

His message reads: *People.*

45

It was a relaxed dinner. As the starters arrived (dumplings in a leek and creamy cheese sauce), General Duncan Maale stood to say a few words.

Praised his late colleague Brigadier Sipho Mpungose.

"He was a man of steel. He was a man of principle."

Lamented the waste of his life.

"Because of the violence that plagues our land we lost a huge talent. We are too quick to pull the trigger. Too quick to kill."

Promised justice.

"As Brigadier Mpungose fought each day for the rule of law, so we will honor him."

They toasted their fallen comrade. (The wine an oaked chardonnay.) Then took to the starter.

"Delicious."

"What a wonderful sauce."

"General, this is fine dining."

And the mood quickly lightened.

Now Colonel Kaiser Vula leans across the table to Brigadier Sithole. "He is a loss to you, Brigadier. Especially. I hear he was supportive of the ICU."

A vigorous nod from the brigadier. "No question. We have lost a pillar. At a time like this when there is so much wrong in the police system, we have lost a strong support. There is not much we can do with our small budget. We need more financial backing."

Colonel Vula lets the brigadier chew through a mouthful. Watches a muscle in the man's cheek catching the light. What does the brigadier really care? He will be gone in a few months. Some other weak fool will be promoted to the position. Unless … Unless the ICU was pulled into Police Intelligence. Where it could be sidelined. Back-officed. Starved of resources. He keeps the brigadier engaged.

"Perhaps you need to ask General Maale for assistance." Watches the brigadier cut into a dumpling, spear it with his fork.

"These morsels are tasty. Don't you think?"

Morsels? Makes Colonel Vula smile inwardly. Something he must remember to tell Lady. She will enjoy it. How did you enjoy the morsels, my dear?

To the brigadier, he agrees they are most tasty.

Then beneath the conversations, hears the brigadier say, "He, I mean General Maale, knows how much we at ICU needed Sipho. He gave us information about police crime. We were talking, Duncan Maale and me, that when I retired in a few months, Sipho could oversee ICU. Maybe even do as you suggest, attach the unit to Police Intelligence. It would make sense. There are what the management gurus call synergies between our areas of operation."

Synergies! Another one for Lady.

"Of course," says Colonel Vula. Clearly, the sooner Sithole retires the better. The man knows he has no power. He knows he is a filler. A useful fool. Vula watches the brigadier gesture round the table. "These are important people. That you are here, Colonel, as someone from the Agency, says many things."

Oh yes, thinks Kaiser Vula. "Do you think so?" he says. "It is within my portfolio to liaise with Police Intelligence. I am sure you agree there should be cooperation between the law enforcement agencies."

"That is what I mean precisely."

"Especially in this climate of corruption."

"Yoh! It is bad. Everywhere in government. Even in the police service, it is out of control. Like a virus that has made us sick to our hearts. It was not like this in the Struggle. We were better people then."

Colonel Kaiser Vula nods. Takes a mouthful of the chardonnay. Something to clean the palate. A better people then! Perhaps Sithole hadn't seen the places he'd seen. Hadn't been with the movement in exile. Hadn't been at the Quatro camp in Angola. Perhaps he didn't know what had happened there. The interrogations. The torture. The rapes. The killings. A better people? He thinks not. Takes another swallow of chardonnay. Still, no reason to contradict Sithole. The man is history. He feels a hand on his shoulder. General Maale.

"General?"

"Excuse me a moment, Colonel, Brigadier."

"No problem," says Brigadier Sithole. "We were talking about the need for cooperation."

"Good. Good. Yes, cooperation. That is what the president wants. He tells me that there will be a great change coming. We will fix this country. But, Colonel," General Maale lowers his voice, "we must talk, you and me. The two of us. Perhaps after dinner we will have time to do this. If you do not mind?"

"Not at all. That is why we are here."

"You are not tired? It will be late. Your good wife won't mind?"

Colonel Vula brushes aside the general's concern with a wave of his hand. Glances at his good wife talking to the Mrs. Brigadier Sithole. Animated. Laughing. She will be pleased to know this.

"Then the Impala Room, next to this one. We can be there," says General Maale. "I look forward to it. We must talk some more about what I proposed to you yesterday. I am sure you have given it consideration?"

"I have."

"Good. Then we should prepare a road map."

46

People!

My lewe fok.

She drives fast to the cottage. Cursing that she hadn't looked at his message when it came through. That she hadn't phoned him back.

Imagining the scene.

Wynston hears a car approaching. Thinks it's her returning. Then maybe picks up a difference in the engine noise. That gets him moving. He blows out whatever candles are burning. Takes his gun from its holster, a flashlight, stands at the window. Sees bakkies stop to the side of the cottage. Men getting out, going straight to the shed. Wynston pads across the cottage to the kitchen window. Sees the shed door is open. The men taking out the crates. What to do? He phones her. She's his captain; she'll know how to handle it. Except he gets no response. WhatsApps the word *People*. She'll go into overdrive with that. Again no reply. What to do? The only thing he can think of: stop them.

Which is as far as Zara wants to imagine.

Hopes he hadn't intervened. Hopes they hadn't checked the cottage. Hopes it wasn't like this at all.

But.

But she fears the worst.

All the way to the dirt-road turnoff, she fears the worst. At the gravel road, stops, racks a round into her pistol, lays the gun in her lap. Kills the headlights. Drives on slowly. Three, four, five hundred yards. She can see the cottage now, dimly in the distance. Enough moonlight between the clouds to hold the scene. No cars visible. No light at the cottage. Another hundred yards. A better visual. Which decides her.

Now she puts foot. The tires skidding on the gravel as the car accelerates. One thought in her head: Wynston.

Zara comes to a hard stop at the cottage, dust swirling round the car. She sits. Watches. Hopes to see Wynston suddenly in the cottage doorway. No movement. No movement in the cottage. No movement in the veld.

Now she is out of the car. Pistol in one hand, flashlight in the other, approaching the cottage. The door open. She calls his name.

"Wynston."

No response.

"Wynston, it's me."

Still nothing.

She clicks on the flashlight, shines the beam into the room. Scans the floor, the beds, the chairs, in the corners. Goes through to the tiny kitchen. The back door closed, locked. Through the window sees the open shed door. One crate visible. Like the thieves have left in a hurry.

My fok.

Goes back out through the front door, round the cottage, sweeping the light beam from side to side. Three crates gone.

Calls Wynston's name again.

Walks around the other side of the cottage. Shines the flashlight into the veld.

No Wynston. No guns.

Shines the beam on the sand patch where her car is parked. The light picking up tire tracks. Two sets. Not the same tread mark as hers. Tracks that showed two vehicles had reversed, headed back toward the tar road.

Catches a glint then in the sand. Picks up a casing: 9mm, rim fire. Sniffs it. Recently fired. Searches hurriedly for others.

Nothing.

Goes over to the cottage door, searches the sand for casings.

Nothing.

Imagines the scene: Wynston comes out of the cottage, gun in hand. Shouts at the fuckers to get down on the ground. On their stomachs, arms above their heads. No shit or he'll shoot. Now. Now.

Then what?

He doesn't shoot. He didn't shoot. No shells to tell a story. But no blood either.

No blood means what? Stalemate? He walks toward them. They're obeying him, getting down on their knees, hands high, one of them telling him, "Nay, my bru, yous got the wrong end, really. We's reserves for the cappie at Saldanha. She says to collect the boxes for proper storage. There inna proper armory."

Wynston ordering, Down, down. Wynston five paces closer.

Then what?

Does one of them shoot him?

She looks at the shell. Not a cop-issue round.

But she can't find blood. The sand this side of the tire tracks is a chaos of disturbance. Would take a forensic to work out the scene. Would take full daylight.

Nine hours till sunrise.

Proper thing to do is report the situation. Phone Sithole. Except Sithole is somewhere to hell 'n' gone on a safari in the bush, out of cell phone coverage. Log the incident at Saldanha police station. Report Wynston missing. Possibly wounded. The proper thing to do.

Which Zara doesn't do. She paces the cottage. Decides she will search through the veld. Circle the cottage, moving further out with each circumference. It is all she can do. It might be wasted effort but at least it is doing something. No reason to wait out the long hours to morning. In case. In case what? In case Wynston has got away, is out somewhere on the veld. Lies out there bleeding.

She goes five circles out by flashlight. About seventy yards from the house, toward the tar road, she finds him. Finds his body shot through the heart.

He's lying face down.

"Wynston! Wynston!"

She knows it. Can see he's dead. But keeps saying his name.

Crouches beside him. The flashlight showing the hole in his back.

Clutches at his shoulder, goes down on her knees to turn him over, his body flopping onto her. His face with open eyes, looking at her. It can't be.

"Wynston!"

She lets his body slide to the ground. Hears a strange whimpering as she kneels there, playing the flashlight over his features. Seeing, not seeing in the shaky light. Gradually realizing the keening is hers.

The tears come. Uncontrollable. She sobs. Howls. No. No. No. Not this. Not Wynston. Bunches his clothes in her fist. Wants to pull him up. Resurrect him. But there's just his dead weight.

Oh fok. Oh my lewe fok. No.

Wet faced. Sniveling. She sways over him. On her knees, swaying over him. For minutes. Long minutes.

And then she will drag, heft, stagger-carry his body back to the cottage. Panting with the effort. Sobbing.

"I can't fucking do this, Wynston."

Giving in to her grief, leaving his body, walking out into the night to scream. Then returning to lay him there on the cottage floor. To cover him with a blanket.

And in the coming hours she will sit on a hardback chair in the flickering candlelight. She will force herself to eat a sandwich, drink water. A foul taste in her mouth, cramps across her stomach. Her body tense, hurting, her ears alert for any change in the night sounds. The quieting of insects, the snap of a stick, the distant barking of a jackal. The infrequent hum of a car on the tar road.

She will look at Wynston's covered body often. If you had not left him, he would not be dead. You as good as pulled the trigger. You were careless. You were reckless. You cost this man his life. Which bends her over, gasping for air. Until that too quietens.

There are no tears now. There is the fact of his body. The fact of his gone life.

In the long dark night she will fall asleep. Always briefly. Her nodding head waking her. And nothing will have changed. The body under the blanket will still be there.

She will have other thoughts too. Thoughts on the consequences that will come from this. Abandoning a colleague.

Disobeying her suspension orders. Not reporting her intentions to a senior officer. Not immediately reporting the theft. There'll be disciplinaries, demotion, perhaps even dismissal. A punishment deserved.

But at the end of those thoughts there is Wynston: dead.

And the dawn will come. The slow brightening of the scrub, the long reach of the sky revealing the mountains. She will stand in the cottage doorway, looking out at this. Behind her the body of her colleague, Wynston. In her chest, the sadness. And the anger. And a pain. Sharp. Relentless.

47

"This is my favorite room," says General Duncan Maale, sliding open the glass door onto the deck. "Especially in the nighttime." He peers at the floodlit waterhole. "You see there are hippos on the bank. And there I see two jackals. The creatures of the night."

Colonel Kaiser Vula propels himself across the room. A room of trophies. On the walls the heads of buck. On the stone floor, zebra skins. Leopard pelts thrown over the settees. The settees are leather, grouped with them three wingbacks upholstered in a brown cloth. One wall is a glassed-in bookcase. In a corner, a bar beneath three elephant watercolors. Sunday paintings in Kaiser Vula's estimation. But still, the room smells of money. Which pleases Kaiser. And of an open fire. The coals burned down in the grate. Maale crouches to stoke the embers, pack on some logs. He straightens.

"Cognac or whisky?" he says.

"Cognac."

Maale pours two snifters. Hands one to Vula.

"To your new appointment as general in Police Intelligence. Do you accept?"

"Without hesitation. It would be an honor," says Vula.

"Then salut. And welcome."

The men clink glasses. Maale sits in one of the wingbacks.

"Good cognac, you agree?"

Vula says he does. His attention half on the general, half on the night sounds.

"French. Eight years in the oak barrels." He swirls the brandy, cups the glass in his hands, brings it to his nose. "Ah, the drink of the gods."

They drink again.

What else is this about? wonders Kaiser Vula. Wonders, too, was that a scrape of shoes on the wooden deck? Clears his throat, says, "I was surprised the minister wasn't present, General."

"She knows about our imbizo but she could not be here. She was to meet with the president about the insurrections last year. Maybe at last they will bring charges against the traitors. I don't know. We have given them our evidence, all the evidence General Mpungose collected. He was thorough. A dedicated comrade. Now it is up to the prosecutors." He pauses. "I am sure you are the right man for his vacancy in Police Intelligence, General. And this is what I will tell the minister on Monday. She will be most pleased to know that you have decided to come across. At the Aviary, you will leave a big hole, that is for sure, but here we welcome you." The general shifts forward.

From outside comes the distant howl of a jackal. Once. Twice.

Now it comes, thinks Kaiser Vula, his left hand tight on the wheel rim.

"Of course," says General Maale, "I have heard your story. There are many people who tell about the man who saved the president, but I have not heard it from you."

Ah, thinks Vula, the shadow of the past. He wants to know if I am still connected to the robber president and his insurrectionists.

"You were on his security unit, nè? The time that it happened, the shooting."

"Correct. Sometime earlier I was recruited to join the president's personal unit. Even on his trips to other countries, I was to accompany him."

"Do I recall, he had dealings in central African countries?"

"Yes." Kaiser Vula looking at the general, their eyes meeting. For the first time Vula seeing there a glint, a cunning. The man might be weak, but he is a general. He has survived. More than survived, attained a position. Says, "Mining. Diamond mining. And at his compound, he kept bees."

"Bees. How strange. I did not know that. I did hear some stories that he lived in a bunker."

"With a glass window onto a swimming pool."

General Maale laughs. "You will tell me next he had women swimming naked there."

"I could. He did."

"That is the truth?"

Vula nods. The truth is worse. The robber president had robbed him of his lover. A sexy woman later murdered. Where is Mpho? Why does he not act?

"Hoh! Man, I did not know that."

The head of Police Intelligence, yet so much he doesn't know. Or says he doesn't know.

"You worked for him despite these strange habits the former president had?"

Colonel Kaiser Vula raises his glass, takes a mouthful. Feels the warmth on his tongue, the fumes in his nostrils. Holds up a hand in supplication. "It is what we do, General, you will agree. Like you, I am a soldier. I obey orders."

Maale's eyes back on him. The man is a snake in the grass.

"Now you work for our president of the New Dawn? He has your allegiance."

"That is my duty."

"That is our duty." The general goes over to the bar, returns with the bottle of cognac. Pours for Vula before he tops up his own glass.

"Salut, again, General Vula."

General. He likes the sound of that. Then hears Maale asking once more for the story of his wounding. Which brings his attention back to the moment.

And Vula tells him, how at a feast within the presidential compound, the great chief had walked among his guests. His specifically invited guests. His supporters. All those he personally knew. What Colonel Vula leaves out is a specific detail. He does not mention the young woman walking with the president, the lovely Nandi, Nandipha Dlamini. The woman who had once been his. Who had been wooed away by the president. How he had walked behind them in a jealous rage but not blinded by his anger. He tells how he caught the assassin's eyes across the heads. Saw him lift the pistol, fire. How he leapt forward, took the killer's second shot in the chest. Which staggered him but he didn't drop. Took another shot in the stomach. Went down with that. Told about the chaos of screaming people. People fleeing, trampling him. Glass breaking, more gunshots. Does not mention that through it all, he heard the clear pitch of Nandi's howl. Tells how, from where he lay, he raised his own pistol, brought down the gunman.

"Extraordinary, comrade, absolutely an amazing story. You saved a head of state. The hitman was security, not so? An officer?"

"He was."

"So often the danger is within."

Vula says nothing. Tense. Straight backed in his wheelchair.

"I am pleased to have heard you tell the story, General. It is an honor." He pauses, cocks his head to listen. "Do you hear that?"

Vula shrugs. Could hear snorting from the waterhole. Says, "It is only animals."

"No. It sounded like something on the deck. I will check."

"I am sure it is nothing."

"Probably. But you never know in the bush." He gets up, goes to the open doors, peers out. Looks left and right. "No. Nothing. You are right, just animals. Perhaps I should close the doors. We do not want strange creatures sliding in here."

"It's fine," says Vula. "I like to hear the night sounds." All the same, shifts in the wheelchair to quickly access his pistol.

"Are you sure? Maybe you are right. We shut ourselves in buildings all the time. I think we have lost our touch with the wild places."

Maale returns to his chair. "That is why I like it here. To sit at night and watch the waterhole. That I find peaceful. But we are not here to talk about what we like. So, yes! Your story. You see, General, I am not so sure if we have such dedication still in our younger officers. I wonder, who would take a bullet for our New Dawn president?" He raises his glass to Vula. "Salut. I must say further accolades, that was good shooting to take down the assassin."

"It was a lucky shot."

"Perhaps. Perhaps you are being modest. That is also something we do not find much anymore in these days. Our young people are quick to say how wonderful they are. Such confidence. Such foolishness, do you not think?"

Vula doesn't say if he does or not. What puzzles him is the general's stance. A New Dawn man. Yet not critical of the robber president. So … a fence-sitter. A survivor. Relaxing there in the wingback, his crocodile-leather shoes toward the fire, his gaze on the flames.

"I have a proposition, General Vula." Again the pause, again the cocking of his head, a frown. "There! Did you hear that? Almost like, I would say, a scraping sound."

"I didn't," says Vula. "Perhaps it is a breeze through the branches."

General Maale stares at the open doors. At the glow of the floodlights over the waterhole. He comes back to Vula. Then flicks his eyes away to the fire.

"There is a matter of a situation you might find that you could support," he says. "It is nothing new. You could say it is like a stokvel, a sort of club. Or maybe like an investment on the stock exchange. But you do not have to buy shares. Your word is your support. And when there are profits, you are rewarded. This I can tell you"—he chuckles deeply, turns his head to grin at Vula—"there are always profits. What I mean is, for example, we could say that we could create a company that is compliant in all legal conditions that wins a tender for a project." His voice trails off. His eyes back on Vula.

"I understand," says Vula. Thinking, How interesting that the noble Maale is running a side business.

"Good, good. It is a small perk in our dangerous jobs. Do you not agree?"

Before Vula can respond, there is Sergeant Langa Mpho in the doorway. For a hammerman, how ridiculous he looks, thinks Vula. Slightly paunchy, too short, wearing camo fatigues. Only the silenced Ruger he holds isn't ridiculous. Held at shoulder level. Double-handed. Steady.

Vula hears Maale exclaim, an intake of breath. Says, "What—" Mpho fires.

Plop. Damn good silencer. Certainly no one could write "a shot rang out."

Vula swivels from Mpho to Maale. Sees the hitman has missed. Four yards at most, yet the guy has missed, the bullet splintering the wood paneling above the fireplace.

Maale drops to the floor, squirms away in a leopard crawl, his glass of cognac clutched in his fist.

Mpho steps in. At two yards, shoots down into Maale's back.

Plop. Good one. Misses the spine. Seems to have missed any vital organs the way Maale keeps up his leopard crawl, mewling. His cognac glass rolling away.

Mpho looks at Vula. Vula nods for him to fire again.

Mpho does. Twice.

Plop. Another back shot, which puts Maale flat on his stomach. Brings out a groan.

Mpho steps closer for a head shot.

Plop. From a yard out. As good as execution style. Maale's head exploding. Matter splatters on the floor, the walls.

Mpho looks again at Vula. Colonel Kaiser Vula raises his Taurus .38 revolver. Needs only one shot, through the mask out the back of Mpho's head. A fine red mist on the wood paneling. This time it could be said "a shot rang out."

Vula sighs. He had been a good man, Mpho. Perhaps overzealous occasionally. Occasionally even out of control. But he'd done what was asked of him. Without question. RIP Sergeant Langa Mpho.

Before he can dial the security detail, he hears boots in the corridor. A man crashes through the door, gun in hand. Wild eyes.

"Everything is under control," says Vula. "We were attacked. You need to secure the lodge compound. There may be more assailants."

PART TWO

Two Months Later

Mutual Love and Understanding

48

Early November. Midmorning on a sparkling ocean. Here's Zara
paddling, as if she's racing death. Her kayak cutting smoothly
through a glassy sea. Left stroke, right stroke. It's a double-blade
paddle, the blade going in, pulled back by her arm, a twist of her
body. This is how it's been since she launched at Three Anchor
Bay. Worked herself into a fast rhythm along the coast toward
Clifton. She's off the cliffs now, still caught in the rhythms of
her paddle. The splash of spray against her face, salt on her lips.
She's wearing gray Lycra shorts, a short-sleeved neoprene vest,
black; a red visor peak with her pony pulled through the Velcro
fastener. Not that there's much of a pony, given her hairstyle.
Above the slap of the sea, she can hear her phone ringing. Lets
it ring. She's not ready to stop her rush. Not ready to get back
into her mind where all the bogeymen lurk.

The ghost of Wynston: Where were you?

Ashton: You're a useless mother, a useless cop.

Vula: We need to talk.

Sithole: You have ruined my career.

Big D: I am not getting involved in this.

Hendricks: Enough, okay? Leave it.

Kutoka: I need protection.

Even her father: What has happened to you?

And Kyle: I don't want to go to Dad.

But also kinder voices.

Jo-Jo: You will get through this. I am here.

Elsi, her mother: I'm worried for you, Zara-sweet. So's your pa.

Janet: I's your help in the troubling times, Mrs. Z. I's your rod 'n' staff.

The ringing stops. She stops. Lets the kayak glide, resting the paddle on the coaming. Realizes then how heavily she's breathing. How her heart is pounding. You're out of training, girl. You need to get your puff back. Which is true. She hasn't been out since that long-ago day back in August. Before the world went dark. Before Wynston was shot. Before her life drained away. Even today took effort. If it wasn't windless, hot, she wouldn't have gone. If Janet hadn't said, "Jirre, Mrs. Z, jus go," she wouldn't have gone. If Janet hadn't said, "Instead of saying you should go jus go, man," and more or less forced her into her gear, shoved the paddle into her hands, pushed her out the front door—she wouldn't have gone.

"You gotta stop with the Wynston-morbies, Mrs. Z. Enough truly."

And maybe she was right. Wynston was dead. Only thing, he wasn't gone. You could hear him. Howzit, Cap. In the office you could catch a movement. A shadow. And turn, expectant. But face his absence.

Which was when Zara would sit at her desk, staring at the wall. Seeing it again: his body in the veld. His body under the blanket. Feel the tight pain in her chest.

But now you're here, Zara, on the sea, exhilarated by the fast, hard paddle, feeling the rush of blood through your body. Smiling for the first time in weeks. Smiling at the sheer joy of being out here. You can do this. You can go back. There are all the leads. You've just got to pick them up, follow through. Track them down until you get to the big guys. Easy. Well, not easy exactly. Takes dedication. Temerity. You've got that. Everyone knows the stubbornness. Zara the tenacious. Which convinces her. Okay, I will. Wynston, this is for you. I'll take them on.

She looks out to sea. At the empty horizon, remembers her phone rang. Fishes it out of the hatch. Unknown number. A Pretoria landline. Curious. Chances are, it's marketing spam. Curiosity wins. She taps the connect icon.

"Yes."

Not spam. A woman's voice.

"Who's this?" Zara asks.

Gets back: "Who are you?"

"You phoned me."

"I phone lots of people."

"Two minutes ago."

"Ah. Then perhaps this is Captain Dewane?"

"Who's asking?"

"Minister Majoro."

The Minister of Police.

Zara: For real? Says hesitantly, "Okay."

"Good. You don't trust this. Good. Certainly we can't talk on the phone. But listen, Captain, I shall be in Cape Town this afternoon and we can meet then. A car park. A beach front. Somewhere not too far from the city. At five o'clock. I will send you a cell number. WhatsApp me the place we should meet."

All very spookish.

"Okay," says Zara to dead air.

Wonders why Majoro would want to see her. The minister hardly an advocate for the ICU. Hardly, in a riven police force, the voice of reason, come to that. Majoro herself under investigation for inappropriate practices. Implicated in a scam about medical protection gear. Let alone the other stains on her CV: irregular expenditure, nepotism, comrade deployment, dodgy tender applications. The last person Zara wants on her side. The last person she wants to be seen with for that matter. Too many cops fallen under the boots of Minister Majoro. High-heeled ankle boots that'd given her kudos in the fashion columns. Elsewhere the nickname: pussy in boots. Which was more Zara's understanding.

The minister brings a decided unease. Every reason why answering unknown phone calls is a bad idea. You should've let it go. You're allowed some time out. Don't have to be at everyone's beck 'n' call. Especially while you're on suspension, cappie. Not beholden to anyone. Beholden's nice. She likes that. Such an old word. One of her mother's words. You're not beholden to Ashton. You're your own woman, Zara. You shouldn't have been with him. Ever.

The smartphone vibrates in her hand. A WhatsApp number for the minister. Oh, to be so honored by the high and mighty. Even in your own time on the sea.

Then another call: Advocate Josephine Lanski.

"Jo-Jo."

"Just bloody checking you've remembered about tomorrow."

"Why wouldn't I?"

"In your hectic life, could be a million reasons."

"I'm on suspension."

"And that makes a difference?"

Zara laughs.

"Where are you anyhow? Lots of static noise."

"About half a kay off Clifton."

"Are you bloody mad? There're sharks out there."

"Not a fin in sight. Couple of seagulls. Some cormorants. A seal I passed earlier. But no sharks. Sharks are all on land today."

"That's for bloody sure. Especially the ones circling you."

"Let them circle."

"Hey, don't be casual. This is serious. I want you cool, calm, and collected, Zara Dewane. Chilled."

"Ja, I know. Don't worry. What's all this about anyhow? What's with a meeting before the hearing?"

"They're calling it a preliminary discussion. That new general, Vula, he's fulla shit."

"I heard."

"Probably just a scare tactic. Don't get freaked. Be chilled."

"Yeah, sure. Chilled's my middle name. Alongside Eloise."

"Just don't say that, you hear me. No my lewe fok, Eloises, not even under your breath. Promise."

"Maybe."

"Not maybe. Definitely."

"Alright."

"Good. You'll be fine. Just let me do the talking, if you can. Gotta go now. See you tomorrow, 10:00 a.m. Got it?"

"Got it."

Zara stows the phone in the hatch, takes up the paddle, makes a slow turn back the way she's come. A certain reluctance in this. Because now reality's kicked in. Suddenly the going's harder, the sea running against her. Takes effort to clear her mind, put her arms into a rhythm. She pushes out Vula, Sithole, her ex, the minister. Focuses on the water ahead until she has become only body.

At the approach to Three Anchor Bay, she sees a kayaker heading toward her. Hears his cheerful "Haven't seen you for a while."

The guy from weeks back. She eases up. Digs in the paddle to stop.

"Haven't been out for a while."

"You should join us. It's more fun in a group."

"Oh yes, that's why you're alone?" Smiles at him.

He grins. His face animated. Even with the shades over his eyes, she can imagine the glint in them. "Sometimes you need to be alone." He shrugs, getting serious. "Listen, sorry about what's happened to you. That shooting. The attack. I read it in the newspapers weeks and weeks ago."

Which catches Zara by surprise. Remembers he knew her rank last time. "Have we met?"

"Nah. But I've seen you around. In court mostly."

"You're a lawyer? An advocate?"

"A lawyer. With the prosecuting authority."

"Ah ha! And you've got time out middle of the day, middle of the week?"

"Couple of days' leave. It gets to you sometimes, that office. The only way to handle it's to get into a different space."

She nods. "I know what you mean."

"The chaos. You've no idea, the chaos. Nobody can get anything done. There's no will. No proper system. Loads of information, actual stuff, hard evidence but no will to nail the buggers. Big names, but the president's got no balls."

Yeah, well, the what-can-I-tell-you moment. They both look off at the horizon. Nothing like salvation's going to come sailing up from the blue yonder.

Zara lifts her paddle. "Nice chatting."

"Sure," he says. "You up for a drink sometime?"

Not been one of those invites for a while. Another surprise. Likewise her response.

"Why not?"

And really, why not? The guy looks alright. He's a kayaker, nogal. They exchange cell phone numbers. His name's Jaco Cilliers. JC for short. He grins that boyish bashfulness. Lovely, thinks Zara.

"Nice boat," he adds. "You don't see them much around here."

"A Dagger Stratos, mostly US, UK," she says. "Bought it from a Brit a while back. It's like new."

They part. His last words: "I'll call you."

Zara thinking she could even hope he does.

49

From the promenade, a man watches the two kayakers. Leans on the railing as if he's enjoying the sunshiny day, come out to get some fresh air after a torrid meeting. He looks like a professional desk driver given the two-tone Skechers, pale chinos, a green golf shirt with an indistinct logo. Something in red and blue. Age? In his early fifties. Slim, gyms two or three times a week. Plays enough squash to keep his eye in. He's taking photographs with his phone. You'd think he was snapping scenic shots: the ocean, the splash of foam against the rocks, the flop of the kelp on the swells, ships in the roadstead, the distant line of Robben Island—you'd be wrong. He's framing the kayakers. Actually, only one of the kayakers: Zara Dewane. He zooms in for a portrait. A little fuzzy even for his iPhone but enough to show you she has a stunner smile, the flash of teeth. Enough to show you she likes talking to the kayaker guy. Which means he's also worth a few closeups. For the record. Because back at the office, in a laptop, there's a file of Zara Dewane photographs the iPhone photographer started two days ago. As part of his due diligence. He stays there taking the odd snap. Watches the kayakers part, Zara paddle to shore, stow her boat, walk to her car, drive away. He doesn't follow. He doesn't have to. He knows where she lives. Also, he's fixed a tracker to her car. And put spyware on her smartphone. All thanks to Pegasus, the non-click wonder.

50

Breakfast in the Vula house.

"I am worried," says Lady Vula. She looks it, standing there beside the table. Frown lines across her brow. A slight tremble to her hands. She's in sweats, trainers. The general's in his full police getup. On the table before him, a plate of pap and sausages. A health smoothie—almond milk, frozen strawberries, spinach from the garden, chia seeds—in a long glass at Lady Vula's setting. She lifts it, you can see the tremble. Sips. Puts it down. A slight smudge of pink on her upper lip.

General Vula glances up at her, puzzled. "You cannot be worried. There is no need to think dark thoughts."

Lady Vula touches her lips with a napkin. "There is Captain Dewane. There is Sergeant Kutoka. There is even Captain Hendricks."

"Ah man. What problems can they be?" Vula cuts the sausage into bite-sized chunks. Forks up a mouthful with white porridge. Talks through the food. "The minister is with me. All the police are with me. Captain Hendricks is my colleague. Captain Dewane is nothing. Soon she will be off the radar. Finished." He swallows. "Sergeant Kutoka! I have plans for him. He will be ..." Kaiser Vula clicks his fingers. "Gone."

"You should be wary of Captain Hendricks. That woman knows too much."

"She knows some things, she does not know everything. Also, you have heard what they say about having skin in the game. Captain Alicia has much skin in the game. She likes it. She likes what it does to her bank balance. This is why she is no problem."

"You will still have to watch her."

"I am watching everyone. Luna will tell me if there are dangers in the shadows."

"Luna, Luna, Luna. Always Luna."

"Because she can see."

"I should not have told you about Luna."

"Bah! Why not? Because of Luna we made the right actions. Look where we stand now. Only eight weeks and we are flying. You have invitations, too many to accept every one. We have been for dinner to the president's Tuinhuis. We meet with ambassadors. We can move to a bigger house. This is what you wanted."

"But you see too much of Luna. If she was not a white woman, I would think you went for phata phata."

General Vula laughs. Heaps more pap and sausage onto his fork. "I have you for phata phata."

"But even that is not the same."

He eats, chews, looking at his wife. "It is this time we live in. You are depressed by the global problems. You are feeling trapped. But there must be things to do. There is Dubai. You can do shopping in Dubai. Or you can cruise. There are ministers' wives who cruise. To Mauritius. To Madagascar. There are these islands for cruises."

"Without you."

"Ah, my true, you know it is too difficult for me to leave, I have a new position. There are things to be done. You know what the robber president did. You know of the state-capture project. This is what we must now end for the New Dawn."

"But you will not cruise with me?"

"I will join you."

"You promise you will come?"

"Of course."

"After you are tired of Luna."

"Enough with Luna. Luna is my counsel. My advisor. I need Luna to tell me what is coming."

Lady Vula holds out her trembling hand. "Look at me, Kaiser. You see how I am shaking. It is because I am nervous. I am anxious. We have done bad things. The ancestors see us."

Vula finishes his meal, points at the coffee pot. "Will you pour?"

She does. Even though her hand is unsteady. She spills down the side of his cup.

"Ah man, you have messed."

"You see, it is what I'm telling you. I can't do this anymore, Kaiser. Their deaths won't leave me. I have nightmares." She puts down the coffee pot. Runs sobbing from the room.

"You need to gym," he shouts after her. "It will make you feel better." Hears her slam a door closed.

The woman has changed. Before she cracked the whip; now she spills the coffee. Before she was firm; now she wails. So quickly it has happened, as if she has been bewitched. Cursed. Depression, the doctor calls it. Prescribes medicine that makes no difference. You need a holiday, the therapist advises. Hence the cruise. "Something different to take your mind off this worry." The worry. The deaths, the killings, she keeps talking about. Obsessing about.

"Maale, Maale. He is everywhere."

"Langa Mpho, Langa Mpho. I cannot stop seeing his face."

"It is a witching," Luna tells him. "Her ancestors are troubled."

"A psychotic state," the psychiatrist diagnoses. "I recommend she be committed."

A psychotic state that has her sleepwalking at night. Whimpering that she smells blood. Once washing her hands in Dior perfume. Sprinkling it about the room. Another time tapping nonsense into her phone. The woman has lost her mind. She is mad.

Ah man, ah man.

He drinks what's in the cup, wheels himself through to the lounge where his driver waits.

"Time to go," he says. There are matters to sort out. There are intelligence reports to read. There are cabinet ministers who need to know that he, General Vula, is watching.

Also, he needs to get away from the lunacy of his wife.

He doesn't call out goodbye to her. She wouldn't hear him anyhow.

The general on his ride into the city. Writing WhatsApps on his phone. Sending emails, messages, making posts.

To the Minister of Police: *There is talk of unrest in the Zulu province. Suggest up visible presence. Arrests.*

To the Commissioner of Police: *Talk of discontent among the chieftains. Suggest indaba. Recommend budget cuts to the traditional leaders. Tighter handouts.*

To the director, State Security Agency: *Threat of unrest by unregistered aliens/foreign nationals/bogus refugees. Will lead to xenophobic outbreaks. Suggest deportations. Arrests.*

To Captain Alicia Hendricks: *My office 2:00 p.m.*

On Facebook as Afrojo: *What's with the Cubans. Send them home.*

On X as @assegai: *The president is weak. When comes the new dawn?*

On Instagram as @hardboy: Photographs of hungry children.

Browses Google: SAPS gun thefts. A page of links. Puts out emails with links to all Police Intelligence heads: Authenticate. Corroborate. Name names, ranks. List offending police stations. Describe the situations. This is Top Secret. Non-disclosure. My eyes only.

Looks out the window at the traffic. Thinks of Luna Maplewood. In his head, the Rolling Stones singing "Let It Bleed." General Kaiser Vula taps his fingers, unsure why that song now.

To his driver, says, "What's happening, chief?"

His driver gives the daily briefing: poached abalone movements; the ratlines of tik (that wondrous crystal meth the youth so love); cash heists in the making; demands for weaponry; coming gang fights.

"And what of Tamora Gool?"

"Nothing there, boss," he says. "Mouse quiet."

"Keep listening, chief, I need you."

51

Captain Alicia Hendricks glances at her smartphone clipped to the console. The bright face of Duifie on the screen. Brushing her teeth.

"You mustn't let him bully you," Duifie says. "That para just takes advantage of being legless."

Captain Hendricks has to laugh. Says, "Don't talk like that."

They're speaking in Afrikaans. Mother tongue for both of them.

Since Duifie flew into Alicia's life, it's been a jol. Fun and laughter where before was anger, disappointment. It's love, Duifie tells her. That's all you needed. Maybe so because it's now four weeks since Alicia stopped smoking. At Duifie's request. Ja, well, stopped smoking more or less. She's got an emergency packet for tense moments in her bag. Tense moments usually involving legless General Kaiser Vula. Okay, blerrie nice that he's got her out of Saldanha. Blerrie ass-end of the world that was. Very lekker to be fast-tracked. Nothing sexier than Police Intelligence. You get respect. A tidy office. Most importantly, you don't deal with rubbish: no drunks, no battered women, no berserk men. Best of all you get to know what's what. You get to see who's stealing. (Mostly everyone in government, it turns out.) Which means you can write up insurance against each one.

Against the day you need to file a claim. Alicia's good at that. She's got files opening up: Minister of Police, Commissioner of Police, Director-General of Police, generals, brigadiers, majors, etc. etc. Top of the list? General Kaiser Vula.

"So you're gonna be okay, skattie?" says Duifie.

"Ja, ja. I'm fine. Why're you brushing your teeth?"

"I ate cilantro. It mos looked like parsley. You know how awful it is. Like eating dead people."

"Ja, of course, you've eaten dead people?"

"If I had, this's what it would taste like."

"Aggenee. Dhania's tops."

"Go slay the dragon, liefie," says Duifie in English. "You're gonna be late if you don't hurry."

"I'm parking," says Alicia. "The oke can wait five minutes."

Turns out the oke has to wait ten minutes. The oke isn't pleased. When Captain Alicia Hendricks walks in, General Kaiser Vula taps his wristwatch, says, "Not good, Captain. Not good."

"You know," says Captain Hendricks, settling into a chair, "Cape Town traffic. What can I say?" Pleased with herself for not kowtowing. Can hear Duifie's giggled "Nice one, girl."

The general glares at her. "You saw Gool?"

"I've just come from her."

"And?"

"She can take the consignment."

"She can!" His voice raised. "What does she mean 'she can'? This woman thinks she's doing us a favor? There are others who would jump high for this. Maybe we should tell Gool to go fuck herself." Doesn't end there, the diatribe going on about the woman's attitude, her demands, her ingratitude, ending with "Who's she? A damned gangster. A lowlife."

Hendricks waits it out. Wonders how the general's going to take the next bit.

He stops. Raises his hands. "So?"

"We have agreed she will make the collection at our storage

facility." Hendricks likes that "our storage facility." The "facility" is a storeroom in a row of storerooms in a suburban industrial estate. One side a carpet dealer, the other a pool doctor's stock of chemicals. The collection would have to be daytime, in plain sight.

"Of course she will make it at our place. Does she think we will deliver too? Does she want a pizza delivery?"

One thing about Vula that puzzles Alicia Hendricks is his temper. Never good. Since the brass went on his shoulders, even worse.

"What about the payment?"

"In diamonds."

"What the hell! Uh uh. No ways in hellfire. We do not take diamonds. Diamonds are big trouble. You try to get rid of diamonds, you have too many problems. You told her cash."

What Alicia Hendricks had said to Tamora Gool was, "Maybe. The general likes money."

What Tamora Gool had said to Alicia Hendricks was, "Take it or leave it."

Which Alicia thought was ballsy tactics. Come on! No ways she'd turn down the weaponry stock. On the street, that stock was worth double their asking price.

But Tamora Gool had held her position. "That's what I'm offering, sisi. Your call."

Alicia Hendricks had said, "I'll get back to you."

"Like when, sisi?"

"Like soon enough."

Which was where negotiations ended.

Now General Kaiser Vula says, "You are telling me she is going to walk away. This gangster is going to say goodbye to serious pink money. No. You are joking. She is joking. You tell her no money, no boxes."

"I have."

"Tell her again. Go now, Captain. Sort it. We are not taking diamonds."

52

He's standing among the parents when Zara picks up Kyle from school. He could be another dad in the waiting knot. He's so close he can smell her. The orange fragrance of her shampoo, the soft jasmine of her deodorant. He likes the secret of being near her. He knows her; she doesn't know him. He steps back as Zara swings round, an arm across her son's shoulders. Hears her say, "How'd you like to do some skateboarding later?" And then they're gone. On his phone, he watches them drive home. Goes back to his office in Woodstock, not far from her home, actually. He has other clients to attend to. Phone calls to make chasing debts. He's good at debt collection. Never threatens. Never has to. Well, never threatens directly. Merely lays out the option that if the debt isn't settled by a certain date, then ... dot, dot, dot. The rest doesn't have to be said explicitly. What he does say is he's a shield, a shield protecting the debtor. Says no one wants the loan shark to get upset. Loan sharks are tough buggers. Merciless. Much better the money's paid back so that phone calls don't have to be made, you understand? Mostly people do understand. Occasionally he's even put up the bucks himself. For a price, obviously. But the gratitude's immense, everyone overlooks the commission. Because bongo-bongo is the final option, an option no one wants. Bongo-bongo means the loan shark doesn't get paid. Also means there's one less borrower in the market. The way the man says "bongo-bongo" so sadly, everyone hears a bell toll. So while debt collecting's his main occupation—even corporations use him—he has an international sideline in bongo-bongo. The tally's rising in that sector. Mostly he works in Africa. Some Latin American jobs. One in India. Two in Taiwan. One in the US, one in the UK, a sprinkling (five) throughout Europe, including the Scandinavian countries. He doesn't mind travelling but prefers working at home. Which is why it's wonderfully convenient that Zara's just up the hill. No more than five minutes away. The moment she moves her car, he can be on her tail. Also, she's a good-looking broad. There are various possibilities.

53

Kyle can't believe his luck. The Battery Park skateboard zone. He's only been there once before, and that was with a friend's family. He's out of the car, running ahead of Zara, shouting, "I can't believe it. I can't believe it." Rushes back to his mother. Hugs her. With Zara calling out, "Be careful."

She finds a bench where she can watch him. And wait.

Wait for Minister Majoro.

"Good choice," had been the minister's response to Zara's suggestion of a meeting place.

Five after five, Minister Majoro sits down beside Zara. Lets out a sigh.

"This is very pleasant." She waves at a boy propelling himself toward a concrete ramp. "He is most happy."

"He's not the only one," says Zara, pointing out Kyle. She's surprised the woman's dressed much as she is, casually in jeans and a long-sleeved shirt. She also has a flimsy blue scarf draped round her neck. Her feet are not in ankle boots but open sandals. Elegant feet. Thin ankles. Polished toenails.

"Straight to the point, Captain: I don't like what's going on. I disagree with your suspension. I disagree with shutting the door on the Internal Crime Unit. I certainly don't like what's happening inside Police Intelligence. Most specifically, I disagree with the department being located in Cape Town. Of course there should be a strong presence here, but the centers of insurrection are KwaZulu and Gauteng. That is where we need attention. Look, Sithole was useless as head of ICU. If he hadn't been retiring, I might have pushed him in that direction. But no, ICU is not good. To clean up the cops, to make our people trust cops again, we need the ICU. Even the president knows this. Unfortunately he is a weak man. He cannot go against our new General Vula."

The minister pauses, waves at her son. "Your boy is good. My Sipho needs more practice."

"He's doing okay," says Zara, giving a thumbs-up to her son; wondering where the minister is going.

"So, here's the thing, as my colleagues say, I have no call to action. I have lost support in cabinet. I cannot get your disciplinary hearing to go away. The president is careful not to take my side. He will not fire me, he doesn't fire anyone, but his eyes will not look at me. But I am still a cabinet minister. I still have some controls. Of budgets. Of people. There are those I trust. There are those who trust me. What I am going to ask you is off the books. Just between us. Yes?"

"Could be," says Zara. "Depends."

The minister laughs. "Always cautious. Okay, Captain, what do I want? Let's see," she holds up her left hand, counts off on her fingers, "Support. Information. Insight. Confidentiality. Commitment. In return, I'll try to get the ICU up again. I'll try to get you as commander of the Cape Town unit. Try. That's the best I can do. Try. No guarantees. Just an intention."

"Alright."

"So, the crunch. I need an investigation into General Vula. I need to know about him. Everything. His habits, his relationship with his wife, his income, where he banks, who he sees. Who his friends are. Who his enemies. As I said, not official, off the books, quietly, quietly. I am asking you if you can do it for me. Help me. I am worried about this general."

Zara thinking she could already tell the minister a thing or two about this general. But doesn't. Doesn't mention the name Exit Kutoka. Keeps his revelations to herself. Because, like all politicians, this minister is not to be trusted.

"I have a discretionary budget, Captain. Funds for strategic operations. What I am saying is we can mutually help each other. I know you are on suspension without pay. That is tough. When the money does not come in, that is tough. Perhaps you have savings, but I can tell you these people will delay your hearing.

They want to make you desperate for money. Maybe you have to borrow money. Maybe you have to take money out of your bond to live. Maybe you have to sell your house. That is how it will go. Believe me, they will knock you down. What I am saying is I could help. We could help each other."

"Why do you think this general is a problem?" Zara's half-turned toward the woman to catch any facial flicker.

A long pause while the minister watches her son. "This is a wonderful place for children. Such freedom to do their thing." Then: "You know about the killing of General Maale?"

"Yes."

"You know that this Sergeant Mpho was the assassin?"

"Yes." Zara thinking she also knew a lot more about Langa Mpho she could divulge.

"You know that Vula was there when this happened?"

"Yes. He had to shoot Mpho out of self-defense, is what I heard."

"That is the story. And that is what I find strange. This man Mpho was there as Vula's security. To me, there is something wrong here. It is too confusing. Do you not think so? Why would Mpho want to shoot Vula as well? It is too strange."

Thoughts Zara has had but not mentioned to anyone. Not even to Jo-Jo. And is not going to say so now.

"I have found out that General Maale planned to make General Vula his number two at Police Intelligence. And then suddenly Maale is dead and Vula is in charge. This man in a wheelchair who was once a top spy for the robber president is now a general in Police Intelligence. I do not like it, Captain. I fear for what is going on. I fear for our country. Maybe even our current president is a target."

Perhaps a bit dramatic, Zara thinks, but then, the woman is a politician.

"Think about it, Captain," she says, for the first time turning toward Zara. "If you can help me, I will help you." Their eyes meet. Zara puzzled that this woman with the dubious reputation should look so beguiling. So open, so confidential. "One other thing. Do you know of some white sangoma called Luna Maplewood?"

"No, I don't. Who is she?"

"Some witch the general has been seeing. Perhaps for reasons other than fortune-telling." She laughs. "But don't quote me." Their gaze meets again. There is no laughter in the minister's eyes now. "Please, remember, you are not alone. We are not alone. But others are afraid. We must show them." With that, stands, holds out her hand. Zara rises; they shake. "I am sorry about your colleague, Warrant Officer Adams. My condolences."

"Yes," says Zara. "He is a great loss." More than that, she's thinking, he's the black mark on my conscience. My shame.

Minister Majoro nods. "I understand. Thank you for meeting with me, Captain." With her free hand, gestures at the surroundings. "This is so much better than an office." Then calls her son, and the boy comes, complaining.

Zara watches them leave, stays on for another twenty minutes. Her thoughts a confusion of what she's been told. She waves Kyle in.

"We've gotta go, boykie."

"Ah, Ma."

But he comes. And they leave with her arm around his shoulders. Kyle saying, "Did you see my kick turns? Did you see my tic-tacs?"

"Rad," she says. Thinking: You better swot the terminology, mommy. And is about to ask him what's a tic-tac when her phone rings.

"Ma!"

"Where are you, Zara-sweet?"

She tells her.

"Oh that's nice. So good for you both. Listen, I'm at your place but I'm not waiting. I've brought you some pickled fish. I'll leave it on the stoep out of sight."

Her mother's pickled fish is to die for.

"Isn't Janet there?"

"It's for you and Kyle."

Her mother, never quite sure how to deal with Janet. Causes Zara to smile, shake her head.

"She might eat some, you never know."

54

He watched the woman and her boy. They drove away like any mother and son. He wondered who she was. She looked familiar, he thought he should recognize her. Maybe she was someone from television. A minor celebrity, perhaps? Some big shot's wife? He gave the foxy Zara a last look, then followed the unknown woman in her BMW. Out of the city to the suburb of Rosebank. The posh Rygersdal apartment block. He knows the place. It's been remodeled for cabinet ministers. All the upmarket touches added. Luxury living for the high and mighty. But an apartment nonetheless. No wonder the woman needed to give her son somewhere to run around, get some exercise. Yet did it without security guys. Interesting, he thinks. Pulls over to the curb to flick through images of top politicians on his phone. There she is: Minister of Police, Lebo Majoro.

55

"This is a surprise. Twice in one day. People will think we are lovers." Tamora Gool to Captain Alicia Hendricks. They're at the Blouberg Beach parking strip. A compromise last-minute rendezvous. This late hour of a fine afternoon. The strip is packed with cars. Alicia lucky to find a space at the circle end. On the beach, walkers, joggers, families. For her, way too many people. But needs must.

Tamora Gool leaning against her shiny M5. Relaxed and casual. Seems she's just back from a run. Water bottle in hand. Towel around neck. Sweaty T-shirt. Cropped Lycra leggings. Bare feet. Green varnished toenails. Actually, Alicia Hendricks has to admit, sexy. Especially with that scar on her face. Gives her an exotic look.

Alicia Hendricks says, "Let's walk." Kicks off her shoes, heads for the beach.

Tamora Gool right with her. "You wanna hold my hand?"

Alicia Hendricks ignores her, says, "Get serious. This is serious."

"Ooh la la, I can hear."

"So, his thing is he doesn't want payment in diamonds. It's no deal."

"No, man, what's his case?"

"He wants cash."

"We talked about this."

"I know."

"You said diamonds were good."

"I know."

"You said diamonds were better."

"Yes. But, end of the day, it's not my call. You know that. He's the boss."

"Shit, man! This makes it difficult. That's a lotta cash to raise. I'm not some bank."

They walk in silence.

Then Tamora Gool: "There's another way."

"Tell me."

"I take the stock. You get the diamonds. We know how much Wheelchair Man wants. You go to your guy for an evaluation. The diamonds'll be more than the price."

"You reckon."

"Guaranteed. Next, you find a buyer to pay out the cash. You take a commission, give Wheelchair Man his share of the cash. Everyone's happy. You especially."

"Why don't you sell the diamonds; give me the cash."

"Hey, Captain, look at me." They stand at the water's edge, doing the face to face. "This is a favor. Anyhow, I don't need more shit in my life like dealing with a diamond dealer."

"So it's okay for me to deal with a diamond dealer?"

"You're a cop. You've got powers. Don't you get it? What I'm saying is here's a chance for you to make a bit more cash. I'm doing you a solid."

"What if I don't want the favor?"

"You're going to kiss off a hundred grand?"

Captain Alicia Hendricks thinks about this. It's a lotta bucks. You can go a long way with that kind of moolah.

"That's what I'm offering, from the goodness of my heart, sweetheart."

"Why? Why'd you want to give away money?"

"So we can stay friends. Because there's gonna be lots more of these situations. We have to play nice."

They walk on. Alicia Hendricks thinking that, for a gangster, Tamora Gool has some unusual traits. Like, handling their trades as normal business. Bringing it down to a basis of trust. Prompts her to ask: "How do I know how much the diamonds are worth?"

"Trust me."

Alicia Hendricks snorts.

Gets a laugh from Tamora Gool. "Yes, what the poes, I wouldn't trust you either. Except I do. How about we go this way: you take the diamonds, get a valuation. Then we arrange the stock collection."

"Ah! You're going to trust me?"

"Why not? Like I said, you're a cop." Another laugh. "Listen, chickie, I know about Duifie. I know where Duifie's ma and pa hang out. You shaft me, I shaft Duifie. Pimple simple. That's how we do it, Captain. Mutual love 'n' understanding."

Sends a cold anger through Alicia Hendricks. She grabs Tamora Gool's arm, pulls her off balance. "You touch her ..."

"Hey, hey, slow down, soldier, slow down." Tamora yanks herself free. "I'm not gonna touch her. I'm just saying. Putting you on the level so you know. Everything transparent. I see you. You see me."

They stare at one another, then Alicia Hendricks turns back to face the sea, the mountain across the bay.

"Alright. You give me the diamonds. When?"

That cynical laugh from Tamora Gool. "Right now, sisi. Right now. They're in my car."

Like, who rides around with a parcel of diamonds in their car? In this city of thieves. Hot diamonds, in addition. They walk back in silence. At the BM, Tamora Gool takes a packet from the glove box.

"All yours."

But when Alicia Hendricks puts her hand on the packet, Tamora Gool doesn't let go.

"A small favor."

"Now what?"

"Two firearm licenses."

"You've got to be joking."

Tamora Gool releases the packet. "Careful with those. I'll send you the details for the guns."

"I don't do firearm licenses."

"Nothing you can't do, my sista. Look where you've got yourself in seven, eight weeks. You're a rising star. Also, not like I'm not gonna pay you. On top of the diamonds. You're talking a winning streak. Ride it."

Captain Alicia Hendricks spins away. Jesus, the woman has cheek. Then again, she feels the stones in the packet, she has the hot rocks. Maybe take Duifie for a weekend up the West Coast, see Big D for an evaluation, maybe sort out the firearm licenses at the Saldanha station.

Why not?

Yeah, why not?

56

General Kaiser Vula lies on Luna Maplewood's bed. She lies next to him. He has been there an hour, for an appointment on his way home. Which can happen two or three times a week. Because the trouble with Luna Maplewood is that Kaiser Vula finds her desirable. Has found her increasingly desirable. Over the weeks he's been consulting her, desire has become lust. Which Lady Vula has intuited. The woman she once called a sangoma is now a witch. She has called her a bitch witch to his face. But the general is not bothered by his wife's distress. His focus is on his advisor. She predicted his future. She can warn about his enemies. Hers is the voice he listens to.

He runs a hand over her thigh, over a skin so translucent he can see the blue veins of her life. She lifts his hand to her lips.

"You must go, General," she says. "You have a wife." She says it playfully, a smile in her tone.

He wonders if she has any feelings for him. Or is she simply hyped by his power?

He is compelled to ask: "Why are we here? In your bed?"

"Because this is what we both want?" she says, swinging her legs off the bed, standing. "You came to me."

"That first time," he says, "when suddenly you rushed out, why was that? What did you see?"

"Shadows," she says from the bathroom. "A man with so many shadows."

"What do you mean 'shadows'?"

"Figures I could not see. They were vague; I could not see their faces."

"And now?"

"Now I am used to them. I have realized they reveal themselves when they are ready. And when I can see their faces, I tell you. You know this."

"I do. But my wife is worried that others are plotting against me."

Luna is back in the bedroom, dressing.

"You are a man of power, Kaiser. Of course others are plotting against you. It would be foolish not to think this."

"Who?"

"I will tell you when I know. When I can see their faces. At the moment they are shadows. Even the closest one."

He watches her zip her jeans, wiggle her feet into sandals. She is a graceful woman. He thinks of her as an antelope, quick, skittish, alert to a world he cannot see or hear. Yet since their relationship moved to the bed, she has changed. At first she was obliging, not freaked by his cummerbund and pouch, adventurous even, but lately he has sensed a resolve in her, as if she is saying goodbye. And she is harder. More forthright. Brings up a violence in him. The urge to hurt, to hit her.

Now she switches on a light, gathers his uniform from the floor, dumps it on the bed. Helps him dress. He will shower at home.

"I need something for Lady," he says. His torso is muscular. He imagines it excites her to dress him.

"Ask her to see me."

"She won't come."

"Why not? She was the one who brought you to me."

She eases his underwear up his legs, then his trousers, lets him zip himself closed. "You know why."

She sighs, swears beneath her breath. "There was no need for her to know. This is a pity."

"She has women's intuition." He buttons his shirt, tucks it in at his waist.

"You should have been more careful."

"It is not of such importance. We have been through this before. We are still married."

Luna shakes her head. "What sort of something does she need?"

"Something to calm her. She is anxious, depressed. She is worried. Before, she was strong with ambition. But that is all gone. Now she sees ghosts everywhere. Washes her hands as if they are stained. I cannot live with her like this. It will drive me mad."

She draws socks over his feet. Laces his shoes. Straightens his tie. In five minutes, he has become General Kaiser Vula. She pulls him into the wheelchair, leads him out of the bedroom to her consulting room. From a cupboard takes a bottle of powder.

"You must have patience with Lady. It is not easy for her. A pinch of this is enough," she says, "in a small glass of water." Holds out the bottle. "Obviously, she knew you would be here today?"

"You are my advisor. My clairvoyant. I need to consult you. Of course she knew I would be consulting you today." He takes the bottle. "Where is your Nurse September? She is never here anymore."

"She is here. So is my intern. She has her own room."

"Why didn't I know of this arrangement?"

"Why should you, Kaiser? It is my business."

"I thought we were alone."

"I have told you we are never alone. The shadows are always around us."

He stares at her. Such a slight woman, yet she can say these things to him. She should be afraid of him. "You should be afraid of me," he says.

"Why on earth?" She smiles at him, playfully. "I can disappear in the click of my fingers, my dear General. And then you will never see me again."

Among the Dead Creatures

57

Another day of endless blue.

There's a whisper of a breeze in the air that will build through the hours. Could be gale force by nightfall. The return of the southeast trade. For days on end, until nerves fray in the haze and dust.

But that's for later.

Now it's 10:00 a.m. in the city center.

More precisely in a building fronting the parliamentary precinct. In a room at the mountain end of the building, a view of the flat top through the window. No cloud wisping there yet. Says something about your status when you get this view.

"Why here?" says Captain Zara Dewane to advocate Josephine Lanski. "This isn't even a cop building. This is where some of the State Security spies from the Aviary hang out."

"Not so loud." Jo-Jo glances round at the open door. "The general may be relocating Police Intelligence."

Hardly news to Zara but she plays along. "That's quick. Into the spooks?"

"Seems like it. At least to be near them."

"And the cops're okay with this?"

Except the minister, of course.

"Not at all. Bloody unhappy. But the Prez is centralizing the security services."

"Old Moonface? He's doing that? How cunning."

"Bloody hell, Zara. Keep it down."

"So Vula's got his backing for this move?"

"That's the talk."

My lewe fok!

Remembers she'd agreed, no mention of Eloise. Looks round the room.

They're sitting at a long table, water jug in the middle on a silver tray, two glasses their side, two glasses opposite. Not much else in the room except a row of six chairs against the one wall. Above them photographs of the democratic presidents, except the one that would be the robber president is facing the wall. He's the one Vula took the bullet for. Against the other wall is a collection of dead birds in a display cabinet. The birds perched on branches, or dangling from a thread, wings wide. Above them is a map of the country patched from the skins of small mammals. Who sews up maps like that? Zara's thinking if it's a metaphor, then Vula's making a point about being the apex predator. Which, if Exit Kutoka's right, means the guy's a walking psycho. Or rather a mobile psycho.

Zara bends her head to Jo-Jo. Says in a whisper, "Remind me, I've gotta tell you about a guy called Exit Kutoka."

"Tell me now."

"Not enough time. Later."

Because there's the buzz of an electronic wheelchair, the clop of approaching heels in the corridor. Enter General Kaiser Vula, behind him, Captain Alicia Hendricks. Both in full uniform. Shoulder decor gleaming. Zara, like Jo-Jo, is business smart. Captain Hendricks closes the door.

Zara and Jo-Jo stand.

"Sit, sit," says the general. "This is informal. You are excused being out of uniform, Captain Dewane. However, the proceedings are for the record, you understand."

"I was told this was a preliminary discussion," says Jo-Jo. "Not for the record."

General Vula maneuvers behind the desk, slaps down a file. Smiles at Jo-Jo. "A preliminary discussion, exactly. Then perhaps afterwards we will not need a disciplinary hearing at all. I believe in talking, Ms. Lanski. It is what you lawyers do, am I not correct? By talking we can work out our differences. We can compromise. Find a way forward. That is what we are here to do for your client, find a way to better our service delivery. For that we need to be on the record. However, for the purposes of this discussion we will ignore the gross violation of your client breaking her suspension."

"Noted," says Jo-Jo.

Vula shifts his gaze to Zara. "I believe you know Captain Hendricks, one of your successors at Saldanha Bay police station?"

Zara nods.

"Good. She is now working for Police Intelligence. So. If you are settled, let's begin." He pulls some sheets from the file, taps them. "I have your statement, Captain Dewane. But I would like to inquire if you would elaborate. This would give us"—gestures at Captain Hendricks—"some context. A background to these incidents. Without this, we are walking in a dark wood." Again he consults his papers. "You say you and the late Warrant Officer Wynston Adams were at the Malgas cottage to apprehend anyone who came to collect the weaponry cached there."

Zara doesn't respond to his quizzical expression.

"How did you know there were weapons stored there? You don't give this information in your statement."

"Because I didn't know."

"Then why did you go out to this place? I don't understand. You must have known something. No one would drive all that way for nothing."

"I took a chance. It was as simple as that. Detectives' intuition."

"That is not good enough."

Zara shrugs. "I have no other explanation, General. We knew that once before weaponry had been stored there. Captain Hendricks can confirm this. Our checking was routine." Certainly wasn't going to tell him about the death threats from Mpho, or that Hendricks was the real reason for going out there.

"You could have asked Captain Hendricks to check. She was much closer. Only twenty minutes away. She could have sent a van."

"My preference is to do my own donkey work, General. I might have been bothering Captain Hendricks for no good reason."

The general shakes his head, drums his fingers on the documents. "I find this most irregular, Captain."

"Except, General," says Jo-Jo, "you have to admit, the captain's 'intuition'"—she gives the scare quotes—"proved accurate. It is one of the measures of a good detective, do you not admit, that they can act on hunches? No one was inconvenienced and my client found an illegal stash of weaponry. Weaponry that, as it turned out, had been heisted from a police van that morning. If we did not have dedicated police people like her, where would we be?"

"You should have reported to me," interjects Captain Hendricks. "That was my policing region."

Before Zara can respond, Jo-Jo says, "Admittedly, that was an oversight, Captain."

Hendricks: "We could have put security out there. Warrant Adams might not have been shot."

Vula: "That is what your client's intuition led to, Ms. Lanski, the killing of Warrant Officer Wynston Adams. We must not forget this. Had Captain Dewane followed proper procedure, he would be alive now. We would not be here now."

Zara doesn't respond, motions to Jo-Jo with a flick of her fingers to let it go. But her face tightens, a heavy grief in her chest.

"And something else," says General Vula, "that I find odd." Looks up from the documents before him, stares at Zara. "Why did you expect someone would come to collect the weapons that weekend?"

"It seemed ..." She clears her throat. "It seemed logical."

"Logical? I'm sorry, how? We are talking about a remote

cottage on the West Coast. Surely as secure a place as any for thieves to cache weapons?"

"The shed had been used before. My sense was that the cottage was a temporary storage. Possibly a frequently used facility."

"Your sense! Intuition! Hunches! Police work needs facts and information, Captain. Hard evidence. Womanly instinct is not exactly science."

"Yet it proved correct, General." Jo-Jo putting a hand on Zara's arm as if to restrain her. Not that Zara needs restraining. She has nothing to say to the general's taunting.

"Luck," he says. With Zara half listening, her gaze on the mountain, wishing she was paddling into the ocean. The sea would be flat. The southeaster not noticeable yet on the Atlantic. She should be there. Instead she's here: pilloried. With her hand in her pocket, rubbing the bullet casing she'd picked up at the cottage. The bullet that'd done for Wynston. Her thoughts distracted until she catches Vula saying, "Your statement is not very detailed on why you left the warrant officer alone while you went off. It is this action which leads to the tragic eventuality."

As well Zara knows. As she has been torturing herself these past months. If only she hadn't gone. If only she hadn't stayed away so long.

"Perhaps you can enlighten us, Captain Dewane."

No. He's dead isn't he! Isn't that enough?

"A break, General," says Jo-Jo. "I need a smoke."

58

General Kaiser Vula watches the three women leave the room. Nice asses all of them. Smaller than Lady's but well-shaped. Even Hendricks in uniform shows form, the material tight around the cheeks. Causes a vague stir in his groin, makes him think of Luna. He pours a glass of water, waits for Hendricks to close the door.

Breathes out. The fucking Dewane woman. What is her

case? Rank insubordination. More than that, she is dangerous. Treacherous.

He grips the glass, drinks off half of it. Thinks of Luna, the translucent whiteness of her skin. Again the brief stir in his crotch. He should phone her. Instead he phones his driver.

"Chief, watch out for me where the women are."

Gets back a "Yes, boss."

He's a good man, this chief.

Vula contemplates calling Luna. But before he can key in her number, his phone rings. The damn Majoro. He collects himself. Counts to three.

"Minister."

"General." Genuine surprise in her voice. "I was expecting to leave a message. Is your informal discussion ended? You can't be finished already?"

"Not entirely. We are taking a break. There are matters Captain Dewane needs to reflect on with her representative."

"I see. Yes. How is it proceeding? Are you getting the information you wanted?"

"In some areas. In others, we will need the protocols of a formal disciplinary."

"But this will be the end of your investigation? You will go to a proper hearing?"

"Certainly. I do believe it is necessary."

"You find her in serious breach of police code?"

"Yes. She broke her suspension order. And she is guilty of negligence. Dereliction of duty."

"How so?"

"In her leaving a junior officer alone at a compromised crime scene. An officer of her standing should have known this was dangerous. She should have considered the consequences. Also …"

"Yes?"

"She lies."

"You know this? You are certain of this?"

"We have statements contradicting her statements. She has perjured herself."

"But this is not a court of law."

"Her statements were made on the record."

"Of course. Then you must discipline her."

"That is my intention, Minister."

"I want you to make an example of her. We need to show that we are cleaning up the police service, General. If that means her dismissal, then that is what we must do. You have my full backing on this. I would like you to keep me informed about this matter. Perhaps when your discussion is finished, you could email me your findings, and how you will proceed."

"Yes, Minister."

"And General ..."

"Yes, Minister?"

"I mean it. This officer is a troublemaker. From what I have read in her file, she has had a number of cautions. We do not want this poor caliber of person in the service. I would not dispute a recommendation for dismissal. Proceed, General, and excuse me for keeping this conversation brief."

Gone before he can reply.

Leaves Vula wondering why the minister would even know about the case. Let alone call for Dewane's file. Makes him wonder why an ordinary matter of procedure has the minister's attention. And her support. Unless there is more to Dewane than he realizes. Perhaps she knows more than he realizes. Either way, it is not good. Dewane is a threat. And threats need to be neutralized. Sooner rather than later.

He taps his fingers on the desk, mulling on the prospect of Dewane neutralized. Maybe even in the coming days. That would clear the path. Is it not what Luna had foreseen? His thoughts return to her. He phones. Gets her business voice: "One moment, please."

He waits. Imagines her leaving the room. Her client sitting eagerly at the small table. On the table, Luna's throw of the bones. The client's future revealed.

She comes on: "I asked you please not to phone me like this. We can meet later."

"It is not possible." He has a formal dinner. "I need to know now: who is the shadow nearest to me? What do you see?"

"I have told you, Kaiser. I have told you. You have no problems except the one. And that one I cannot see clearly. I have told you: I do not know if the figure is man or woman."

"Dewane?"

"Maybe. I do not know. Sometimes the shadows can be clever in how they hide themselves. I must go. Come to me later. I would need to throw the bones again."

Which was when he changes tack. Needs to punish her for her insolence the previous night.

"What are you wearing?"

He has done this before with women. He has done this with Luna before. In the early days, had found her quickly obliging. On that occasion, it had been nearly midnight. Lady asleep in their bedroom down the passage. He was in his study. He'd WhatsApped Luna on phone without video. He preferred it that way: the dark anonymity. She'd come online. To his question said, pajama bottoms, a short-sleeved T-shirt. Beneath that? Nothing. Touch yourself. She had, or said she had. Then said to him, And you? He had. Which was how it had gone on. Something they'd not repeated. Until now.

"What are you wearing?"

"What?"

"What are you wearing?"

"Kaiser, no. Not now."

"A dress? Jeans? One of your Mandela shirts?"

"What I always wear. My long dress. So what?"

"Underneath?"

"I'm sorry, no."

"Touch yourself?"

"No. You cannot do this, Kaiser. This is not our arrangement. You do not control me. So now I am going. I have a client. When you can, come and see me. There is something I must tell you. Something important."

"You can tell me now."

"I cannot. I do not do these things over the phone. You know that." She says goodbye. He stares at her profile picture on his phone.

Wena! This mlungu.

59

They stand in the shadows of Parliament Street. Zara and Jo-Jo well separated from Captain Alicia Hendricks. Who's on her phone, smoking furiously.

Zara steps away from Jo-Jo's exhale, says, "This is bullshit."

"Of course it is. It's a fishing expedition. The investigators decided there was no case. Which there isn't, which was why they pushed it upstairs. On this basis, there was no reason to close down ICU. No reason to suspend you. But Vula wants you gone. For bloody Christ alone knows what reasons." She sucks at her cigarette, eyes on Zara. Exhales. "And you're not going to tell me everything, are you? Actually, I don't want to know."

Not that Zara has any intention of telling her. Some of it, yes. But definitely not all. Not yet.

Jo-Jo grinds out the cigarette in the gutter. Leaves the butt there. "This is a bloody fiasco. Come on. Let's get it over with."

"We don't have to be here," says Zara. "It's not official. It's not part of procedure."

"True. But we can't walk out. That would look bad. Besides, it's useful for us. We get to learn how little they have. So be vague."

Back in the mountain-view room, Zara kicks off with an observation. "It's a bit bizarre sitting with all these dead things. Let alone that map."

No response from General Vula.

"Don't tell me they're your trophies, General?"

He looks up, smiles, no teeth showing, just his lips drawn

tight. "No," he says, "I do not shoot birds; I do not hunt four-legged animals. The trophies belonged to one of our former presidents, the one they called the big crocodile, P.W. Botha, the Groot Krokodil. A savage man with savage tastes. We keep the room as a reminder of past barbarities." He glances from Zara to Jo-Jo. "Can we proceed?"

They acquiesce, showing open hands.

"I want to move on to your absence when the gangsters arrived. What we do not understand, Captain, is why you left Warrant Officer Adams alone."

"We needed more provisions."

"Provisions! According to your statement, you went into Saldanha to buy these items."

"Yes."

"You obviously felt it was safe to leave Warrant Officer Adams?"

"I did."

"Why?"

"It was early in the evening. I did not expect anything to happen until much later. Even days later."

"Again, this is supposition. You are relying on your instinct? Your sense? Your intuition?"

"Yes."

"I see." A pause while he makes a note. Then, raising his head, "There is another possibility. But let us park that for the moment. We can return to it later. Firstly, can you tell us where exactly you went for these provisions?"

Jo-Jo held up her hands. "I'm sorry, General, I can't see the relevance of these questions."

"Then let me be more specific and return to the other possibility: it is in the time that the captain is away buying these provisions that the gangsters arrive to take the weaponry and Warrant Adams is shot dead. To me and Captain Hendricks, this coincidence is suspicious. How convenient is it that Captain Dewane is not at the cottage when the guns are collected? You see my point?"

No response from Zara or Jo-Jo. Zara thinking, Wynston's death, this shitshow, all for the sake of a few bottles of wine. From such trivial decisions are lives—or deaths—determined.

"Let me help you and your client, Ms. Lanski. You might argue that the coincidence is 'just one of those things.' They happen all the time. We are so used to them; we do not even consider them. They are what you could call a happenstance. But in the police and the secret service, we do not believe in coincidence. Coincidence is too convenient. When we find coincidence, we become worried that there are, how shall I put it, underlying causes."

Jo-Jo stands up, walks to peer at the map of skins. Zara wondering why the theatrics. "Alright," she runs her hand over the map, "what you are implying is that Captain Dewane knew when the thieves would come for the weaponry and made sure that she was not there. Perhaps you are even suggesting that she was working with the thieves? That she is complicit?" She turns from it, faces Vula and Hendricks.

"We would not go so far but you see there is this possibility. The incident is so neatly timed."

Jo-Jo examines her hands. Brushes off hairs. "This map is shedding fur, General. It is going to disappear unless someone preserves it." Rubs her hands against one another. "No matter. Your point, General. There is one thing you are not considering: if my client knew all this, why would she go out there in the first place? Why would she take a witness with her? Why would she deliberately put the warrant officer in danger? This does not make sense."

Now it's General Vula's turn for theatrics. He rolls back, away from the table. Swivels to look at the mountain. Swivels back. "We have considered this, Ms. Lanski. This is why we have an investigation: to get to the truth. There are too many odd things, what we could call imponderables. And these things only Captain Dewane can answer because only she knows."

Jo-Jo sits. "She has told you she does not know who the gangsters are. She is not in some sort of conspiracy with them.

You have, General, the wrong end of the stick. And now I have to admit, I cannot see the point to continuing."

"Ah, that is where you are wrong, Ms. Lanski. We have cell phone records that show Warrant Officer Adams messaged Captain Dewane and got no response. He even phoned her and got no response. Why did Captain Dewane not answer her phone? Where was she? You can see how this looks. This looks very odd. Would you not agree, Captain Dewane? Would you not agree that, as a responsible officer, you should have kept in contact with your subordinate? So, I must ask again, why did you not answer your phone?"

"There could be reasons, General. She may have forgotten it in the car while she was shopping for the provisions. She might not have heard it ringing in her bag. She may have been driving. Surely there are times when you miss calls or text messages?"

"Let her reply, Ms. Lanski."

Zara does. Says, "I didn't hear my phone ringing."

"That's it? You didn't hear your phone ringing."

"Yes."

"This is odd. Would you reply the same under oath?"

"Yes."

"Is it possible you didn't hear your phone ringing because you were in the hotel pub buying wine?"

I was. That's why he's dead.

"I'm sorry, General," says Jo-Jo, "I can't see the point to your question. It is irrelevant. It has nothing to do with my client's suspension. In fact, we are both unsure why she has been suspended at all. What is your disciplinary hearing to be about? If we knew that, perhaps we could answer the relevant questions."

"Surely you can see, Ms. Lanski, it refers to your client's attitude. First she leaves the warrant officer alone; then she doesn't answer his calls for help."

"But she doesn't know they are calls for help. I am finding this very frustrating, so I think we're done, General. If you want to continue, serve a notice for a formal disciplinary hearing."

Jo-Jo stands. To Zara, gestures with a toss of her head toward the door.

Before they can move, Captain Hendricks says, "You were at a crime scene, Captain. You were in violation of your suspension order. You were there without permission. You were disrupting an ongoing investigation."

"You see," adds General Vula, "this is why you will face a disciplinary hearing. In addition, your attitude toward your colleague, Warrant Officer Adams, toward other police colleagues such as the late Sergeant Mpho, demonstrate that you should not be in the service. We need disciplined officers, Captain. Not reckless mavericks."

60

Where to let off steam?

They settle on the café in the Gardens. Terrible coffee but it's outside, under the trees. Perfect in the spring mildness. It's a short walk there from the general's museum: down Parliament Street, cut along the lane beside the Slave Lodge, then up Government Avenue and over to the café.

Enough of a distance for Zara to walk off her irritation. They dodge through the pedestrians, peanut sellers, beggars without speaking. Jo-Jo pulling seriously on a cigarette. At the café, they sit in the dappled shade.

"The bloody bastard," says Jo-Jo.

"Ditto," says Zara. "A complete prick."

No sooner said than Captain Hendricks is at their table. Standing over them, hands on hips, panting a bit, as if she's been running.

Which she has.

"Now you're in the kak, Dewane," she says. "We're gonna nail you."

"My lewe fok," says Zara, "what hole'd you spring out of? You followed us here? Jirre, man, what for?"

"To tell you you're gonna see your ass. No more ICU. Ever. No more SAPS. You're finished. Joining the unemployed. You wanna play with us, we're gonna do this the formal way: full-on disciplinary, Dewane. Finish 'n' klaar. End of story."

"You ran all this way to tell us? What a good little doggie."

"Thank you, Captain Hendricks," says Advocate Lanski in her formal voice, no implied sarcasm. "The advance notice is appreciated."

Captain Alicia Hendricks looks ready to spray more invective but doesn't. Backs away, her finger raised. Then turns, struts off without a backward glance.

"Well, that sorts that out," says Jo-Jo. "I guess we must have pissed them off."

"I should go back to boxing. I've been meaning to."

"No. You're not going to hit anybody else."

"Never said I would."

"I can see it in your face, Zara Dewane. You'd like to klap our Captain Hendricks."

"Nothing could be further from my thoughts."

"Of course not."

They stare at one another, until they both laugh.

"Thing is," says Jo-Jo, "for the life of me, I can't see what they hope to gain by pressuring you. They've got nothing but a cockeyed conspiracy theory. But tell me you weren't at the hotel buying wine."

"I was."

"Oh, bloody hell."

"And bumped into someone who our Captain Hendricks had seen about some diamonds."

"You're only telling me this now?"

"It's also all I'm telling you now. It's part of an ongoing investigation." She grins.

"You're not supposed to be investigating anything."

"Shhh. I could be. With higher blessing."

Jo-Jo groans. Knocks out another cigarette. "I don't think I should hear this."

"I don't think so either. What I do think you should hear is about Sergeant Exit Kutoka."

"Coffees, ladies?" says a waiter. "Or maybe a house wine with an early lunch?"

They go with the house wine, a plate of chips to share. On Signal Hill, the cannon fires. It's midday.

The way Zara tells Jo-Jo the story, she begins with Exit Kutoka knocking on her front door one afternoon. In fact, one afternoon a week back.

"I'd just fetched Kyle from school. We were in the kitchen having a snack with that crazy Janet. She's okay, really. Gets a bit much now and then but she picks up my vibe. Knows when to back off. I told you she's living mostly in my outside room these days. Apparently I'm at risk. Her words exactly: 'Yous vulnerable, Mrs. Z, yous at risk. Yous gonna need on-site protection services. But I's not gonna charge because the room's mos quids in pro quo.'"

Jo-Jo snorts. "She said that?"

"Word for word. I like her. Like having her around. Anyhow, back to Exit. There's a knock on my front door, I open, there's a guy, a cop in uniform on my stoep. He says he's got to speak to me about an ICU matter. I tell him I'm on suspension, there's no ICU in the Western Cape at the moment. I even suggest he speaks to you."

"Thanks for that."

"Pleasure. But he's not interested. No, he says, he's got to speak to me. All the time he's standing there, he's looking round into the street up and down. Really nervous. But the street's empty. There's no one. I ask him in. We sit down and I say, Okay, how do you know where I stay? He tells me this long story about how he was working with Sergeant Langa Mpho ..."

"Our guy from the rape hearings?"

"The very same."

"The guy who shot Maale?"

"Yes, him."

"Who General Vula shot."

"Exactly."

"He was working with Mpho? How?"

"Hang on. I'll get there. Go back to the day someone took pot-shots at me and killed my neighbor Studs. Turns out, he, Exit, was driving the car. Mpho was the shooter."

"Bloody hell."

Their wines arrive; they clink glasses. Zara going straight on with the story.

"The next day it was the two of them attacked me after Mpho's disciplinary hearing. Which was why I went to their police station. Kutoka's based there too."

"And you let this guy into your house."

"And gave him tea and biscuits."

"Bullshit."

"Yeah, bullshit. I didn't."

"I should bloody hope not."

"He's sitting there, edge of the chair. Not looking at me. Even when I say to him, Look at me, he can't. He catches my eye then looks away."

"Did he apologize?"

"Yes. Later. I'll get to that. He tells me that he and Mpho did the weaponry heist on the highway. Took the weapons to the Malgas cottage where they met with …?"

"Let me guess, our delightful Captain Alicia Hendricks."

"None other. But here's what they call the kicker: Mpho told Kutoka he was flying to some wildlife lodge with Vula because Vula had a job for him. Then he, Mpho, WhatsApps Kutoka …"

"What sort of name's that, Kutoka?"

"Kenyan apparently."

"He's a foreigner? In the cops?"

"It seems."

"O-kay. Go on."

"Mpho WhatsApps him from the lodge to brag the Vula job's worth R400,000. Doesn't tell him what sort of job, that's obvious, just tells him how much money he's going to make."

"For bloody popping Maale?"

"Ja."

"Jesus! Where's this guy Kutoka now?"

"I'm getting to it. The thing is that Vula's been onto him, onto Kutoka, said he was recruiting for Police Intelligence, offered him a position."

"Hokaai, slow down. How does Vula get onto him?"

A basket of hot chips arrives, splashed with vinegar, sprinkled with salt. They ask for more wine. Pick at the chips.

"Kutoka reckons Vula got hold of Mpho's phone, saw the WhatsApp Mpho had sent about the R400k. Could also see from the WhatsApp record that he and Mpho were buddies. My feeling is he pulls in Kutoka because he's a handy Mpho replacement. Intimidates him. But also showers him with moolah."

"Yes, sure. One way of looking at it. So what position does he offer?"

"Probably a place in some sort of investigations department that Vula's setting up in Police Intelligence. Nothing in writing yet, but he's already got Exit running little errands."

"This Exit is happy to do that?"

"Not happy. But feels he has to. Feels pressured. Not even the money's taking the edge off."

"What sort of errands?"

"Deliveries of the odd pistol, the odd packets of ammunition. On one occasion, to collect a payment."

"I'm sorry, you've lost me. How? How does this happen? How does Sergeant Exit Kutoka get a pistol to deliver?"

"Simple. It's given to him. From what I've heard, a standard modus. He reports for duty at his cop shop, there's a package waiting for him. Actually delivered by a courier company. Inside the package is a pistol, say, or a box of ammo from an unknown gifter who is probably Alicia Hendricks. Also instructions of where to make the delivery. This way he gets drawn into their system. He becomes complicit. That's how Vula told him it would work. And that's how it works."

"Interesting operation. And where is he told to take these gifts?"

"To beaches. Blouberg once, Monwabisi, Strand, Camps Bay. Park benches right here in the Gardens. The Sea Point lawns."

"You're kidding me!"

"Not at all. Classic way you see it in the movies. You sit down on a bench. A pretty young thing comes along, sits next to you. You wait five minutes, then get up, leaving said package behind. The PYT walks off with it."

"That's how it happens?"

"According to Exit. That's what he told me."

"Bloody hell."

"Thing is, Exit's getting nervous. The whole wheelchair thing disturbs him. He doesn't like Vula."

"Who does?"

"He doesn't trust him. Doesn't like what's going on. He wants out. He comes to me because he knows I was ICU, he knows I was onto Mpho. Now he wants protection. He gives us the dope on Vula, the payment he promised Mpho for the Maale hit, we give him protection. I told him there's not much I can do but I'd try if he gives me information incriminating Vula. Honestly, the best thing is he takes leave. Disappears for a while. Seriously disappears. Maybe even goes back to Kenya if he's got family there. But I didn't tell him that."

"All the same, you think this is what he's going to do?"

"Don't know. I've got another meeting with him."

"Where? When?"

"Don't know. Still to be decided."

The waiter puts down another carafe of wine. Zara fills their glasses.

"Cheers."

"Cheers."

"You realize that you should report all this? That if you don't, you become an accessory. To not one but two killings."

"I'm a cop."

"On suspension. About to face a disciplinary hearing. That means you're not a cop. You're an ordinary citizen gal withholding information. Serious bloody information. Bloody sake, Zara, get a grip."

Despite the earlier hint, what Zara doesn't tell Jo-Jo, certainly doesn't intend telling Jo-Jo at this point, is about her meeting with Minister Majoro. Knows that this would send Jo-Jo into orbit. Especially the bit about investigating General Kaiser Vula. Which she's decided to take on. Why not? He was causing major upset in her life, so why not reciprocate?

"I don't like it, Zara. You're in the bloody crap as it is. Why dig yourself in deeper?"

Because.

Because my lewe fok, Eloise, there's kak in the land.

While she's in the vicinity, Zara reckons no harm in checking out Captain Hendricks's other office again. Air kisses Jo-Jo goodbye, heads into the back streets. Is soon enough climbing the stairs of the musty building. On the first floor goes down the quiet passage, gets in at Umuzi Trading in twenty seconds flat. She's been back a couple of times over the weeks. Always surprises her, the lock is still the same. Same bank statements too. Never anything new.

She's at stalemate with getting the banks to release their client's information. Their line is: Come with a subpoena, you can see who signs for Umuzi Trading. Fat chance of anyone giving her a subpoena.

Thing is, Umuzi Trading's seeming more and more like a shell. Completely empty. No one even visiting.

The traps she'd set—a flyer slipped under the door, the angle of the desk chair—unmoved.

By her reckoning, it's been four weeks since Hendricks was last here. Why even keep this place?

Zara pulls down one of the beach posters, leaves it draped across the filing cabinets, as if the sticky tack dried out. Show Hendricks her world's coming unstuck.

Le Weekend

61

Come Saturday morning, Zara wakes to the quiet. The wild night wind has died down. Unusual for this time of year. This time of year it should be days of salt haze, dust, discontent. She lies still, listens to the silence of the house, slowly hearing the soft hum of the city. There's sunlight yellow on the curtain. There's the sweet scent of Yesterday-Today-and-Tomorrow coming in the window.

Her first thought is: Take the kayak out.

There'd be glassy conditions, soft swells, maybe dolphins, and maybe, just maybe, the kayak lawyer. Not that she's given him even a passing hallelujah before now. Anyhow, he'd said he'd phone but hadn't. Not that he seemed the shy type. Unless he was worried there'd be rub-off. Didn't want to associate with contaminated goods.

Which brings in other thoughts, dire thoughts about money, for starters. Bond, car repayments, school fees, food, petrol. Another couple of weeks would shred her bank balance. Ashton would gloat. Her mother and father would offer support. She'd feel twelve years old. She'd be Eloise. She sits, hugs her knees in consternation.

No.

Never.

She'll take the minister's offer: investigate Vula. My lewe fok, Eloise, you're halfway there already. What's the big deal? Just do it.

The big deal is that she'd be in debt to. Beholden to. Controlled by. No longer a free agent.

On the other hand: what good is being a free agent if you're cash-strapped?

Nothing to be gained.

Except, as much as she was the minister's tool, the minister would be hers. Courtesy their pact of reciprocity.

Which enlivens her.

Gets her out of bed to open the curtains, let the sunshine in.

Lets her look on the Foreshore: the container ships in the harbor; the tankers in Table Bay. All caught in the bright light of the rising sun.

When she hears the key in the back door. The door creak open. The pad of bare feet across the wooden floors, down the passage to her bedroom. Knock, knock.

"Mrs. Z. Mrs. Z."

"Ja, Janet."

"Mrs. Z." A gasp as Janet enters. "Oh la la, Mrs. Z. Mrs. Z's mos sexy in that thingie, shimmery outfitting. Even I can say so, 'n' I's not lesbianism." She gets a feel of the material between her fingers.

"Heavens, Janet, it's just Woolies PJs."

"No man, Mrs. Z, it's how you fit it. Yous need a man for this sorta gets up."

Zara detaches Janet's hand, steps back. "Okay, okay. What's happening?"

Janet holds up her phone. "It's Exit. He's phoned me now-now."

"He phoned you? How's he get your number?"

"From when he was here, mos."

"He asked for it, you gave it."

"Ja, of course. We's like spies. Because he doesn't wanna use your phone. You's buggered, he says."

Probably only too true. The reason she has three others. "And so?"

"He's wanting a meeting."

"That's it?"

"Down there where you do the canoe paddling. He can make it about whatever time."

It's possible, Zara reckons. She can drop Kyle at a surf spot. Get out on her Dagger as well. Kill lots of birdies with one stone.

"Fine. How d'we do this?"

"I WhatApps your commandments."

"You're now his handler? Our handler?"

Janet grins. "Of special agents running in the fynbos field. I know the lingo."

Which makes Zara want to laugh, but she doesn't. She plays it straight. "Tell him ten o'clock. He say anything more? Like what it's about?"

"Not a Bo Peep."

Understandable.

Except, whatever it is, it's not good.

At least that would be the message in the world according to Zara Dewane.

62

He's diligent. He has a reputation for detail. It's why he's in demand by corporates, government, foreign agencies.

So when his target's car moves, he's on it. Despite this being a Saturday morning at nine.

Leaves a half-finished bowl of cornflakes, pours a too-hot cup of coffee into a flask, heads for his car. He can see she's on Philip Kgosana Drive, direction Gardens. That's where he finds her stopped on Mill Street, her kid and another boy strapping a surfboard to the roof racks.

She's looking as beautiful as the morning.

Then she's over the Nek to Camps Bay beach, drops the boys

there. Off again. He takes a bet to Three Anchor Bay. This sort of morning, the woman's not going to miss a damn paddle. Means he has to kill a couple of hours to make sure that's all this is about. He's switched on her phone mic but all he's getting is Linda Perry.

At Three Anchor Bay she parks, stays in her car. He drives on, finds a curb space, walks back, a stroller among the strollers. A fit, rugged guy in a dark green jacket. Takes a seat on a handy bench.

Waits.

Five, ten minutes.

An old Honda Ballade stops behind her. Looks like someone painted it white with a hand brush. He recognizes the car. Recognizes the driver. The driver's a low-priority target, but a target all the same.

63

Zara's out of her car the moment she hears the Honda. Says to Exit Kutoka, "What's the problem, Sergeant?"

"I am going," he says. "This is too dangerous for me."

He's looking harrowed. Zara's seen this on people before: the pinched skin at the eyes, the sallow complexion. The tight mouth. The shifting from foot to foot. Like they're about to run.

"This is new. Last I heard, you wanted to blow whistles. What's happened? You've been threatened?"

"Every time, it is a threat to me. I cannot stay here. Even you knowing it is a problem for me. If Mpho can be killed, the general can do it to me. I am no one in your country."

"I have told you, we have witness protection."

"No. That is worse. That is a big problem." He goes silent.

Zara waits him out.

"I must find a safe place."

"What are you going to do?"

"Soon I will disappear."

"To where?"

"No. I cannot tell you."

"Will you stay in touch? You can do it through Janet. That's best."

"This might be possible."

"Your evidence is vital, Sergeant. I will need it."

"You have my affidavits."

"If you are not there to support it, they will throw it out."

She keeps her eyes on him, watching for any tick in his face. But it's passive. Emotionless. Impossible to tell what he's thinking. He stares past her at the long reach of the sea. Then abruptly bends to take a package from the back seat of his car.

"I have brought one other thing for you." Gives it to her. It's a courier bag from a company in the city. "This was waiting for me at my station. My orders are to take it to the Strand beach this afternoon." He gives her a piece of paper with the meeting details.

"How did you get this?"

"A WhatsApp message."

"Can I see it?"

He shows her.

"Who's this person who sent it?"

"I don't know. It is always a different number."

"Is it Vula?"

Exit shrugs. "He has another person."

"Captain Hendricks?"

"Yes."

Zara thinks, Ja, Vula wouldn't do it himself. He'd use a proxy. Who better than darling Alicia? The trouble with scumbags, they duck and dive.

She decides: "Send it to this number." Gives him the number of another of her phones. Has a stab of remorse about Wynston. He would have tracked the origins of that WhatsApp down chop-chop. It'll take her longer but not impossible. Tries another tack with Exit. "You must go to the Strand. I can watch you make the exchange. Even video it."

A vigorous headshake. "No. I am finished with this matter. For me it is too dangerous. Look in the package. Open it. See what is inside, then you will know."

Zara bites down. If Kutoka's a lost cause, she can't blame him. The guy knows what he's up against.

A time of terror.

A nine to the head.

A grave in the Atlantis dunes.

Eloise, get real. Tears off the plastic courier bag, opens the box. Within: two Z88s.

Cop guns.

"But you don't know where these come from?"

She does. Although not exactly.

They could be from the weapon heist. Or the evidence lockers. Most likely from the police armory. Doesn't matter where. Not in the long run. What matters is nailing these to Vula.

Even then she's going to need Sergeant Kutoka.

"I know." Said so quietly she isn't sure that's what he's said.

"You know where they come from?"

He nods. "There is a place. It is not always the same place. But for now I know it."

"Tell me."

He tells her it's a storage facility out at Philippi.

"You've been there?"

Again the slight movement of his head. His eyes off scanning the scene.

"And?"

"There are many guns. Ammunition. Much weaponry."

"Do you know where it comes from?"

"All over. Some is from heists like I told you. Some is from the army storage. Some is from the police what they call the armory. Some from citizen people, guns that should be destroyed. Some is from the Struggle, the AKs."

"They move all this from storage to storage?"

"Yes. It is easy. Everything is in crates."

Zara thinking, Maybe, but even moving a crate means you need manpower. Means others know what you're doing. Where the treasure is. You wouldn't want that.

"Who moves the crates?"

"Me." He taps his chest.

"You can't do it alone."

"There is always another man to help. Not the same man. Always a foreign man who wants the quick money."

Neat.

A tidy operation for General Vula and Captain Hendricks.

Except there'd be security cameras in the streets. Visuals of comings and goings. You wouldn't want that.

"Such a place," she says, "there'd be security. Patrols. Cameras."

"In the daytime, there's too much business. Lots of trucks. Lots of bakkies, cars, the deliveries. It is just another place for delivery and dispatch."

"They only move crates during the day?"

"Always. It is safest."

Safest undoubtedly.

Very cool.

Although Exit is shifting his feet, his eyes never on her face. The man's anxious. His fingers alive, the jiggle-jiggle of his car keys. Like any moment he's going to run.

"You know what name the storage is under? Who rents it?"

"I do not know."

"Maybe it's a company?"

"This information I do not know."

"Okay, alright," says Zara, "are there a lot of crates? Is there a lot of ..." She hesitates. Was about to say "stock." Like this is some shop in a mall. Which in a way it is, of course. Your handy cash 'n' carry for gun toters.

"Not so much. There has been more."

"But there's stuff right there, right now?"

A quick step, yes.

"Any big buys about to happen?"

"I don't know. I don't know that sort of thing. They use me for small jobs only."

"And hard labor." Zara laughs to ease Exit's St. Vitus dance. Gets a grin from him that's more nerves than humor. The man's the link in her case. He's vital. He goes, the case goes. "You have to stay in touch with me."

She suspects he won't. She's got nothing to dangle. With the exception of: it's the right thing to do. But that's a cliché she's not going to voice. She has to let him go. Hope to hell he won't vanish.

"I must go now," he says.

"Stay in touch, Sergeant. Please, man."

He gives her a slight smile. Then he's dancing away, drives off in his throaty, hand-painted, white Honda Ballade.

64

From his handy bench the man in the dark green jacket watches. Sees the one target drive away. Sees the other target place the package in the boot of her car. Sees this target head for the kayak lockers. She's damn well going for a paddle. God, she's got a body! Easily it moves. Silky it would be. He can almost taste her on his tongue. He shakes his head in mock vexation. Refocuses. What amazes him is that she's going to leave the package in her vehicle. He can't believe it. Can't believe that someone can be so trusting in this city. Implies the package can't be worth much. Yet would still be worth checking. Except the car would be alarmed. The man sighs. Sometimes it is best to do nothing. Except file a report. Let the principal decide. He taps a message on Telegram.

65

General Kaiser Vula wakes, wonders what has woken him. Doesn't move. Does not even open his eyes. A habit from his MK guerrilla days: to lie still, listen. It had paid off once.

Then.

He was in an abandoned house on a farm with two comrades. They'd jumped the border the previous night. Walked through the day. A wary walk across a wildlife reserve. Had heard the cough of lions, often been startled by the crash of animals in the thickets. They reached the house at nightfall. A long-deserted place of empty rooms. Sand creeping over the floorboards. Empty except for a keyless piano in the lounge, a wardrobe with wooden coat hangers in a bedroom, in another a chair without cushions. On the kitchen wall a calendar for 1977, the first three months crossed off. It was October 1986. They had come here for the weapons. A cache buried in the yard. They dug up the guns. Ate a cold supper, too cautious to make a fire. Then fell asleep in the backrooms. At first light, Vula had woken inexplicably. Kept his eyes closed, listened. Realized there was someone in the room. Someone near him. He smelled meat breath. Deodorant.

As the story went, he rolled over, fired twice. Heard the wap-wap of the 9mms going in. A man's grunt. The rest was wildfire. He'd escaped. His comrades hadn't.

It was one of the legendary stories about Vula. Or was it a lie? Either way his waking habit had never changed.

Now.

He lies still. Feels with his right hand across the bed; Lady's side is cold. He doesn't remember her getting up, dressing, leaving. Not good. Where is the instinct that once had saved him? He opens his eyes on a dark room. An outline of daylight around the curtains. On the digital clock, the time is 10:03. The screen of his smartphone is lit up. That is what must have woken him. An incoming WhatsApp.

From Luna Maplewood: *Phone me when you get this.*

He levers himself into a sitting position against the pillows. Drinks from the glass of water on his bedside table. He hasn't spoken to her since she cut up huffy. Even though she said she had something important to tell him, he hasn't been to see her. If it was that important, she would come to him. He scratches at his crotch, phones his consultant.

She sounds breathless. Does not say hello, does not ask how he is, says bluntly, "I have seen them."

"What? Seen what? What are you talking about? Why are you husky? Are you playing down there?"

"Kaiser. Stop. Listen to me: I can see them."

"Yes. You have said that. Who are you talking about?"

"They have come closer. Two of them have come out of the shadows."

"So what does this mean? You said I had no problems with them, only with one."

"But now I sense a danger here."

"You can see their faces? You must describe them to me."

"No. I have told you, not on the phone. That is impossible. Come to me, Kaiser. Come to me."

This last said softer in her bedroom voice. Perhaps she is ready. He smiles. The mlungu can't resist. Says, "Put on your video. I want to see you."

And there she is, wearing a thin jersey.

"Happy now?"

"Take it off."

His video screen goes to her profile picture. She says, "Come to me, Kaiser. I cannot reach them without you."

She disconnects.

The bitch. He can't believe that she treats him like this. All the same, he summons his driver. Tells him to be there in an hour.

Then goes looking for Lady. Expects to find her in the garden but she's not there. Nor is she in the house. Finally, he wheels through to the garage. There she is in her car, staring at the closed garage door. He raps with his knuckles on the side window.

"Why are you sitting here?" He realizes she must have been there for an hour or more. She should be at her yoga class.

He watches her overcome by tears. She leans her head against the steering wheel, weeping. He can see her body wracked by the sobs. It's the last thing he needs. She should pull herself together. This is weakness. He cannot stand weakness.

He swings open the car door. Says, "Did you take the muti?"

She shakes her head, turns to him, screams: "No, no, no. Stay away. You have put me under a spell. You are poisoning me. You and the witch are killing me."

He slaps her face. Once. Twice. Pulls the keys from the ignition. "Get out. Get out of the car. You will take the medicine. You will stay here while I am on business. This is enough. You cannot be like this. Not now when we have our position. When I have my position."

Lady shoves him back. Bolts from the car. He hears a door slam in the house, knows she is in the spare room. Fine. Let her bawl herself dry. He has other matters to consider. She must calm down. Accept his path of action. She who once was all for plots and plans, now falls apart.

Kaiser Vula wheels himself back into the house. Pauses outside the door to the spare room. Can hear her crying. This is nonsense, her behavior. But he says nothing. Moves on.

66

Zara paddles onto a still ocean. There are other kayakers about in groups. There are shouted invitations to join them. But she waves no thanks, heads out toward the Island. Finds herself wondering where the lawyer is. JC for short. The boykie who was going to take her for a drink. Finds herself thinking, You actually hoped to see him. Somewhat surprised at her disappointment. Thinking, You're a little old to be mooning. You're not a teenager. Yet it would've been nice to see a cheery face.

She powers up her pace, blots the boykie from her mind. To have him replaced by Exit.

Exit teetering. Almost a lost cause. Unless she can protect him. Get him out of the line of fire. The way you did with Wynston!

My fok, Wynston. So often, lurking Wynston crosses her mind. Maybe she needs to see the shrink about Wynston. Sort out the black thoughts. The guilt. It's been two months now. Coming and going. Filling her headspace. Hurting her heart. A real chest pain. Or maybe talk to Jo-Jo rather. Yeah, Jo-Jo'd be a better bet. Which resolve puts more power into each dip and stroke of the paddle. Gets her thoughts back to Exit.

If he could do one last courier job. Then she could get cameras on the lockup storage. Her dad was good at that. Maybe he'd come to the party. Next, with a bit of luck, a lot of luck, actually track down the cell phone number. Because getting the phone, the owner of the phone would be a major coup. A leap. Only thing, if the owner was Hendricks, only a subpoena would crack it. Yet what chance of a subpoena? The legals would laugh at any request from on-suspension Captain Dewane. Comes back to Exit: he's the link. Without him the two pistols don't mean a thing. Without him there's no case.

She's out on the water for an hour plus before heading back to Three Anchor Bay feeling almost stoked, as Kyle would have it. Still no sign of boykie JC. Again a tinge of disappointment. She stows the boat. Changes. Dawdling a bit. Then clicks her tongue. Heaven's sake. Takes the seaboard road to Camps Bay. Thirty-five minutes later she's standing on the white sands, waving for her son to come in.

And there is Ashton. Striding across the beach at her in full rage. Stumbling through the soft sand, shaking his fist, his face hard. Bitter.

Where have you been?

How could you leave him here alone?

You are completely irresponsible.

You selfish bitch.

You are unfit to be a mother.

I am his father. I want custody.

You people ... You people are rubbish.

It's the "you people" that gets to her. She knows what he means: the quick racist jab.

She squares up to him.

"Why're you here, Ashton? How do you even know Kyle's here?"

He smirks. "I've got a tracker on his phone."

Fok. The guy doesn't stop.

"So you thought what? You'll pitch up, play the good father. Earn some brownie points. Show your lawyer pictures of dad and son doing togetherness. Even on his off weekend."

"You, you, you ..." he splutters. When he's angry, he splutters. Until he's over the glottal stop, then the words come out, high pitched. Manic. Stream-of-consciousness style. Zara's always found it something to behold. Like a performance. That should end in applause.

"I am his father he is my son who belongs with me where he can get a proper life with love and care in my security away from you people and your rubbish family from the sand dunes with your nonsense business that this is your place here below the mountain you dregs you animals you shame you are a scandal you are disgraceful how can you show your face in the streets you cop scum on suspension for being a stupid woman with shit for brains that you cannot even see how the darkies despise you you sewer crap you trash get away from my son before I have you charged you you you cunt."

At which point Zara wants to clap but says, "You don't have to say these things, Ashton. You're better than that." He stands before her, blue-lipped, hands trembling, his eyes dodgy. She had never realized how small, how pinched his face is until this moment.

"I'm not going to argue, Ashton. I just don't see things the way you do. Please, now, can you leave? Kyle is with me this weekend. He is not alone here; he is with a friend. There are lifeguards on this beach, there are other surfers on that break and, yes, he has his cell phone to contact me. Or you, if he wants to talk to you." Although why he'd want to do that I don't know. But she doesn't say this aloud.

She waits. Keeps her eyes on him. If anything, a sadness in her expression.

Ashton shakes a finger at her. She knows his rage consumes

him. He is panting. As if he cannot get enough breath. He will
have to leave now. And he does. Mumbling something she doesn't
catch. Isn't interested in hearing. As she watches him cross the
beach, cross the street, disappear.

Only then does she realize she is wound up. The way she
gets facing the hard crims. Yet this guy was once her husband.
Once her lover. Even so, there'd been that tweak of instinct, that
warning, when they first met. And she'd ignored it. Gone with
the smooth, love-bombing Ashton. And lived to regret it. Was
still regretting it. Would only be free of the creep when Kyle
was older.

She phones Jo-Jo.

"Yeah, doll, what's it?"

"That fucker Ashton. But that's not it. You got a moment
soonish?"

"Natch. Today? Tomorrow?"

"Tomorrow. Your place."

67

"Where's this?" says Duifie as Alicia Hendricks pulls into the
Port Owen Marina. She's been asking where they're going all
the way.

Each time Alicia has responded, "You'll see. Just enjoy the
ride." And Duifie has leant over, stroked the back of her hand
down Alicia's cheek. Thrilling. Comforting. Alicia pleased she
decided to make a weekend of it.

Now here they are at the Marina, signed in, the gates opening,
the smiling guard waving them through. She finds the rental
without a problem. It's bright, airy, the lounge opening onto a
deck that steps down to the water.

Duifie is in raptures. Has changed into a bikini under a silk
gown before Alicia has made coffee. Pads barefoot across the
tiles. Gives her a hug.

"Perfecto."

After coffee on the deck, Alicia breaks the news. She has to go off for half an hour. No problem for Duifie. She'll lie in the sun. Drink bubbles and orange juice.

"Like it's the south of France, my liefie."

Maybe it is, thinks Alicia, on the drive to the house of Big D.

He opens at her knock as if he was waiting for her. Stands there barefoot. Grubby shorts. T-shirt smudged with stains, flecked with fish scales. A knife in his hand.

"Not going to shake, I'm cleaning fish," he says. Stands back to let her in. Leads her to the kitchen. On the block: two fat Red Romans. "You want one?" he asks. "They're fresh. Two hours fresh."

She nods thanks, yes, wow, how can she repay him?

He says it's a gift, slips the blade's point into the fish's belly, slices it to the gills. Puts his hand in, pulls out the guts.

Alicia grimaces.

"You haven't cleaned a fish?" he says. "You're a Capey, you haven't cleaned a fish! No, man, can't be." Holds out the motley innards, adds them to a pile on a sheet of newspaper. Rinses the fish, wraps it in paper. "All yours. Enjoy." He washes his hands. "Now, what's the scene?"

"These." Alicia gives him Tamora Gool's packet of diamonds.

Big D spills some into his palm. Whistles. "I'll tell you for free whoever's dealing these is big-time. This time you going to tell me where you got them?"

Alicia shakes her head.

"No. Didn't think so. The usual cop stuff, hey." He spills the diamonds onto a plate. Fetches a loupe. Scans through the haul. Picks some out for closer attention. "So whadda you want from me, Captain?"

"A value."

"It's gonna be a thumb suck."

"The last one was accurate enough."

"This is a lot more. There're good stones here." He bends to focus his loupe. "Exceptional."

Captain Alicia Hendricks waits him out.

"You want some coffee? Tea? A cooldrink? A drink? A glass of white wine? This is a big haul. You should celebrate."

"How big?"

He gives a figure that's twice the price tag on the guns she's sold Tamora Gool. Did Gool know how much the packet was worth? Was this Gool capturing her? Maybe. Maybe not. Either way, too good an opportunity to miss. She could pay Vula. And bank a treasure trove. Take Duifie to the south of France.

"A glass of wine," she says. "Why not?"

"Hey, okay," says Big D, all smiles. "That's the way we roll then." Opens a bar fridge in the lounge. "Chardonnay? It's unwooded. Sauvignon blanc? Riesling? Chenin?"

"Chenin," says Alicia. Her tastes on the sweeter side. Impressed that he keeps that many varieties in his fridge. In hers, you'll find some chenin. Her go-to after a hard day: a rich amber late harvest. Unlike Duifie, who's more a bubbly girl.

Big D pours two glasses. Sits down on the sofa opposite her. Leans over, clinks his glass against hers.

"So you left us, Captain?" he says. "You pleased to be out of Saldanha?"

Alicia flutters her hand. "It was interesting here. Quieter. You know, mostly the problems were domestic. Even that can get hectic with the wife beaters, the rapists."

Big D nods along. Says he knows it's a major problem. "And now. Where're you now?"

She sips her wine. Tells him Police Intelligence.

"Which means what, you're like a cop spook?"

She sips her wine. Tells him "You got it."

"Come on, it can't be that mysterious."

She sips her wine. Relents. Thinks a bit of info is better than no info. A bit of info can be a smokescreen. "We get information about syndicates, organized crime, that sort of thing."

"You missed getting intelligence before the July riots, hey!" He laughs. "The insurrectionists caught you guys fast asleep. Your own people stoking the fires, and you didn't know it. Suppose you can't be on top of all the scumbags. So, what's with the diamonds? IDB? Some cabinet minister doing a dirty?"

She shrugs.

"C'mon, you can tell me. Like, who'm I gonna tell in this paradise we call home? Who's even going to care?"

The way he's looking at her, quizzy, flirting, she wonders if he's alone, without a love interest at the moment. Which would be unusual for Big D. Women are moths to his candle. There was that woman last time. Hears him saying, "You've come to me twice for valuations. You could go to a real dealer. You guys've got to have those types on your books, not so? That'd be way easier than driving up the coast to see a diamond diver. I can't even give you a professional opinion."

"You're pretty accurate."

"Ja, well, should damn well hope so. I've seen plenty of these beauties." She catches that flirty look again. "Also, you come to me there's no record, hey. Cutie on the QT."

"There is that." Time to get out of there before Big D gets big ideas. She finishes her wine in a couple of swallows. Stands.

"But, if you want a professional price, I know a guy. A legit trader."

"Who'd that be?"

"Man called Straight Abe Margulies."

"Which sounds dodgy."

"He isn't. Got all the right paperwork. I can make the introductions."

"Alright."

Big D nods his head. The smile never leaving his lips. Takes her by surprise what he says next. "You here with a cherry? You wanna bring her over tomorrow for a fish braai?"

Alicia thanks him. Says, "Maybe not a good idea."

"Your call," says Big D. "Would be worth your while. Would be fun too." Gives her the wrapped Red Roman. "Pan fried's best, hey. Good scoop of butter, not olive oil."

Before she gets back to Duifie, Alicia Hendricks sends Tamora Gool a WhatsApp: *You can make the collection chop-chop.*

Seconds later comes the reply: *Chop-chop is Thursday.*

Hendricks: *I want to get this done. Earlier than that.*

Gool: *Thursday, cop chickie. Don't push me.*

68

"Chief, tell me, do you have men you can trust?"

General Kaiser Vula sits in the back of the black Mercedes. Sees the driver's eyes in the rearview mirror.

"Yes, boss. There are some of us."

"That is good for me to know."

"You can believe in us," says the driver.

They go on in silence to the suburb of gabled houses. The driver stops at the driveway gate.

"Stay here," says Vula. "I will do it myself."

He propels his chair to the front door. Knocks. The door opens. She stands there looking down at him. She is austere. Tight. Not the woman he has phata-phated. She doesn't smile. She gestures for him to come in.

Mlungu bitch.

They sit in the lounge as they did the first time. Sit on opposite sides of the coffee table. She in the straight-backed chair. He in his wheelchair. Her clutch of bones on the coffee table. A pack of tarot cards beside them. He is the first to speak.

General Kaiser Vula says, "What is this going on?"

She holds up a hand. "Stop. Don't speak. Wait. They are coming."

"Who?"

Again the stop hand. Her stern eyes.

He clenches his fists. Bites down on his irritation. She has been right before. She foresaw his future. He must let her do it her way.

Now she releases the bones onto a cloth. Peers at them. "There are three. Two are close. One stands in the shadows. She will not reveal herself."

"A woman?"

"I feel it is a woman. Yes."

"And the other two?"

"Wait. They are showing me cards. This one, the close one, holds the Devil. And the one a step behind shows me the Tower reversed." She stops, leans forward, fans out the tarot cards. "Pick one," she says. "Do not turn it over." He does as she says. She shuffles the deck, fans out the cards again. "Pick another." He does. She withdraws the deck. "Now turn them over. Place them side by side."

This is new to Kaiser Vula. She has never used cards before.

"What is this?" he says. "You are a fortune teller today?"

"Do not joke, Kaiser. You need all the insights I can give."

"But these? What good are they? European tricks."

"Respect, General. You must not think Africa is the only place with sangomas. Wherever there are people, there are connections to the other world. We can use all the channels."

"Bah. It is white monkey business."

"I can stop." She sits back. "It is your choice."

She has not been like this before. Challenging. Dismissive even. Her expression nonchalant. It irks him. But he is curious about these strange pictures.

"Do you want to know about the cards?"

"Yes. Go on."

"You understand they are what you have chosen."

"Impossible. I could not see what I was choosing."

"Your fingers drew them out. One among many options. That is choosing."

Again he has to tighten his resolve. She is testing him. Riding his temper. "Go on."

The first shows a person in a chariot drawn by two animals with the bodies of lions, the heads of men. The other is a king on his throne.

"What does this mean?"

"We are coming to it, Kaiser. Wait." She looks down at the cluster of bones.

He waits. The house is silent. No street noise either. He studies the impassivity of her face. No tic. No emotion. But her eyes bright, focused. Her chin resting on the fist of her left hand. She lifts her head. "The one who stands closest is a man."

"Can you see his face?"

A hesitation. "No, his face is turned away. Oh. Now he is showing me the card again, the Devil. The Devil means that he must stop, he is going the wrong way. Or maybe he means you must stop."

"Ah man, which one of us? Him or me?"

"It is him. He holds it close to his chest, his heart." She glances at Kaiser Vula. "The Chariot is your answer to him."

"And what is that? What does it mean?"

"Your willpower. You will move forward with your plan."

"There is no question of not doing that. This man is foolish to think anything else. Are you sure you cannot see his face?"

"Yes. But he knows you. You know him. I would say he works for you. He does what you ask. Perhaps he is a courier. Your runner. Not a high-ranking man, someone more menial. That is why he will not show his face."

Exit Kutoka. Could it be? The name flashing through Vula's thoughts. The man is a danger. He knows about Mpho's message. Maybe he has become weak. Maybe he is frightened. A frightened man is a problem, his fear makes him crazy.

General Vula points at the bones, perhaps he can surprise this man holding the Devil card. Says, "Sergeant Kutoka, I see you." To Luna he says, "This Kutoka has a job to do for me."

"At a beach?"

"How do you know that?"

"I can see it. He is sitting on a bench. There are blocks of flats behind him. It is a beach I recognize."

"What beach?"

"It doesn't matter. Where is not important. He is doing a job for you."

"Good. What of the other figure?"

"That is a woman."

"You are sure?"

"Yes. She holds the card in front of her face. It is the Tower reversed. Your card was the Emperor."

"And what does all this mean?"

"The Emperor is about power, authority. It is a strong sign of your strength. But the card she holds foretells of destruction. Perhaps there will be sudden changes. It is a warning, Kaiser. The shadow woman is warning you."

General Kaiser Vula stabs at the Emperor card with his finger. "This is my card. This is my authority."

Luna Maplewood nods.

His finger moves to the Chariot, hovers above it. "And this one you say is about my position. That I am in charge. Yes. That is what you mean?"

She nods again. "Yes. This is how the cards are read. But can you not see you are facing difficulties?"

"We are always facing difficulties. This is nothing new. It is what comes with leadership."

"Except these two are close to you. This means it is urgent. You must listen to them."

"Ah man, wena. I get it."

They sit in silence. Vula thinking, There was a third figure. She had mentioned a third figure. Why has she not said anything about this shadow? He asks.

Luna Maplewood bends over the bones. "She is still there. It might be the Hermit she holds but there is too much smoke hiding her."

"What is this Hermit?"

"A lonely person. Someone who seeks truth."

"I don't know anyone that could be like that."

"You do. That is why she is there."

"Ah man. These cards, they are too vague!"

"They are warnings, Kaiser."

"And you, who are you?"

"I am the messenger. Do not shoot the messenger. You are my client."

"We are more than that."

"We were more than that. But it is over now."

He stares at her, thinking, She has no heart, no feelings. This woman he thought could see him as a whole man had used him for her pleasure. He is nothing but another walk-in with ready cash. Has it all been mumbo jumbo? He realizes she is talking to him. Asking him about Lady.

"Is she feeling calmer? Has she taken the muti?"

"Yes," he says dismissively, "she has found herself." He grips the wheel rims, turns the chair, wheels himself from the room. Hears the woman say, "These figures are real, Kaiser. These warnings are true. You must beware. You are a man at risk."

What does she know? This woman. This mlungu bitch.

69

Zara's phone rings while she's waiting for Kyle. Of course he's still in the surf. Getting Kyle out of the water takes persuasion and patience. And pizza. Fifteen minutes ago, he signaled that he wanted one last surf. To Kyle, one last surf is a flexible concept. Zara knows this. For the moment, is happy to wait him out. Especially as she's feeling good about getting one up on Ashton. Also, it gives her a chance to think about Exit. So she sits on the beach, watching her son. He's pretty good. Hits the lip once. Puts in a good zigzag on one of the other last waves. In between gets seriously dumped twice. Par for the course. All the time, she's thinking about Exit. Thinking that Exit has to be persuaded into doing the drop this afternoon. Then witness protection. No arguments. The general's gone rogue. Exit's the best chance, the only chance, of stopping him.

Which is about where her thoughts are when her phone rings.

Big D. "Howzit, Cappie."

"Hello, D."

"I just had a visitor, hey. Quite a surprise-surprise for me on a Saturday morning. The last person in the world I'd've expected. But life's full of interesting stuff while it's a life. You wanna guess who it was?"

Zara says she doesn't.

"Lovely female. Well, lovely lezzie female."

"Alicia Hendricks!?"

"The very same personage. Did you know that?"

"What?"

"About her. Her persuasion."

"Sort of. I've got a friend who guessed."

"Ja, well, I don't have a friend. I've got intuition."

"Good for you. So tell me, what did she want? And don't tell me she wanted you to buy some diamonds."

"Hey, man, jackpot almost. But ja, not quite. Still not a bad guess for a detective. No, Cappie, she wasn't gonna sell me stones. Anyhow you know I'm not a buyer."

"Course not. As you've said plenty times before."

"You're damn right, course not. I don't do IDB. I've heard about the kind of jails you lot run. I'd be raped every night."

"That's Prisons Department. Not my lot. Though not sure why you're telling me all this. You've probably heard my lot don't want me in their lot."

"I got the whisper. Can't see why they have you outside the tent pissing in."

"One way to put it. What'd the lovely Alicia want with you?"

"Same as last time, to show me a bag of stones. Tells me there's more where they came from."

"Oh yeah? Interesting. Like how much?"

"Thumb suck, give or take: the right place, this lot you'd get quarter mil."

"Wow."

"Very wow. My guess is the stones are from the same source as last time. Probably Namibian. Clean ocean stones. Beauts, hey. Real beauts. But that's all I got from her. She's a smarty, that one. She one of those you're lining up?"

"Now I'm going to tell you, aren't I?"

Which gets a laugh from Big D. A laugh she remembers. A laugh that thrilled her. And she gets a proposition. "Why don't you drive up? I've got fresh from the sea this morning Hottentots and Red Romans. Very lekker. Cold beer. Cold wine. Juicy reds. We could have an evening braai in the warm air. It's really tit here today. Bring the boy. Tomorrow I'll take him to a kif spot: a clean left break. The guy'll cream. Serious."

For all of a second, Zara thinks it would be fun. But this is Big D. Capital D for dangerous. A glass of wine too many, she'd be on the wild frontier. No accounting for. Stay-away signs flashing at the corners of her eyes.

"I take it you're fancy free. Where's what's-her-name? The pretty poppie."

"Elmari."

"Ja, her."

"Gone home to Mamma."

"Sorry for you."

"Nah, it's okay. Easy come, easy go, hey. So, what d'you say?"

"Another time."

"A pity. But okay. I'll hold you to it."

"Sure."

"I've got a long memory."

"Sure. Anyhow, listen, thanks for the heads-up about Hendricks. She didn't drop anything else?"

"Nada. Nyet. Niks nie."

Zara's thinking could be a simple IDB investigation Hendricks was on. Part of a Police Intelligence gig. On the books, on the level. But with rogue Vula now at the head? How likely was that? Unfuckinglikely. Rather more likely part of a deal. Payment in lieu of cash.

Says to Big D, "Thanks. I owe you."

"You owe me a visit." That laugh.

Maybe she does. Maybe she should. Some other time.

"You might get lucky," she says. Disconnects before he can say anything. Sees Kyle and friend coming out of the sea. Thinks she's got to work on Exit.

70

General Kaiser Vula stares at the pictures on his phone: two of Exit Kutoka and the suspended ICU captain, Zara Dewane. Pictures taken today. The mlungu bitch was right with her tarot cards. Kutoka has crossed the line. Now he has short time.

Keep on him he messages back to the man who sent the photographs.

General Kaiser Vula sits in the car being driven home. He sits with ramrod back, flexing his fingers, releasing the tension. Stares at the passing scene: the Black River, the waste ground, the new development stopped while the first peoples squabble over heritage sites. Who cares who grazed their cattle on this confluence of rivers four hundred years ago! Now it is a different world. He looks beyond the dispute to industrial areas, suburbs, shopping centers, highways, the entire city below the mountain. Yet still these people demand respect for their ancestors. The same ancestors who let the settlers come ashore in the first place. And what happened after that? Centuries of shit happened.

Ah man, suka wena, fuck off.

Kaiser Vula settles back on the leather seats of the Merc. A Merc as new as it smells.

His fury at Luna bitch with her tarot cards is quieting. He has decided on a plan. An exit for Exit. "The one who stands closest is a man. He knows you. You know him." Her words, spoken from the tarot cards.

Maybe the cards spoke the truth.

Maybe.

Kaiser Vula gets home to a moody house. Lady's car is still in the garage. Yet she doesn't answer his greeting. The door to the guest bedroom is still shut. He doesn't knock or attempt to enter. He stops his chair to listen. This time he can hear nothing but the barking of a distant dog.

He wheels down the passage to his study. Closes the door. Wonders if Sergeant Kutoka has compromised the afternoon drop? Probably. He would like to act quickly against Kutoka. Finish him. But knows it would be better to wait. Let others reveal themselves. He phones Captain Alicia Hendricks. It takes a while for her to answer.

"Where are you, Captain?"

"Away for the weekend," she says, her voice hesitant. "I was going to phone you. Is there a problem?"

"A small matter, perhaps, about Sergeant Kutoka. But I feel it can wait."

"What is it?"

Ah, the woman's curiosity.

"He has been talking with Captain Dewane."

"You are sure?"

Of course I am sure he wants to bark at her. Why would I not be sure? Why would I even say this if I was not sure? But he lets the insolence go.

"I have pictures of them. Two pictures. They look very much in earnest, the way they are standing. Unfortunately, it is too far to see their faces. But this is not good that he has gone to her."

He pauses, knowing how Hendricks will respond.

"You have a spy on him?"

The surprise in her voice makes him smile at his image in the window. She is so very predictable.

"I did not trust him. Do you?"

She does not reply.

Again, he considers himself. "My feeling is that we should have the patience to wait. We must not do anything for the moment. We know about Kutoka, but he is ignorant of this. We will see if he delivers this afternoon. It is not so urgent we cannot wait until next week."

"Next week Thursday we have a collection at the storage."

"What is this? Come again?" Why didn't he know about the collection? When was this arranged? "I did not know of this arrangement."

"I am sorry. I said I was going to phone you. It has only now-now been sorted."

"With which person?"

"Tamora Gool."

"She has paid?"

"We are arranging."

"Cash?"

"It will be cash."

"Nothing else. We do not want diamonds. You understand me, Captain? No fancy stones. I do not care if it is more than the cash value, we do not want gravel from the oceans. These people always have real money. They must pay that way."

He wheels himself closer to the window to look into the garden. In the last month, Lady has let it become a riot of weeds. Where once had been order and vegetables, now were creepers and sagging deadheads. Such a waste.

"Anyhow, my Captain, you must go back to your relaxing weekend. I shall keep an eye on our impimpi sergeant. Do not speak to him. Do not tell him about the collection. Everything is in order." Before she can reply, he taps her off. She is good, the captain, but she has to be watched. She has to know that he is in control. That there is only his way.

For that, he has the man. And the driver.

71

At home, Zara gets to work on Exit.

She gets Janet; she gets Janet's phone. Except Janet's not giving it up easily.

"Jirre, Mrs. Z, I's got no data to spare yous." Holding the phone tightly, hand against chest. "You know mos they charging like wounded buffaloes for airtime."

Zara holds out her hand. Fingers waggling. She could use the other phone number but they'd agreed on Janet's phone. "I'll sort you out, Janet, don't worry."

No change in Janet's posture. The phone still clutched.

"Yous gonna have to, cos I's a connected person to my networking. They's calling me an influencer on social media."

"An influencer?" Zara playing it straight. "Ja, seriously. Doing what?"

"Market gardening."

"Really?" Hardly taken Janet for a daughter of the soil.

"There by the tampon towers, we got a patch. You know mos the towers?"

Zara does. Who doesn't. It is a local eyesore. Three tubes of apartments at the edge of the city under Devil's Peak.

"All types of vegetables. I get the street peoples in actual market gardening." Her eyes go cunning. "You give me a hundred smacks, I can bring you fresh-as-dewdrops tomatoes, cauliflower, courgettes, baby-sweet carrots. Taste of the Cape."

"Okay. Deal. Your phone?"

"For a hundred airtime."

"Okay, okay."

The phone changes hands. Janet not moving an inch. Zara gets a haunch up on the kitchen table, eyes on Janet. Wondering should she tell her to scram. Decides what the hell. Contacts Exit.

Says right out: "You've got to do that live drop this afternoon."

No response.

"You hear me, Exit, please, man, you must. I need to get hard evidence. You know how it is. National Prosecuting's going to laugh at me otherwise. Please, Sergeant. Nobody'll see me." Going for his rank as a call to action.

Doesn't work. Again no response. This time she lets the silence drag. Eyes on Janet. Janet mouthing at her: You gotta talk more, Mrs. Z. Say something. Zara does.

"Look, I know this is difficult for you. I know you don't want to do it. But it's just a handover. You put the box on the bench.

Someone sits down. Few moments later, walks away with the box. No problem. Isn't anything going to happen. Anyhow, I'm going to be there, watching."

Janet giving her the thumbs-up: Way to go.

"I want to see who we're dealing with."

Lets it hang there.

Then he says, "A gangster nobody. A youth."

Yes.

"That's how it's been before?"

No response.

"You don't know which gang?"

"No. It doesn't matter. Sexy Boys, Americans, Mongols. They are the same."

"Please. One last time, Sergeant. As a policeman. Do this."

A long gap. Zara comes off the table. Paces the floor. Catches Janet leaning against a counter, watching her.

"What?"

"Wait, Mrs. Z, this is fishing. You gotta leave time. Don't tug on the line."

Zara can hear the guy breathing on the other end. Cop duty fighting cop instincts. She counts. On twenty's going to tell him the story of little Levana. How little Levana, seven years old, was skipping with friends in the street when wannabes from the Mongols started shooting at wannabes from the Born Free Kids. Bang, little Levana takes a 9mm to the head. Doesn't kill her. Puts her in hospital. Many operations later, she's still with us. Now she's nine years old. But she can't skip in the street anymore. She hasn't got friends anymore. She's going to need someone to feed her, dress her, wash her, wipe her ass for the rest of her life. Nice life, hey!

Zara doesn't have to tell Sergeant Exit Kutoka the story of little Levana because he says, "Alright. Okay."

Says it so quietly she's not sure she heard correctly. But she isn't going to question him. Goes straight into arrangements of where and when. Exit tells her: the car park at the Vincent Pallotti Hospital, 3:00 p.m.

Which gives her a couple of hours to organize her life: get pictures of the guns; line up her parents to take Kyle; get Kyle to them.

"Ah, Mom, do I have to go?"

"You do.

"Can't I just stay here?"

"No. Listen, be grateful you got a whole morning surfing. If you're nice, you might get a repeat tomorrow. Any rate, what's your problem? Gran feeds you choc muffins. They've got fast Wi-Fi. G-pa'll take on your chess moves."

"He always wins."

"So get smarter."

She phones her mother to make arrangements. Then talks to her father. Asks him: "Can you help me fix up a camera tomorrow?"

He comes back with "At your house?"

"No. For surveillance of a facility."

A pause. "Where? Is it legal?"

"Isn't illegal."

"Not the same thing."

"It's a case I'm working."

That considered pause. "You're on suspension. You're not supposed to be working any cases."

True. She's got no response to that.

72

Vincent Pallotti Hospital, 3:00 p.m. Zara turns into the parking area, finds Exit Kutoka's hand-painted Honda in a bay against the fence. He's standing at the car, peak, sunglasses, jeans, T-shirt, a hoody top draped over his shoulders. Doesn't look anything like a cop. She pulls up; he's quickly into the passenger seat.

No niceties. No smile.

She's looking at him: "This's a strange place to meet."

He's staring straight ahead. "My car is safe here."

Perfectly true.

Zara wants to say, Relax, Sergeant. This is just a handover. No big deal. You've done it before. Plenty times. You're not going to have to do it again. Bit of luck you'll get a medal when I've nailed this down.

Goes with, "Hang in there, Sergeant. Next week you can drink beer, watch Netflix all day long."

She takes the N2 highway to the Strand. They find the bench on the promenade with fifteen minutes to spare. It's a fine afternoon. There're kids in the shallows. Moms and dads on the beach. The citizenry taking an afternoon constitutional along the front. Plenty of crawl traffic doing a zooty car parade. Your ideal spring Saturday without the wind.

Zara does a couple of circuits to check out the scene. Here and there, low-riding jeans hanging around. Then again the collect-guy could be in broads and T-shirt, your average surfer dude. Far as she can see there's no setup planning to ambush Exit. Turns off the front to find parking in a back street.

Their plan: she'll make her way to the beach. Find a spot where she can easily video him. He'll give her five minutes, walk slowly to the designated bench. Sit down, wait. Afterwards, he stays there for fifteen minutes. She'll give him the all clear. He goes back to the car, writes out an affidavit of what went down. Ten minutes later, they're on the road home. Mission accomplished.

At least, that's the plan.

The first part works out. Zara finds a low wall she can sit on. Straddles it. Gets the sea on her right, a long view to an ice-cream van straight ahead, the bench off five, six yards to the left. She's wearing a floppy hat, pretends she's reading stuff on her phone. Watches Exit come out of a side street, cross the main road, buy an ice cream. Mr. Ever So Cool. He's toting the box awkwardly under his arm. She's thinking, Hell, Sergeant, the ice cream's not a good idea. Couple of times looks like he's going to drop it. He doesn't. Makes it to the bench. Sits on the furthest side, the box to his right. Zara gets some video going. Ja, that's nice. Could have done with a Choc 99 herself. Nothing like a soft-serve at the beach.

Exit finishes the ice cream, wipes his mouth with a tissue. Fastidious guy. Shifts his position to lounging. His legs stretched out. His hand on the box, the only nervous tic his fingers moving in a rhythmic pattern: tip tap, tip tap. Tip tap, tip tap. She wants to tell him, Stop it, chill, my bru.

And then, who's this?

Not some wannabe shooter from the ganglands.

Not some fifteen-year-old tikhead stonked on crystal meth.

No, my lewe fok, Eloise, it's Tamora Gool herself in actual stunning person. Also licking at an ice cream. Also a Choc 99. Taking her time with long licks at the vanilla. Now sitting next to Exit, saying something to him, pointing at the beach. Zara follows the direction to a bunch of kids kicking a ball. Then Gool's standing up. Zara knowing if she glances her way, it will be to gloat: Clocked you, bitch. But she doesn't. Which doesn't mean she's unaware. Could be she's just being smart. The usual Tamora Gool style. Now looks back at Exit, shakes her head, goes off across the beach toward the boys playing football. Gool's not ten paces away when a teenage low-rider slides onto the bench. So far, so stereotypical. Gangsta wannabe says something to Exit. Exit points at the box. The low-rider gives him the two fingers safe-my-mate, whips away with the box into an idling car. Throaty exhaust and they're off. Zara getting it all on video. Itching to know what Tamora Gool had to say. She's about to walk, leave the scene, when a white woman takes a seat next to Exit. Sits close to him, her knees, bare knees, almost touching his thighs. Starts talking straight away. Urgently. Even touches his arm. The woman's in her thirties. Dressed for jogging. Trainers, Lycra shorts, crop top. Hair pulled back in a tight pony. Clutches a runner's water bottle. Is really into Exit. My lewe, the guy's a babe magnet. Then the woman's off the bench, crouches in front of him, seems to be pleading. Exit looking awkward, leaning forward, trying to get her to rise. She does. Mournful expression on her face. Zara wonders should she intervene? Rescue the poor man. What's with the woman, anyhow? Unless Exit had a thing with her. Handsome guy like him could leave a trail of broken hearts. Then sees the woman's off, not turning round. Zara checks on Gool. She's with the boys, a long way down the beach. It's a quick glance before Zara looks back at Exit, searches for the woman. The woman's gone. Like poof, disappeared. Not a trace of her among the pavement strollers. Not a glimpse of her crossing the street. The bird's simply flown. Vanished.

Fifteen minutes later, Sergeant Exit Kutoka opens the passenger door of her hatchback. Came up from behind. But she'd caught the movement in the wing mirror.

Her first words to him: "Where the hell have you been, Sergeant?"

"We said fifteen minutes. It is fifteen minutes."

No point arguing that one. What Zara wants to ask is: who was that woman, the jogger?

What she goes with is professionalism. "What'd Gool say?"

"That she was pleased to meet me. She hoped that there would be more business like this."

"You knew who she was?"

"From pictures."

"That's all she said?"

"She said she would meet me at the storage on Thursday to make the collection."

"Storage? The place you told me?"

"Yes."

"She's going to make a collection on Thursday only?"

"Yes."

"She knows where it is?"

"I do not think so. They will only tell her one hour before."

"She didn't ask you?"

"No."

"What time would it be, the collection?"

"Early probably. It is always early, at eight o'clock."

"You knew about this collection?"

"No. I have not been told this. I told you this morning I know nothing. I'm guessing the time."

"But you're the one who's on site? You supervise?"

"That is the captain. She has the key. She makes the organization."

"The collection could happen without you?"

"It is possible. I do not know. The captain will tell me if I must be there."

"When?"

"Later. This is too early. She will only tell me in the exact morning."

Zara's impressed. Last-minute instructions always the best. Less chance of anything going wrong. Comes back to Exit. "Nothing more? Gool said nothing more. It seemed like she did. When she was pointing at the beach."

"Not about the collection. Only she says her boy is playing soccer on the beach."

Yeah. "Miss Perfect Mom."

You had to give the woman her chutzpah.

"And the other woman? Who's she? You have a thing with her?"

Exit Kutoka snorts. "Bah, never."

"You know her?"

He turns his head to frown at her. "How must I know her? I've never seen her before."

Zara lets this go, looking intently at Exit's face now in profile. Not a twitch of emotion there. He's focused on the empty street.

"So what'd she say? Seemed like she wanted to eat you."

"She said that I must run. They are going to kill me."

"Who's going to kill you?"

"The general."

"Vula?"

"Yes."

"She said him by name?"

"Yes."

"And you don't know who she is? You have no idea? She's just some arb came jogging along, thought she'd better stop 'n' tell you you're gonna die. Plonks down on the bench. Grabs your arm, says, 'Exit, my love, there's this general's going to take you out. Beware the wheelchair man.' That's what she says? My lewe fok, Exit, what's she? Some kind of informer? Some spy from the Aviary who's got an inside track on General Vula? What I want to know is how does she fit into the frame? You got any answers?"

Exit stays staring at the street.

"She even give you her name?"

He mumbles something.

"Say again."

"I dunno. Maybe she said something. She speaks too fast."

"But you heard General Vula's name."

"I heard it."

"But not her name?"

"No. It was too quick."

Zara starts the car, heads back to town. On the highway, says, "What are you going to do? Are you still going to run like you said this morning?"

A nod. A quiet yes.

She's been thinking about this for the last five miles. If she puts him into a safe house, she's got a witness. If she captures the storage collection on video, she's got evidence.

"I can help you. I can make a plan."

He waits a long time to say "Alright."

She tells him how things will play.

73

The man praises the Israelis. Oh, how they have simplified his life. And all thanks to a winged horse. Before Pegasus, life had its hidden moments. With Pegasus, life is more, well, transparent. And all it takes is a WhatsApp call to install the software on the target phone. In the lingo—which he loves—a "zero-click exploit." In short, he can switch on her phone mic whenever he wants to, listen to whatever's going down in the vicinity. He can switch on her phone camera if needs be. He can listen in to whatever she's saying. And she doesn't know it. Wasn't that difficult to get her number either. You know the right people, you can get anything. And then, oh baby Israeli, what a wonderful world, what a bright, blessed day. He's had Pegasus flying on Zara's phone since the job started. Which is why he got an earful of Linda Perry earlier. Not that he doesn't like Linda's singing. She's got a helluva voice. "What's Up" could be his theme song as well. He just wishes Zara was more attached to her phone. If she held it in her hand everywhere she went, life would be easier still.

But never mind.

We shall overcome.

He's heard her talking to a third party. Heard her arranging to meet said third party at the Vincent Pallotti Hospital at 3:00 p.m.

And there she is at the appointed time with none other than the easily recognizable Sergeant Exit Kutoka.

He follows them to the Strand. He watches Zara Dewane set herself up. So attractive for a cop. That black hair, lithe figure. Her surety of movement. She's good. As good as he is. There is a moment she even looks in his direction as she scopes the surrounds. He has to move away, relocate. Wait until he's sure she's not onto him. She settles down; he settles down. He watches the sergeant eat an ice cream. He videos him have a conversation with an unknown female. She's a stunner in skinny jeans. What's it with these brown ladies, they're all walking models. Has to stop himself watching her walk away across the beach, that tight bum. With a sigh, keeps himself focused. He videos the low-rider gangbanger slope off with the package. He videos the sergeant being talked to by an unknown white female. Not bad looking either. Especially in the jogging gear. Got to give it to Exit Kutoka, he pulls in the broads. Brings him back to Zara

Dewane, sitting there unobtrusively. In all the videos, she's in the foreground, her back to the camera. He watches his two targets leave separately. Switches on the useful Pegasus but no luck. Her phone's buried somewhere. Can't even hear muffled voices. Twenty minutes later, there they are, driving past him in Zara Dewane's white Polo hatchback. On the N2 highway he catches up, overtakes, is waiting at the hospital parking lot when they pull in. Still the stupid bitch's got her phone stowed away. Nothing for him but to follow the sergeant.

Which he does. Into Gugulethu, past Mzoli's Place down the neat NY115 to a house with columns, sliding gates. Here the sergeant goes in. He must drive past. Okay, he knows where the man stays. Now what? This is a tricky situation. A white man in a parked car in NY115 is wrong. Two choices: stop for a beer at Mzoli's or go home. The first option appeals. It's been a long afternoon; it's time to hang loose. He'd love to kick back with a short No17. But he doesn't. Does the white man in a parked car in NY115 getting WTF glances from passers-by. Hasn't been there ten minutes, he catches a WhatsApp from Zara Dewane to Exit Kutoka.

You are booked in at the City Lodge, Pinelands.

He Telegrams his principal. Attaches all the videos. Why not? Give the dude a thrill.

Gets back a green tick.

Telegrams: *Bongo-bongo?*

Gets back a green tick.

Mzoli's is tempting. Professionalism triumphs. He follows Exit to the Bellville Town Lodge. The cunning bitch. Must've got to Exit on another phone. All the same. Nothing lost.

74

Zara slides the phone she uses for miscellaneous stuff into her pocket.

"How many of those burners've you got?" asks her father.

"Three."

He smiles, shakes his head.

"Just playing it safe."

"You cannot conduct such a case alone, my bokkie. You must report this."

"To who? The brass would laugh at me. I'm on suspension."

They're in the backyard, drinking beer from bottles, sitting round the braai, more specifically her father's Weber. He's cooking lamb chops, small porkies, jacket potatoes wrapped in foil. It's a paradise night: no wind, warm, there's still light at gone seven o'clock. Kyle's inside on YouTube. Granma's making a mixed salad. Domestic bliss.

Father John says, "There is your legal colleague, what's-her-name?"

"Jo-Jo. Josephine."

"Her. Also, there are structures, you know? And you said you've met Minister Majoro. You could go straight to her even."

Zara sighs. Takes a pull at her beer. He's right. It's an option.

"You're right, Pa. After next week, of course I could. But I need that evidence first."

"No, Zara, you need to stay away from that collection." He lifts the lid to check the meat. Turns over the sausages. "You need to tell Serious Crimes for the right people to handle it. They are trained for such things. They have tactical units."

"Oh yes, that's going to make a big difference?"

"What're you now, Superwoman? You can't do everything alone."

"Which is why I'm asking you. Help me put up a camera tomorrow. No one's going to see us. C'mon, Pa. I mean, who's going to be at that place on a Sunday? Nobody in their right mind. We can fix it with a motion sensor. I get the whole collection on digital. That's evidence. I don't even have to be there. You know how these things work. You can do it."

"You reckon!"

"Look, Hendricks will be at the collection. She has to be, to open up. My feeling is Gool will be there too. She's hands-on. These two girls think they're putting one over on the big boys. So I want them both in the frame."

Her father flips the chops with a fork, rolls over the potatoes. Takes a drink from his bottle, turns his eyes on her. Skeptical eyes, like hers. She's seen them plenty of times over the years.

"You don't have to look at me like that."

He sighs. "Ag, Zara, what can I say?"

"What's on your mind. You always do."

"You know as I know that real evidence is catching them loading up those crates. That's proper evidence. Indisputable. That's what you need. You position a unit there, that's what'll happen; you'll get real evidence."

"Sure. And I'm going to get that to happen how?"

"Phone the minister. Now. Phone her. Tell her. This is where it ends for you. Your job's done. You've got that sergeant safe. You got evidence this afternoon. Next week Thursday, let Serious Crimes wrap it up."

She knows he's right. She's been through these thoughts herself. Any other time, she'd have gone by the book. But this isn't any other time. This time she's got other ideas.

"If I do that …"

"Not if. Do it."

"Listen, just listen. If I do that, it doesn't lead to Vula? He can still duck it all."

Her father does more braai inspection. Sits back. "How so?"

"He's a general. A war veteran. The man's connected."

"Doesn't matter. Your Captain Hendricks will give him up."

"So what?"

"What d'you mean so what? She says she's in with the general, that's what you want."

"He'll say she's gone rogue. He knows nothing about her activities."

"When she's caught, it'll get nasty. People're like the fish that's taken my bait. They fight like hell. They don't want the hook in their cheek. From what you've said about this captain, she'll fight. Also …"

"Also what?"

"I'm getting there." He puts a hand on her arm. How many times hasn't he done that? "Let me finish, okay?"

She smiles. Acquiesces.

"Thank you." A pause while he takes a drink. "You've got your sergeant's evidence. That gets you to Vula."

"Again, it's his word against Vula's. That's all I've got. A sergeant against a general. The man leaves no paper trail."

"And the captain. That's two witnesses. That's leverage." Her father stands. "We're all done here." Forks up the chops into a pot. "What's wrong with collaborators' testimony?"

"They're deniable. No hard evidence of complicity."

"So why is getting video evidence of this collection going to be any different? I don't see it." He uses his fingers to lift the potatoes, the pork sausages. Flicks his fingers at the burn.

"Because all I'm planning is to show it to Vula. Tell him I'll be talking to Hendricks. Putting a Section 22 search and seizure on Tamora Gool. It's bait, Pa. Something to put a hook in his cheek."

"I think it's a crap idea. You're taunting him."

"Exactly."

"I don't know. One minute you're telling me no brass will listen to you, the next you want a Section 22. How're you going to get that?"

"Like you said, there's Jo-Jo. They'll jump for her."

She grins at him. Takes his arm. Hears him grumble that if she listened to him the first time …

"Yeah, I know we wouldn't have to go round and round. But that's the thing, that's the way we do it."

"Right, come you two," says Elsi from the kitchen doorway. "Enough with the cop-talk, time to eat." Her mother standing there, hands on hips, trying to keep a stern face. Now beckoning them with an impatient hand.

What'd we do without her? Zara wonders.

75

Couple of minutes after 10:30 p.m., the man drives into the parking grounds at the Town Lodge, Bellville. Parks in a row one back from the entrance. Above him lighted windows. Behind one of them, Sergeant Exit Kutoka probably stretched out on the double bed, watching television. Probably thinking this is the safest night of his life. Probably a tray with supper remains on the dressing table below a mirror. Probably can see the reflection of himself relaxed, living the life. No doubt whisky miniatures gone from the minibar.

The man has a standard idea about hotel behavior.

Now, from the glovebox, takes out a black Ruger SR22. Really nice polymer grip. He's got the grip with a wider palm swell to fit his hand. The man's hands are large. The clip for the SR is ten up plus one .22LR rimfire cartridges. He's tried them out hunting gray squirrels in Newlands Forest. With the .22LR, there's no kickback, not much noise. Fit the new lightweight Silent-SR sound suppressor, you've got no more than a watery plop on execution. You can shoot squirrels without anybody knowing, even in a walkers' paradise like the forest. Then again, the SR22 is also highly effective at an intimate range. He has a preference for intimacy: ideally two yards, max three.

The man screws on the silencer, tucks the weapon into a holster beneath his jacket. A bunny jacket he fancies on a job like this. A sober navy-blue zip-up with a round collar, side pockets for his gloves. Lifts a package from the back seat. It's a padded envelope sealed with brown tape addressed to Sergeant Exit Kutoka, from Captain Zara Dewane. Doesn't weigh much, feels like documents. Which it is.

The man gets out of his car, remote locks as he steps away.

At the hotel's reception desk, he asks if he can deliver the package to the sergeant.

Unfortunately not, he's told. Hotel rules. Said with a no-offense smile.

He lays on it's an urgency.

No problem, a messenger can do it immediately.

Much obliged, he says. Asks for directions to the men's loo.

When the hotel staffer takes the stairs to deliver the envelope, the man is not far behind. Watches the exchange happen at room 115. Hears the hotel staffer wish the sergeant a good evening, head off down the long corridor, leaving by the service stairs at the end. The man reckons no time like the present. Best to sort matters while the sergeant's still reading through the documents. The documents being the ins and outs of witness protection the man's pulled off the internet.

Toot sweet, he knocks on the door of room 115. To the "What?" from inside, explains, "From reception, sir, another envelope."

The door opens. The sergeant's standing there: barefoot, wearing maroon tracksuit pants with white stripes down the legs, a long-sleeved T-shirt (green). Looking tense.

"Evening, sir, sorry to barge in," says the man, barging in, sending Exit staggering back to sit on the bed. The man closes the door, swivels on Exit, his long-nosed Ruger SR22 with the ten .22LR loads plus one in the breech steady in his right hand. "You wouldn't want to do anything foolish, Sergeant," he says.

Before Sergeant Kikiha "Exit" Kutoka can respond, the man takes a pace forward into the two-yard intimacy range, fires. Opens a hole in the sergeant's forehead. Neat. No exit cavity. No Jackson Pollock splatter on the wall. The sergeant collapses backward on the bed. Neatly laid out. For surety's sake, the man leans slightly forward, shifts the barrel downward, fires into the sergeant's heart. The body gives a weak shudder. The man holsters his weapon. Draws on gloves. From the bedside table, takes the envelope of witness-protection documents, still unopened. Leaves without a glance at the dead man, going down the long corridor to the service stairs as the staffer had done. Brings him out into a lane with wheelie bins of rubbish stacked neatly on both sides. The metal gate at the end is unlocked, opens onto the far end of the car park. Five minutes later he's in his vehicle, sending a Telegram text.

Gets back a green tick.

The man's all heart, thinks the man. Drives home to the songs of Linda Perry. He's quite taken to her music. Thank you, Zara Dewane.

76

"Enough," says General Kaiser Vula aloud. She has not answered his knocking. She has not answered his calling her name. The door to the spare bedroom is locked. Her recalcitrance is now annoying. Extremely irritating. He should have her support. This was what she wanted. She should be basking in the power. Instead, she hides away.

It is Sunday morning. He phones the driver. In the half hour it takes the man to arrive, he sits in his study, staring at the overgrown garden. Lady is not uppermost in his thoughts. Uppermost are Sergeant Exit Kutoka and Captain Alicia Hendricks. And tarot cards. The childish figures of the tower, the chariot, the devil, the hermit. What nonsense. Yet the words of Luna Maplewood. They are warnings. And Lady's words: "I am worried. The ancestors see us."

He hears a car arrive. Wheels himself to the front door. Opens it on the driver's knock.

"Boss?"

"Come." He reverses, sets off down the passage. Until they stand outside the bedroom door. He looks up at his man. A gym and steroid individual. "Break it."

The driver frowns at him. "I must hit the door?"

"Break it, chief." Vula holds up a hammer. "It is a hollow door. Break it there at the handle."

The driver smashes through in four blows, clears a hole using the claw.

As Vula expected, not a peep out of Lady at the destruction. He inches forward, peers through the hole. He can see the neatness of the room. He can see her on the bed. She lies unmoving. He knows why. He shouts her name. He thumps on the door.

"Lady! Lady!"

This is no longer irritation. Now this is an ache in his chest that surprises even him. A rasp that comes into his voice. He backs away from the door. To the driver, he says in a low voice, "Put your hand in. There is a key in the lock, you can turn it."

The door opens. He grips the wheel rims, propels himself across the brown carpet toward the bed. On the side table is an empty glass. A bottle of whisky, half consumed. An empty vial that had contained the little pills she'd taken to popping nightly.

He feels at her neck, there is no pulse. Her skin is cold. She has been dead for hours. He looks at her face. What can you tell from a dead face? You can see peace. You can see relief. Or you can see horror. You can see fear. General Kaiser Vula does not want to see horror or fear. General Kaiser Vula sees humor. A pull on the lips as if she is about to smile. As she once smiled at him. And he knows he did not want this to happen to her.

Ah man.

He turns to the driver. "You can go, chief. There is nothing for you to do here."

"I can stay, boss. I can help the general."

"No. It would be better for me alone. I must make the arrangements."

"I am sorry, boss. I am sorry for your loss."

Vula nods. "One other thing. Last night? It is sorted, that business at the hotel?"

"It is, my boss."

"There were no problems?"

"No problems."

Vula nods again. "You are a good man, chief. Do you want payment on book or cash?"

"Book, my boss. I am making savings."

The general grunts his approval. "Ah ha. Then maybe one day, I will come to you for a loan."

"It is never possible," says the driver. "The general, he is too rich."

They both bark a laugh at this idea as Vula wheels himself out of the room.

When the driver has gone, he makes the phone calls.

To Minister Majora. She is in town. She will come over immediately.

To his doctor. He will be there in half an hour.

To the funeral parlor, Angel Wings. They are also sorry for his loss. Has the beloved been seen by a doctor? The arrangements for the beloved's burial or cremation can be arranged later. Attendants will be there in an hour to take care of the beloved.

And then to Luna Maplewood, because he is puzzled. What did she say to Exit Kutoka? Why was she there? How did she even know about it? But he's decided, he's not going there. He will save that for another time. Right now, he needs to tell her about Lady. He starts with: "She is gone."

"Kaiser! I'm sorry, what? What are you saying?"

"She is gone. Lady has died. She is dead."

Silence. "My god! My heavens! How is this possible?"

"She took the sleeping pills."

"But what of the muti I gave you for her?"

"That doesn't matter. She is dead."

Silence.

Then: "I am so sorry, Kaiser. I don't know what to say. Do you want me to come over?"

"No."

"Do you want to come here? I can fetch you."

"No."

"You shouldn't be alone."

"I am not. There will be people all day. Minister Majora is coming. And there will be others from the Service. I have the domestic to serve the biscuits and tea. And I must answer the phone. The news gets out. There are condolences from many people."

77

On this Sunday morning, Zara's thinking a repeat of Saturday would be good. Kyle hardly going to object. She's standing at the bedroom window, looking at another morning without wind. Unheard of. Especially in November. She takes a pee, brushes her teeth, thoughts of Exit now uppermost. Should she call him? She should call him. She should. But maybe not at 8:00 a.m. Going to be another forty-five minutes before she's got Kyle moving. She'll ring at nine.

Which she does.

She and Kyle in the kitchen in surfskin tops, wetsuits pulled up to their waists.

"Isn't this cute," she teases him. "Ocean dudes." He squirms away.

Now champing, "Ah c'mon, Mom, can't we go already?"

Zara saying, "Hang on, okay. Just hold it for a moment."

Janet saying, "Yous wanna use my phone again, Mrs. Z? I's gonna have to charge a commissioning fee."

Zara holds out her hand. "Whatever, Janet. It's a goddamned WhatsApp call on *my* Wi-Fi. In case you'd forgotten."

"No never, Mrs. Z. I knows that. But this's my device from my capital expenditure."

Zara waggles her fingers. "Give."

"Just one call, hey."

She connects via WhatsApp. Lets it ring for a long time before she disconnects. Tries a direct call. Again no pick up.

What's the problem with the guy? He's switched his phone off? Would he do that? Is he dead to the world? Does anybody sleep through a ringing cell phone? He's got it on silent? Maybe he's in the toilet? Maybe he's taking a shower? Maybe he's heard it; he'll ring in a few minutes.

"Come on, Mom," nags Kyle. "I told the guys we were on our way."

"Two minutes, Kyle. It's not going to set your life back. You want to wait in the car, that's fine. I'll be there in two minutes."

Kyle slouches off; she times two minutes.

Before they're up, Janet says, "Give him another ring, Mrs. Z, these mens like their sleep time. You gotta wake him."

Zara phones again. To no avail. Now thinking, Do I take the boys to the beach, then check on him? Do I check on him first? Decides, Get rid of the boys.

"Look, I'm going. When he rings, you phone and tell me. Yes?"

"Jawohl." Janet snaps a heil Hitler.

Zara hands back the phone, deadpan. Would like to scream "My lewe fok, Eloise," but doesn't.

All the way along Philip Kgosana Drive, has Exit on her mind. The guy is her responsibility. Or that's how she sees it. At least her responsibility until she can get him into witness protection. Comes off the highway into Gardens, stops outside the home of Kyle's friend. Said friend's standing in the driveway, surfboard under his arm. His mother hovering behind.

It's right then that Zara changes her mind. Tells Kyle, "Out of the car. Now. Please." Is out of the car herself, moving fast toward the friend's mother, saying, "Listen, I'm sorry to do this. I've got an emergency, a police thing, could you take the boys to the beach?"

The woman, alarmed, steps back, says, "Yes, sure, no problem. I didn't realize. Hope it's not serious."

Kyle's protesting, "Mom, you said you would?"

When Zara realizes she must look weird, being dressed to kayak. Stammers out, "I've got to get home and get changed. This's a mess." To Kyle, "I'll see you later at the beach. As we said, one o'clock." To the mother, says, "That okay with you?"

The mother saying, "Of course. We can pick them up if you want? WhatsApp me what's happening."

With a "Will do" and to Kyle, "Don't get eaten," Zara's gone.

At home, changes into her uniform: jeans, T-shirt, red leather jacket. Has Janet standing at her bedroom door, telling her, "Ooo la la, Mrs. Z, yous on the war path. That's a nice sports bra like I wanna buy."

Zara thinking, Yeah, I know where this is going. Runs a brush through her hair. Says, "Has the sergeant phoned?"

"Not a peep-peep."

"Try again."

Janet does. No answer. "You better find him, Mrs. Z. I got a bad feeling coming on."

"You 'n' me both, Janet."

78

The man's been watching his tracker zip to Gardens, return to Woodstock. Minutes later, it's off again. Gets onto the national highway. He knows where this will end. He's getting no joy from her phone. The camera shows a black screen. The mic gives muffled voices. As if she's twigged that her phone's hot. Is keeping it pocketed.

He sits in his kitchen with its view of the mountain, the blue sky above. The weekend newspaper spread out on the table, a mug of tea at his hand. The man's a Ceylon addict. No local rooibos. No vegan herbal mix. No fruit teas. He wants Ceylon black tea leaves. Not tea bags. Never tea bags. Those are filled with dust, floor sweepings. He buys his brew of choice direct from a wholesaler.

On his iPad, he watches the tracker stop. Believes she's in the Bellville Town Lodge car park. Then he gets visuals. She must have her phone in her hand as she walks. He gets her black trainers, tarmac, a door opening, carpet pattern.

Hears: "Can you tell Sergeant Kutoka I'm in reception."

On the screen, a flash of people standing around, others at the desk checking out.

Then the receptionist: "There's no response, I'm afraid. Perhaps he's eating breakfast."

"I'm going to his room."

"We can't allow that, ma'am. It's hotel rules."

"I'm police."

"I'll get my manager. He can go up with you."

"Get him."

On screen, he's got the receptionist summoning her manager. Then the manager saying, "How can I help you, ma'am?"

The man sips his tea. Watches the swinging images as the captain and the manager take the stairs. No conversation between them.

Hears the manager say, "This is the room, 115."

There's a knock. And again.

The swipe of the electronic card. He's getting all this on video. They go in, the room's empty. No suitcase. A whisky glass on the bedside table. Empty miniatures on the bar fridge. No toiletries in the bathroom. The bed rumpled but not slept in.

"My god," says the manager. "The guy's done a runner. I don't believe it."

My lord, thinks the man. That's amazing. Got to hand it to the general. He's organized.

79

Alicia's worked a deal that they don't have to be out of the weekend pad until after lunch. So they're still in bed, sliding door open onto the marina. There are Egyptian Geese (nowadays renamed ducks) out there paddling around with a string of little ones. Alicia and Duifie are propped against the headboard, Duifie in a long T-shirt; Alicia, let's say she's got a sheet covering her lower extremities. The bed's a mess because earlier Duifie put her tongue into Alicia's ear. Woke her with its soft probings. One thing gets Alicia fired, it's a tongue in her ear. Gives her what she calls "the grils." Goosebumps up and down her back, her arms. The insides of her thighs. A situation Duifie exploits to the max. She's got a wicked tongue. Among other techniques. A whole Kama Sutra that Alicia'd never dreamed of before. Which is why the bed is a mess. Rucked undersheet, discarded duvet. Afterwards, after the tongue thing, Duifie spoilt her in other ways. With bubbly and orange juice in flutes. A poached egg on buttery toast. Blueberry muffins. Coffee.

Alicia breaks off a piece of muffin, pops it into her mouth. Washes it down with the last of her coffee. "So've you ever been to the south of France?"

Duifie laughs, licks a dribble of egg off her chin. "Ag, no man, what a question. Like when's that been possible in my lifetime. Working girls such as moi don't mos go jolling at Saint-Tropez. Maybe a week on Clifton Fourth Beach or up to Durbs on a cheapie flight. I haven't even got a foreign stamp in my passport. Are you crazy?"

"Me neither," says Alicia. She looks at Duifie sitting cross-legged on the bed, her hair bunched in swirls, thinks, Ja, what, this's the girl. You can get lost in her. You can go places with her. Can see them at some harbor café on the Med eating bouillabaisse. Swimming topless in the moonlight. Why not? She's going to have the bucks. She's got more leave owing than days in a month. Seize the moment, poppie. Now's the time.

"Would you like to go?"

"Ah crap." Duifie scoops muffin crumbs from the bed. "These blerrie things always break for me." She stuffs muffin into her mouth. "Ja."

"Ja, you'd like to go?"

"Of course, that'd be such fun." She leans forward, plonks a kiss on Alicia's nipple. "Only thing is, how're we gonna do that?"

"With my savings."

"Wow, you can't pay it all."

Alicia has to smile. Strokes the back of her fingers down Duifie's cheek. "Why not? I've got the bucks."

"Really?"

"Really."

"Ah, liefie, you're mos so nice, I can't believe it." She snuggles in.

From the outside comes a voice: "Yoohoo, ladies, enough with the shagging. Time to socialize."

From Alicia: "Oh shit. Oh kak." Raises up on an elbow to see a canoeist beyond the jetty, waving his paddle.

Duifie lifts her head. "Who's that?"

"The fish man."

In the canoe is Big D now holding up a kicking crayfish.

Duifie's out of the bed, wraps herself in the duvet, bounds from the room onto the deck. "Hello, Mr. Fish Man, that was lekker fish you gave us."

"How about some of these?"

"That's amazing. Any time."

"Right then, tell your lazy partner there's someone she needs to meet. And a couple or ten of these crayfish you'll want to eat. What d'you say?"

"Lekka smekka. We're coming."

"My place in an hour. See you there 'n' then, pretty chick."

80

The door of room 115 opens. Entering is Advocate Josephine Lanski, looking unhappy. Actually looking seriously pissed off.

"You took your time." Zara gets up from where she's sitting on the floor in the corner of the room.

Gets a "Bloody hell, Zara, it's Sunday morning. Some of us have lives, you know? We're not all at your instant beck and call." She's in colorful Soviet trainers, jazzy leggings, an orange T-shirt, a peak cap. "We were having breakfast out. In case you were wondering. For the first time in a while. Just the two of us. Until your bloody call."

"Okay, sorry, okay?" says Zara. "But, look, this is strange."

"Doesn't look like anything strange to me. Looks like a hotel bedroom." Jo-Jo has her arms folded. Sunglasses dangling from her fingers.

"Listen. First thing this morning, I started phoning him."

"This is Sergeant Kutoka?"

"Yes. No answer. I come here and find he's gone. Can't you get forensics for me to do the room?"

"Oh yes, of course. Like, I can snap my fingers and they'll come running. Seriously. How'm I supposed to arrange that? On a Sunday. When it isn't even a crime scene."

"It may be. That's the thing. The room has to be checked out."

"May be? Christ alone, Zara, listen to yourself. Getting forensics to a crime scene is bad enough. Getting someone to a 'maybe'"—Jo-Jo does scare quotes with the fingers of one hand—"is going to get me a 'ha, ha, pull the other one.' So just forget it. It's a lovely day. Go paddle your canoe."

"Kayak."

"What?"

"It's a kayak. Not a canoe."

"Kayak, canoe, boat. It floats. You take it out where sharks swim. Aren't there enough sharks for you on land? Anyhow. Aren't we having a heart-chat later?"

"Don't know. Depends. Maybe not now. Maybe another time."

Jo-Jo's about to sit on the bed when Zara grabs her arm, holds her back.

"Don't sit there. That's what I need forensics to check out."

From the doorway, the manager says, "Excuse me. Are you finished yet? We need to prepare the room. We can't hold it any longer."

Zara glances at him. "This is a police matter. We need to secure the room."

"What for? I don't understand."

"I've told you."

"But you can see nothing's happened here. Your sergeant's skipped. That's it. His car's gone. You checked yourself, you told me yourself. Now, please, Captain Dewane, can we service the room?"

"No. Not yet."

Jo-Jo ushers the manager from the room with whisperings that Zara can't hear. Closes the door. Turns to Zara.

"Briefly. Words of one syllable, what's the problem?"

Zara catches her eyes. Holds them.

"I've got a witness …" Starts again: "I had a witness in protection. A Sergeant Exit Kutoka."

"That much I've gathered."

"Then let me finish. He's in with Vula and Hendricks, running a deal selling guns. Guns out of the armory. Guns supposed to be destroyed. Anyhow, yesterday we set up a live drop. I got video of a gangster collecting a gun from him. Afterwards Kutoka wanted to disappear but I persuaded him witness protection was the way to go. It was me organized this hotel room for him until Monday. Then we could do things properly. Get him into the system."

"Except now he's ducked."

"I don't think so."

Jo-Jo runs an arm of her sunglasses over her chin. Skeptical. "What do you think?"

"Best case, he's been taken. Worst case, he's lying dead somewhere."

"And you believe someone, some ones, came in here and did that?"

"Yes."

"Sneaked in. Sneaked him out. Alive or dead. No one heard a thing. No one saw a thing. Come on, Zara. This's a hotel. There's front staff. Kitchen staff, cleaning staff lurking in the corridors. How likely is it anyone'll pull this off unseen? Not bloody likely. Anyhow, how come they even knew he was here? You made the arrangements. The only people who knew were you and him."

"That's what I've been sitting here thinking about."

"And?"

"And after the gun collection, we drove back in my car. No one followed us. Everything was hunky. He got into his car, went home to pack a bag. He was okay about what he was doing. Well, okay, as okay as you can be, given the situation. Meanwhile I fixed up the hotel. Phoned him the details from one of my burners. He told me he was clean. No worries, no one following him. But someone must've been." She knots her fingers behind her head. "Or the problem's my phone."

"What sort of problem?"

"I've been seriously hacked. Kutoka thought so on my main phone. Didn't want to take calls from me. But I used one of my backup phones to make the hotel booking. Then WhatsApp'd him from the burner after I'd booked the room. WhatsApp is encrypted so I wasn't worried. Now I'm thinking my backup phone's been done as well. How'd that happen? This is weird. Completely spooky. How else would anybody have known if they hadn't caught the call? They couldn't." She lowers her arms. "All the time I've been sitting here, it's the only thing I could think of. That's how they got to him. That's the only way anyone could have known where he was, if my phone's bugged. But like bugged with serious spy software."

"Where's your phone now?"

Zara takes it out of her jacket pocket, wrapped in tinfoil. "It's switched off. I've taken out the SIM."

"And the tinfoil?"

"From the kitchen. Supposed to be one way to stop the cell phone working."

"You're paranoid."

"I don't think so. All I want, Jo-Jo, is for forensics to check."

"What for? Blood? There's no blood. You can see there's no blood."

"The bed cover's missing. That says something. Why's that gone? It'll just take one guy to flash around a blue light. That's all I'm asking."

"It's not going to happen." Jo-Jo sighs. "Face it, Zara, your guy took off. It happens all the time. He's scared; he's freaked. Maybe he took the bed cover cause he's going to sleep in his car. You've just got to wait until he gets in touch."

Or he's found dead in the sand dunes.

Which is how Zara thinks this will play out. If the white woman at the beach was right, the one who told him he was going to die. But this detail's best not told to Jo-Jo. Too freaky.

81

Alicia is at Big D's under duress. Not that she's showing it. She couldn't disappoint Duifie. Duifie begged to go. Was really excited at the prospect. It would be an adventure. And crayfish right out of the sea. "Ah, please, liefie." And Alicia had caved. Also, Duifie is hyped on jet-setting to France. Which makes her even more attractive, if that were possible.

Now she's on Big D's deck where he's steaming the crayfish, drinking bubbles from a champagne glass. He's flirting with her; she's flirting back. Which Alicia can see from the lounge where she's talking to Straight Abe Margulies. She's not concerned about Duifie's flirting, more amused at her liveliness. Although with Duifie she knows things sexual can swing both ways. Have swung both ways in the past. However, with France on the horizon, a swing isn't likely any time soon.

"These are very nice," Abe is saying. "Nice high color. Great clarity. I could certainly be of assistance."

Abe has a magnifying eyepiece plugged to his right eye. He's probably in his early fifties, Alicia reckons. His hair is patchy brown, being subsumed by gray, the skin of his face softening, folds beginning under his eyes, under his chin. He's wearing a blazer with silver buttons over a fawn open-necked shirt, beige chinos. Slip-ons without socks. He's told her he drove up this morning at Big D's request. Big D's always got something interesting going on.

Alicia's wondering what made Big D expect her to take up his offer of lunch.

"Big D had you come up all this way to see me?"

"No, we've got other business. He thought I could do you a favor. And I can."

Other business, Alicia's thinking. What'd Big D be doing with a jeweler? Although in this situation, better not to ask.

"You're a cop," Abe asks or says, it's unclear to Alicia. He takes out the eyepiece, glances at her. "It's alright, I'm not going there."

She shrugs.

"I can help you here though." He points at the package of diamonds. "Big D told me what he thinks they're worth. I'd have to assess to see how high I can go. Certainly, I can take them off you for probably a bit less than he's suggested. Big D's always top or bottom of the scale, depending."

Even a bit less would still give her a healthy profit. Make the south of France a comfortable holiday with change. Then again that nag that maybe Tamora Gool was capturing her. But she could live with that for the moment.

"Okay," she says. "In cash."

"That's a lot of cash. I don't know if I can manage so much. Not straight away. Half maybe. The rest we'd have to apportion. You happy with that? Or maybe we can do a deal. Things you want I can pay for. That's a way of handling this."

Alicia begins to see an opening here. Pay off the general, get Abe to sort out the French expenses, flights, accommodation. A couple of thousand could go through the Umuzi Trading account. The rest in cash over a spread of months. If she trusted Abe. Was there any option but to trust Abe? Abe with his faint tang of garlic. Now that she wasn't smoking so much, she could smell other people. Sometimes this wasn't a good thing.

"I can probably live with that." Thinking she needs to find out where the guy stays. Get some security for her investment. "So how do we do this?"

He spreads out the stones on the kitchen counter. Uses the palm of his hand to separate a batch. "I'd have to weigh them, but I'd say, off the cuff, these should cover as much as I can manage in cash. You want me to weigh them? Give you a price for each one."

"Why not?" Alicia looks at Big D and Duifie fooling around on the deck, Big D lifting the crayfish off the steam. "Looks like we're about ready to eat."

"Here." Abe scoops the remainder into her Ziploc bag. "I've taken ten stones. My scales are with me. You go out and eat. I'll get a weight and price for each one, join you then?"

"You'll give me some sort of accounting?"

"Sure. You want to see the weight for yourself, we can do it together. Or you can trust me. Personally, we should do this together."

Alicia likes that. Straight Abe. Or else he expects to disarm her, have her say, No, she trusts him. Which she doesn't.

"It's best I watch," she says.

"Spoken like a cop." He doesn't make eye contact, doesn't grin at her. Fishes about in a leather bag, the sort doctors used to carry, brings out a scale. "What happens is this. I give you a carat weight, that's 200 milligrams. That's the scientific part. The rest is my valuation, considering color and clarity. Based on that, I'm going to give you a cash figure. Someone else might give you more. Someone else might give you less. Up to you. You've got Big D's assessment, I've told you he's over the top. I'm going to be level. You want a second opinion, be my guest." He hands her a business card. "There's my address. If you want to think about it, that's fine by me."

Straight Abe playing straight. Alicia can't believe it. But can't see a catch.

Looks at him looking at her, his eyes smiling. He's amused. Amused at her lack of trust.

"Sometimes," he says, "you've just got to trust people."

From the deck, Duifie shouts, "We're eating."

"You start," Alicia calls back. "We'll be right out."

Abe has a piece of A4 paper on the counter, the diamonds dotted down the page. He weighs each one, writes the weight alongside, picks up the stone, looks at it against the light, sets down a valuation. Less than ten minutes he's done. There's a total price at the bottom of the page.

"If you're happy with that, I've got the cash here. Even brought my banknote counter so you don't have to do it by hand."

Alicia wondering what sort of guy travels with a banknote counter. What sort of guy even has one. What sort of guy travels with that much cash. Says, "Ja, that's okay," having visions of Duifie spread topless on the sands of a Saint-Tropez beach (wherever that is), her little cherries ripe for the licking.

Just got to get through to Thursday.

Sweet Thursday

82

Which everybody does. And now it's here: sweet Thursday. The torments of Monday, Tuesday, Wednesday are history. The day's come that they've all waited for. More specifically, it's ten minutes before collection time.

The zone is busy. Overly busy for Zara's liking. Trucks delivering, trucks dispatching. Scooter drivers loitering over takeaway coffees. Smokers getting their hit, talking on their phones. Not an easy site to pull off an arrest of scary gangsters. She's got a feeling it'll be a cock-up.

Even with this tactical team. Twelve true officers. Trained. Experienced. Disciplined. You put them face to face with the Mongols, there's going to be shooting. The team is in three vans kicking their heels in a back street two minutes away.

Their commander, a major, sits with Zara in a surveillance vehicle. Positioned at the back of a parking area. They've been there fifteen minutes. Have line of sight on the storage unit. Which is at the end of a row of similar units. Beyond is a high wall topped with razor wire. Beyond that: vacant land. The unit marked Umuzi Trading is fronted by a metal roll-up security door locked down with two padlocks. Behind it wooden doors. High up on the wall the major has rigged a mic which transmits to the vehicle.

To test it he'd said, "You getting this?" Practically all he's said to her.

The major is short on words. Sucks at a Fisherman's Friend, giving off a faintly minty scent. He's offered Zara one. She's declined with a smile, a shake of the head.

The major's got a radio handset in one hand, his phone in the other. Binoculars in his lap. Sits so still, Zara would swear he isn't breathing.

She's keeping her breathing even, her hands loose. There's adrenaline in her blood making her antsy, but she fights it. Won't let the trembles show.

Five minutes to kick-off.

One thing about this, it keeps her from thinking of Exit Kutoka. How he's gone *phuff* into thin air. Not so much as a stranger's come bearing tidings of his whereabouts. She got his address from a contact at his station. Took a drive past late on Sunday. Nada. No badly painted white car under the awning. No lights on in the house. She's called him from Janet's phone. Called him from one of her secret phones with a new SIM. Mostly the calls went to voicemail. Then stopped connecting. Playing into Zara's worst suspicions: the man is dead. Like Wynston. She has to live with it. As she lives with Wynston's killing. Eventually Exit's car would turn up. Eventually his body. If she hadn't made the WhatsApp call ... If she'd used another phone. If, if, if. You can beat yourself up on ifs. If you hadn't flirted with Big D that time. If you weren't so insistent. My lewe fok, Eloise, where's your heart? You're supposed to be more of a person. You've got feelings. Compassion. A thought which makes her squirm on the seat.

The major gives her a look: What's your case? Ants in your panties?

She ignores him. Slots him away as another swinging dick.

Three minutes to kick-off.

And here's Captain Alicia Hendricks in her Mazda, parks in a bay opposite the storage.

The major says into the radio handset, "Prepare."

To Zara says, "You stay here, got it? You do not leave the car. At all. No shit, hey!"

Alicia Hendricks is on her cell phone. Her voice too soft for the mic until it picks up: "I will confirm afterwards."

The major grunts, "Good tech, hey."

Zara doesn't comment, wonders who the captain's talking to. Watches Hendricks end the call, bend to unlock the roller door. Lifts it to reveal wooden doors. Unlocks these. Opens them. In the dimness, a stack of boxes visible against a wall.

The major has the binoculars to his eyes.

"You want to check?" he says.

Zara takes the bins, counts five crates against one wall, possibly three further back. Ms. Gool'll need a small truck to take that load away.

"Vehicle approaching," says the major. Into his handset says, "Stand by."

Zara swivels right, through the binoculars gets a closeup of a cargo truck coming on slowly. Driving, she'd swear, is Tamora Gool. The woman is all out for glory.

Beside her, she can hear the major clicking his fingers. "Give, give."

Pig. But she hands him the binoculars.

They watch the truck reverse, back up close to the storage unit. Captain Hendricks standing to the side.

Yes, it's Tamora Gool who leaps from the truck's cab. All bouncy, like, Isn't this fun.

"Three persons," says the major into his handset. "One female driving. Two males. No weapons visible. Assume they are armed. Stay. Repeat. Stay."

Over the speaker, they hear:

Tamora Gool: "So where's your sergeant, sisi?"

Alicia Hendricks: "He's not coming."

Tamora Gool: "Why's that? He's a cool guy, hey. We had a little chat on Saturday afternoon, him and me. There at the seaside eating ice creams. I like him."

Alicia Hendricks: "You don't have to wait. You can start loading."

Tamora Gool: "Sure. There's no panic though."

Alicia Hendricks: "Maybe not for you. For me, I've got a job."

Tamora Gool: "Ja, well. Okay, okay. Keep your broekies on."

In Afrikaans, says to the men to start loading up.

Tamora Gool: "So tell me, Captain, you're happy with the little stones? Your guy gave you a good valuation? You know it's way above a cash payment for this lot, yes? So you see what a commission I'm giving you. But that's our life. You help me; I help you. Sisters with power."

Alicia Hendricks: "They're still only pretty stones."

Tamora Gool: "'Strues. You want some help there?"

Alicia Hendricks: "What sort of help?"

Tamora Gool: "You know, someone to make a plan with. To convert those extras into cash money."

Alicia Hendricks: "Who's this?"

Tamora Gool: "A guy I know. Lives in the city. International trader. You see his flat, you wouldn't say that he's stacked up. Guy has top government on his books. You go to him; he gives you a price. It's gonna be the same as your valuation. Maybe better. He's not a cheat. He's fair. At least you got two prices to compare."

Alicia Hendricks: "Alright. Write it down for me, his address." Takes out a notebook, hands it to Tamora Gool.

Into his handset, the major says, "Go."

To Zara, says, "They're going to come in fast. There'll be kak. Like I said, you stay in the car. This's my scene. Understand." Not a question.

"Yes, Major, sir." All she can do not to salute.

The major sir looks at her like he's going to say something. Raises a warning finger.

On the speaker, Tamora Gool says: "There you go. Give him a call, go 'n' see him. It'll work out. The other thing is, where's my gun licenses?"

Alicia Hendricks: "Be patient."

Tamora Gool: "I've got another matter we could talk about."

Alicia Hendricks: "What's that?"

Tamora Gool: "Evidence."

Alicia Hendricks: "Oh no, no. Not that."

Tamora Gool: "It'd be worth it. Stuff goes missing from your evidence storage all the time. You know how it is."

Alicia Hendricks: "Not my scene."

From the right, Zara hears engine-roar, the squeal of tires. Sees armed members in field gear leaping from the vans, running toward the cargo truck, shouting. A bullhorn commanding attention. "Police. Police. Put down any weapons. Down. Down. Down."

She can see Alicia Hendricks and Tamora Gool standing behind the truck, not visible to the task team. The major heading toward them, radio handset in one hand, pistol in the other. The gangsters still in the darkness of the storage unit, also not visible to the task force.

At the loudhailer commands, Hendricks takes a pace toward her car. Ducks down. Gool's out of sight, probably in the unit. Coming out of the unit are the two men, guns drawn. They fire. Wild shots that do nothing to stop the task team.

The bullhorn telling them: "Put down your weapons. Put down your weapons."

No deal.

Zara sees one of the gangsters stagger backward, collapse against the wooden door. A spread of blood blooms across his chest. The other bends to snatch his comrade's gun, now fires two-handed at the task team. Then he's backpedaling, crab-running toward the high wall, swiveling to shoot. Bullets zing off the cargo truck, smack into Hendricks's car.

"Put down your weapon."

Zara's out of the surveillance vehicle at a crouch run, Z88 held beside her thigh. She's going diagonally across the car park toward the high wall. Can hear to her right the crack of handguns.

Watches ahead the banger go full tilt into the major, knock him ass over kettle. Fire down at him. Then he's up onto the wall, engaging with the razor wire. She comes to a halt, shouts at the scrawny bugger.

"Hey, dickface."

He grins at her. "Yous fulla shit, lady." Tosses away one of the guns. Points a finger at her, points at himself. "We's the same. We's got no twis to cause a quarrel."

"Just get down before you die."

He aims the other pistol at her. "I's not wanna kill you, yous not wanna kill me."

My lewe fok. The guy thinks now's the time to debate. Zara puts one in his shoulder. Can't but grimace as he screams, falls among the barbs to dangle there.

"You poes bitch. Djy het my fokking geshoot."

"What'd you think, pal? This isn't cops 'n' robbers play-play."

"I's gonna make charges. See you inna court, my hoerkie."

Yeah, yeah, dream on. She turns toward the storage unit, sees the major sitting on the tar, massaging his heart. Thank you, Kevlar vest. Beside him, a member's kneeling on Hendricks, getting her cuffed. The major's about to stand when Gool breaks free of the men restraining her, comes in with a solid boot kick to the major's kidneys, sends him sprawling again. Does a stamp on his hand before she's taken down. Again, gets Zara's reluctant admiration. The bitch's got fight.

Puts a smile on Zara's lips. She walks up to the captain.

"Howzit, Cap Hendricks. What a place to meet again, hey? What a thing, you and sisi Gool going into the haulage business. Sisters with power. I'd never have guessed."

The wheezing major straightens, leans against the captain's car. "This is not your operation, Captain Dewane. Leave the scene."

Zara hesitates. Not finished gloating at the women. "Lots of time for cozy chats where you're going, ladies. Strategy meetings. Financial planning. Targeted marketing. You got all the time you want." Puts her Z88 away, pulls out her jinxed phone. Does a quick video of Hendricks and Gool.

When the major shouts. "Captain!" A shout that ends as a wheeze. "Enough. Go. Now."

"Always happy to help, Major." Zara moves off, videos the inside of the cargo truck. Zooms into one of the crates. A tidy display of handguns: mostly .38 pistols, a couple of heavy revolvers.

"Captain! Leave."

"Yes, Major, sir." Gives a mock salute. Pockets her phone. Whoever's snooping in her phone's going to enjoy this clip.

83

Zara leaves. But doesn't go far. Pulls over outside the industrial estate, phones Jo-Jo Lanski. Tells her what's happened. Asks her to keep a watch.

"That's bloody nice but I've got a job," Jo-Jo says. "I'm in court this morning."

"When you're not. You know …"

"Go home, Zara. Or take out your kayak. You're all stoked up. No one's going anywhere. When I'm back in the office, I'll let you know what's what."

Which is not good enough for Captain Zara Dewane. Sure, she could put the boat on the water. A nice-enough morning. The wind would be a factor in a few hours. But until then a paddle down the coast would be mind-clearing. A distraction. A way to think things through. After a couple of hours of that, Jo-Jo would be back in the office, could let her know the situation with Hendricks. Could maybe arrange for her to talk to Captain Alicia Hendricks. That would be good. And then Ms. Tamora Gool.

But Zara does not do this. What Zara does is find a parking space outside the police station where Hendricks and Gool are being held. She's got a clear line of sight to the front door. And here she sits for almost two hours. Twiddling her thumbs. Being patient. Doing what good cops do: keeping the scene under surveillance. Also, wondering how to get to Hendricks. Wondering when Exit's corpse would pitch up. Wondering what it would feel like to hear Ashton had crashed and died.

About an hour into her watch, sees a black Merc pull up. General Kaiser Vula exit, powers himself up the ramp into the station. The general in full uniform. The driver stays sitting in the Merc. Forty-five minutes later, there's Hendricks leaving with General Vula in his wheelchair. They get into the general's car. The Merc pulls out, Zara's right behind it all the way to the industrial zone. Where Hendricks retrieves her car. The black Merc with Vula goes off. Hendricks heads in a different direction. Zara behind her. Where to now?

When her backup phone rings: Jo-Jo. Who tells her Hendricks is out.

"Yeah, I know," says Zara. "I'm driving not far behind her. Heading toward the northern suburbs, I suspect."

"Bloody hell, man, Zara. What're you doing? Be careful."

A laugh from Zara. "Relax. I'm a cop. Not like I haven't done this a zillion times."

"Yes, okay, sorry. How'd you even get to know where she was?" A pause. "Don't tell me. You've been stalking outside the station?"

"I have to confess."

"Are you mad? Do you want to land in more shit?"

"No one saw me. Like I said, I've done this sorta thing a zillion times. So what you got to tell me?"

A whoosh of air that Zara reckons is Jo-Jo exhaling smoke. "You won't bloody believe this."

"Try me."

"They bloody let her go on Vula's say-so, can you credit? He claimed the operation was a sting to catch Tamora Gool. What could they do? We're talking about the head of Police Intelligence pulling rank. They had to let her go."

"Not surprising for Vula to do that. He's arrogant. Has no problem putting himself out there. Interesting. What about Gool?"

"Comes up for a bail hearing tomorrow. You can pretty much believe she'll get it."

"Of course. Listen, would you do something for me?"

"Doll, for you, anything." Laced with sarcasm.

"Ah, aren't you the sweet one."

"What's it?"

"Could you check the numbers on those weapons before Police Intelligence put a claim on them? Would be handy to have a list."

"And how'm I going to do that?"

"You're Advocate Lanski; you can do anything."

"Of course. I keep forgetting I'm Wonder Woman. One word from me and … Jirre, give me fortitude."

"That's not what Wonder Woman said in the movie."

"You know what I mean."

They disconnect. Twenty minutes later, Zara watches Captain Alicia Hendricks drive through the security gates of a block of flats. Now what?

Nothing for it but to sit again. Twiddle her thumbs. Play Linda Perry tracks. Think of maybe meeting the kayaking prosecutor guy again. Maybe he could be useful in all sorts of ways. As it happens, she doesn't have to wait long. Thirty minutes, then there's Captain Alicia Hendricks driving out of the security gates—two bullet pockmarks in the back of her SUV.

There's also a WhatsApp message from Jo-Jo: *Just heard that Lady Vula committed suicide, last Sunday. Will confirm.*

Fifteen minutes later, she does. *It's true.*

Poor woman. For the general, Zara has no sympathy.

84

Hardly a sweet Thursday. A shit day. To be strictly accurate, a shit morning.

Because above the city, on Signal Hill, the noon gun has just been fired. Yet the afternoon does not promise anything. These are the dark thoughts of Captain Alicia Hendricks as she heads back to town. In bumper-to-bumper traffic. In tailbacks longer than forever. Her mind buzzing with anger and fear. At the indignity of the takedown, at General Kaiser Vula, at Captain Zara Dewane, at Tamora Gool, at Sergeant Exit Kutoka.

First General Kaiser Vula. Relieved as she'd been to see him power into the police station, afterwards he'd wasted no words. Berated her for incompetence. For stupidity. For recklessness. They'd sat in his black Mercedes-Benz, Vula in full voice. The driver smirking in the rearview mirror.

"What is your problem, Captain, that you cannot see a setup? Right in front of your own eyes. If you cannot see it, can you not feel it? For us when we were fighting in the bush, we could feel the attacks coming. But you, you walk right into the trap. Are you stupid? You make it easy for them. You have to look around. You have to notice the small signs. There are always small signs of a trap. But you are a blind woman wandering in the darkness. You see nothing. You feel nothing. You hear nothing. How can you be a police and not have the instincts? Ah man, Captain, I cannot believe this incompetence. I cannot understand how this has happened. There are always signals. I ask you, how did this happen?"

His outrage had repeated. Even to tell her that she was reckless. Yet how was the collection to be made otherwise? Sometimes the man made no sense.

And then had come his persistent "How did this happen? How in the name of the glorious ancestors did this happen?" Tapped out on her arm.

She had told him that the collection date was only known to her and Gool and Kutoka. The time known only to her and Gool. She had tried to phone Kutoka from early in the morning but his phone was off.

To which Vula had said nothing. Waved a dismissive hand.

Then she'd dropped the whammy. Captain Zara Dewane was there.

That stopped the tap, tap, tap.

"What? How come?"

How come had been the question on her mind since Dewane said, "Howzit, Cap Hendricks. What a place to meet again, hey?" Either she'd got to Kutoka. Or Gool's Mongols were leaking.

She had told Vula her thoughts.

"Gool," he'd decided. "If Kutoka did not know the exact time, it has to be from her side. A spy or a wiretap. Do not worry about Dewane. I will sort her. She is on suspension. I can finish her. For good. She will not be a trouble for us."

Fine.

Which had left Gool and Kutoka. Except Gool wanted her diamonds back. Or their weight in cash.

Had said while they were handcuffed in the van: "You sort this, captain chickie. Don't fuck me around. If this's a setup for you to get the money, keep the guns, you're dead."

Alicia had held up her cuffed hands. "Does this look like a setup?"

"Could be. Depends on what happens next."

Which was Vula opening the same playbook. How weird was that?

Kutoka? Kutoka AWOL was a problem.

But the general had been dismissive.

"We will find him. If he did not know the exact time, he is not the problem."

Maybe so but where was Kutoka? AWOL for days.

A problem for later as she stops outside the house of Straight Abe, the diamond dealer. For Sea Point, a modest house. In a back street. No view of the sea. A Victorian terrace row. She knocks. He opens.

"Welcome to my abode."

No smell of garlic this time.

In she goes to chaos. Shelves stacked with files, boxes, books, ornaments, vases of dead flowers. Threadbare runners down the center of the passageway. More piles of boxes on the wooden floors. Towers of books. Paintings hanging at random from picture hooks. A pervading smell of old vegetables. Not the sort of house she had expected Abe would live in. The way he dressed was not the way of the house.

Today, Straight Abe wears two-tone black sneakers, new jeans, a lightweight beige V-neck jersey. No shirt or T-shirt underneath. Mr. With-it.

"You live here?" she says.

"Not often," he answers. Casts his glance about. "It's a mess, hmm?" He laughs. "You can say so. I don't mind. It is a mess. I know it is a mess. A mess of lives. All the bric-a-brac of other lives. You see, the house belonged to my late father. He was born here. Lived his life here. I was born here too. What do we do with these places when we inherit them? Throw everything away? Sell them? Move on? As you see, I can't do that. He is still here, in the dust. So is my mother. If I vacuum clean, they will disappear." He laughs again. "All I can do is keep the past as it is in the present. I have no siblings. No children. When I am dead, someone else can turn our lives into smoke and ashes." He looks at her. "So, Captain Alicia Hendricks, what's up?"

He leads her into a lounge. Which is as littered as the hallway. Except, here there are also piles of newspapers: *Cape Argus, Cape Times*. Old, yellowed, bound in twine. And stacks of magazines, *The New Yorker, Popular Mechanics, Good Housekeeping, National Geographic, History Today*.

The curtains are closed. He flicks on a central light that casts the room in a brown haze. On a table against the furthest wall is his counting machine. They stand amid the clutter. Even the chairs offer no space to sit.

"You do not look happy, Captain. Last weekend was fun and games. Today is darkly serious. Is there a problem?"

"There may be."

"You have a second opinion who is offering you more?"

"It is not that."

She sees that smile he has, the one suggesting he can read her mind. "Then how can I help you?"

"I need more money."

"Achso." Said with a German accent. He perches on the arm of a highbacked chair. "I can help you a little bit perhaps. All depends on how much."

"Another R300k. I have more ..." She'd first thought two hundred thou, then topped it up because, what the hell!

"My word! As much as that!"

She watches him staring at the floor. The fingers of his right hand circling in the dust on a magazine cover. Eventually he looks up. No smile now.

"Alright."

She's relieved. Now there's an out. Quick purchase of air tickets. Arrange a month, two months on extended leave. Put a fix on Tamora Gool before she got bail. Let the general tidy up the rest.

"Tomorrow. I can't do it today. But tomorrow would be in order. Shall we say midmorning, yes?"

"Yes." Knowing she has no option.

85

Zara's parked up the street in sight of the Victorian terrace row. Sees Captain Alicia Hendricks go in empty-handed. Sees her come out ten minutes later empty-handed, drive away. Whatever her business, why didn't a phone call cut it? She waits another ten minutes, then she's knocking on the door.

The door opens, a man says, "Hello, how can I help?" Stands smiling at her, all friendly.

"Can we talk inside?" says Zara.

"Depends," says the man. Right hand now in his jeans pocket; left hand blocking her way, holding the door frame. Left foot crosses over his right foot. Relaxed, staring at her with bright eyes. Like he's enjoying this. "All these lovely women coming to see me."

Zara gives him the stone face, the cold-hooded eyes.

His smile fades. "What's it you want to talk about?"

"Captain Alicia Hendricks," says Zara. "The person who just left here."

"Who're you? What's this about?"

"Police investigation. Internal Crime Unit."

"You got ID?"

She has. It's a fake. But good enough to look like the real thing in a quick flash. She shows him a plastic appointment certificate, won't let him take it. He bends to squint at her name.

"Captain Dewane."

"Ja. That's me. Can we go in now?" Behind him, the passageway is filled with junk. "You're who?"

He hesitates. "I'm not sure why you're here."

"Nor'm I, Mr. ... Mr. who?

"Margulies." He doesn't move.

"Okay. Look, I don't know who you are or what you do or why Captain Hendricks was here but she's under investigation. Maybe you're a friend. Maybe you're one of her informers. I don't know. But I'm interested in her, so now I'm interested in you." She gestures at the clutter behind him. "If there's no space to talk inside, we can speak here if you want, I don't mind. You can start by telling me what you do."

He looks at her. She can see him coming to a decision. A decision to take this indoors.

He steps back. "Come in."

She squeezes past him, stands next to a floor-to-ceiling rack of shelves. Not a space on them. He closes the front door. Says, "Go straight down."

She does, turning sideways to get past jutting sideboards, bicycles, a supermarket trolley full of jars, bottles, glass containers.

"Go on."

She enters a kitchen. Small but neat. A bar fridge, a gas hob, a small oven. No clutter on the counter tops. No dishes in the sink. Plates, mugs, cutlery in the drying rack. There's a table and four chairs. A ginger cat curled asleep on one of the chairs.

"Now, how can I help you?"

"You want to tell me what you do, Mr. Margulies, for starters."

"Bric-a-brac. Jewelry. Precious metals. Gemstones. I've got a license."

"Diamonds?"

"Yes, like I said, I'm certified. People are always selling diamonds. Grandmother's rings. Memories of bad marriages. People want to get rid of that sort of thing, so they come to me."

"What about rough diamonds?"

"I see them, yes, obviously. I buy them."

"Even when you don't know where they come from?"

He shrugs. "Who knows where they come from. You can't tell. No one can tell. It's just a stone. It could come from Congo, Namibia, South Africa, Brazil, Venezuela. Anywhere. Captain, every day there're millions of diamonds being traded around the world. This's just how it is. It's currency."

"Is this why Captain Hendricks was here? About diamonds?" Zara thinking maybe she should have another chat with Big D. Watching the Margulies man handling this like it was part of his day.

"She wanted an evaluation. I've done that before for you cops."

Fair enough.

"You going to tell me how much?"

He considers this. Looks out the window at the house behind. Decides. "No."

"You should."

"Captain, you come with the legal paperwork, I'll tell you. Without that, all you're getting is all you've got."

"Why is that?"

"Because this is sounding like I need a lawyer."

"I don't think so. Simple questions. Simple answers. You'll only need a lawyer if you're withholding. Are you withholding?"

"Withholding what?"

"I dunno. Maybe the captain only wanted an evaluation. Maybe the captain wanted to sell some diamonds. I dunno. That's why I'm asking."

"She's the one you should be asking."

"I will be. Absolutely. Then I'll come for your affidavit. Meanwhile you can help. Because this is something you don't want to be involved in. Believe me, the captain's going down. You don't want to end up with her."

Mr. Margulies is giving it some thought, she can tell. He's again staring out the window, comes back to her with a shake of his head.

"If I have to, I'll get back to you," he says.

"Your call," says Zara. "Look forward to our next meeting."

Back in her car, Zara phones Big D.

Gets his happiness: "Sunshine. You and the boy coming up to brighten my life?"

"You never know your luck."

"How about this weekend?"

"Maybe."

"Maybe with Zara Dewane means not likely. Which means this isn't about getting together."

"Uh uh. Not really. This's about Mr. Margulies."

"Oh yeah, who's he?"

"I thought you'd know. You sure you don't know? You diamond guys all know one another."

"Nah. Not really. Margulies. Margulies. Nah, never heard of your coot. Perhaps he's new on the scene."

"By the looks of his house, I'd say not. I'd say he's been here forever. I'd say he had a local rep, a national rep, could even be an international trader. That'd be my guess."

"Sounds like an interesting oke."

"You could say. Remember how you told me Captain Hendricks came to you with a bag of diamonds."

A drawn out "Yaaarr-ah."

"Well now she's talking to Mr. Margulies. Is that a coincidence or what?"

"Who can say, sweet Captain? It's labyrinthine, what goes on."

Which is where Zara leaves it. Hopes there'll be movement in the labyrinth.

86

And lo.

There is movement in the labyrinth.

Only, Captain Zara Dewane is not privy to the scene. A scene which takes place midafternoon when she is otherwise engaged.

The setting for the scene is General Kaiser Vula's home, his lounge to be exact. It is the only place he feels free to speak his mind. Every three days, he has his man sweep for bugs. To date, it has been clean. The room was swept this morning. After all the medics, the police high-ups, the politicians, the colleagues who had come with their condolences over the previous days, Vula believed he needed surety. Anyone could have left behind a little device. Surprisingly—to him—no one took the opportunity.

Which is why he can meet here with Captain Alicia Hendricks. He offers neither tea nor coffee. She asks for water. He has a decanter brought in on a silver tray with two glasses. She pours for them both. He notices a tremble to her hand. Good. She is nervous. She should be. He takes a different tack from earlier.

"You have the money?"

She is hesitant. Sips at her glass of water. Has to clear her throat. "Not yet."

"What do you mean, not yet? Gool was loading up the crates this morning. How could that happen without payment?"

"We had an agreement."

"Nonsense, man. You do not have a lady's agreements with gangsters. When the collection happens, they give the money, then they get the merchandise. You are too friendly with Gool. I ask again: where is my money?"

"The general will have it tomorrow."

"Why not today?"

He waits. She does not respond.

"Because you do not have it?"

"I have surety."

"Surety? What surety?" Then he realizes. "Ah man, you did

not take cash. You have diamonds. She has given you rough stones. She is a wily fox that one. Never to miss a chance. Let me see them?"

He watches Alicia Hendricks spill the stones onto the silver tray. They could be gravel he's looking at.

"These are worth the collection?"

She nods. Sips again at her glass of water.

"You are sure? You know this?"

"I have two valuations." An easy lie to convince him.

"You are telling me there are two people who know you have these rough diamonds?"

"Yes."

"That was not a good idea."

"They don't know me. I am a stranger. There is no problem."

"No problem. But these stones are illegal, without question. There is always danger in flashing them around. You have a buyer?"

"Yes. I have come from him now."

"You can trust him?"

She shrugs. "He gives me the money; I give him the diamonds. That is what we have agreed."

"Who is this?"

A shake of the head. "No. This is my side. I will give you the money tomorrow."

She is destruction, the witch Luna had said. The upside-down Tower. Is that Hendricks? Is she a warning? He has to smile inwardly. How can Hendricks be a warning? Maybe she takes risks, but she protects him.

Then he has another thought: perhaps the diamonds are worth more than she says. There is always that possibility. She could be cheating him.

"I want to know the valuation."

She has it in her notebook. Shows him the calculation. His share. Her share. A payment to Exit Kutoka. It is the value at which he'd priced the weapons. But he wonders if there were more diamonds. Diamonds she has kept for herself. She could do this. He looks at her. She meets his eyes once, quickly looks down. He can read nothing there.

"I am not crooking you."

"Good. That would not be a wise idea." He wheels backward. End of their meeting. Watches as she shepherds the diamonds with her palm. Scoops them into the bag.

"Tomorrow," he says. "We will meet here in the afternoon. Stay away from Gool. When she is on bail, she will want to see you. Stay away. That is an order. Stay away from Dewane too. That is another order."

But whether they will be obeyed or not, he can't be certain.

After the captain has left, he gets a Telegram message. It outlines where Captain Zara Dewane has been throughout the morning: from the raid at the industrial site to the police station where Hendricks was held, to a street in the northern suburbs, to a street in Sea Point, to her son's school, to her home. Where her car is parked now. Each trip is timed.

A busy girl. Looks like she followed Hendricks to her flat in the northern suburbs. And then to the buyer. This is worrisome.

He sends a note: *Watch her. Let me know her movements.*

Perhaps the nosy captain needs another warning.

Sends an instruction.

Gets back a thumbs-up emoji.

87

Zara fetches Kyle after school, drops him at home.

Says, "Give me another couple of hours or so then I'll take you for a surf. Do your homework, okay?"

Even before Kyle's out of the car, Janet's bobbing down the steps. Like she's been waiting for them to arrive.

"Mrs. Z, Mrs. Z, wait man, hokaai. Hold up the horses; there's been a development."

Zara leans into the passenger seat as Janet bends toward her. Grimaces at the waft of wine fumes.

"Ag sorries, hey, sorries for the chardonnay breath. But I been worried. There was a man here now-now. A white man wanting to know if our place was where the other man was shot. I told him, no, that was mos next door."

Our place, hey? Which raises Zara's eyebrows. Says, "That's two months ago. What'd he want?"

"To see if it was for sale. But Mrs. Z, Mrs. Z that wasn't the odd moment. No, jirre, what spooked me in the stomach was he says he woulda thought it was safe living next to a cop. Like he knows yous a cop."

"The whole street knows I'm a cop."

"Ja, but what I mean is he knows you lives here so why make the confusion with the killed man?"

Zara waves goodbye to Kyle, thinks, What now? Who's this guy? Decides to reassure Janet, says, "It's probably nothing. Look, I'm gonna be another while. Can you make some toasted cheese for Kyle? You see that man again, you phone me. Straight away, you phone me."

But Janet's not ready to let her go. Says, "I got his picture, sneaky peaky." Flips through her phone's gallery. "And his number plate." Holds the pictures toward Zara. There's a man in a green jacket. Fit looking, maybe in his fifties. Big face. Bristly eyebrows. Your chinos and checked-shirt member. Drives what could be some sort of hatchback. Mr. Ordinary when he's out and about.

"Send those to me," she says. "Keep a watch out. Don't open the door to anybody. Nobody. Got it?'

"Of course, Mrs. Z, I's not like a moegoe."

"I hope not. See you in a few hours."

Before Zara can close the car door, Janet says, "Strange mens mustn't come snooping here, Mrs. Z. I got antenna. Like I say, I'm your asset running in the field, nè, Mrs. Z!" Which makes Janet laugh until she coughs.

My lewe, Eloise! thinks Zara, driving off. How the hell did Janet walk into my life? Although, all hallelujahs, not a bad back-room guest.

Traffic heading north is worse now. But thirty minutes, one bumper-to-bumper grind later, she's doing a parallel park into a curb space. Almost right outside the block of flats where Alicia Hendricks lays her head at night.

For the hell of it, Zara buzzes the flat. To her surprise, a voice answers.

Zara introduces herself by rank, says she's a friend of Alicia's, is she home?

"Just now," says the voice. "You wanna come in 'n' wait?"

Zara does wanna come in 'n' wait. So the gate clicks open, as does the foyer door. She takes the stairs, only three floors after all. Isn't even breathing heavily when she knocks on the door.

It's opened instantly by a slight twenty-something woman in a sleeveless T-shirt, tracksuit pants, bare feet.

"I'm Paloma," the twenty-something says, sticking out a hand. "You can call me Duifie."

Zara shakes, waltzes in, all friendly, all "Wow, this is lovely. Parquet floors. You don't see that often anymore. These 1950s blocks are amazing. You said your name's Paloma? What's that, Portuguese?" Follows her host through to the lounge.

Duifie's hair is pinned up, loose strands floating round her face. She tucks one behind an ear. You're sweet, thinks Zara. Where the hell did Alicia find you?

"From my granma, Ouma Palo," says Duifie. "She was Spanish. But I only ever heard her speak Afrikaans."

"And what's this, the map?" says Zara, leaning over the coffee table. "The Mediterranean? I've never been there."

"Me either. We're planning a holiday."

"That right? The best part for me's always the planning. Exciting stuff. Where're you thinking of?"

"Paris first. Then the south of France."

"Very nice. Not Spain though, to see where your ouma lived?"

"Maybe. I'd like to. Alicia says it depends if she can get extra leave. You never know what she can work. Sit, sit."

They sit opposite one another on sofas.

"Can I get you coffee or anything?"

"I'm good, thanks." Zara still hunched forward looking at the map. "So when do you think this'll happen? Flights aren't easy right now with everyone wanting to travel."

She's thinking, Not cheap either. Keeps up a gentle probing, learns of the weekend at Port Owen, of the amazing guy Big D's place right on the water, of a fish braai, and real French bubbles.

There's a thing. Zara's of a mind to phone Big D, ask him why he's not sharing info the way he used to. Let's Duifie bubble on about her weekend treat, the surprise of the possible French holiday. How wonderful Alicia is to her.

And there, at the mention of her name, Alicia walks in. Stops. Zara watches her face go from smiley to hard mask in an instant. Always fascinating. That change. Says, "Duifie's been telling me about your coming trip. Nice one."

"Out." Said calmly. Alicia Hendricks taking up a position behind Duifie's couch, arms folded. "Get out."

"Don't you want to know why I'm here?"

"Out."

"You should hear me."

"I don't think so. Get out. Now."

Zara stands, holds up her hands. "Okay, okay. Keep your hair on. This's your funeral." Makes no move toward leaving. Says to Duifie, "I wouldn't bank on the south of France. It's not gonna happen."

Alicia Hendricks comes round the couch, hand on her pistol. Gets into Zara's face. Says, "Right now you're not a cop, lady. You want a charge of harassment added to your record, that's no problem. You're trespassing. You want to know something: the only funeral's gonna be yours. Ashes to ashes."

Zara backs away. Keeps her hands visible. Face serious. "Here's the thing, Captain: I know about the diamonds. I know about your man Abe Margulies in Sea Point. I know about Umuzi Trading. Yeah, I even know about the Maale shooting. What really happened that night in the bush lodge. You see, I know the what-what of General Vula. I know that Kutoka's dead. I were you, I'd want to get on the right side of all this. You know what I mean: now might be the moment. Save your skin. And probably Duifie's as well. Clock's ticking, you gotta believe it."

She can smell a rankness in the captain's breath. That's fear. Stomach curdle. It's a smell she's known before. In the tight moments before the guns come out. Takes another step backward.

"I'm going, okay."

"You better."

Zara steps round the couch. Still facing Alicia Hendricks, flicking her gaze between the captain's hands and the captain's eyes. There's also confusion in those eyes. Like Alicia's heard something new. Which bits? About the Maale shooting? That was truly flying kites, mentioning that. Nothing more than sixth sense based on the info from Kutoka. Or was it about Kutoka's killing? Again a gut feeling. Yet it's rattled her cage.

"This isn't over, Captain."

"Fuck off."

"We can still talk."

Hendricks has her gun out now. Pointing down, but there it is in her hand.

A scream from Duifie.

Zara thinking, Cool it. Just go. Get out of this right now. But, my lewe, can't resist a last quickie. Once more not entirely the honest truth. "Mr. Margulies is giving me an affidavit. Complete with evaluation. Something I can take to General Vula."

Captain Alicia Hendricks raises her gun. Points it at Captain Zara Dewane.

Again Duifie screams.

88

The man's at his desk, eyes on his laptop screen. He's tracking two targets. One is in the southern suburbs making a house call. This one's nothing to worry about. The target is an insurance salesman. House calls are what insurance salesmen do. Where he makes those calls is what the man's client wants to know. This sort of work is easy money.

The other target is Captain Zara Dewane. He's watched her pick up her boy from school. Drop him at home. Drive all the way north out to the flat of Captain Alicia Hendricks. The car's stopped outside the block of flats. Been there for thirty minutes. At forty-five minutes it's on the go again back toward the city center.

Fifteen minutes later she's in a traffic jam. Still at least twenty minutes from home.

He gets a Telegram message: *Proceed as arranged.*

This is followed by confirmation of a deposit into his bank.

The man doesn't like this side of the job. It's messy. There's a high random factor. In other words, there's plenty of risk. Much could go wrong. And, truth to tell, there's an emotional cost. Watching someone die is a reminder of your own mortality. Not a comfortable thought. Fortunately, it's only a fleeting concern. Something he's learned to quickly quash. Very effectively actually. To this end, he only takes on black clients. He's only interested in black targets. By black he means anyone who is not Caucasian. And then the reward helps. You see, the money's good. Really good. It is also half upfront. Technically he feels recompensed with the half. That covers the job: gloves, travel expenses, ammunition (when necessary), hourly rate. The remainder is, strictly speaking, surplus, i.e. profit. Thus, if the remainder's not paid he's not out of pocket. He is, however, put out. Collecting can be a hassle but is easily solved when families are involved, particularly if there are young children. Also, he knows where all his clients live. He doesn't take on any work until those boxes have been ticked.

In the case of the Captain Zara Dewane commission, all the boxes have been ticked. He knows where both the client and the target live.

The assignment now is akin to bongo-bongo. For this he uses a Mini Uzi. It's light at about a kilo and a half. Has ammo sticks that take twenty 9mm rounds apiece. Why the Mini Uzi? Because, surfing the net, he came across a YouTube short clip of blonde Lea shooting the gun. Very cool. Put through an order with the general. And voilà, the piece was delivered.

For this job he's loaded up two magazines with full clips. Wore gloves throughout the loading process. When there's going to be a spray of shell casings left behind, best not to have them fingerprinted. An on-site inconvenience at both points of contact is that he will have to drive across the road onto the right-hand side to fire out the driver's window. But nothing he hasn't handled before. On such jobs he wears a flat cap, sunglasses, a black mask. His gloves are your standard brown leather, fastened with a press-stud, designer holes over the knuckles. Very sexy, in his opinion.

His car for this job is hardly sexy. Your bog-standard white Polo. No revved-up engine, no fat tires, no rumbly exhaust, no distinguishing body features. Except the plates are false, but then they would be.

He has the Mini Uzi on his lap as he eases into a side street, then into the Main Road traffic. It's busy but moving. Unlike Captain Zara Dewane still stuck in bumper to bumper.

89

"Fok, Eloise," Zara Dewane says aloud in her car. Has to laugh. My lewe. Has to sit there shaking her head. Anyone saw her, they'd think she was looney. Or on the phone. Mostly everyone in a car's on the phone these days. Gesticulating. Chatting away. Hardly paying attention to the traffic.

But you have to give it to Alicia Hendricks, Zara's thinking.

Her performance was surreal. Crazy. A cop pointing a gun at another cop. Hectic, hectic, hectic. Your dad would despair, Zara Eloise Dewane. Thoroughly. Two grown women playing bang bang you're dead. Well, not quite, but heading in that direction. The woman is losing it.

Zara can only imagine what's happening up there in the flat right now. Duifie going ballistic. Throwing her toys. Alicia doing the calming, trying to hug her, hold her hand, saying, "Let me explain, it's not what you think, we're still going to France, nothing's changed, she's bad that one, on suspension, you can't believe anything she says." All the time wanting to get Vula on speed dial.

When she does, she tells him they are in shit street. Deep in the kak. The fucking Dewane knows all about their extra curricula activities. The heisted guns. The diamonds. About Umuzi Trading. Is making wild allegations about Exit. That he's dead. Is that true? That she knows about the Maale shooting. WTF. What's she on about?

And Vula telling her what? "Leave it to me. Dewane knows nothing. She's trying to scare you." Some sort of pacification like that.

Yes, well, Hendricks has it coming. Just a pity about dovey Duifie. The cruel world showing its hard side. Ag siestog. The poor girl is going to be so disappointed. Will have to watch her dearly beloved putting on orange overalls. Mind you, might find that sexy. Could be an erotic side to a zip-down onesie.

The erotic leading to a: what if the prosecutor guy, JC, was going kayaking? It could be. An after-work paddle to get rid of the frustrations. Another reason to pick up Kyle, drop him at Rocklands, then make for Three Anchor Bay. Paddle into the ocean with NPA guy, head for the horizon. Time to maybe take it a bit further.

These thoughts roiling through her mind as she sits in a traffic jam. Two lanes of cars not going anywhere fast. There's the Foreshore cluster of high-rises up ahead. So near. She gestures to the driver on her left that she wants to move into his lane. Holds up her hands in prayer. Will he let her in? He shrugs. Lifts his hands off the wheel: what-can-I-do sort of attitude. Doesn't look at her anymore. Doesn't open a gap when they inch forward.

Zara considers flashing him her cop accreditation. Hoots to get his attention. Gestures: wind down your window. Slides down her passenger window. He's ignoring her. She hoots again. This time he looks. She holds up her plastic ID card. This time she gets his attention. She's shouting at him, "Let me get in front of you." He's shaking his head. Looks like he's saying, "Fucking cops."

But he lets her in, despite a cacophony of objection as she jams the left lane. Then she's through. Checks that the shoulder strip's free, then belts down it toward the exit, hand on hooter.

She's off the highway at a red light when her phone goes: Janet. A hyper Janet.

"Yous better come home quick-sticks, Mrs. Z. We's shot to shit. All over the place bullet holes. What's Mrs. Z say, 'My lewe fok?' It's a madness, I don't know in this time of pandemonium." The women in full flow.

Zara breaks in: "Janet, Janet. Stop. What's going on? What're you talking about?"

"Someone's shot your house, Mrs. Z. Lots of bullets."

"Kyle? You?"

When the connection breaks.

90

She tries to get back to Janet. No answer. Not even voicemail. If Kyle had been hurt she'd have said. Wouldn't she?

Wouldn't she?

No guarantees with Janet. Someone's shot your house, Mrs. Z. Lots of bullets. My lewe fok, this job! If only there was Wynston. If only there was help. Your own fault, Cap, doing the lone ranger thing. What the hell were you thinking?

But she's not going there. Because she's driving wild. Spins off at the red light at a gap in the traffic. Leaves cars hooting.

Even as she's overtaking on the solid line. Flashing her lights for oncoming vehicles to give her space.

And the mad driving clears her mind, keeps her focused. There's adrenaline pumping into her blood. Giving her the shakes. So she grips the steering wheel with her left hand. Has her right pressing the hooter.

Kyle.

If Kyle was hurt. Janet would have said. This repeating. And repeating.

Until she skids to a stop outside her house. Leaves the car in the middle of the street. Has to push away neighbors to get to her gate. Where Janet's holding court. Kyle on the stoep with another boy taking smartphone videos. The front of her home is pocked: chunks taken out of the brickwork, windowpanes shattered.

"Hey, Zara," shouts a neighbor. "Twice in two months. It's getting dangerous living near you. Last time the journalist guy died."

Zara does her cop thing, asking people to move back. Everyone's picked up the casings, like no one watches police movies. Like no one felt any need to preserve the crime scene.

A man comes over, shows her a fuzzy clip on his phone of the gunman's car. Says, "I saw it. Right there from my stoep." Points to a house across the street. "I checked this car coming up, next thing it swerves across to outside your house. Bam, bam, bam. Jesus, I don't know how many, the oke's got it on automatic or something. Any rate, doesn't even get out of his vehicle, just sprays your place one-handed. Man, I got such a fright, I ducked down. Still I held up my phone to take this. Tshoo, someone doesn't like you plenty."

"I need to see my son," Zara's saying, heading through the gate.

Janet tugging at her: "The cops're coming, Mrs. Z. I called them right after yous."

The neighbor saying, "You'll be lucky you see them this side of Christmas."

"That's the same car as the other one, Mrs. Z. Look, look."

With one hand trying to stop Zara's rush toward Kyle. With the other scrolls through photos on her phone. "Ag, no man, it's a different number plate. Doesn't mean nothing at all, at all."

Zara reaches Kyle, grabs him, hustles him into the house. "Are you okay?" Can see he is. More excited than shocked.

Telling her, "We were at the back in the kitchen, Janet and me. And then bang, there was this hectic noise, like the house was falling down. What'd he use, Mom? Has to be something like a machine pistol. A Beretta. Or a Mac. Or a Czech Skorpion. That can fire like a thousand rounds a minute. Totally awesome."

Zara thinking, How does the boy know about these things?

When her phone rings. Her old phone. It's Ashton.

He's: "What the fuck almighty's going on there, Zara? I'm coming to get Kyle. I'm on my way. He's not safe around you."

She holds the phone against her leg, says to Kyle: "Did you call your father?"

He shakes his head. "He was phoning me when it happened. To find out if I'm coming."

Shit.

"It's okay, Ashton. You shouldn't come here. Kyle's fine. There'll be police, they're going to be taking statements. I do not want you in their way. I'll get Kyle to phone you later."

In truth, no police yet, but he doesn't need to know that.

"He's not sleeping there tonight. Get it. I don't know what crap you're working on but he's not staying with you anymore. You're a target, pretty face, in case you haven't worked that out yet. Someone wants you dead. And they're not killing my son in the process."

Zara sighs. The last things she needs right now. "Everything under control, Ashton. Honestly. Just stay away. Kyle's going to be perfectly safe tonight." Thinking, she'll get him to her parents.

"You're right about that. He's going to be with me."

"I told you don't come here."

She smothers the phone again, says to Kyle: "You want to sleep at your father's tonight?"

He gets agitated. "No, Mom, no. This is so cool." Then a frown of concern. "We'll be alright here, won't we? With armed guards and such."

"We'll be fine." Not wanting to tell him just yet that they'll be at her parents. She walks into the house, into her bedroom. There's glass on the floor. Three bullet smacks high up the wall opposite the window. A dusting of red brick on her pillows. Chips of plaster.

Gets back to Ashton: "I've asked him. He doesn't want to come to you, okay? Look, I'll talk to him, see what we can work out. It's just not going to be tonight. Please, stay away. Kyle's alright. He's safe. I know you're worried but this is under control."

"No, you listen to me. He's my son. My son. You hear me? My son."

"I'm well aware of that, Ashton."

"I'm coming to get him. Not you or the whole of SAPS will stop me. Not a judge south of Timbuktu won't give me custody."

With that, he's gone.

Her phone rings: her father.

"You must come here quickly, Zara. Quickly."

"I can't. There's …"

"Now."

"What's going on, Pa?"

"Come. Just come."

91

He drives back to Main Road, in a side street changes the registration plates. Leaves the old ones in the gutter. They'll end up on some bergie's trolley; he doesn't care.

Now takes Newmarket south, follows his nose: Albert, Malta, Liesbeek Parkway, round the Rondebosch Common to Milner, eventually a left into Imam Haron. There is traffic but it keeps moving, he's making good time. He trawls down Belgravia Road until he finds the house. From the garden gate, it's about ten yards to the stoep. Front door is off the stoep. He knows the plan of these houses. Behind the stoep would be the lounge. Off the central passage on the right the main bedroom. This job's not as easy as the first one. Not something he can do from the Polo. Also there's a man washing his car three houses away. Young kids playing in the garden next door.

He goes past. At the first intersection, makes a U-turn. Drives slowly back to the target house. Stops at the curb, keeps the engine running. Gets out, reaches back in for the Uzi. Flashes on blonde Lea's YouTube moment with the Uzi. There she is with amber sunglasses, wearing a black plunge-neck T-shirt, the studs in her ear, the stud in her nose, her secret cream-pink smile. Whispering, "Hey! Did you guys order some Mini Uzis?" What a dream.

The man leaves the door open, walks round the front of the car. The kids are ignoring him. The car washer has looked up, is watching. No bother. This will be quick. At the gate, he levels the gun, keeps the stock folded as a grip, moves his arm fast from left to right, his finger on full auto. Empties the clip. Strides round the back of the car, tosses the gun onto the passenger seat. Gets in quickly. In the rearview, sees the car washer running out of his property. The booger takes up a shooting stance in the street. Feet apart, both arms extended. He's got a pistol in his grip. Cracks off two shots like he's at a shooting range. Both miss. The trouble with these suburbs, you sometimes take return fire. It's a hazard.

The man opts for the long way back. That means making for the leafy burbs along the mountain's skirts. In a street of arching trees, changes the registration plates once more. The old ones he slides under a hedge. Will be a long time before they're found. Not that he's bothered one way or the other. In truth, he's now a bit shaky from the adrenaline rush. Hadn't affected him on the first job but the end of an operation always brings a kick. He pops a benzo to steady himself. Takes a long drink of sparkling water. Then winds through the forest road toward the city. On the way, gets in the groove with Linda Perry. She's a great find.

"Bang the Drum."
"In My Dreams."
"Knock Me Out."

92

She'd told Janet to hold the fort. Janet hopping about her, tugging at her arm.

"What'm I gonna tell the gattas if they come?"

She'd shaken free. "That I've got an emergency."

"This is an emergency. Right here, Mrs. Z. A big emergency that could've had killings included."

She'd pulled her aside. "Janet, Janet. Don't argue. Tell them they can phone me."

Then hustled Kyle to the car. Kyle taking up the complaint, going on about what was the problem? Why'd they have to go?

Because you take someone shooting your house seriously.

On the way had tried her father again. Voicemail. Her mother's phone: voicemail. Had got hold of Jo-Jo Lanski, told her about the shooting. Asked if she could go there to her house. As her proxy.

"Of course, Zara. I'll bloody drop everything, get over to your house chop-chop. Jesus! Why's your life like the bloody Wild West these days?"

Zara had pleaded, knowing the desperation in her voice would turn Jo-Jo in the end.

"What's going on?"

"I don't know. My dad wouldn't say. Told me he needed me there urgently."

A quieter voice from Jo-Jo: "Let me know."

Twenty minutes later, Zara turns into Belgravia Street. There's cop vans outside her parents' house. An ambulance.

As they stop, Kyle says, "Shit, Mom, they've been shot up like us."

As true as.

Bullet pocks in a sweep across the house frontage, window-panes shattered.

She's out of the car, rushing down the garden path. There's an officer on the stoep tries to stop her. She shoves him away, belts into the house, comes to a stop in the passage. There's her father at his bedroom door.

"Pa!"

The bedroom is crowded with medics. They're moving her mother onto a gurney. She's strung up to IV bags. She's out of it.

Her father's in tears. Zara's got Kyle clutching at her.

Her father sobs. "She was having a rest. I was out the back. Oh god, Zara, I don't want her to die."

On the way to the hospital, Zara gets the story from him. How that morning, they'd gone to the nursery to buy seedlings, basil, rocket, parsley. Then to the library, afterwards to the Lebanese Bakery for lunch. "In the afternoon Ma read on the bed as she likes to do most days. I was in the backyard potting the herbs, getting the veg patch sorted. You remember my old sergeant, Lappies, big man with a loud laugh, no, well, it doesn't matter he was coming round for a drink later. I had chairs out so we could sit with a beer. Everything was so normal. Tomorrow your mother was going to her craft circle. That's her best times with the other ladies making things for the church fêtes. And now ..."

He stops. Choked up. Holding back the sobbing.

"You shouldn't have brought Kyle. He shouldn't see his granma like that."

She can see Kyle in the rearview mirror. He's crying too. Roughly smearing tears from his eyes.

"We were hit as well."

"Oh god." He turns his head to look at her. "You didn't say. Why didn't you say?"

"I couldn't. You can see we're fine, Kyle's fine. Jittery. But fine. No one was hurt. Just the house front got shot up. It's the same guy that hit you, the same gun probably."

"Maybe you must leave the cops."

"You never did."

"Nobody ever shot at my family. Even in the bad days, nobody did this."

"Of course they did, Pa. You know cops were always being killed. In the townships, what cop stood a chance?"

"It is too dangerous what you're doing. You have to think about Kyle."

"You think I don't?"

"That's not what I mean. You know what I mean."

"Ja, but then what else am I gonna do? This is the job I want. I just didn't think I'd be a police target."

"You know who's doing this?"

"Sort of. I've got links but no evidence."

"I don't want to tell you this, my bokkie, but you can't win. Not against these people."

"You never said that. You had worse people in the ranks."

At the hospital, they have to wait.

Kyle sits close up against her on a bench in the waiting room. Keeps wanting to know, "What's happening, Ma? Is Granny gonna be alright."

"It's okay, boykie," she tells him. An arm round his shoulders. "They'll fix her." Although she's not really sure if that's likely.

After half an hour, Zara can't stand the sitting any longer. Says to her father that she's taking Kyle out for a walk around the block.

Her father's got forlorn eyes. Like he's lost, maybe frightened even. "Don't be long." His pleading voice cracking.

"I won't." Zara shepherding Kyle to the door, thinking between her father and her son she's not sure who's affected the most. Let alone her own emotions. This one being on her. Again.

My lewe fok, Eloise, maybe you've gotta leave the cops.

Not going to happen.

She and Kyle head for a park not far from the hospital. There're two boys there flying a kite.

"That's a stunt kite," says Kyle. "They're awesome."

Mother and son stand watching the boys zoom the kite. Kyle's backed up against her, her arms draped over his shoulders. Not often, not ever, does he want this. Gives Zara a lift, this intimacy, then she remembers her mother.

"We'd better get back, boykie."

So they leave the boys, with the stunt kite dipping, swooping over the park, return to their reality.

"Still nothing," says her father. "They say we've just got to wait."

After an hour, a nurse comes out to tell them Elsi's still in surgery. The problem is a ricocheted bullet in her brain. The best surgeons working on it. When the nurse leaves, Zara goes after her.

"I'm her daughter. Tell me, tell me is my mother going to make it?"

"You must pray," says the nurse. "That is the best."

Cop Chickie, Get Real

93

Zara had spent the night at home. What was left of the night. Slept in Kyle's room, her Z88 on the bedside table. Spent a lot of the dark hours awake.

You're going to play at being bait, you'd better stay up for it.

Spent a lot of time fretting about her mother. Would she make it? She'd survived the operation. Would she survive the induced coma?

Concerned for her father. A shrunken figure in a hospital chair refusing to leave the waiting room. How'd he cope if her mother didn't make it?

Anxious about Kyle. His vulnerability. How to protect him during the day. What sick fuck went targeting a family! She'd tossed and turned about that one. No family out of town she could send him to. Could pack him off to Big D. He'd like that: surfing, diving, eating crayfish. Big D was certainly an option. Though Ashton would never agree.

"You're gonna hear from my lawyers, first thing," he'd said. This at the hospital where he'd tracked them down. "Come on, Kyle, come with me."

Kyle had refused. Said he was going home with his mother. That pleased her. Especially watching Ashton backing away, shaking his forefinger at her. Made her wonder what she'd ever seen in him. His hard face. The slackness starting at his belly. His insignificance. The man was completely without presence. How could she ever have been mad for him? Unbelievable.

After that, she'd got Kyle home, told him he'd be sleeping at Jo-Jo's.

"But Mom ..."

"Kyle, please. You can't sleep here, end of story."

At which Jo-Jo had said, "Young man, you're not thinking straight. Your mother needs one less worry on her mind tonight. So let's get out of her hair."

And with that, Kyle had gone quietly.

Much to Zara's relief.

At some point toward dawn, she'd fallen asleep to be woken by Janet.

"Mrs. Z, Mrs. Z, it's mos sunrise and shine. I hope today there's not gonna be some mens come round 'n' shoot us up some more."

Ditto, Janet, ditto.

Then Zara'd checked in with her father. He was okay. No change in her mother's condition.

She'd got over to Jo-Jo's to get Kyle to school. Told him she'd fetch him at the end of the school day. Or Jo-Jo would. He was not to go with anyone else.

Now she's in court to hear Tamora Gool get bail. Which means she fastens a hand on Gool's arm in the street. The woman jerks free.

"Voetsek." A pause. "Hey, I know you from long years ago. You're the cop chickie. You're the one pounced on Hendricks. What you want, cop chickie?"

"Tell me about the diamonds you gave Hendricks."

A laugh. "What diamonds?"

"The ones you were using to buy the guns."

"There were no diamonds."

Zara shakes her head. Gazes up at the bright blue sky. Smiles. "Look, don't give me crap. I know there were diamonds. I've got pictures of you giving them to Hendricks. I've got affidavits from the man who bought them from her. My lewe, woman, you're in deep shit. Fifteen, twenty years of deep shit."

"That's what you think?"

"Ja."

"I think I'm fine. I'm not going nowhere. Not even to court."

Zara does the quizzical frown. "Face it, Ms. Gool, they caught you. Lots of witnesses. Lots of video. No dispute. You were taking boxes of guns. And now they've got your diamonds, they've still got the guns. They don't care about you. You're just another gangster in a big market. Lots like you they can trick."

"You think?"

"I know. Listen, I don't care about you. I want Hendricks, I want her boss."

"Ja, ja, listen to you. You think you can clean up the cops. You've got to be joking. The cops're just another gang. They'll fry you."

"Then give me something; I'll give me an out."

"To make the charges go away? Ha! I'd like to see it. You've got no chance."

"Try me."

"Cop chickie, get real. I play with you, how long d'you think I've got? Huh! How long? One day I'm at the beach; one day I'm sitting at a café; one day I'm even maybe at home watching Netflix, they get me, pop, pop. My people, your people. Doesn't matter who points the gun, I'm dead. I help you, I'm a target. I'm saying, 'Shoot me. Come to my funeral. Drinks on me.' Uh uh. No thank you very much. You're on your own, lady. Okay you've got guts, I like that. Takes guts to say no to this lot. But don't ask me to help. No ways." She leans toward Zara, taps her on the head. "I'm not fucking stupid like you."

With that, turns away.

"I'm going to get them," Zara shouts after her. "You're going to be in court testifying."

Tamora Gool gives her the middle finger. "Try your luck, cop chickie. We'll see who's still alive for Christmas."

Zara goes for one last throw. "You heard of a cop called Exit Kutoka?"

Stops Tamora Gool. She looks back over her shoulder, flicks her hair. "Maybe. What about him?"

"He's disappeared."

"So what?"

"Probably been killed. You talked to him on Saturday at the beach. I saw you. I was there. One of your boys got a gun from him."

"In your dreams."

"They're gonna get you."

"Them and the Sexy Boys, the Americans, the Foxy Ladies, they're all trying to get me. It's how we live."

How you'll die, thinks Zara. Watches a black M5 stop next to Tamora Gool, hold up the traffic while she gets into the back. No rush despite the irate hooting of the citizenry.

94

From his operations desk, the man is watching various clients active in the city. For instance, he knows Captain Zara Dewane has parked in Harrington Square. That her car has remained stationary for most of the morning. Another client has stopped for a brief interlude with a paramour. He is also monitoring phone calls, thanks to Pegasus. Right now he has Captain Alicia Hendricks (a new target) speaking with an unknown. Most of the captain's calls are routine. Some are lovey-dovey to Duifie. These calls he listens to. Has even activated her phone at night in the hopes of getting visuals of their action. The current call he starts recording when the caller becomes angry.

"Don't crook me, chickie. You hearing? You listening? Don't you go buggering me around. You think you're so clever, you 'n' the general telling them it was an operation. So neat, hey, chickie, so neat. But don't crook me one bit. That's not a clever thing. Because you heard what they say on the TV, I know where you live."

"Is that a threat?"

"It's like information. For you to consider in your own free time. Now tell me: where's our deal standing?"

"We have to wait."

"There is no time to wait."

"There are charges against you. You are on bail."

"You think that can't be changed, hey? Plenty times I've been here in this situation before. Nobody's gonna bang me up anytime soon. So. Our deal. You've got the payment; I want the goodies. Like we agreed. I put trust in you. You gotta honor me. One for one. This time, no funny stuff."

"I can't do it just like that."

"What d'you mean, just like that? This isn't just like that, chickie. This a day later we're talking. And Cap Alicia's sitting pretty with the money. And the product. Crates of product, I heard. You gotta cough up."

"It's not that easy."

"Bullshit."

"I can get maybe one crate."

"Howzat! We got a start. When? When's this coming?"

"Later."

"Tomorrow is Saturday."

"That's too soon."

"Ag, nonsense. Not for me. Today's not too soon for me."

"I'll see."

"No, no. That's not enough. Not 'I'll see.' 'I'll see' means you're gonna do nothing. This time you gotta play nice, chickie. You wanna kiss Duifie's tits again, you better play very nice."

"You leave her alone."

"Such a pretty little birdie. Maybe I'll go see her, buy a new pair of shoes."

"Leave her out of it."

"Nobody's out of it, Captain Hendricks. We gotta all be fair 'n' square to stay in this game. Tomorrow's our day, my captain. No more monkey business. Everything on the level playing field. You give me something so I know you got skin in the game. One crate minimum."

"Just like that."

"Why not?"

"And we do this where?"

"How about … How about at a beach. How about somewhere different to where we've been. Like way down there at Muizenberg's Sunrise Beach. That's a big parking ground. What d'you say: no surprise at Sunrise. No tacticals hiding in the sand dunes. You put the merch in your smart CX-5, all we gotta do is load it into my smart M5. Coolio."

"Then what?"

"Then we do it again on Monday somewhere else."

"You're mad."

"That's what happens after a night in jail. You go lady gaga. [A pause.] I want my merchandise, Captain Hendricks. This time no tricks 'n' treachery."

End of.

Hotties, thinks the man. That would be something to watch: these two taking guns out of one car, stashing them in another. What he needs is to get a tracking device onto Captain Hendricks's vehicle. Shouldn't be too difficult a task.

Another call registers from Hendricks to a male unknown.

"Can we meet this afternoon?"

"Three o'clock suit you?"

"Can you make it earlier?"

"Unfortunately not. Nothing grows on trees, you know."

[Silence.]

His voice again: "I'll take that as confirming three o'clock, my place."

"You better be there."

"Why wouldn't I be?"

While they're talking, the man notices Captain Zara Dewane's car is on the move. Threads round the Parade Ground into Strand Street, High Level Road, drops down Glengariff to Main Road, winds up where she was the day before. There she sits. What happens in that street? Maybe something he should check out.

Could always claim it under a rubric such as "extraordinary expenses." Most government types did these days. The general would be used to it, wouldn't think twice.

95

Zara's phone rings: Jo-Jo. She taps her to speakerphone.

"I've dropped Kyle with Janet," says Jo-Jo. "You sure this is okay?"

"Ja, of course. I'm gonna be home now-now. Janet knows to keep him inside."

"Alright. I can't wait."

"I know, I know. It's fine. Really. Was he alright?"

"Perfectly. Sure. No problem. He asked where you were. I said you'd be home soon."

"I owe you."

"Big time, baby doll. Big time."

It's not but fifteen, twenty minutes and Zara'll be home.

Then Ashton rings. "I'm coming to get Kyle."

"Don't. Okay? Just don't."

"I am. He needs me. He needs stability. Safety."

Zara breaking in with: "His grandmother's in a serious condition, Ashton. You know that. He's been through a helluva experience. Just let us get through this. He's perfectly safe with me."

She's about to drive off when there's a car coming up the street that looks like Captain Alicia Hendricks's Mazda. It is Hendricks. Zara watches the captain execute an expert parallel park. Hop out, remote lock over her shoulder, stride up to the diamond dealer's door. Knock, knock.

"Like his grandmother was perfectly safe. Nobody's safe around you, Zara. You're a dead woman walking."

"Thanks for that."

"It's true. Look what happened to your neighbor."

"Just back off, Ashton."

Down the street, the diamond dealer's door has opened. He's

not visible. Captain Alicia Hendricks steps inside. Oh, to be a fly on that wall. If there was space for a fly on his walls.

"You're going to hear from my lawyer. You're a disgraced cop. You're a disgraceful mother. Shame on you, Zara. Shame on you."

She disconnects. Turns the ignition.

Would so much like to nip down the street, join in the fun and games among the dusty relics. Or even wait? Follow Hendricks to see where she spends what's left of the afternoon? Is about to pull off when there is Hendricks coming out of the house, clutching a plastic bag. Your common supermarket plastic bag. Standing behind her in the doorway is Abe Margulies. Who doesn't move even after the captain's driven away.

Zara ducks down as Hendricks passes. Now she's hyper to get going. But can't follow Hendricks until the Margulies man's gone inside. If she pulls a tight U-turn in the street, he's going to recognize her. Warn Hendricks she's being followed.

Heaven's sakes go inside.

Which he does.

When his front door closes, she's after Hendricks, who is no longer in sight.

What about Kyle?

He's with Janet. He's safe.

My lewe fok, make a decision.

At the top of the street, Zara goes left.

Hendricks would be heading back to town. Zara bets on the office of Umuzi Trading. She gets it right. Going up High Level Road she sees the Mazda ahead. Follows the captain into the city. Stops in a loading zone a hundred yards back from the Mazda. Sees Hendricks rush into the building.

What about Kyle?

He's with Janet. He's safe.

Go now.

She doesn't. She waits. Five minutes and Hendricks is back. This time heads out of town.

What about Kyle?

He's with Janet. He's safe.

Who're you kidding!

She phones Janet. "All okay?"

"Yes, man, Mrs. Z. I's with Kyle right here inna kitchen doing toasteds."

"Keep him inside."

"Roger that, all loud 'n' clearly."

My lewe, that Janet!

And now here she is in Parklands where tailing is impossible. These are suburban streets. There is no traffic. Zara has to hang back, let Hendricks get ahead, then hope to hell she can find her again.

She's in luck. In a side street there's the bullet-holed Mazda parked at the curb. She drives past. In a driveway is a black Mercedes-Benz. From the driveway to the front porch a wheelchair ramp. Hooza.

Two hundred yards away she stops under a tree. Angles the rearview mirror.

What about Kyle?

He's with Janet. He's safe.

Two minutes. Three minutes. If nothing after five minutes, I'll go.

Meanwhile fires off WhatsApps: to her father for an update on her mother; to Jo-Jo for an update on Vula; to Janet to say she's on her way home.

Also responds to a voicemail: please report at the Woodstock police station to make a statement about the shooting at her house. Sends a voicemail saying she'll be in first thing Saturday.

And on six minutes there's the captain trotting across the street to her Mazda. Zara wavers: confront Vula or Hendricks or go to Kyle?

What to do?

Go home.

Get the affidavit from Abe Margulies first.

Check out whatever Hendricks left at the Umuzi Trading offices.

Then take on the captain. She'll save her own ass when push comes to shove, no question.

Before she can swing the ignition there's a response from Jo-Jo: *Vula not in the office. Compassionate leave. Thursday's weaponry not registered in the SAPS armory. Origins unknown. His wife's funeral tomorrow. Maitland. 10 a.m.*

Zara thinking, That's something you can't miss.

Then her father. A voice call: "I think you should come to the hospital. Your mother's not good. The doctors say ..."

Whatever it is the doctors say, her father can't say it. He's sobbing. "Just come."

She says, "Pa, Pa" to dead air.

Tries to phone him. But is stopped by another voice call: Janet.

"I can't find Kyle, Mrs. Z. He was mos here one minute and then he was mos wasn't."

Now it's Zara who can't get the words out.

"I been all throughout the house, Mrs. Z. Kyle's nowhere I can find."

"Outside," says Zara. Her voice strangled. She clears her throat. "Outside, Janet. Maybe he's in the street with his skateboard."

Although she's told him many times not to ride in the street.

"Mrs. Z, I's on the stoep; I's down at the gate; there's nobody in the road."

She disconnects. Dials Kyle's phone. Gets voicemail.

Shit, shit, shit.

Goes back to Janet. "Is his phone gone? Has he got his phone?"

"I'm checking, Mrs. Z. I heard it ringing."

Shit.

"Here's it. On his bed."

Fok!

"I'll call the security. You stay there; don't go anywhere. I'm coming. Half an hour, okay? I'll be there in half an hour." Then the obvious thought, My lewe. "His father hasn't been there? He isn't hanging around somewhere?"

"Not a chance I let mister anywhere near us."

Kyle wouldn't go with his father without saying so. But then again not beyond Ashton to bribe him away. By dangling a new surfboard, for instance. Or a new phone.

Now she calls Ashton. Gets his voicemail.

The bastard. She starts the car, heads out of the suburb onto the highway into the city. The bastard's testing her. That's what's happened. The bastard has him. Which is no consolation. She's got no way to Kyle. He's got no way to her. Ashton has everything stacked to his advantage. He can dictate when it happens. How it happens. Except, she knows where he lives.

Her phone goes. Her father again. "Where are you? Are you nearly here?"

He's more lucid.

"What's happening with Ma?"

"She's dying, bokkie. She's dying." Which brings the heart-wrenching sobs. His grief's too much for her; Zara stabs him off. Puts her foot down hard on the accelerator.

Does Ashton's flat first. It's kind of on the way. A dog leg but doable despite the evening traffic. Except Ashton's not there. And he should be. And she can't wait around. He's still not answering his phone. She leaves a message: "Get the fuck back to me."

Not her usual style but she's stressed.

Also, she's convinced Ashton's bribed Kyle to make a point. But it's gone 6 p.m., the point's been made.

She phones Janet to check Kyle's not back.

"No, Mrs. Z, I'd've mos told yous chop-chop."

You better. Except she doesn't say it. Says she's going to the hospital.

Where she learns her mother's still hanging in. She finds her father.

"Where were you?" he says. "You should have been here. They thought she was going to die."

But she hasn't, has she! She's still in the ICU ward. Drips in, electric monitors recording her living signs. To look at you'd think she was sleeping peacefully. Her face at rest. Okay, her head is swaddled in bandages; there's bruising at her eyes. What you can't see is the other skim wound across her chest.

Zara's father is sitting beside the bed, clasping his wife's hand. Head bent. Shoulders slumped. The man's had it. In all her years she's never seen him defeated. Thwarted, frustrated, foiled, yes. But not crushed. Not like this: broken. On her tongue to tell him Kyle's missing but can't. The man's dealing with enough. This is your freak-out, bokkie, keep it that way.

Asks instead, "How's Ma doing?"

He shakes his head, can't speak.

A matron overhears her question, takes her aside.

Says: "Maybe you shouldn't let your dad stay here much longer. It's not too good for him. He needs you now, nè. He should go home. She's going to be okay, your mom. That was a terrible moment earlier but she's strong, she's got through it. I've seen patients get bad like that, then, wha-za, they come back. Your ma's come back, lovey."

Which is what Zara wants to believe. Sees the earnestness in the matron's face. That she's convinced of her prognosis.

"Honestly, lovey, tomorrow your ma's going to be smiling. Take your pa home. We got this one."

Nothing in the matron's expression that's anything other than confident.

"Okay," says Zara. "You'll ring me if there's any change?"

"Of course. But the only change is going to be the plus side."

Okay.

Sometimes you've got to trust fate. Or the professionals.

Zara coaxes her father out of his chair, has got him a bed at the home of his old sergeant, Lappies. On the way there, her thoughts a swirl of dark repetitions: am I doing the right thing? Will he be alright? Where's Ashton and Kyle? Ashton's phone still going to voicemail.

It's well gone eleven. Zara's in her car outside Ashton's flat. She's been up there twice to bang on the door. No response. Except the next-door neighbor asking what's her problem.

No, he hasn't seen Ashton. Or heard him come home.

So where the fok has Ashton taken Kyle?

She's tried his lawyer. Got nothing from him either. "He's the boy's father. I'm sure there isn't a problem. Go to sleep, Captain Dewane. You sound hysterical."

But what if there is. What if Ashton's not to blame? What if he's with a girlfriend? Not answering calls because he's screwing his heart out. What if Kyle's been kidnapped?

That's a thought she pushes away. That's a thought that keeps returning.

All she wants is to have her boy with her. Have him asleep where she can see him. Be back in her own house. Safe 'n' sound. Be able to drink a glass of wine. Fall asleep in her own bed.

After Kyle, all Zara wants is to think about her mother getting better. Her mother suddenly back from the edge.

But finds she can't.

Keeps dreading a world without her mother. How close that came. All that life on Thursday, gone on Friday. But it didn't happen. So no point in dwelling on what might have been. Nothing to be gained by imagining the dreadful. Yet she can't help going there. Imagining how her father might have blamed her. Maybe still does for putting her mother's life on the line. Maybe doesn't blame her in so many words. But he'd have had these thoughts. Maybe even wished she'd never been born.

Which agitates Zara. Gets her driving back to the hospital. Back in her mother's ward, sits in the chair, agonizing.

How could this have happened to her? She knows there is no answer to this question. Knows it is not even a sensible question. But it keeps coming. If it wasn't for her investigations her mother wouldn't be fighting for her life. If, if, if ...

She blacks that one. Switches to Kyle. How she'd told him not to go outside. Not to skateboard in the street. Not to go off with his father. If he did. If he hadn't been forcibly abducted.

Fok no.

Drives home eventually. In the small hours. Lies on Kyle's

bed. The light on. His posters of monsters looming at her. And then Wynston. For god's sake, why now, Wynston? I can't be everywhere. I can't do everything. I couldn't be with you, couldn't be with him, all the time. Give me a break. I'm only human.

That's your problem, Wynston says. Deal with it.

96

Saturday. Outside the Full Gospel Church of God, 10:35 a.m.

Spaced-out. Dark-eyed. Agitated Captain Zara Dewane waits in her car for the Vula cortège to leave for Maitland Cemetery. Sits there drumming on the steering wheel. Impressive array of black vehicles parked in the streets. Drivers, protection muscle hanging around. She stops well back. No line of sight to the church. But that doesn't faze her. To leave the suburb, the mourners will have to come her way.

Already this morning, she's been to Ashton's flat. No sign of him. No sign that he'd been home. Still not answering her calls. Just voicemail, voicemail, voicemail. And she's left increasingly agitated messages. Also got one of Wynston's contacts to locate Ashton's phone.

An hour later the contact came back, "Can't find any trace, Captain. The guy's got to have his phone switched off, battery out, SIM card out. He's gone black." Actually used the word "black."

A light moment in Zara's grim morning.

It'd been another sleepless night of worry.

He has to be with Ashton. If he's been kidnapped, there'd have been threats already. Kidnapping's not the style here. Drive-by is the style here. He has to be with Ashton. This is about Ashton showing his power. Playing I'm the Big Daddy, I can do as I please with my son. All the same, not knowing for sure he's with his father, freaks her out.

After the drop-in at Ashton's flat she'd taken her father to the hospital, spent half an hour with her mother. Elsi was still in an induced coma. Still attached to an electronic array of devices. But the signs were positive, according to the nurses. She'd left John looking hopeful. Less stressed. The father she'd never known to show his anxiety. Even so, hadn't told him about Kyle. The man had enough to deal with.

Also, she'd been to the cop shop to write her statement. Where she learned that the bullets were all fired from the same gun. That the shooter must have changed his registration plates. Twice. "You're talking a careful man, Captain," as the sergeant taking her statement put it. "There's lots of white Polos on the traffic cameras. Any which one could be his."

Not that she'd expected much to come of that.

The other thing she'd had was a list of gun numbers from Jo-Jo. They matched her list. Those were the guns in the crate in the Malgas shed the night Wynston was shot. Guns that should've been in an evidence store. Guns Hendricks planned to sell to Gool.

Gotcha, Alicia.

With a bit of luck.

Now two traffic cops on bikes pass slowly, followed by the hearse, followed by Vula, followed by Minister Lebo Majoro, followed by brass she vaguely recognized, followed by Captain Alicia Hendricks (alone), followed by a white woman in a mini Suzuki SUV, a face she recognizes. The woman who talked to Exit at the beach. Zara jots down her reg number, then joins the cortège. Everybody driving sedately, headlights on in deference.

At the cemetery she leaves her car well back, walks to where a group is gathered around the grave. Packed close to look at the coffin being lowered. Except the white woman in a floaty scarf hanging back on the fringes.

From behind her Zara says, "How'd you know Exit Kutoka? D'you maybe have a clue to his whereabouts right now?"

The woman spins on her. Hisses, "Leave me alone. It's a funeral."

"He's missing. He might be dead."

"I know nothing of that." She moves away.

Zara lets her go. She can get her address from the traffic department, visit her quietly. At least now scarf-lady's spooked.

Next on her list is Cap Hendricks. There she is, standing behind the top brass. A tap on the shoulder, a quiet word. They move away from the brass.

"What do you want?" Hendricks to Dewane.

A cocky response: "To give you a heads-up."

"About what? I don't need it."

"No? I think you do, Captain Hendricks." Zara thinking, Why not lay down another scare? "You see, I've got affidavits of IDB. Evidence of illegal gun deals. Bank statements of Umuzi Trading. Your fingerprints all over all of this. You want to help yourself, we should talk."

"You're lying."

"Try me." She holds up a thumb and forefinger mils apart. "That's how close I am."

Leaves Captain Hendricks to ponder this, moves through the crowd nearer to General Vula. Impressive how many have turned out for the general. She gets a quick moment with him as people disperse. Bends toward him.

"My condolences, General."

He glances up. Waves her off with a sharp flick of his wrist.

Again she bends. "You should talk to Captain Hendricks, General. She is my sweet spot. I know about the diamonds. I know about the guns. I know about Sergeant Kutoka." With that, straightens. "Think about it, General. I am coming." Moves quickly away as men gather round the general.

Zara is nearing her car when a black Merc stops beside her. A muscleman jumps out. Says, "Get in." Holds open the rear door.

"I didn't expect to see you here," says Minister of Police Majoro from inside. "How come?"

Zara slides into the back seat. "Paying my respects."

"It didn't look like it."

"Well, you know, sometimes people don't appreciate a gesture."

The minister laughs. "He didn't. Why's that? What did you tell him?"

"Nothing he doesn't know already."

"Like?"

"Trading guns for diamonds. Guns from a heist. A heist about seven, eight weeks ago. The weapon numbers were inventoried. I've got a list."

"Well done, Captain. I want a full report before you take any action."

Which gives Zara pause. What? "I'm sorry. Do I understand you?"

"I think so." The minister lays two fingers on Zara's wrist. "There is more here than you know. You must come to me first. I expect it."

No soft-spoken mother of a young skateboarder now.

Zara keeps a bland face, says nothing.

"You hear me?"

She nods. Edges herself out of the car.

Before the muscleman can close the door, the minister calls out, "Captain, Captain." Zara leans back inside. There's the minister's serious eyes looming at her. "Don't let me down, Captain. I wouldn't like that."

Zara walks away. Considering how this is the first time she's been threatened by a politician. A minister, would you believe! Begs the question: What's going on?

At her car, she waits until everyone has left before driving away.

Hardly the start of a traditional funeral. No after-tears party. No feasting. No drinking. No long speeches.

Suits Zara.

Means she can get on with her day. With worrying about her son. Also has her wondering: Should she take on the diamond dealer or see if Hendricks has gone to Vula? No reason she can't do both. Vula's place first.

En route puts through a call to a little helper at the traffic department. Second time in the morning she could give praise for Wynston's contact book of little helpers. Asks for a trace on a reg number.

At Vula's house, there's his Merc in the driveway. Parked at the curb, a Mazda CX-5. Who'd have guessed?

Oh, to be a fly on the wall.

97

What the fly would've heard is this:

"She's got nothing, Captain Hendricks. Nothing. She said those things to scare you."

This is General Kaiser Vula in his wheelchair, facing Captain Alicia Hendricks sitting on the couch. The room is bright with midday sunshine. Vases of flowers on every available surface. Condolence cards that were hand or courier delivered stand between them. Pride of place on a corner table, a memorial pamphlet with a cover photograph of the lovely Lady. Said photo taken at the safari bush retreat, the day after Vula shot General Duncan Maale.

Vula looks away from the worried face of Alicia Hendricks into the garden. Out there sits his driver, smoking a cigarette, absorbed in his phone. A placid scene. In here, Vula roils. He presents as calm, yet his mind is restive. Alicia Hendricks is the harbinger of destruction. He remembers the words of Luna Maplewood: "It is a warning, Kaiser. She is warning you. She can turn the world upside down."

No. She is more than a warning. She has broken a good thing. The mlungu bitch was right. The captain is chaos. She must go.

But he gives no hint of this.

Says, "Now you see why I say we must do business in cash. When you exchange like this, there are always problems."

Ah man, how often has it not happened, that he needs to act himself? If he does not do it, it is not done right. How often do others fail? They lack the will. They lack the blood. Like this one.

Who now says, "Dewane has talked to Margulies."

"Margulies?" Who is this Margulies?

"The diamond dealer."

There it is: another person. Another person who knows about the diamonds. Another weakness. But Vula keeps his grip, pacifies.

"So what? If any commissioner asks, you are investigating a case of illegal diamond smuggling. In the course of this inquiry, you have been led to question certain people of interest in the diamond trading environment. As part of this operation you exchanged diamonds for cash. You see, Captain, there are always reasons for our actions. But you will never have to tell anyone such stories. Especially not the commissioner. You can relax. Maybe if you want to take a holiday, this is a good time."

He watches her face loosen. First an easing of the tension at her eyes, then a softening of her lips. In the beginning, she was a good comrade. Organized the fieldwork, kept a wall between him and the interactions. And so it could have continued, were it not for the diamonds. Were it not for her own stupidity. Her greed. Were it not for the Dewane person. He has to take charge. He is protected; he has the power.

"Where are they? The rest of the diamonds. You have them?"

She digs in her briefcase. Hauls out a Ziploc bag.

Ah man, she carries them around. This woman is losing it for sure.

"Perhaps I should keep this." He takes the plastic bag. "For the moment. In case there are problems."

"What problems?"

He wheels toward her, reassured by the alarm suddenly back in her eyes.

"I cannot say. You must be careful. This Captain Dewane is a tsetse fly. She stings when you are not looking. But like all tsetse flies, we can eradicate her."

He likes that, the tsetse fly reference; it's better than jackal. In the bush war, the tsetse flies had been a big problem. Some of the comrades who'd been stung had recovered, many had died.

"You mean …"

"I mean, as you know, she is on suspension. I am her superior. I can have her discharged. I have been too lenient with Captain Dewane. Now she must feel the edge."

Who was Dewane to threaten him with affidavits, testimony, bank accounts, eyewitness statements? Even on suspension, she tries to sting. He must deal with her. But first there is Captain Alicia Hendricks. She knows everything about him. Perhaps not what happened to Maale but most everything else. She can also sting. She can drop him fast. Turn whistle-blower to save herself. Women against a man. The sistahood banded up. Ah man, ah man!

He wheels yet closer to her. Their knees almost touch. The captain shifts her legs sideways. He smiles reassurance.

"You have paid yourself from these diamonds?" He lifts the Ziploc bag.

"Yes."

"Good." Of course she would have. She looks after herself. "As I have said, you should use the money for a holiday. Perhaps outside the country." Vula eases some of the stones into the palm of his hand. "Have you been to other countries? Senegal? Kenya? Tanzania? The island of Zanzibar? Madagascar?"

Hendricks shakes her head.

"Now is your opportunity." He examines the diamonds in his hand. "You say these are top quality."

"Namibian ocean diamonds. Washed down by rivers."

"Interesting."

"That's what I was told."

Vula funnels them back into the bag. Presses closed the Ziploc. Raises his head to look at her. "Why don't you take immediate leave? Put the form on my desk, I will sign it when I am in on Monday. By then you can be on a plane to paradise. It will be better this way."

When the captain has gone, Vula pours himself a whisky. Powers from the drinks cabinet to the side table to stare at the photograph of Lady. It is regrettable she weakened. Could not enjoy the power. He lifts his glass in a toast, says aloud, "It is a pity you are not here." Takes a sip, letting the liquid lie on his tongue. Then swallows, enjoying the slide of its warmth to his stomach. Now turns from his dead wife to focus on his phone. Pity has no place today. He sends a Telegram to the man. Fortunately, there are the diamonds to meet these extra budget expenses.

98

The diamonds, at least one of them, also come in handy for Alicia Hendricks. She has kept back two stones. For emergencies, for off-book expenses. Like this.

The first thing she does is call Duifie. Do you have to go in tomorrow? Can you take a month's leave?

"Liefie! Wow, babe, that's hectic sudden."

"It's a police thing."

"I can take a month's leave but I gotta work tomorrow morning. It's my Sunday shift. But, jissis, man, how we gonna get visas that quick?"

"We aren't. Sorry, have to be south of France next time."

"Ah, you said …"

"I know. Not possible. What about Zanzibar? Or Mauritius? No need for visas there."

A moment's thought. "Zanzibar."

"Okay. My first choice too."

"Really?"

"Really. Your manager won't mind?"

"I dunno. I'm coming even if I must resign."

The second thing is a travel agent. Alicia finds one in a nearby mall.

Yes, there are seats on a Kenyan Air out of Cape Town on Sunday night. Accommodation? Yes please. A beach villa for a month? Easily arranged. Payment upfront on her credit card. Half an hour, it's all done and dusted.

Third thing: foreign currency. No problem. There's five grand US hidden in a couch in the offices of Umuzi Trading. Plus Straight Abe Margulies will surely cough up dollars for the diamonds. More than enough.

She does all this. Even gets thirty grand out of Margulies for one of the stones. Undoubtedly less than it's worth, but she's not arguing.

Back at her flat, Alicia reckons she'll go in tomorrow morning, clear her in-tray, submit the leave form to the general. Plenty of time afterwards to pack. As for Tamora Gool, she can get stuffed. By the time she realizes what's what, the flight will have taken off. Up yours, chickie. Alicia sticks a bottle of sparkling wine in the freezer. Waits for Duifie to get home. This is freedom. Away from the woman Dewane. Away, away. Looks at the brochure of the beach villa. Wooden deck. Shutters. Palm trees everywhere. A path between them leading to white sands, a turquoise sea, far skies. Maybe they'll never come back.

99

When the general's message lands, the man is on a surveillance job in the city. His target is sitting at a sidewalk café. He, himself, is parked in a twenty-minute stop zone, thirty yards away. He doesn't need binoculars. He has clear line of sight. His target is approached by another man. There are handshakes, back slaps. A brown A4 envelope is placed on the table by the newcomer. Without fuss. Without comment. More handshakes. The men part. The target sits down again. Drums his fingers on the envelope. This target is the man's first concern this afternoon. He cannot abandon his surveillance at another client's whim. There are professional standards at stake. Nevertheless he notes the general's demands. On a notepad tallies his possible expenses, his fee. Telegrams this to the general.

By return: *Urgent bongo-bongo.*

"Only as urgent as my schedule allows," mutters the man. There is nothing here that cannot wait until the morning.

He does not respond to the general.

His focus is on the target settling the bill. The man picks up the envelope. And then the line of sight is broken by a boisterous group of young men. When the target is clear again, he no longer has the envelope.

"Fuuuuck!" curses the man, while admiring the neatness of the brush-past. That envelope could be with any one of the young men. Or it could have been slipped elsewhere. He watches his target enter a car park. Five minutes later, he exits in his Audi. Nothing for it but to follow. Some jobs have their setbacks. As the man well knows, this work requires patience.

Hellcat

100

In the late afternoon Zara fetches her father from the hospital. At his request. "Your mother's improving. We'll come back again later. I need to get away for a bit."

In the ward there's a bouquet of flowers signed from the politician Rings Saturen.

"And that?" she says to her father.

"A long story. I'll tell you later." He takes the flowers; in the hospital parking lot dumps them in a bin.

"Pa! What're you doing? I wouldn't have minded those."

"From that man everything's tainted," he says.

"So what's the story? Please tell."

"Another time." And that's all he'll say. She knows not to push things.

She takes him home to collect his car. Change his clothes. Suggests he stays at Lappies for a few days. It's closer to the hospital.

Maybe a minute passes. He doesn't look at her. Then says, "Ja, Lappies doesn't mind."

While he packs a small suitcase, Zara wanders through the house. There's knitting beside the chair in the lounge. Like her mother had put it down to fetch something.

Be right back, Zara-sweet.

The words clear, as if she'd heard them. She spins round, catches a flicker of movement in the doorway. Her father.

"It's my fault," she says. "My fault she was almost killed."

"No," says her father in the cop voice she remembers. Stern. No bullshit. "It's not the first time it's happened. In my day we had bricks through the window—three times. Even an attempted Molotov cocktail. You probably don't remember that. You were only five or six. This is cop life, bokkie. We get hit. But it's not our fault for doing the job. It's them. The criminals. They're the killers. The man who pulled the trigger wounded your mother."

Of course.

But.

But if she'd not threatened Vula he would not have set his dog on her. That this is Vula's doing she has no doubt. She will take it to him.

John: "Do you know who it is?"

"Yes."

"But you don't have all the evidence?"

"No. Not yet."

"Some high-up?"

"A general. Selling guns. Trading in illegal diamonds. Probably behind at least two murders. Maybe three."

"You can't do this alone. You need backup."

She knows what's coming next.

"Let me help."

"You're retired."

"You're on suspension."

They stare at one another. In cop-speak: considering their options.

"I'm not yet sixty-three for Chrissakes, bokkie. Not some old man." He digs around in his overnight bag, pulls out a 9mm Ruger. "I'm even tooled up." Laughs as he says it.

She takes the gun. It's clean. Oiled. Ejects the clip. It's fully loaded at fifteen. "Where the hell did you get it?"

"I've always had it. Since about 1989."

"You never told me."

"Lots of things I never told you."

My lewe fok. What the hell! Her dad as backup. Madness, Eloise. But the guy is fit, he knows the scene. Why not?

"Alright. But you don't interfere. This's my gig."

He shrugs.

"Please, Pa, no problems."

"It's okay, bokkie, you're the boss. What's the plan?"

Instead she says, "There's another thing, Pa. Kyle's missing."

"Uh! What? What you saying? My Jesus, Zara. Since when?"

"Yesterday night."

"Now you tell me."

"You had other things …"

"Jesus fucking Christ, my girl." From the father who seldom swears. "What the heck, bokkie. You've got the cops looking for him? You sure he's not with his father?"

"The cops, not yet. I'm pretty sure he's with his father. But Ashton's not answering his phone. Actually got his phone switched off. His lawyer tells me to stop freaking, Ashton's got rights."

"Not to kidnap his own son. Not tell the boy's mother. We should be looking for him."

"Like where, Pa? Where? For god's sakes, where?"

"I don't know. You've tried Ashton's friends?"

"Some. They tell me to relax. They tell me Ashton's okay. He just wants to be with his boy."

"We're going to the station. First things first, hey. We get them onto Ashton."

Which they do.

Because John Dewane is still Sergeant John Dewane in this cop shop. He's remembered. They do things for him. Which irritates Zara. The condescension: Ag shame, Captain. First they shoot your house. Now your boy's gone. This is wild South Africa these days.

"They'll find him," says her father as they leave.

Yeah, thinks Zara, like they found the guy who shot my neighbor. Shot my house. Bloody cops!

She tells him now they're going to Sea Point. To the house of a diamond dealer. He's to stop well away from the target house. She goes in. He doesn't. She's going to get an affidavit from the dealer. It's not a big production. No cause for concern.

"Alright?"

"Got it, bokkie, loud and clear."

They head off in two cars, her father following.

She's decided to hit up Abe Margulies first. With his affidavit she could get Hendricks to roll. She could get Gool to a plea deal. She could hang an arrest and charge on Vula.

Especially backed with the Kutoka evidence. You're going down, General.

As agreed, her father parks higher up the street; she stops outside the house of Straight Abe Margulies. Knocks. No response. Phones him. Gets voicemail. The curtains are drawn at all the windows. Clearly nobody's home. Zara tries a neighbor. Is told: "Oh no, Mr. Margulies left in a taxi about two hours ago. Looked like he was going away from the size of his wheelie suitcase. Mr. Margulies often goes away. Actually, he's more away than at home. Such a strange bloke. Often has people coming and going from his house. Nice man, though, very friendly. A perfectly quiet neighbor. Can I give him a message next time I see him?"

Zara says, No, she has his cell number. Walks up the road to her father waiting quietly in his car.

"What now?" he says.

"I phone him again."

Margulies answers. "Captain Dewane."

"Where are you? I need an affidavit."

"Sorry for you," he says. "I am on a plane about to take off for destinations distant. I do not like the heat, Captain. And you police are too hot. Goodbye. Totsiens. Auf Wiedersehen."

Dead air.

My lewe fok, Eloise.

"What was that?"

"He's gone. Leaving. Running away. He's scared."

"A wise man."

"So now what?"

"I confront the general."

Her father's got his eyes fixed on her. "You should wait. You can't force these things."

"I know."

"Then why are you going to do this?"

"Because if I don't he'll get away with it. I know it."

"You're speculating. You need evidence."

"I've got enough. I need to force him to act."

"That's not a good idea."

She knows this. And there was the police minister's warning. But. This is not a time for caution. She needs the general to incriminate himself.

"I'm doing it for Ma."

"That's also not a good idea."

"Can't think of a better one."

He thumps the steering wheel.

She holds up a finger. "Pa."

"I know, I know." He closes his eyes, takes a deep breath. "Your gig. When do you plan to do this? Tonight?"

"Tomorrow. First thing."

101

Zara stays over with Jo-Jo. Just the two of them. Jo-Jo's wife is away on business. They sit in the kitchen, opposite sides of the table. Pick at a salad. Drink wine. Talk long into the night. About Kyle. Ashton.

Zara letting it go. "I'm freaking out that I don't know where he is. My stomach hurts. I can't think straight. I can't sleep properly. What the fuck am I gonna do?"

Jo-Jo holding it together. "Hellssakes, Zar. You've done all you can do. The techies are on it. The cops are on it. You've just got to wait. He's got him, I'm telling you. No question about it."

"It could be he's been kidnapped. That's also possible."

"By Vula or Hendricks? No ways. It's not their style."

"By the gunman."

"Not his style either. He shoots people. Shoots at houses. That's his style. No, this is Ashton punishing you."

"For what?"

"Ah c'mon. For kicking him out. For calling him an asshole."

"That was ages ago."

"Men don't forget. That's the way they are. You know that. They bear grudges." Jo-Jo drains her glass. Gets up to fetch another bottle from the rack. Uncorks it. Fills their glasses. Throughout Zara twirling a fork between her fingers. Distracted. Fighting the rise of emotion in her chest. Thinking: Just keep this together. Hold back. Swallowing hard. Keeping her eyes away from Jo-Jo. Doing what Zara does best: bottling.

All the same. Just as well Jo-Jo changes topics.

"I need a smoke." She opens the kitchen door. Lights up, blows smoke outside. "So tomorrow you're going to confront Vula?'

"Ja."

"Maybe you shouldn't drink any more?"

Zara holds out her arm. Steady. No shake. No tremble. Straight as a plank. A woman in control. Again.

Jo-Jo laughs. "Hardgirl Zara. What's that prove?"

"Proves I'm gonna confront him. I've got all the info, the evidence. You've seen it. He's going down."

"And you think it's as easy as that? That he'll come quietly with the Lone Ranger."

Zara rocking back on her chair. Frowning. "Hey, what's this Hardgirl, Lone Ranger stuff. It's a simple arrest."

"And your backup. Seeing as you're on suspension."

"My dad."

"John?" Jo-Jo crushes out her cigarette. Leaves the ashtray on the outside step. Closes the door. "He's not even a cop anymore. He's retired. I'll come."

Which gets a quick retort. "No. This is cop business. I need you for after. For the actual arrest. For charging. Processing. Getting the paperwork lined up."

Jo-Jo shrugs. "Sometimes I give up." Toasts: "May you have all your ducks in a row."

"I have."

"Okay, then. Let justice be done." They clink glasses, drink. "You remember, we were supposed to talk last Sunday. You wanted that."

"I know. Last Sunday got weird."

"So what was so important then?"

Zara pauses. Takes another sip.

"This is alright wine."

"Wolftrap. Not your malbec, but a good blend. So back to your problem."

A sigh from Zara. "It's Wynston. The guy's haunting me."

"Of course. That's called grief, Zar."

"I know. But still. It's months ago. But it's like it isn't."

"You guys were colleagues. Close colleagues. You feel guilty about his being killed."

"No kidding."

Jo-Jo reaches across, covers her hand. "You know what?"

"What?"

"Some bad news. There's nothing you can do about it. You can go for therapy all you want. You can spill it now to me. Weep. Gnash your teeth. Pull out your hair. Rend your clothing. It's not going to help. This is your story, you're just gonna have to live with it."

"Oh thanks. That's so encouraging."

Jo-Jo releases Zara's hand. "It's how it is, doll. Wynston's not through with you yet. Despite what I said, go see your shrink. At least you'll feel like you're doing something to come right." She knocks back what's left in her glass. "Enough now. Bedtime."

Bedtime. Hours lying awake. Doing the turning, tossing thing.

Sometimes letting the tears roll. Then sleeping as the light comes.

Until Jo-Jo wakes her. "What's your plan?"

"Simple. Confront General Vula."

102

On this Sunday, the man also has a plan, an order of events.

First up is Captain Zara Dewane. She is the easiest to hit. The MO here is to knock on her door. She opens. Bam, bam, thank you, ma'am. Two 9mms to the chest. With a silencer, no disturbance to the suburb. As she collapses, he'd push her backward so he could close the front door. A hop and a skip to his car, head off for target two: Captain Alicia Hendricks.

Target three is Duifie. He has no surname for her. But he does have the address of the shoe shop where she works. He knows she'll be there this morning. Last night, he'd thought to fulfil some of the general's order. Gone so far as driving out to the flat of targets two and three. Then seen security cameras in the street, at the entrance to the block of apartments. With security cameras you need to know the lay of the land well in advance. He stood himself down. Instead, fixed trackers to the cars of both targets. That was easy enough to achieve. Sometimes he can't believe how professional he is.

He checks his weaponry. All 9mms. Always best to spread the tools in hand.

For Target Dewane, a Beretta APX.

For Target Hendricks, a damn expensive CZ 75.

For Target Duifie, an unused (except for target practice) Sig Sauer. The P320 semi auto.

He'll dispose of all three pistols off the rocks at Cape Point. Down in the kelp beds, they're not going to be found for a long, long time, if ever. Afterwards, stop at The Scone Shack for carrot cake and hot chocolate. Make something of the morning. Truth though, it's a pity about the CZ, but not as if he laid out the bucks. All three weapons were handed in as part of the amnesty on firearms. All three were diverted before they could be destroyed. And ended up with the man.

Right now, he's still in his office. He has Target Hendricks on Pegasus talking to a female unknown. It's amusing because he knows all about the paradise island holiday. How Target Hendricks and Target Duifie are scheduled to board a Kenyan Air flight that afternoon and fly away. Yet she's saying this stuff.

103

Here's what's happening between Target Hendricks and the female unknown.

Who is Tamora Gool.

Captain Alicia Hendricks doesn't need lip from Tamora Gool. But she's getting it. And has to suck it up.

Tamora Gool wants confirmation that nothing has changed. That everything is set to go ahead. No surprise parties jumping out of the sand dunes.

"You don't pull any shit, Cappie."

"I told you what's what."

"You told me kak stories last time. This isn't playschool, chickie. No more police hotel for this lady. You got it?"

"You need to calm down."

Tamora Gool whistles. "Careful, chickie, careful what you're telling me. Who's the exposed one here, hey? Who exactly? It's me. It's not Captain Hendricks, it's me, the girl who's been landed in the poo-poo. I need to calm down? No, no, chickie. I'm only nice and calm when I see you this afternoon. Only you. No oukies in funny hats with big guns. You hear me? Yes? You got it?"

"I said I will be there."

"With the crate."

"With the crate."

"Sunrise Beach, 3:00 p.m."

"Ja, man, I said I'll be there."

"You better. For Duifie's sake."

"You leave her out of it."

"She's not in it if you keep your side. Up to you, Cap Chickie."

Which is where Alicia Hendricks ends the connection.

104

The man smiles. Unknown female is going to be the hell in angry when Hendricks doesn't pitch. Not his problem.

The man is ready to rock 'n' roll. He checks the monitor. Sees Target Dewane is now heading west out of the city. Which is an inconvenience. He shifts his priorities to Target Hendricks. Her car's in motion, direction the city. Going quickly downstairs to his car, activates the app on his phone. There she is coming off the highway, threading through the streets toward her office. This is far from ideal. But the man believes that luck favors those who make themselves available. He's an opportunist.

So he latches onto Captain Alicia Hendricks in her battle-scarred Mazda CX-5 at the Sir Lowry Road intersection. He's two cars back, following her left into Canterbury, down to Harrington. She curb parks near New York Bagels. Buys a cup of coffee. While she's waiting on the sidewalk, the man drives slowly toward her. Has a scarf covering his mouth, wears sunglasses, a brown peak cap. As he pulls opposite her, slides down his window.

Says, "Excuse me, excuse me."

Watches Captain Alicia Hendricks turn toward him. She's two yards away. The road ahead is clear. There are no cars behind him. People standing around but eyewitnesses are going to have their own stories of what happened.

He brings up the damn expensive CZ, now fitted with a silencer.

105

Captain Alicia Hendricks orders her latte to go. Walks over to the service hatch. Thinks, Two hours to clear her desk. Thirty minutes' drive back to the flat. Duifie would be there by then. Change from cop to citizen. Call an Uber. Make it to the airport two hours before departure. Once through customs, she could breathe.

Up yours, General Vula.

Get stuffed, Tamora Gool.

Piss off, Captain Dewane.

This going through her mind when she hears: "Excuse me, excuse me."

Turns toward the street.

There's a white Polo drawing level with her.

The side window comes down to reveal a guy wearing a brown peak cap, dark glasses.

"Can I help?" she says. Used to people asking for information when she is in uniform. Can't tell if the guy's smiling or anxious. His right hand coming off the steering wheel, dropping out of sight. She takes a step toward him. Sees him shift slightly to his left, raise his right hand. Extend his arm. He's aiming a silenced pistol at her head.

WTF.

106

Pop, pop, pop. Head. Chest right. Chest left.

As the captain staggers backward, he drives off. No haste. No wheel-spin. Takes the first left, the next right. In no time, he's on Philip Kgosana Drive gliding through the curves below Devil's Peak.

On his sound system, Linda Perry sings "Fly Away."

He gets off the highway at the hospital, winds through the streets down to Observatory. In a quiet spot, changes the number plates. Probably unnecessary but the man's a professional.

His tracking app shows Duifie's car stationary near the shoe shop. As it should be.

He's not sure how this target is going down. Depends on the

situation. If there are no customers, then in the shop's good. If there are customers then maybe on the street is the better option.

Turns out this early on a Sunday morning, there are no customers. Just Duifie and the woman relieving her at short notice. Not even the manageress hanging around. As luck has it, there's space in the loading zone right outside. He zips in there. Leaves the engine running. From the box on the passenger seat, picks out the Sig Sauer, screws on a silencer. Now he's wearing ordinary reading glasses, a tartan flat cap. He wants people to notice the cap. It'll be distracting.

At this time of the morning, not many pedestrians. A bergie pushing a shopping trolley. Couple of women window shopping at the appliance place next door. The traffic's not heavy either. Nothing he can't force his way into.

He checks the scene for security.

No visible orange jackets.

No visible cameras.

Go.

He's out of the car, scoots round the back, in three strides is into the shoe shop.

Says, "Hello, Duifie."

The two women look up. Which one the fuck is Duifie? You're faced with two young birds in jeans, T-shirts, trainers, how're you supposed to know who's who?

Jesus.

His hand is forced.

He does them both. Single shots to the forehead. That's an instant takeout. No suffering.

All the same, he's annoyed. Contract is one thing. Collateral is another. He regrets collateral. That's not nice. Some poor woman who just happened to be in the wrong place at the wrong time snuffs it. That's a loss all round. He'll have to insist on a gratuitous expense.

Even though he's angry, the man stays calm. That's the thing about the man, he keeps his head. He hides the gun under his jacket, flips the open sign on the door to closed, pulls the door shut as he leaves. Fortunately there's no one desperate for a pair of shoes.

He gets into his car, drives off slowly, taking the second left to stop a couple of blocks up. On the tracking app, he locates Captain Zara Dewane. There she is, entering the suburb where General Kaiser Vula lives. Interesting. Should he maybe head that way, check out the scene? Decides it's a good idea.

Before that, Telegrams the general that targets two and three are bongoed.

107

Zara's ahead of her father by three cars. She phones him on a secure cell phone. Uses the voice of Captain Zara Dewane.

"When we get there, stop well back."

An audible sigh. "I've done this before, bokkie."

She laughs. "I know. Just fooling."

Gets: "Stay focused. This general's not some stupid cadre deployment. He's been through MK. The presidential guard. The spy Aviary."

"A joke, Pa. Okay? A joke." Trying to keep the irritation out of her voice. "I know this snake."

"You're carrying your sidearm?"

"Of course."

"And the Hellcat?"

"At my ankle."

"Good girl."

She bites down. Sometimes Pa should stop being Pa. If only.

Zara turns into a neat suburb. Mown grass sidewalks. No electric fences. Low boundary walls. Sometimes no walls. You can walk between the flowerbeds, look in at the windows. Like this isn't murder-capital Cape Town. Three-bedroomed houses. Double garages. And here is where the general chooses to live? It amazes Zara. Suburbia doesn't get more suburban. No view of anything from these streets. You could be in Johannesburg. Wouldn't even know you were just three miles from the ocean. Wouldn't know you were that distance from gang wars.

She drives slowly down the general's street. All the house numbers prominent. Stops one beyond his. Sees her father pull in fifty yards behind. Walks back. There's a black Merc in the short driveway. She takes the garden path to the front door. Rings the bell. Waits. Rings again.

The door's opened by a huge guy.

"Yebo, yes!"

"To see the general."

"Not possible."

"He'll see me."

"You think, sisi?"

"Tell him Captain Dewane."

"Go away, lady."

She pulls out her ID. Thrusts it in his face. "Read, bhuti." He makes to grab it. She's faster. Snatches it away. "I said read. You use your eyes, not your hands. Go tell him."

He doesn't have to. She hears the hum of the electric wheelchair, hears the general behind mountain man.

"It's alright, chief. Let her come in. Take her gun."

Chief holds out his hand.

"This is not necessary."

The man waggles his fingers.

Zara gives him the cold eye. Relents. Hands over her pistol.

"I'll have that," says the general. Takes the gun. The man steps aside, indicates for her to follow the general. She goes into the house, notices the lingering smell of fried bacon. The walls without pictures. The tiled floors without rugs. In the lounge, the general wheels to face her.

"Close the door."

She does, the chief leering at her from the passageway. Wonders how to play this. She's here without a plan of action. Wants to see how Vula responds. Thinks to present herself as the unsure female detective. Not fully prepared. Not fully switched on. Feed into his stereotypes.

Checks out the room. It's barely furnished. Two small sofas, a gas heater in one corner, a square rug over ceramic tiles in the middle of the floor. No wall decor, a big window onto the garden. Vula has positioned himself in front of the heater. She stands opposite him in front of one of the sofas.

"Why do you come armed? Are you expecting a gunfight?"

"I'm a cop. Cops carry guns."

"Correction: you're a suspended cop. That means no cop at all."

He ejects the clip from her pistol, slides the rounds into his palm. Dumps them in an ashtray.

"And one in the chamber." He clears that. "How well prepared is our suspended captain." Vula pushes the magazine back into the grip. Hands the gun to her. "You can take the bullets when you leave. I wouldn't want you to accuse me of stealing your police ammunition." Said with a smile. "Now, Dewane, what do you want? You harass me at my wife's funeral. You taunt me. You show no respect. And now you are here. In my home. You come to persecute me in my grief. What sort of woman are you?"

Zara's about to tell him the determined type. But he stops her with a raised hand.

"You are on suspension, Dewane. You face being discharged. I am your superior officer. Your little ICU is within Police Intelligence. I can have you discharged. On my signature, you go. End of career. Disgrace. Disgrace to the Service. Where will you get a job then? Huh! You will be finished. Maybe you can be a supermarket checkout teller." He laughs. "You can ring up my groceries."

"I have come to charge you, General Vula."

"You? Don't make me laugh. You can't do that. You come here alone. Who will even know you are here? You should come with an active member if you want to charge me. Or even your friend, the advocate. But no, former Captain Dewane comes alone. You are out of order, Dewane. You have no rank. You have no position. Now you have seen me, you can go. You are dismissed."

Zara likes the hint of anger in his tone. Time to push another button. She holsters her gun.

"I know about General Maale."

That takes him by surprise. The quick frown. The narrowing of the eyebrows. Then the dismissive hand.

"What is there to know? He was assassinated. I was there. I shot his assassin before he could shoot me."

"You mean, you shot the man you commissioned to shoot the general."

She meets Vula's eyes. Can read the anger in them. Their unblinking stare. And holds them until he wheels himself to the window. Faces into the garden. A long minute passes.

Then: "This garden was once my wife's joy. Flowers, vegetables, abundance until she became ill."

Now a softening in his voice. How quickly the man can control himself.

"An illness of the mind. It is the saddest thing to experience, Dewane. The person looks healthy but in their mind they have become someone else. Someone you do not recognize. Even after years of marriage, you do not know this person. That is what happens when the mind weakens. Sometimes I wonder if it was that weekend when General Maale was killed that she ..." He stops. Zara waits. "I wonder if it was then that she became fearful for me as my position changed."

She watches Vula turn to face her. His eyes have lost their fire. They are hooded. But he still holds himself stiffly in his chair. Zara makes to sit on a couch.

"No, don't sit," he says. "You will not be here much longer." He smiles.

She shrugs. Knows Vula is unpredictable. Can strike unexpectedly.

"Why would I have General Maale killed? That is nonsense, Dewane. It makes no sense."

She keeps her arms by her sides, her fingers loose. "I have WhatsApp recordings."

"What WhatsApp recordings?"

"From Sergeant Mpho to Sergeant Kutoka. Mpho told Kutoka what you had instructed him to do."

"And you believe this Kutoka?"

"I do."

"Then let him testify. Let him swear an affidavit. Bring him into the station."

"You have had him killed."

General Vula laughs. "Oh now, what are you saying? He is another of my victims? You believe that?" He clicks his tongue. "You are a creative thinker, Dewane. All these men I have murdered. But look at me. You see I am in a wheelchair. I cannot walk. How could I shoot this Kutoka? In your daydreams, how am I this murderer?"

"I have Kutoka's evidence on Captain Hendricks. He let me photograph him handing a gun to a gangster. He told me about payments from Captain Hendricks for similar jobs. He told me that he and Mpho heisted a truck of guns for Captain Hendricks."

"What has that to do with me."

"I have photographs of the captain getting diamonds from the Mongols leader, Tamora Gool. I have testimony that she sold these diamonds for cash. Captain Hendricks is your number two, General. You brought her in from Saldanha to that position. The fingers point at you."

"You think Captain Hendricks will admit these things?"

"I do. To save herself."

"You do not know Captain Hendricks."

Zara's burner phone rings. It could be her father. It could be Jo-Jo. It could be Janet.

"You can answer it."

"It can wait. They will leave a message."

Then her compromised phone rings, a call tune assigned to Jo-Jo.

The general raises his hands. "So many phones. So important you are. Answer it. Be my guest. Someone wants you urgently."

She takes it from her jacket pocket, her eyes on the general.

108

Target One's car is still in the vicinity of General Vula's house. The man is a few miles away. He was there once, in the general's street, as part of his due diligence when the general became a client. He likes to know where his clients live. What types of houses they occupy. The general was a referral from one of his old mates in the Force. As the police service was called in those days. They'd first met at a wine estate in the Constantia Valley, he and the general. Sorted out the details. The terms of engagement. Surveillance, mostly. Possibly escalating, dependent on developing situations.

"Understood, sir."

A deal without a handshake.

Here he is now, nearing the client's house. Surprise, surprise, a call to Target Dewane. He'd suspected she'd realized her smartphone was bugged. But now Advocate Lanski is phoning her and Pegasus can listen in.

Josephine Lanski: Where are you? Do you know what's happened?

Zara Dewane: Not now. Not on this phone.

Josephine Lanski: Bugger that. Hendricks has been shot.

Zara Dewane: What?

Josephine Lanski: Outside New York Bagels.

Zara Dewane: You're sure?

Josephine Lanski: Bloody hell, Zara, you think I'd make this up? One of my interns was there with her boyfriend for breakfast. Saw the whole bloody thing. She's a bit freaked out.

Zara Dewane: So you've got details?

Josephine Lanski: As much as could be expected. A white man. Sunglasses, brown peak. A blue or navy jacket with a round collar.

Zara Dewane: That's pretty good.

Josephine Lanski: Was driving a white Polo.

Zara Dewane: Oh yes, sounds familiar.

Josephine Lanski: My thoughts exactly. The guy used a silencer. Speaks of professional.

Zara Dewane: Surely. How? I mean, from the car?

Josephine Lanski: From the car.

Zara Dewane: While he's driving! Did your person get a number?

Josephine Lanski: Yeah, we're checking CCTV.

Zara Dewane: When was this?

Josephine Lanski: About an hour ago. I've only just got back from the gym. Where are you anyhow?

Zara Dewane: I've got to go. We can talk later.

The man thinks, Christ, a white Polo's not the best car to be driving, even with changed plates. Nothing he can do about the car. But he can discard items of clothing. He pulls into the curb, throws into the long grass the brown peak cap. Even his jacket. Continues toward the general's house. This is not going as he would want. But he has the upfront payment. Also, he is a professional. That was his training back in the day. Get jobs done.

109

Zara disconnects the call. Sees the general is watching her. Puts away the phone but makes no eye contact. She's thinking, No Hendricks, no Kutoka, no Margulies, what has she got? Fok all. Less than. She meets the general's gaze.

"That sounds serious, your phone call."

"You could say."

"I hope it is not about work. You are not in service. I remind you again, you are on suspension."

Leaves Zara wondering, Should she surprise him? Gauge his reaction? Say, That was Advocate Lanski to tell me your Captain Hendricks has been shot dead. Decides, No, she should leave. Quickly. Doesn't take a rocket scientist to realize this is Vula cleaning house.

"I have to go," she says. Makes to scoop her bullets from the ashtray.

"Sit, Dewane," says Vula. "We are not finished."

"We are."

"No, my sisi, we are not. You say you came to arrest me. You think I am guilty of all these wild stories, that I have done bad things. You think I can say that is alright, you have made a mistake, it is just stories, do not be confused. No, my former captain, you must stop with this nonsense. These are lies. These put my name in the mud. You cannot tell these lies about me."

He digs inside his jacket, comes out with a service pistol, a Z88. "Move away from me. On your knees and hands on the floor."

"You're crazy."

"I mean it, sisi. You don't want to ride my kindness. Now, hotnot. Now."

She gets down as ordered, thinking she could roll behind the sofa, draw the Hellcat, maybe get one or two into him before he got one or two into her. She stays on all fours, her head raised watching him.

He holds the pistol in one hand, takes out a phone from a pocket on the chair. Puts through a call. His eyes flicking between her and the screen as he selects his contact.

"Yes. Listen to me, I am paying you for a job. Must I do the work for you?"

He listens.

"I do not care about that. That is your problem. You must come here to collect the other target."

He listens.

"That is not far. A few minutes away. How come you already know she is here?"

He listens. Splutters a laugh.

"You are a careful man, my friend. I am sure you know my house."

During this, Zara has listened, not moved a muscle. The gun and the general's focus on her throughout.

Now she moves. Lunges at the wheelchair, hoping to shove it backward, upend it. But the general's as fast. Puts a bullet into the floor, tile chips lacerating her face. Zara rolls sideways, comes up on her knees. Steadies herself against a sofa. The rug is rucked, had caused her to slip as she sprang at him.

"That was a warning, sisi. The next one will not be so kind. Down on your hands."

The lounge door bangs open, the chief stands there, waving his gun around.

"It is alright," says Vula. "Fetch cable ties for my guest." Into the phone, he says, "Your target is being a problem. Come. I have had enough of her." He returns the phone to its pocket. With his gun, indicates for Zara to move back. "Go where you were. No more funny jinks-jinks."

Zara does. Thinking, Now. Do something now before you've got both him and the chief in the room. Her face is stinging from the cuts, she can feel ceramic splinters under her palms. She backs against the wall. *Now.* It's an easy roll behind the sofa.

She hurls herself to the side, drawing up her knees. Hears three shots. One into the wall behind her. Two high into the sofa. Either Vula's a poor shot or has not been practicing for a while. She draws the Hellcat. Comes away with blood on her hand. Looks at her ankle, there's blood leaking into her jeans. Probes at it with her left hand. It's a score, not a through and through. Which is some relief. Weird thing is she can't even feel it. At least not yet.

Vula fires again over the couch into the wall. The bullet gouging in. One thing: he's not much worried about destroying the room or the furniture. Question is, how to take him? Blind shots from the side or over the top? Or a stand-up. Draw down on him. The best option. Also the riskiest. It'd be full exposure. She'd have to be fast. On three.

One.

"Get up, Dewane. Enough with the games."

Two.

The door opens, there's the chief with the cable ties.

A clear line of fire for Zara. She takes it. Sees the man jerk sideways. Scream. Curse. Disappear from view. Hears the general shout, "Stop, Dewane."

Three.

She stands, raises her right arm with the Hellcat, fires. Once, twice. A miss. A hit. That propels Vula backward, he topples. Still manages three shots: the first zings somewhere above her, the other two into the ceiling.

Zara vaults the sofa, comes down on her bleeding ankle, slips on the rug to end up crushed against Vula. Body against body. With her gun at Vula's cheek. He's lying on his side, his weapon pressing at her temple. She can smell his breath. Surprisingly minty. Like he's just used mouthwash. Or sucked a Fisherman's Friend.

"You fucking shot me," he says.

"You're fucking right," she says. Shoots him again. This time there's brain splatter all over the gas heater.

That's when the pain throbs in her ankle. It's eye-watering. Zara bites down on her lip, pushes herself away from Vula's exploded head. Gets to her knees. Wipes hair from her face leaving blood smears. Stands. Looks down at the man she's killed. Thinking, Him or me. It was him or me. The sight of him disappearing as she listens. Can't hear any movement in the passageway. Can hear a car's engine starting.

In the passage, there's blood on the wall, blood on the floor. A track to the kitchen. The back door is open, the Merc being reversed out of the driveway. Zara lets it go, limps into the street. With a raised hand still holding the Hellcat, signals to her father. Then sees a white Polo slowly approaching. Driven by a white man. Hobble-runs toward the car.

"Hey! Hey, you! Stop."

The Polo drives at her. Zara lurches backward. Watches the car accelerate away.

She stands in the middle of the street, breathing heavily, her shoe sticky with blood. Her ankle screeching pain. Her face scratched to hell 'n' gone. Pieces of the general in her hair. The adrenaline trembles firing up. The realization of what she's done. Killed. Had to kill. You or him. You had to. No question. Her mouth gone dry. She bends over, tries to still her rapid heart.

My lewe fok, Eloise.

Her dad stops his car beside her.

"Jesus Christ, Zara. What's going on? Are you alright?"

She straightens, nods. "Ja, ja, more or less." The words barely audible. Takes out her smartphone. "I better call Jo-Jo to clean up this mess."

110

Zara's outside Vula's house. Waiting for Jo-Jo and the cavalry. Sitting in her father's car. Shaking. Not trembling. Shaking. Her whole body gone live. She can't stop it. Tenses her muscles. Relaxes her muscles. Nothing works. She's no longer even feeling the pain in her ankle. The stickiness of the blood.

Playing over and over in her mind the mess of Vula's head.

"I've gotta walk, Pa," she says, swinging her legs out of the car. "I can't sit still."

"Watch it, bokkie. Your ankle's not good. Rather you want me to go get you something? Buy you a coffee?"

"A double brandy."

"I can get that if you want."

"I'm joking."

"I'm not."

"Okay, just walk slowly. Maybe it'll stop the shock."

Don't know about walk. She wants to run. To get away. Get to the sea. Get in her kayak, paddle for the open ocean. Keep going to the horizon. Not think, You could've died, girl. You could be lying splattered inside that house. Waiting for Vula's cavalry. Then what happens to Kyle?

Kyle.

Eloise, what about your son?

She's limping along now. Counting out the paces. Fifty, sixty, gets to a hundred. She comes round gingerly, starts hobbling back. Has her phone out, tapping through to Ashton. Still voicemail.

"Fokkit, Ashton. Get back to me."

Maybe he's got them both, the man in the Polo. Maybe that's what's going on here. He came after Kyle. Ashton got in the way. Is now collateral. Fully deserved. But it's no comfort.

She comes down too hard on her ankle. Which sends daggers of pain.

Zara stops. Tries Kyle's phone. "Hullo, Mrs. Z, this is mos Janet the answering service. I's at the window looking at the street. All Sunday quiet. The boykie's not made any contacting."

"If he does ..."

"Ja, man, I know, Mrs. Z. Yous the first on the speedo dial."

Zara disconnects. Limps on again. Twenty, thirty, forty. Pain etched in her face. When her phone rings.

Ashton.

"Where the fok is Kyle?"

"You're on speakerphone. Kyle's stoked."

"Hey, Ma. This's been the best." Kyle rushing his words in excitement. "Dad's been super cool. Bought me a Chew Toy. That's like the hottest surfboard."

Zara cutting in, "Where've you been, boykie? I've been going frantic."

"At Elands, Ma. Up the West Coast. In ace surf. Like Dad told you."

"Sorry, Zara, forgot to tell you," Ashton shouts over his son. "My bad."

Zara's speechless. Actually can't talk. Her vision gone black. She's stopped breathing. Has to support herself against a lamppost.

Slowly the world returns. The street. The houses. Her father standing at his car, anxiously calling her. She breathes again. Deeply.

Sees Jo-Jo pulling up.

Hears Kyle saying, "We're coming home, Ma. See you soon."

With that the connection cuts.

Kaffeeklatsch

111

One week later. Sunday morning. The hospital parking lot.

There's Zara (with bandaged ankle and elbow crutch) and father John pushing mother Elsi in a wheelchair. She's been discharged. The head wound still covered by a bandage. The wound in her side healing nicely. Aside from all this, Elsi Dewane is still Elsi Dewane. Has a lot to say all the way home:

I hope you've bought fresh veg and fruit, John.

I need a home-cooked meal.

I want to sleep in my own bed.

What I wouldn't do for a cup of my own coffee.

To Zara, the thing about her mother's coffee is that it's always weak. Plunge-pot coffee doesn't cut it. But you can't tell Elsi that.

What does impress Elsi is the plaster repair work John's done to their house. Gone the bullet pocks outside. A new front door fitted.

"That's solid, John. Where did you find it?"

Scrapyard, he tells her.

"It looks new."

"Pa restored it, Ma," says Zara. Then brings up the matter of the Rings Saturen bouquet.

"He sent me flowers, John?" says Elsi.

"He did."

"I hope you threw them away."

"I did."

Which makes Zara laugh. "What's the thing with Saturen and you guys?"

"It was long before your time, Zara. And best forgotten. The man's a crook, not to be trusted."

"I know his story," says Zara. "From the streets to the corridors of power. Just can't see where you'd fit in."

"And best you don't. That's enough of Mr. Rings Saturen for now. You go and make us a nice cup of coffee."

Being the obedient daughter, she does. Decides there will be another time to discuss the dodgy politician.

112

Wednesday afternoon. Battery Park skateboard zone.

There's Minister Lebo Majoro on the bench watching her son. This time men in black stand around. Not trying for discreet. Four of them, shaven heads, hands clasped at the crotch, black sunglasses, don't-try-it attitude. Makes Zara Dewane smile.

"All yours," she says to Kyle. "You got half an hour."

No sooner said, he's off with his board to get some action. Zara, still using an elbow crutch on her right side, joins the Minister of Police.

The woman glances up at her, says, "I thought it would be best to meet here. Gives the boys a treat."

Zara sits, hands easy in her lap.

The minister assesses her. "How're you doing, Captain? How's the ankle wound?"

Zara tells her it's fine. Mostly healed. She doesn't really need the crutch. Can drive without a problem.

"So I see," says Majoro. Laughs. "Glad to hear you're mended." Gets serious. "I was sorry to hear about your mother being shot. That was truly an awful business. You got my card, the flowers?"

"Thank you."

"She's recovering?"

"Out of hospital. At home now."

"I am pleased."

A pause.

"Good. Now, we must go on despite the hardships. Straight to the point, Captain."

"Okay," says Zara. Not too sure what's coming next. Not too sure what this off-field meeting's about in the first place.

"So, Captain, as you know, I can't interfere in these matters but I have the police commissioner's ear. And his full confidence. We have discussed this matter, he and I. We are of the same mind. Accordingly, he will reinstate the Internal Crime Unit. It has a valuable function to perform. It gives the service transparency. It reassures the public. And you have done good work. For this, you will get to increase your staff complement to three or four for the moment. Future operations will determine if a larger task force is necessary here in the Western Cape. We are open-minded. Approachable. The ICU will stay based in your current offices. In the chain of command, you will report directly to the provincial commissioner. He will also reinstate your position, scratch the suspension from your record. Given your investigative work, you will be recommended for a medal for outstanding service, silver. All this he will convey to you within the coming days. Any questions?"

A number.

The most pressing: Why this change of attitude toward her?

She shakes her head, no questions.

Thanks the minister.

What rankles is that the medal is silver not gold. Given that she had her life on the line. The miserly bastards could have gone large. Then again, bright side, she's back in the game.

The minister turns from watching her son to look at Zara. Their eyes meet.

"As you know, we are no nearer to catching whoever shot Captain Hendricks and her friend Duifie-whatever. That was tragic. That was unnecessary. Captain Hendricks was guilty of many crimes but Vula did not need to have her assassinated. This was unforgivable. Especially to also kill an innocent woman. Two innocent women. You saw the killer, nè?"

"I think so. A white man in a white Polo. It could have been the shooter. It could have been anyone. Except Vula had phoned some man to come collect me."

"For a grave in the sand dunes."

"I am sure."

Minister Majoro shifts her attention back to the skateboard park. Shouts, "That's my boy, Sipho. More. More." To Zara, says, "He is getting better each time we come here." She stands. "But now we must go. Time to deal with affairs of state, as we like to say to the president. Perhaps we will be treated to cupcakes at the cabinet meeting. Did you know our president has the nickname Cupcake? There are many stories about that. But then, there are many stories about our president." She laughs.

Zara keeps a straight face. As if she hasn't heard the stories. How a lover called him Cupcake. Sent him a text message that went viral.

"Goodbye, Captain Dewane. I am sure we will meet again. Keep up the good work."

Zara watches her walk away, Sipho running after his mother, complaining about leaving so soon. The men in black flanking her one pace back. There goes a woman on the make, thinks Zara. There goes a woman more bent than a question mark.

113

Three Anchor Bay.

The man has a new commission. A new client. Anonymous. Contactable via an intermediary. Except he knows who he's dealing with. He has his sources. Has established that the originator of the commission is a cabinet minister. That in itself is intriguing. Equally fascinating is that he's back with the same old target: one Captain Zara Dewane. Surveillance only. For now.

Which is why he's here, observing his target. She's still wearing a waterproof ankle guard. Completely steady these days. Even so, using her paddle as a crutch, she gets into a kayak, sits upfront. Behind is her son. In another kayak is a woman who is clearly terrified. Her partner is a man of about mid-thirties, an experienced kayaker. Seen often before at this location. This man is an advocate at the National Prosecuting Authority. There is a developing relationship between him and the captain. To date: a coffee, a two-up kayak outing down the coast one Sunday morning, a drink at Rockpool, a midweek lunch at La Colombe in the Constantia Valley. No dinners as yet. No home visits. As yet. The man still has Pegasus installed on her one phone. She uses this as if it is not bugged, which puzzles him. So he gets her routine cop appointments, her fiery relationship with her ex, family stuff with her mother and father, arrangements with her son. Even the appointment with Minister Majoro was set up through this phone. Only conclusion, she's playing him. Except, she doesn't know who "him" is. Him in sunglasses, wide-brimmed leather hat pulled down, sitting five or six yards away from her on the Three Anchor Bay beach. Listening.

The frightened woman says, "Ag, jissis, man, Mrs. Z, yous putting me right into the jaws of Jaws."

"You'll be fine," says Zara. She's got her paddle dug into the sand, ready to punt out of the shallows. "You've got a human engine behind you."

"I dunno, Mrs. Z, Great Whites ahead, great whitey behind, how's a girl supposed to be safe? My lewe fok, Eloise, as yous always saying."

Glossary of words and expressions

ag siestog: (Afrikaans) oh what a pity
aikona: (Nguni group of languages/colloquial) never
asseblief: (Afrikaans) please
babbelas: (slang) hangover
bakkie: (Afrikaans) pickup truck
bedonnerd: (Afrikaans) angry, crazy
bergie: (Afrikaans colloquialism) vagrant
bhuti: (slang) brother, informal way to address a man
blerrie: (Afrikaans slang) bloody, damn
bliksem: (Afrikaans exclamation) damn
bokkie: (Afrikaans diminutive, term of endearment) little buck
broekies: (Afrikaans diminutive) panties
charra: (derogatory slang) Indian
doos: (Afrikaans, vulgar) box, vagina, cunt
dop, doppie: (Afrikaans) a drink, to drink
eish: (urban slang, exclamation of surprise/disappointment)
eina: (Khoi, exclamation of pain) ouch
finish 'n' klaar: (urban slang) over and done with
fok, fokking, fokkit: (Afrikaans) fuck, fucking, fuck it
gabba: (slang) friend
gat, se gat: (Afrikaans) asshole, your asshole
gatte, gattas: (slang) police
haaita: (urban term, an exclamation)
hamba: (Nguni/urban) get away

heita: (urban slang) hello

hoerkie: (Afrikaans diminutive) whore

howzit: (contraction) how goes it, hello

imbizo: (Nguni) meeting

impimpi: (Nguni, urban slang) a police informer

indaba: (Nguni) meeting/to talk

ja: (Afrikaans) yes

jol: (urban slang) to have fun, to party

joller: (urban slang) a cool cat, also a gangster

jirre: (Afrikaans urban slang, exclamation) Jesus!

jislaaik: (Afrikaans urban slang, exclamation of surprise)

jissis: (Afrikaans urban slang, exclamation) Jesus!

julle: (Afrikaans) all of you—can be accusatory

kak: (Afrikaans slang) shit, crap

kif: (surfing slang) nice

klap: (Afrikaans) hit

larney, larnies: (urban slang) posh

lekker: (Afrikaans) nice

liefie: (Afrikaans term of endearment) lovey

lobola: (Nguni) bride payment

moegoe: (urban slang) a stupid/naïve person

mos: (Afrikaans colloquialism) in fact

mlungu: (Nguni) a white person

my lewe fok: (Afrikaans slang, vulgar, from "my liewe fok")
my fuck

nè (Afrikaans) you understand? hey?

nogal: (Afrikaans) and, also, in addition to

oke, oukie: (Afrikaans colloquialism) guy, young guy

patha-patha: (urban slang) sex

perlemoen: (Afrikaans) abalone

poes: (Afrikaans, vulgar) cunt

poppie: (Afrikaans diminutive) little doll

sangoma: (Nguni) traditional healer

sisi: (slang) sister, informal way to address a woman

skattie, skattebol: (Afrikaans) darling

skollie: (Afrikaans) thug
snoep: (Afrikaans slang) miserly
sommer: (Afrikaans colloquialism) just, simply, merely
tit: (slang) nice
tsotsi: (urban slang) gangster, thug
twis: (Afrikaans) conflict
voetsek: (Afrikaans colloquialism) be off!
wazimu: (Swahili) crazy
wena: (Nguni) you
hokaai: (Afrikaans/Southern Sotho) hold on, wait a minute
woes: (Afrikaans) wild, furious
yarrah: (urban slang, exclamation) my god!
yebo: (Nguni) yes
yoh: (urban slang, exclamation) wow!
zol: (various languages) a hand-rolled dagga cigarette
zooty: (urban slang) flashy

Mike Nicol is the author of twenty-five books. He has written novels, works of non-fiction and poetry. His thrillers have been translated into Afrikaans, Dutch, French, and German. His books have featured in the KrimiZeit top 10 list in Germany and have been shortlisted for the VN Thriller of the Year award in Holland and the Prix SCNF Du Polar 2016 in France. He lives in Cape Town, South Africa.